J·U·N·I·O·R

BBC BOOKS

King Street Junior is a Radio 4 series, written by Jim Eldridge and produced by John Fawcett Wilson, starring Karl Howman as Philip Sims and James Grout as Mr Beeston, the Headmaster.

Published by BBC Books
a division of BBC Enterprises Limited
Woodlands, 80 Wood Lane, London W12 0TT
First published 1988

ISBN 0 563 20068 3

Set in 10 on 11pt Times
by Phoenix Photosetting, Chatham
Printed and bound in Great Britain by
Richard Clay Ltd, Bungay, Suffolk
Cover printed by Fletchers Ltd

CONTENTS

This book is dedicated to the cast and production team of King Street Junior, especially John Fawcett Wilson, without whom there would have been no book; and to the staff and children of Denbigh Junior, without whom there would have been no show in the first place.

Jim Eldridge

CHAPTER ONE

THE NEW TEACHER

I don't believe it! thought Harry Beeston incredulously. The first day of a new school year and the place is still full of decorators and pots of paint. Well, all right, just two decorators painting the corridors; but in a school filled with 350 rushing kids, even two decorators was a guaranteed recipe for disaster. He could not believe that anyone in County Hall could be that idiotic! Well, yes, he could believe it. On County Hall's past record of policy-making decisions, it was par for the course. And, all right, King Street could do with repainting. It could have done with repainting years ago, but surely even someone with an IQ in single figures could have worked out that the worst possible time to do it was when the school was filled with children. That was why he had asked for it to be done during the six-week-long Summer break. He had pointed this out to the foreman painter when he had come into the school the day before term began and discovered them still there.

'The job sheet got delayed in being issued,' the foreman painter had defended himself petulantly. 'It's not our fault.'

'Well whose fault is it, then?' Beeston had demanded, nonplussed. One look at how far they had got so far showed that they would be there for weeks.

'County Hall's,' said the foreman.

'But you work for County Hall,' Beeston had pointed out.

'Yes,' the foreman had agreed, 'but we're only dogsbodies. We're not the brains.'

Brains? Beeston had nearly snapped at him. There are no brains at County Hall. They all leave them outside when they get a job there.

And then there was the problem caused by Brown leaving. He sighed. A pity that, Brown had been a good teacher. Just the sort of teacher the kids at King Street had needed. Intelligent, enthusiastic. Too good to be true, really.

The door of his office opened and Fred Holliday ambled in, pipe in mouth, looking exactly the same as when he'd walked out of the school six weeks before. Beeston was sure he was even still wearing the same jacket. It was as if the holiday had never happened.

'I see the decorators are still here,' commented Holliday lugubriously. 'I thought all the painting was going to be done while the kids were away?'

'So did I,' said Beeston. 'So would anyone with half a brain. How was your holiday?'

'All right,' said Holliday, not exactly bursting a blood vessel with enthusiasm. 'We went to Swansea.'

Not exactly a tropical resort, thought Beeston. He supposed the Hollidays had been to visit one of their apparently endless supply of relatives. Every vacation time Holliday and his wife got in their dormobile and motored off to various locations around the United Kingdom visiting sons, daughters, nephews, sisters, cousins. Beeston suspected that was why Holliday kept putting in for early retirement – they had countless more relatives dotted around the rest of the known world and wanted to see them all while there was still time.

'What was the weather like?' Beeston asked.

'All right, I suppose,' said Holliday, unimpressed. 'For Wales. Anyway, what's the replacement teacher situation? The last I heard was when you phoned me during the holidays and said Brown had decided to go to Millford after all. Drops us in it a bit, doesn't it?'

'True, but you can't blame him,' said Beeston resignedly. 'As we both said before, better catchment area, better equipment, more money available from the PTA, and the promise of a scale post. It's a career move upwards, we can't knock him for that.'

'Yes, but we could have done with a bit more notice,'

said Holliday. 'As it is we're left with a class without a teacher. I'm surprised County Hall approved the move at that late hour.'

Beeston gave Holliday a rueful smile. 'I don't want to be accused of being cynical,' he said, 'but remember that Millford have got two parents on the Education Committee, and Millford wanted Brown. Anyway, we've got a supply teacher coming in for this term while they advertise Brown's job.'

'Oh?' said Holliday. 'Who?'

'None of our usual supplies, I'm afraid,' said Beeston. 'None of them can take on a whole term. This bloke who's coming in is called Philip Bradley Sims.'

Holliday raised an inquisitive eyebrow. 'Hyphenated?' he asked.

'No, but when I spoke to him on the phone he said he liked to use his full name,' said Beeston. 'All I could think was, thank God he's not a member of the Royal Family – the amount of middle names they've got, it'd take a day to introduce him to people. Anyway, I've called an emergency staff meeting to fill everyone in on the current situation, both decorating and teaching.' He looked at his watch. 'Quarter to nine,' he said. 'The hordes should be gathered in the staff room by now. We'd better get along there.'

• • •

In the staff room Mrs Rudd, King Street's music teacher, had cornered Yvonne Patterson and was holding forth on the subject of the residential music school she had attended.

'This year the School was centred on choral singing,' said Mrs Rudd. 'A superb sound, the human voice in all its purity.'

'Yes,' said Patterson flatly. She looked around, wondering if there was anyone she could rush over to with an important question, or some similar excuse to get away from Mrs Rudd. She could always try just smiling at her and walking off, but there was a good chance that Mrs Rudd would follow her, still talking. She often did.

'Did you go away?' asked Mrs Rudd.

At last, thought Patterson, a chance for me to talk about what I did, which makes a change. 'Yes,' she said. 'I went to the Greek islands for two weeks. Northern Crete was particularly beautiful . . .'

She never got a chance to expand on her visitor's view of northern Crete. Mrs Rudd gave a knowing nod and jumped in with: 'We had a Greek meal while we were at the summer school.'

'Did you,' said Patterson flatly.

'Very oily,' said Mrs Rudd, expressing her distaste of all things Greek in that one short phrase. She beamed brightly at Patterson. 'Going back to the subject of choral singing, I don't know if you know much about the works of Thomas Tallis . . .'

She was cut off by Beeston's voice calling for his staff's attention. He watched as those who had been last to arrive, or last to read his notice calling the emergency meeting, scrambled for the hard and rickety chairs. The early birds sat comfortable and smug in the soft armchairs, savouring their cups of tea.

'First,' said Beeston, 'welcome back to all those of you I haven't yet said hello to, and I hope you all had a good long six weeks' holiday.'

He looked around the staff room, taking in those, like Mrs Patterson, who were so tanned that he was sure their re-entry into Britain after their holiday would have presented momentary illusions of power for any racist Immigration Control Officer, and those like Mrs Rudd and Mr Marchant who remained the same pasty colour. He wondered if the intensely devout Marchant spent his holidays inside a religious retreat. They looked at him expectantly, although most of them had already guessed what this staff meeting was about.

'As you know,' Beeston felt it necessary to remind them, 'I was planning on not having a staff meeting until the *end* of the first day, in case anything happened on the first day that needed to be raised at a staff meeting, thus saving two staff meetings one after the other.'

A general nodding of heads and murmurings of agreement were the responses to this announcement.

'However,' he continued, 'as it turns out two things have occurred that weren't planned. As you may have noticed, the decorators are still here painting the corridors.'

'I thought they were doing all the decorating during the Summer holiday so it would all be finished by the time school started again,' said Miss Lewis.

Beeston nodded. 'So did we all, Miss Lewis.'

'What provisions are we making against children getting paint on them?' asked Patterson.

'Apart from putting them all in plastic sacks with their heads poking out, there's not a lot we can do,' said Beeston. 'I plan to give a warning talk to them in assembly . . .'

'And a lot of notice they'll take of that!' snapped Mrs Rudd disparagingly.

On form, thought Beeston. Just back five minutes and she's sniping for me already. He smiled at her. Hypocrisy it may be, he thought, but there's no sense in courting trouble.

'Well, let's hope they do,' he said. 'Apart from that, all we can do is keep reminding them to stay away from the corridor walls.'

'What actually went wrong?' asked Lewis. 'Why are they still here?'

'From what I can make out, when the painters came to do the classrooms the job sheet didn't include the corridors, and the omission was only spotted during the last two weeks of the school holidays,' Beeston explained. 'At that time they were decorating the toilets at County Hall, which ranks far higher than a mere school, and so they couldn't get here until this week. And that, in a nutshell, is it.'

'Well I think it's ridiculous,' said Mrs Rudd indignantly. 'If I get any paint on me I shall send County Hall the bill.'

If you get any paint on you, thought Beeston vengefully, it'll be me chucking a bucket of it over you.

'That's one of the important things that have happened,' he said. 'The other is that Mr Brown won't be with us. He decided to take the job that was offered to him at Millford.'

The reaction to this was a hubbub of surprise, Mrs Rudd's voice rising above it, as usual. 'One would have thought he would have given us more notice,' she said in tones of condemnation.

'If you remember, Millford didn't exactly give him much notice,' Beeston pointed out. 'They only asked him at the end of last term. However, that's all water under the bridge now, as far as I'm concerned. To take his class for this term until we get a permanent appointment, we have a supply teacher called Philip Bradley Sims.'

The staff exchanged glances, at the same time looking around the room to see if there was any sign of this new teacher. When it became obvious that there wasn't, it was Long who posed the question: 'Where is he?'

'A good question, Mr Long,' said Beeston. Like the rest of them, he looked towards the door of the staff room. 'To be honest I'd have thought he'd be here by now. Anyway, if there's nothing else . . .'

It was a delusion to even ask such a question, thought Beeston. A wild hope that everything had been dealt with. Experience should have told him that nothing was ever dealt with at King Street, problems just lingered on. This time it was Mrs Patterson who had a problem she wanted to raise.

'The bell will be going for the start of school any minute, Mrs Patterson,' Beeston reminded her.

'This won't take a second,' Patterson said quickly. Another of the Great Lies of the Twentieth Century, thought Beeston. Like: 'the cheque's in the post' and 'the engineer's on his way at this very moment'.

'While we're all here I'd like to point out that the new timetable changes are all wrong,' Patterson said.

Oh God, Beeston groaned inwardly, not the timetable. If there was one thing he hated it was working out the timetable; it was like trying to do a crossword without any clues. Anyway, he was sure that Holliday had sorted it all out at the end of last term. He turned to his Deputy. 'There shouldn't be any problems, should there, Fred?' he said, passing the buck.

Fred shook his head. 'I can't see why,' he said. 'If you remember, last year we had problems with use of the hall in wet weather because of sports taking priority. So what we've done is move the hall periods to mornings, where possible. That's all.'

'That's all very well, but have you seen how it affects the library periods?' said Patterson, and she produced a copy of the new timetable from her bag and passed it across to Holliday. 'Look at Wednesdays and Thursdays. The new timetable means that I lose the library periods with my remedial groups.'

Holliday frowned at the timetable. Beeston turned back to Patterson. 'Are you sure?' he asked.

'Positive,' nodded Patterson. 'I was looking at it this morning. You see, there was general acceptance that when the library wasn't in use, I used it for my remedial reading groups . . .'

She stopped, and Beeston turned and looked over his shoulder to see what had caused her to leave off making her point. A man in his late twenties had walked in, had taken a brief look around, and was now striding towards them a genial smile on his face.

'I'm looking for Mr Beeston!' he announced.

'Yes?' said Beeston, suspiciously. Who the hell was this? he thought. It could be a senior decorator from County Hall come to supervise the painting, it could be a parent, or it could be just some loony off the street who felt like walking in and having a chat. Whoever it was, he obviously didn't believe in knocking at doors or not interrupting meetings. God help us if he's the new teacher, he thought.

The stranger thrust out his hand towards Beeston. 'We spoke on the telephone,' he said. 'Philip Bradley Sims. Your school secretary said I'd find you here, but I got lost in one of your corridors.' He smiled ruefully. 'A bit of a maze, aren't they?' For the first time he seemed to become aware that something had been happening before he walked in, and that was why all these people were gathered in a large circle. He looked around at the faces all looking at him, and then back at Beeston. 'Sorry,' he said with an apologetic grin, 'am I interrupting something?'

'No, no,' said Beeston, 'we're used to people popping in during staff meetings. We're expecting the complete Band of the Grenadier Guards in a minute.'

Before Sims could respond to this, the bell went for the start of school. 'There she blows,' announced Beeston. 'I'll see you all in assembly.'

As his staff eased themselves unwillingly out of their chairs, Beeston stood up and gestured towards the door. 'Welcome to King Street, Mr Sims,' he said. 'If you follow me, I'll show you to your class.'

• • •

Beeston stood at the wooden lectern at the front of the school hall, and looked out at the sea of children's faces, all looking back at him. Well, most of them looking back at him – he could see one or two of the older children more intent on nudging each other and other assorted dubious activities. He'd have a word with their teachers later.

On either side of the hall sat the teachers, their ears still ringing from Mrs Rudd's enthusiastic piano playing and the children's loud and off-key rendition of 'Farmer, Farmer, Sow Your Seed'. Philip Bradley Sims, Beeston noted, seemed to be taking it all in his stride, just sitting there with that beam on his face. Maybe the man was deaf.

Beeston cleared his throat and then moved away from the lectern, smiling benevolently at the youngest children in the front row. He knew what a shock it was for them coming to school at their age. God, it was still a shock for him at his age! The last thing they needed was their New Headmaster towering over them, glaring at them, as his

Headmaster had done when he had been seven. He had felt like Jack of the Beanstalk when faced with the Giant, terrified.

'Now,' he said, gently, but loudly enough so that those at the back could hear him, 'This is our very first assembly of this new school year. A time when I can welcome back all those children who were here last year, and say a special big Hello to those children who are starting at King Street for the first time.

'I like to think of King Street as one big family, where we all help each other: the big children helping the younger ones, the teachers helping you children, but most of all teaching you how to help yourselves. Because we are a family. As the hymn says, the family of people . . .'

At the side of the hall Long leant across to Patterson and whispered: 'My class last year always *did* help themselves. Biggest lot of kleptomaniacs you've ever seen.'

'Sssh,' Patterson hushed him.

'Like all families in any house, sometimes there are interruptions when people like the plumber or the electrician come in,' said Beeston, building up to his Main Topic. 'Well, we have got the decorators in at the moment. Our decorators use paint and, as most of your parents know, paint gets on clothes . . .'

• • •

'How did it go?' asked Mrs Stone.

Beeston dragged his gaze away from the enormous pile of memos that County Hall seemed to spend its days sending to him, and looked at his School Secretary as she slid another sheet of letterheaded paper into the typewriter.

'How did what go?' he asked.

'Assembly,' she said. 'What did the new children look like?'

'Terrified,' said Beeston. 'But then, wouldn't you be? All except for some small child right in the middle of the hall who spent most of my speech picking her nose. Frightened the life out of me. I thought she was going to get her finger stuck.'

Mrs Stone grinned. 'What about the new teacher?' she asked, typing again. 'Mr Sims.'

'Philip Bradley Sims,' Beeston corrected her. 'I must admit, when he walked into the staff room I thought he was a parent or somebody. When he started introducing himself in the middle of our staff meeting I thought he'd escaped from the local lunatic asylum. Still, he seems all right, so far.'

'What's he been doing before?'

'Apparently he's worked mainly on supply in high schools.' Beeston shook his head in wonder. 'It doesn't exactly qualify him to work in a junior school, but that's the current philosophy of employment in teaching, isn't it? The square peg in the round hole policy. Find an A-level metalwork teacher and stick them in a nursery class, teaching reading.'

'Come on,' Mrs Stone scolded him, 'it's not as bad as all that. Which high schools was he at?'

'St James, and the Manor, to name just two.'

'The Manor?' echoed Mrs Stone, almost adding a whistle. The Manor was well known in the area as the place where one teacher had asked to be issued with a crash helmet before he went into a particular class. 'That's a tough school.'

'I know,' agreed Beeston. 'If he survived that, he can survive anything we can throw at him.'

'Have you phoned up their Heads to check him out?'

'Yes, and they're complimentary enough. But then they would be, wouldn't they? I'm always suspicious of glowing references, it usually means they're keen to get rid of someone.'

'That hardly applies in this case, does it, as he was on supply,' pointed out Mrs Stone.

'No, that's true,' Beeston admitted. 'Well, all we can do is see how he shapes out and hope he doesn't offend too many people.'

• • •

If he had seen Sims in conversation with Mrs Rudd in the

staff room at morning break, he wouldn't have been so confident in expressing such a hope.

Mrs Rudd, keen to find out all there was to know about the new teacher, had homed in on Sims like a bird of prey. So far she had discovered that he seemed to be charming, if inconsiderate (he had taken two sugars in his coffee and then replaced the sugar bowl without offering it to her), and that he had originally trained to be a solicitor, which moved him up a few social grades in her eyes.

'But frankly I found it so boring,' he grinned genially. 'All I was doing was conveyancing. What I really wanted was to do criminal work, but then after I'd met one or two criminals I found them pretty boring as well. Most of them, that is. I mean, now and then you meet the odd interesting chain-saw murderer, but usually it's just taking and driving away. So then I did a postgraduate course in teaching, and here I am.'

'I see,' said Mrs Rudd. Then she moved on to what, as far as she was concerned, was the major question – was his name really indicative of social standing? 'Tell me,' she asked, '"Bradley Sims". Is that hyphenated?'

Sims shook his head. 'No,' he said, 'I was called "Bradley" after my Uncle.'

He didn't appear to notice Mrs Rudd's disappointed 'Oh', because he carried on blithely: 'I think my parents called me after him in the hope he'd leave them some money when he snuffed it. As it turns out, when he died he left everything to be divided between a cat's home and two mistresses.'

Mrs Rudd blanched at this, but Sims ploughed on: 'Still,' he said, 'I found it useful. After all, just plain Philip Sims is pretty boring, don't you think?' Before she had a chance to answer, he added: 'I think most people's first names are fairly boring. What's yours?'

Pleased that the conversation was getting round to her at last, Mrs Rudd smiled and said: 'Mine? Well, it's . . . Lilian.'

'See?' Sims beamed at her. 'Proves my point.'

Mrs Rudd glared at him. Well really! she thought.

When the bell went to announce the end of morning school, Beeston was still on the phone to County Hall, still trying to get something sorted out about the painting that was still going on in the corridors. He checked his watch. Five past twelve already? Good grief! Where had the switchboard operator gone? He'd asked her to put him on to the Works Department ages ago, and since then there'd been nothing but silence. What had happened, had she died? No, she was back on the line, questioning if he was really sure he wanted the Works Department.

'Yes,' he said patiently, 'the Works Department. The Department that deals with the painting and decorating of County property. In this case our school. . . . No, I'd already been on to the Education Department for half an hour before I discovered it was nothing to do with them. I want the Works Department. . . . What do you mean, there's no one there at the moment? Why not? They can't all be out painting walls . . . Oh, all right, I'll try later.'

He put the receiver down. Give me strength! he thought, exasperated. I don't know why they don't get a bunch of monkeys to organise the place. It'd run a lot more efficiently.

A knock at the door made him look up. 'Come in!' he called.

The door opened and Philip Bradley Sims peered in. Good grief, thought Beeston, that's an improvement, he's learnt how to knock on a door.

'Can I see you for a minute?' asked Sims.

'It's not a complaint already, is it?' asked Beeston suspiciously. 'You've only been here a morning.'

'No, no,' said Sims, 'I've got an idea I want to try out on you.'

Before Beeston could put him off, Sims was in, shutting the door behind him. He's sitting down, groaned Beeston to himself. That means it's going to take ages. I thought all this had ended when Brown left. I knew I should have gone straight to lunch instead of hanging on for County Hall.

'Will it take long?' he asked.

'No, no, only a few minutes of your time, but I think you'll like it,' Sims reassured him with a hearty smile. 'What I'd like to try out here at King Street is a history game.'

'A history game?' asked Beeston warily. He had seen many enthusiastic young teachers and nearly all of them meant chaos. He could feel it in his bones with Sims.

'Right,' nodded Sims. 'I've already used it with the lower age ranges in two of the high schools I've worked at, and the kids loved it.'

'Yes, but they were high schools . . .' Beeston pointed out.

'Believe me, it covers all ages,' countered Sims. 'And there's only a year or so difference between those children and the ones in my class here.'

'Yes, I suppose so,' Beeston admitted grudgingly.

'It's based around the theory of teaching history by living it . . .' continued Sims, warning to his theme.

Beeston could feel shivers of apprehension stirring already. 'Is this like that TV programme where you build a cave in the middle of the playground?' he asked.

'No, nothing like that. This is more like a history game. You take one group of classes and involve them all in a particular project. What I thought we could do is enact 1066 using three classes from one year – say the third years. One class would be the Normans, one class the English, and one class the Vikings.'

'We're not going to have battles taking place all over the school, are we?'

Again Sims shook his head in denial. 'No, no, nothing like that. The idea is that we prepare an overall game plan to show where each country starts from, and we plot historical events leading up the the Battle of Hastings. To score points each class has to achieve certain objectives, such as the Vikings have to reach an agreement with the Normans that they will combine against the English; and the English have to form a political alliance with William.'

Beeston frowned. 'It all sounds a bit complicated,' he commented.

'Don't worry,' Sims beamed, 'the children will be able to follow it.'

'I wasn't thinking of the children, I was thinking of the staff,' said Beeston. He shook his head doubtfully. 'To be honest, Mr Sims, I'm not sure if it'll really work here . . .'

'It will, believe me,' said Sims. 'The children will love it! And they'll learn so much from it!'

'All right, it may work with your class,' conceded Beeston, 'but I'm not sure about involving the others. For one thing, it will mean juggling the timetable around so that all your year do history at the same time . . .'

'That's true, but I've already looked at it and it shouldn't be a problem,' said Sims.

Beeston looked at him, astonished. 'Already?'

'Yes, I asked your secretary if I could look at the main timetable.'

That woman's a traitor, thought Beeston, giving out timetables to all and sundry. What amazed him particularly was that Sims appeared to have grasped the main timetable so quickly; it always looked to him like the Dead Sea Scrolls written in Egyptian hieroglyphics.

'Well,' he said, 'you certainly storm into a place, Mr Sims, I'll give you that. All right, when do you want to get this off the ground?'

'As soon as possible,' said Sims. 'This week, if we can, before people get their various projects under way. And also it would be good for me, help me to get to know my other year teachers better.'

'All right, let's have a look at the timetable,' said Beeston, and he and Sims walked over to the large version of the main timetable pinned to his wall. 'Now,' he mused, 'we've got your class, Mr Long's and Mr Holliday's . . .'

'That's the teacher with the pipe?' asked Sims.

Beeston nodded. 'My Deputy Head,' he said, just to clarify things. 'Now while it's possible that you and Long could work together at the same time, if Long agrees, that is . . .'

'I'm sure he will!' Sims enthused. 'Everyone loves this idea!'

Beeston grimaced at Sims's enthusiasm. I hope this soon wears off, he thought, otherwise this man is going to wear me out. He tapped the timetable. 'But Mr Holliday's class have music with Mrs Rudd at that time,' he said.

'Oh, yes, but I'm sure if the value of it was explained to her . . .' said Sims confidently.

'Well, if you think you can do it, Mr Sims,' said Beeston.

For the first time, doubt seemed to flicker across the new teacher's face. 'Me?' he said. 'Well . . .'

'Who else is better equipped?' said Beeston. 'For one thing, listening to this scheme of yours, it'd take me a year to work it out, so I'm hardly likely to make a good job of explaining it, am I? You have a word with her and let me know how you get on. And believe me, if you can talk her into dropping music, you're in the wrong job. You should be a used car salesman.'

• • •

The next day Sims swung the plans for his history game into operation. It was important, he reasoned, to get the teachers concerned on his side. He decided to start with Mr Long. He appeared to be the most reasonable of the three, less set in his ways. Then he could go to the others and say that it was already agreed by the rest of the year group, thus making it harder for them to say no. Lunch time found Sims in the staff room, selling the idea for all he was worth.

'So one class are the Normans, one are the English, and the third are the Vikings,' he said, rounding up his sales pitch.

Long frowned dubiously. 'I didn't even know the Vikings were in the Battle of Hastings,' he said.

Sims nodded. 'They were at Stamford Bridge,' he said.

'Chelsea's football ground?' asked Long.

'No, this Stamford Bridge was up north. Yorkshire.'

'A bit far from Hastings,' observed Long, 'Did they get lost on the way?'

'They weren't intending to go to Hastings, they were invading from the North.'

'I see,' said Long, uncertainly. 'I think.'

'Anyway, are you in?' asked Sims.

'I suppose so,' agreed Long. 'It sounds like it could be fun for the kids. Who's going to be the third class?'

'Well, I thought the third one in our year: Mr Holliday's.'

'Yes, but when our classes have history, his has music with Mrs Rudd,' said Long warningly.

'Don't worry, I'm going to see them both,' said Sims confidently. 'I thought I'd better talk to Mr Holliday first, as it's his class that'll be involved.'

Long looked around the staff room. 'I'm not sure if he's down from lunch yet . . .' he said.

'He is,' said Sims, 'I saw him talking to Mr Beeston, but I thought I'd leave seeing him about it until after school. It will give me more time to outline the idea to him.'

'And Mrs Rudd?'

'I'll see Mrs Rudd before school starts in the morning,' Sims said genially. 'I'm sure she'll agree.'

Long smiled to himself. Oh yes? Give up her music? The man didn't know what he was letting himself in for.

• • •

Holliday left the school buildings at the end of that afternoon, his brain still pondering the problem of the timetable and Mrs Patterson's remedial groups. It was all because she'd been doing things unofficially, he growled. Taking her group and claiming squatter's rights in the library like that. Next thing everyone knew, her unofficial library periods had become a matter of right. It really wasn't fair.

He had just reached his car when he heard someone calling his name. He looked round. It was, what was that new fellow's name? Bradley Sims, that was it. What did he want?

Sims caught up with him, a jovial smile on his face. What's he got to grin about, thought Holliday? Give him a few more weeks here, that'll soon wipe the smile off his face.

'Mr Holliday,' said Sims. 'Have you got a minute?'

Holliday looked at his watch. Four o'clock already. 'Will it take long?' he asked. 'Only, even though they've removed the contraflow on the bypass . . .'

Sims shook his head reassuringly. 'No, not long at all,' he said. 'I've got an idea that I'd like to try out on you. It's a new way of doing history which I think all our three classes will enjoy. We take a particular historical event, in this case 1066, and we divide the three classes up into three historical groups . . .'

• • •

Holliday was still fuming next morning when he bumped into Beeston on his way into school. 'You'll never believe what happened to me last night as I was leaving school,' he said. 'That idiot Sims.'

'Oh?' said Beeston.

'Collared me just as I was about to drive off, and then launched into this huge long story all about 1066, and how he wanted to play some sort of history game involving everybody's classes. I had the complete history of why the English lost the Battle of Hastings plus the complete family tree of William the Conqueror. It was twenty past four before I got away. My wife thought I'd left home.'

Beeston did his best to stifle a grin. He knew how important the correct timings on car journeys were to Holliday. 'Still, it sounds interesting,' he said, trying to take the wrath out of Holliday.

'It's all right for you,' grumbled Holliday. 'You didn't have to listen to him.'

'I did,' said Beeston ruefully. 'I was the first one he collared about it. So what did you say?'

'That's the point!' exploded Holliday. 'After half an hour of it I suddenly realised I don't even have my class the periods he's talking about, Mrs Rudd does. So I told him to go and bother her.'

• • •

If Sims had had an easy ride in selling his idea to Long and Holliday, he was not having the same luck with Mrs

Rudd. He had cornered her in the school hall as she was getting the music stands ready for assembly, and started in on his same spiel with the same genial grin. Mrs Rudd had half listened as she distributed the hymn sheets and recorder parts, still baffled as to what all this had to do with her. When she did realise, she was as firm as only Mrs Rudd could be in her refusal.

'No, Mr Sims. Absolutely not.'

Sims had met his first brick wall. 'But Mr Holliday has no objections,' he pointed out.

'Mr Holliday does not take his class for music,' countered Mrs Rudd. 'I do, and I have no intention of giving up my music to take part in some silly game.'

'It's not a silly game,' defended Sims, 'it's a learning experience.'

'So is falling off a bicycle,' stated Mrs Rudd with unerring logic, 'but that does not mean that I wish to experience it.'

'But . . .' began Sims. He never finished.

'You new teachers tend to throw these words into the air as if they mean something,' said Mrs Rudd. 'There is only one real learning experience, and that is putting children in a classroom and teaching them something. Now, if you'll excuse me, I have to assemble the choir for assembly.'

• • •

The decorators, as everyone had prophesied, were having problems.

'I 'ate this job,' grumbled Mick, perched on a ladder and working with slow downward strokes of his paintbrush on the bits above the internal corridor windows. 'The kids keep sticking their 'ands on the wall when we're not looking. There's fingerprints all the way along it. I 'ave to keep going back and repainting it.'

Ben, the foreman, stepped back to admire his handiwork. 'Maybe we ought to put up a barrier,' he said.

'I did,' said Mick. 'I put a plank on two chairs, and when I come back this kid was walking on it. It's worse than that outside wall we was doing last week. D'you remember, we'd got it all lovely and finished when that dog come along and peed on it. Embedded in the paintwork, it was.'

Ben put down his brush and reached out for a fresh tin of paint. He stopped. He looked around, puzzled. ''Ere, Mick?' he said.

'Yeah?' said Mick, still brooding.

'What've you done with that other tin of paint?'

'Which tin of paint?'

Ben indicated the now empty space at the foot of his ladder. 'The one that was down there,' he said.

'I ain't touched it,' said Mick.

'You must 'ave,' said Ben.

'Not me,' said Mick. 'I've been using this one.'

Suddenly the penny dropped.

'You'll never believe this!' said Ben. 'The kids have nicked the perishing paint! Right, that does it. Fingerprints on walls is one thing, nicking our paint is quite another. I'm going to see the Headmaster.'

• • •

'The kids have done what?' said Holliday, poking his spoon into his dessert bowl and trying to identify what awful concoction Mrs Purkiss had served up for them.

'Stolen a tin of the decorator's paint,' said Beeston.

The dining hall was as noisy as ever. Even when the kids were just whispering it sounded like an earthquake, Beeston thought. After eating at King Street he reckoned he could sit down to a five-course meal in the middle of a riot and not be affected by it.

'Do they know for sure it's the kids?' asked Holliday.

'Well, who else could it be?' asked Beeston.

'The caretaker? Maybe he needed it.'

Beeston snorted dismissively. 'Do me a favour!' he said. 'I'm not even sure if our caretaker knows where this *school* is, let alone things in it. It's our second day back and the only way I know he's still alive is because he phoned to say he was off ill.'

Further along the staff table, Miss Lewis and Mr Long

were eating with Sims – although Sims wasn't quite sure if 'eating' was the correct word. He'd eaten in quite a few school dining halls in his time as a supply teacher, but very few had hit a standard of cooking as low as King Street's.

'So what did Mrs Rudd say about the game?' Long asked.

'Well I suppose the short answer is no, she doesn't want to join in,' said Sims with a sigh. 'She's a tough old bird, isn't she?'

'You can say that again,' said Long with a grin. He'd thought Sims would meet his match with Mrs Rudd, and he'd been right.

'Is this about your 1066 history game?' asked Lewis.

'I told Miss Lewis all about it this morning,' explained Long.

'I must say it sounds a lot of fun. I wish my class could play it,' Lewis said.

'I wish they could as well, but the trouble is it's designed for each group to be as equal as possible, and with your first years being so much younger . . .' said Sims somewhat ruefully.

'Can't you adapt it in any way?' suggested Long. 'For example, if we count the Vikings as the losers anyway, then Miss Lewis's class can be the Vikings . . .'

'That's not fair,' protested Lewis.

'No,' said Sims agreeing with her. 'The idea is that there are no losers before the game begins, so anyone can win.'

'Yes, but unless we have three classes playing it, we can't play it at all,' Long pointed out.

'Yes, that's true,' admitted Sims gloomily. He thought about it. 'I suppose we could adapt it to give your class more advantages to take into account the fact that they're so much younger,' he said.

'And simplified it so that they could understand what they were doing,' said Lewis. 'At least it would give them an insight into how history works.'

Sims ran it through his mind again. Yes, yes it was quite feasible. All it needed was a little bit of work. 'Yes,' he said, pleased. 'Yes, it could be done. Right, I'll get on to it so that we can start tomorrow, and blow Mrs Rudd.'

• • •

The next morning Sims was able to tell his class that a simplified version of the history game was now under way. 'The arrangement is that we are the English, Mr Long's class are the Normans, and Miss Lewis's class are the Vikings,' he announced proudly.

'Cor,' said Hanif gleefully, 'we should beat them easy then. Couple of wallops and it'll all be over.'

Sims regarded him sternly. 'There will be no wallops,' he declared.

Obviously his original outline of the game as an intellectual exercise to his class had not struck home, because this statement was met with puzzled looks. He decided that it all needed saying again in simpler terms.

'We will not be having actual battles,' explained Sims, as they'd obviously missed that point the first time round. 'This history game is a game of cunning and skill, like chess. It's better than having battles, because it calls for brains.' He thought he spotted disagreement in some of the eyes looking back at him, but ploughed on regardless. 'Now, there are rules. Every two days we have to decide what our next move will be and we put that move on a piece of paper, which we put into an envelope. Mr Long's class and Miss Lewis's do the same.'

There was such an outcry of disappointment at this that it seemed as if an actual battle *was* about to break out.

'Quiet!' yelled Sims, and the near revolt subsided into low murmurings and grunts of disapproval.

• • •

Mrs Rudd was also having problems with a class at this time, and over the same topic. Her attempts to teach Mr Holliday's class the mysteries of the crotchet and the minim were meeting with sullen resistance. It was not overt rebellion, but she could feel that the class were not wholly with her. Finally a hand went up, and Andrew asked: 'Please, Miss, why are we doing this?'

The whole class held their breath. This was bravery indeed! They all looked at Mrs Rudd, wondering what she would do. Would she suddenly breathe fire on him? They'd all heard Mr Beeston muttering to himself about her as 'that old dragon'.

Mrs Rudd, for her part, was quite relieved at the interruption, recognising it as a chance to get to the bottom of this lack of enthusiasm and to find out what was going on. 'What do you mean, why are you doing this? To learn the finer points of music, of course,' she said.

There was a long pause, with Mrs Rudd waiting, giving the children a chance to Reveal All. When it was revealed, it was the brave and bold Andrew who was again the class's spokesperson.

'But shouldn't we be doing this history game?' he asked.

So that was it! said Mrs Rudd to herself. Sims and his history game, trying to lead these children astray, divert them from lessons. 'Absolutely not,' she said. 'You are timetabled for music, and music it will be.'

'But the new teacher's class . . .' began Andrew.

'Mr Sims,' said Mrs Rudd, 'and what Mr Sims' class are doing is totally irrelevant. You might as well say that because Mr Marchant's class have games at this time, you should have games.'

It was the wrong analogy to make, because there was no doubt at all from the enthusiastic reception that greeted this suggestion that Mr Holliday's class would far prefer to have games.

'Quiet!' barked Mrs Rudd, and the cheering that had almost started up stopped, and the smiles vanished from the children's faces. Mrs Rudd glared. Andrew's hand went up again.

'Put your hand down, Andrew,' said Mrs Rudd sternly. 'We have heard quite enough about this ridiculous so-called history game.'

Andrew wasn't going to give up that easily. He had committed himself this far, he might as well go the whole way. After all, the worst that could happen to him was a tongue-lashing from Mrs Rudd, and he'd had those before and survived. 'But the new teacher's class and Mr Long's class say the only reason we're not doing it is because we're scared of them.'

Mrs Rudd noticed a nodding of heads in agreement from the other children. She looked around the class. 'Ignore them,' she said. 'Such talk is for fools.'

Andrew took a deep breath. The next bit required courage, but nothing ventured, nothing gained. 'And they say you're scared as well.'

Mrs Rudd regarded him with a glare, and for a moment Andrew remembered a story Mr Holliday had told them in history, where if a messenger brought bad news they killed the messenger. Right at that moment he felt like just such a messenger. He swallowed again. 'They say you're scared because you know you'll lose,' he said.

Mrs Rudd looked around the class, and again noticed the nodding of heads. 'Who has had the audacity to suggest such a thing?' she demanded, angrily. 'Was this Mr Sims and Mr Long?'

'No, their classes,' said Andrew. 'But it's the same thing, isn't it?'

The nodding of heads was now added to by the murmurings of vocal agreement, resentment at Mr Sims's and Mr Long's classes welling up.

'Quiet!' snapped Mrs Rudd, and the nodding stopped and silence fell. 'I've never heard such an outrageous suggestion in my life, and I shall deal with it in my own way. Right now, return to your music sheets, and mark time with me. First,' and she indicated the musical notation on the blackboard, 'the crotchet: "Taa".'

• • •

The afternoon for Beeston started badly. He was just leaving his office to find Holliday and see if there had been any resolution to the problem of Mrs Patterson and the library, when the foreman painter pounced on him.

'They're at it again,' he said, his tone registering his annoyance.

Good God, another loony in the school, sighed Beeston to himself. Aloud he said: 'Who are?'

'My brushes have disappeared.'

'Well don't look at me,' defended Beeston.

'They're your kids,' said the foreman accusingly.

'And it's your Department that were crackpot enough to fix it so that you painted when they were all here,' retorted Beeston.

'Yes, but we didn't expect them to start nicking all our stuff,' the foreman complained petulantly. 'We've had a pot of paint go, three brushes . . .'

'That's because you're not keeping a very good watch on your equipment,' argued Beeston. 'How do you know it's the kids?'

'Well it ain't us,' said the foreman, 'and if it ain't the kids, it's got to be one of the teachers.'

Oh God, don't start on the staff, thought Beeston. 'I can assure you,' he said, 'that my staff are not in the habit of stealing County Hall materials.'

'One of them might,' said the foreman insinuatingly. 'You know what it says in the papers.'

'I know what it says in mine,' snapped back Beeston. 'What does it say in yours?'

'Well, the pressures of teaching,' said the foreman. 'It makes teachers do funny things. Maybe one of them's unbalanced.'

Beeston gave a snort of derision. 'Frankly,' he said, 'I think any Department that sends decorators down to paint a school when it's full of kids are the last people to talk about being unbalanced.'

• • •

Mrs Rudd caught up with Sims and Long as they were talking in the corridor at the end of school. Long was just complimenting Sims on the game, and telling him how much his class seemed to enjoy even the early stages, when a voice from down the corridor made them both look round.

'Mr Sims!' Mrs Rudd called. And then, before he could escape, she added: 'You as well, Mr Long.'

By now, she was upon them. It was very odd, thought Long ruefully, that one person like Mrs Rudd could give this impression of surrounding two people.

'It's about this history game of yours, Mr Sims,' she said, and from the tone of her voice it was obvious to both of them that whatever she wanted to say to them was not going to be in the nature of a compliment. 'I deeply resent the inference that Mr Holliday's class are not taking part because I am "scared".'

Long and Sims both started to protest together, each disclaiming any responsibility for such a charge. Mrs Rudd waved aside their protests.

'I do not wish to argue over who said what,' she said tersely. 'I am merely here to tell you that Mr Holliday's class will take part, and I shall lead them.'

Sims and Long stared at her. 'But Miss Lewis's class have already taken over the part of the Vikings . . .' began Sims.

'Have they,' said Mrs Rudd sniffily. 'Then we shall join forces with them.'

Sims was furious. How dare this woman suddenly chop and change her mind like that and expect everyone to jump at her merest whim?! 'What do you mean?' he snapped, his voice full of righteous indignation. 'You can't do that!'

Mrs Rudd acted as if she hadn't heard him. 'I shall see Miss Lewis and we shall work our tactics out together,' she informed him. 'We shall see you in the morning.'

And with that she walked off, leaving Sims staring after her, open-mouthed. Beside him, Long chuckled. 'Welcome to King Street,' he said with a grin.

• • •

When Beeston arrived at the school the next morning, Sims was waiting for him at the entrance. 'I've got a complaint,' said Sims.

'Can I take my coat off first?' asked Beeston forlornly.

Beeston walked down the corridor towards his office, with Sims following, filling him in on Mrs Rudd's action in moving in on the history game in indignant tones. My God, groaned Beeston. The man's only been here a few days and already I'm under siege from him.

They passed the decorators, who were now mounting guard over their equipment, and then marched into the outer office, nodding a 'Good morning' to Mrs Stone, and finally into Beeston's office, with Sims still talking.

'And then she just came in and took over,' raged Sims.

Beeston hung his coat up on his hook. 'Not exactly "over", as I understand it, Mr Sims.'

'But we already had three classes taking part!' Sims protested.

'Yes, but as I recall you said the game was intended to have three classes from the same year?'

Sims paused in his angry tirade, and grudgingly admitted: 'Well, originally, yes . . .'

'So that's what you've now got,' said Beeston.

'Yes, but Miss Lewis is furious,' said Sims, starting up again. 'And quite rightly, too.'

'All right,' said Beeston wearily. 'What do you want me to do about it?'

'Tell Mrs Rudd she can't join in. I'd do it, but I'm only a supply teacher and I don't think she'd take much notice of me.'

Beeston thought it over. The new school year, and already an inter-staff Civil War was on the point of breaking out. 'Can't you absorb another class into the game?' he asked, hopefully.

'Well, yes, we can,' admitted Sims, 'but frankly . . .'

'Frankly, I agree the manner in which it's been done is high-handed,' said Beeston, 'but you've got what you originally wanted and, in my view, if you can't sort it out between you then it'll be better if you scrap it.'

Sims stared at Beeston aghast. 'Scrap the game?' he said. 'Just because I've upset the school's music teacher?'

'No,' said Beeston, 'because I would rather run a school without a lot of strife, than run one with constant bitching going on. And, in my opinion, the sooner this gets sorted out the better. So my suggestion is, play the game and get the whole thing over and done with.'

Sims weighed it up. He wasn't happy about it, but then, what clout did he have in this school? None. He was the new teacher, and a supply teacher at that. He could refuse and take on Mrs Rudd, but then what? No, he thought, let her have this one. There would be other opportunities. He'd get his own back in his own way, and in his own time. 'All right,' he conceded, but without grace. 'We'll see if we can work it out. But I'm not happy.'

'No, I'm sure you're not,' said Beeston.

Sims went to the door, irritation still writ large on him. 'I'd better tell Miss Lewis,' he said, making it more an accusation than a statement.

'Right,' said Beeston, blithely ignoring the implied criticism. 'Oh, by the way, Mr Sims . . .'

'Yes?'

'Have you taken a tin of paint?'

Sims frowned at him, bewildered. 'Paint?' he said. 'What sort of paint?'

'From the decorators. Or paintbrushes?'

Sims shook his head. 'No,' he said.

'I thought not,' said Beeston, 'but you never know.'

• • •

It was two days later that Holliday discovered what had been done with the decorators' missing paint. He had arrived at school that morning, convinced that he had at last worked out the timetabling answer to Mrs Patterson's library problem. He sauntered in from the car park, a smile almost on his face as he reflected that Patterson would at last stop bothering him with unfounded and unfair allegations that her remedial group were being discriminated against. As he turned the corner and was about to walk into the school buildings, he stopped, and the smile was wiped completely from his face.

'Oh my God!' he said.

• • •

'Someone's what?' said Beeston incredulously.

'Painted huge letters on the wall of the playground:

"Down With English. Norman Rules OK." I spent half an hour racking my brain trying to work out if we had a Norman in the school, and what he might have against English lessons, before it clicked.'

'Sims's history game.'

'Exactly,' said Holliday. 'I'm surprised you didn't see it as you came in.'

'I came in the other entrance,' said Beeston. 'My God. How big is it?'

'About twenty feet long and three feet high.'

Beeston groaned. 'I suppose we ought to be grateful they wrote something clean,' he said.

They turned as Patterson's voice came echoing down the corridor towards them. 'Mr Beeston!' she called. 'Have you seen what someone's painted on the wall outside?'

• • •

Beeston and Long stood side by side in front of the wall on which the slogan had appeared. It was big, there was no doubt of that, thought Long. It must have taken them ages to do it. Beside them, children jostled to get a better view of the message, all admiring the bravado that had gone into doing it.

'It still doesn't follow that it was my class who did it,' said Long defensively.

'Of course it does,' said Beeston, irritated. 'Your class are the Normans. Who else is going to paint "Normans Rule" on the wall?'

'It doesn't exactly say "Normans . . .",' Long pointed out.

'I can see what it says, and all it means is your class can't spell.'

'It may have been someone trying to make trouble for us,' suggested Long, loyally defending his children.

'Well if it was they've succeeded,' Beeston scowled.

'Hello,' said Sims, arriving beside them. 'I hear there's been some trouble concerning the history game.'

Some trouble?! Beeston nearly exploded. This was the man who was to blame. He should have persuaded Mrs

Rudd to kill him when she was in the mood.

'Did you?' Beeston fumed. 'Well if you look straight in front of you, you can see it. Are the letters big enough for you? I thought we could try and get that wall into the *Guinness Book of Records*.'

'I don't really think you can blame the game . . .' said Sims.

'No?' demanded Beeston. 'Who should I blame? The Science Department? The Art Department? It doesn't say "Picasso rules OK", it says "Normans Rule OK".'

The children nudged each other. This was great, teachers arguing amongst themselves, and out in the playground, too. Normally they only did it when they thought the children couldn't see. Sims, aware of the audience, felt it was important that he didn't lose too much face in front of them.

'Actually,' he pointed out, 'it says "Norman rules OK".'

Beeston turned and glared at him, wondered whether he could successfully claim temporary insanity if he killed Sims on the spot in front of all these witnesses, then counted to ten and stomped back inside the school. Sims and Long watched him go.

'I think I won that last little point,' said Sims.

• • •

'It's all this Philip Bradley Sims's fault,' complained Beeston bitterly. 'Him and this history game of his. I should have been warned the first time I laid eyes on him, when he just breezed into the staff room. He should be made to wear a sign saying: "This man is dangerous".'

Mrs Stone looked up from her desk where she was finalising the numbers of the new children, and said in a placatory tone: 'I'm sure he means well.'

'Means well?' fumed Beeston. 'Most of the world's great disasters are caused by people who "mean well". The people who designed the Titanic meant well. The point is he's caused more ferment and chaos in a few days than Brown did in a whole term. Why couldn't Millford have offered Sims that job?'

'I'll tell you one thing, though,' said Mrs Stone. 'This history game has certainly got the children interested.'

'Only because they're painting on walls,' snapped Beeston. Honestly, what was the matter with the woman, defending this obvious danger to the education system. Was there no loyalty any more?

'No,' Mrs Stone disagreed, 'I've been talking to Mr Long and Miss Lewis, and even Mr Holliday agrees that this game has got their children wanting to know more about history, and how and why it happens. I think you've got a good teacher there.'

Beeston was not convinced. 'You're far too soft,' he said sourly. 'You'd say that if Hitler turned up for a job.'

'No, I mean it,' said Mrs Stone. 'In the short time that he's been here, he's made quite an impact.'

She can say that again, thought Beeston ruefully. Walls graffitied. Mrs Rudd upset.

'All in all,' said Mrs Stone with quiet confidence, 'I think he's going to be all right.'

• • •

By the middle of the following week, the two decorators had finally finished their work and had gone, relieved to be away from the school. Holliday had indeed cracked the Mystery of the Library Periods on the timetable, and Mrs Patterson's remedial reading groups were now happily accounted for. All in all, a kind of peace seemed to have settled over King Street. That peace was about to be very rudely shattered.

The point of the history game, as Sims had informed his class and everyone else involved in the game, was to make moves, either diplomatic or military, which advanced each country's cause. All these moves were to be placed in sealed envelopes, and then all opened at the same time. Points were scored depending on the move, with a move that outwitted the other 'countries' scoring the most points; and the first 'country' to gain ten points was the winner. After several days of scheming, plotting and move-making, each 'country' now had six points. Miss Lewis's and Mrs Rudd's Vikings were counted as separate contingents, primarily because Lewis and Mrs Rudd weren't talking to each other. Now that the peripheries of the game, the painting on walls and the Norse battle cries, had all died down, the game was continuing on its proper course and on an even keel. Or so Sims thought.

In the belief that it would encourage the children to think for themselves and arrive at their own conclusions, Sim's policy was for his class to discuss their next move amongst themselves and place it in the sealed envelope. Then Sims would discuss the implications of the move they had chosen, and the other possible moves they could have made. Learning by making mistakes, learning by doing. The time had now come round again to find out what his class had decided their next move would be.

'Right,' he said, adopting the role of military and diplomatic adviser to his class, 'in our last lesson we agreed that we English have three options for our next move: either to make an agreement to side with the Vikings, or to pretend to sign a treaty with the Normans to give us more time, or to attack the Norman fleet while they're in the English Channel. Agreed?'

There was a general nodding of heads and murmurings of excited agreement amongst his class at this. This is really good, thought Sims, they're really getting into this.

'And what did you decide?' he asked.

'To attack the Normans, sir,' announced Chandra.

'And you're all agreed on that?' asked Sims.

'Yes, sir,' nodded the children, a few of them adding uncalled-for and undiplomatic phrases such as 'Smash the Normans'. However, these things could be overlooked, thought Sims to himself with a smile. The main thing is they are learning how and why history works.

'Right,' he said, 'if you give me the envelope with your move, I'll keep it safe until they're all opened later today.'

Chandra and the others exchanged bewildered glances. Then Chandra said: 'I haven't got it, sir.'

Sims looked at him, puzzled. 'Then where is it?' he asked. 'I thought you had it all ready?'

'We did, sir,' said Chandra. 'Mrs Rudd took it.'

Sims's mouth dropped open in shock, and the class tensed. This, they knew, was Trouble. 'Mrs Rudd . . .?' began Sims.

Chandra and the other children nodded. 'Yes, sir,' said Sarujeet. 'She came and told us to give it to her.'

'She's not allowed to do that!' exploded Sims. Whatever next!

'I know, sir,' said Chandra, 'that's what we told her, but she said she was a teacher so we had to give it to her.'

Sims was already moving towards the door. 'Class,' he said grimly, 'stay here.'

With that he stomped out of the room. Immediately the whole class moved as one huge excited mass, rushing for the door to lean against it in the hope of hearing what was going to happen.

For her part, Mrs Rudd was giving Mr Holliday's class a lesson on early Norse music as part of the history game, when the door to the classroom burst open and Sims burst in.

'Mrs Rudd!' he raged. 'You took our move!'

Holliday's class sat in their seats, stunned. This had never happened before. Well, hardly ever. Not between teachers, anyway; it was usually an angry parent who suddenly arrived like a vigilante at the classroom door, intent on avenging some wrong they believed their child had received. This was Big Time. This was Teacher against Teacher. Mrs Rudd took it all in her stride.

'Do you mind, Mr Sims,' she said coolly, 'I am in the middle of a class.'

Sims did mind. 'You took our class's move,' he fumed. 'And I want that envelope back, unopened.'

Holliday's class watched, hardly daring to breathe. This was better than the television.

'I haven't the faintest idea what you're talking about,' said Mrs Rudd primly. 'Now if you will please leave my classroom . . .'

'Not without our class's move,' snapped Sims.

He meant business, she could tell. Good God, she thought, the man's unbalanced. 'Certainly not,' she said. 'I shall see you later.'

Sims felt a great wave of despair washing over him. This woman was worse than a brick wall, she was, she was . . . Words failed him. He decided to change his tack, appeal to her sense of reason. That was assuming she had one. 'But it's our secret move and you're not supposed to know it until after all the moves have been made,' he said. 'Those are the rules of the game.'

Mrs Rudd was unmoved. 'Mr Sims, in real wars people don't stick to rules,' she said. 'That is the truth of history.'

Sims gaped at her. What was the woman saying? 'But you can't just confiscate our move like that . . .' he said, incredulously.

Mrs Rudd almost smirked, but restrained herself. It wouldn't look good in front of the children. Instead she just said smugly: 'If you must know, I also got hold of Mr Long's move the same way. Frankly, I just did what any good Viking would have done. After all, we are the Vikings.'

'But you cheated! You stole our move!'

'Exactly,' said Mrs Rudd. 'Therefore, our class has both your moves, and we have topped them with our move.'

'But you can't do that!' Sims stormed. 'It isn't fair!'

'It may not be fair, Mr Sims, but that's history,' said Mrs Rudd. 'We now have ten points, we have won, and the Vikings are now the new rulers of England in 1066, having defeated both the English and the Normans. Now, if you'll excuse me I do have a class. If you wish to discuss it further I suggest we talk about it at break in the staff room, rather than in front of the children.'

The children exchanged disappointed glances. And miss out on all the fun of this big battle? 'We don't mind, miss,' said Andrew hopefully.

'Quiet,' said Mrs Rudd shortly. She turned back to Sims with a smug smile. 'Well, Mr Sims?' she asked.

Sims glared at her for a moment, then at Holliday's class, all watching him, wondering what he was going to do, then back at Mrs Rudd. Was Mr Sims going to attack her? Holliday's class were to be disappointed.

'Right,' Sims snapped tersely. 'I'll see you at break time.' And with that he stormed out of the classroom.

Mrs Rudd permitted herself a little satisfied smile, and held up a warning hand to quell the cheers that appeared to be about to break out from her delighted pupils. A victory, perhaps, but it wouldn't do for Mr Sims to hear them celebrating. It would only bring him back for another round.

'Attention, class,' she said. 'The Vikings, who were nearly always successful in wars,' and here she gave a little smirk, 'preferred the sound of the horn to the more melodious stringed instruments . . .'

• • •

Soon it was all over the school, mainly because Holliday's class spent the whole of break time running around the playground chanting 'We won! We won!' As Lewis and Sims were on playgrond duty together, this did not go down well with either of them; and for the first time Sims found himself wondering if he had done the right thing in taking on a contract to do supply teaching at King Street.

For Beeston, sitting in his office with Holliday, it was a relief that the game was finally over. Also, much as he hated to admit it, it had been a brilliant move on Mrs Rudd's part. In her own way, the woman was a genius. 'So your class won,' he said.

'So it seems,' said Holliday, a little bit of the pride rubbing off on him. 'Big-headed little blighters. They'll be insufferable for days. Sims, Long and Lewis are demanding a rematch, though, claiming the result was won by cheating.'

Beeston shuddered at the thought. 'Not on your life,' he said. 'Once is enough for that game. Let's quit while the school's still standing. And if you ask me, Mrs Rudd's method of winning was quite valid. The politics of wars are totally unfair. She's taught your class a valuable lesson in history.'

'I don't think Sims appreciated it,' said Holliday with a smile.

'He'll learn,' said Beeston. 'You know, after due consideration, I think he'll be all right.'

'Oh?'

Beeston nodded happily. 'Anyway,' he said, 'thank God it's all over. Now we can hopefully get back to a quiet life.'

There was a brief knock at his door, then it opened and Mrs Patterson looked in. 'Ah,' she said, 'there you are.'

Beeston felt his new-found happiness evaporating. 'Yes?' he said.

'I've got another problem with the timetable.'

CHAPTER TWO

FIREWORKS

It was, reflected Harry Beeston as he walked across the playground, the time of year he hated most. Firework Day, November the Fifth. Perhaps that wasn't quite true – there were quite a few times of the year that he wasn't impressed with. Early winter, with its damp and mornings that made him cough and sneeze. New Year's Eve, with its hordes of drunks lurching around singing songs at him in a loud voice and offering to First Foot wi' him into his house at one o'clock in the morning, bearing a lump of coal in one hand and a large bottle of beer in the other. Maybe, he thought, I'm just getting old.

No, he said to himself, the rest I can cope with, but the run-up to Firework Day is the worst of them all: bangs and explosions going off and frightening every form of life in Great Britain, whether plant or animal, that was over sixteen years old and under ten; gangs of miniature Fagins roaming the streets demanding 'a penny for the guy', whether they had a guy or not. And most people didn't have a clue as to whether they were celebrating the attempt to burn down Parliament or the fact that the attempt was defeated. Current sympathies, he was sure, would lie with Guy Fawkes. He had recently seen a piece of graffiti painted on a wall: 'Guy Fawkes, where are you now your country needs you?'

'Good morning, sir,' piped a cheery voice, rousing him from his thoughts.

'Good morning, Asim,' he said. Ah well, he mused, the reflective part of the day was over. 8.40am. Time to enter reality.

• • •

Fireworks were also dominating the conversation in the staff room, for once taking precedence over the usual major topic: who was the last person to have a cup of tea and who'd used up all the water in the kettle? Fred Holliday was particularly incensed.

'Let me get this straight, Sims,' he said, 'You're saying that Guy Fawkes was framed?'

'Absolutely,' said Sims. 'King James needed to turn people against the Catholics for political reasons, and this was an ideal way to do it. Hitler did exactly the same with the Reichstag fire, getting his own people to set fire to it and then finding a suitable scapegoat and a fake confession, thus putting the blame on the Jews and the Communists.'

'Yes, I know all that,' said Holliday, 'but that was Hitler's Germany. We're talking about English history here.'

'What makes us so special?'

Holliday stared at him as if not fully comprehending that Sims could actually be saying what he was saying. 'You're suggesting it was a government conspiracy . . .'

'I'm not suggesting it,' said Sims, 'I'm stating it categorically. From a historian's viewpoint all the evidence points to it. For a start, how else other than with official sanction could so much gunpowder have been brought into the Houses of Parliament? Don't forget we're not talking about a miniature bomb, we're talking about huge barrels of the stuff. Then there's the evidence of the Guards at Westminster . . .'

Holliday just managed to interrupt him before Sims could present the whole case for the defence. 'So according to you,' he said indignantly, 'the history that has been faithfully taught in schools for hundreds of years is a tissue of lies? And our time spent in teaching history has been wasted. No, worse than wasted. You're suggesting that we teachers have duped generations of children.'

'There's nothing unusual about that,' said Sims, unruffled. 'It's been happening since time began. Look what happened to the official Soviet history books after the Russian Revolution: history was rewritten to suit the new government.'

'But that's Russia . . .' protested Holliday.

'British governments have been no different. Look at Shakespeare.'

'Don't try and dodge off the issue,' said Holliday, convinced that he now had Sims in retreat on this argument. 'I thought we were talking about Guy Fawkes.'

'It's the same thing.'

'Of course it's not. Shakespeare's nothing to do with Guy Fawkes. Or are you going to suggest that it was Guy Fawkes who wrote Shakespeare's plays?'

'Shakespeare rewrote the historical truth about Richard III and the Princes in the Tower to the orders of the ruler of the day, Henry VII. In fact, many historians now think that it was actually Henry VII who had them killed. The two Princes were certainly alive after Richard had been killed.'

'Where do you get all this stuff?' fumed Holliday, getting more indignant by the second. Good God, he reflected, this man Sims was nothing more than some political extremist, throwing slurs on English history like this.

'It's all on historical record,' said Sims, 'if only people would look at the evidence instead of reading the fictional version. Going back to the death of the two Princes, most people now accept Shakespeare's version that Richard killed them, which is completely false.'

'So you say.'

'So the evidence says. But that's how rulers and governments operate, they give the public propaganda, not truth. That always has been common practice amongst governments throughout history. And still is today. It's a conspiracy to maintain power.'

Holliday looked at Sims quizzically. 'Are you sure,' he asked, 'that you're not some kind of subversive?'

On the other side of the staff room Mrs Rudd was fully in her stride, haranguing Yvonne Patterson on the dangers of fireworks and stating the case for their complete and utter banning with such force that Mrs Wilberforce had been forced to take refuge in the ladies' toilet.

'Banned I said and banned I meant,' said Mrs Rudd, in case people had missed her point.

'But they are fun,' countered Patterson.

'Fun?' demanded Mrs Rudd. 'Fun?! Frightening animals to death? Children having half of themselves blown away? Fun?'

'If it's in a controlled situation . . .'

'There is no such thing as a "controlled situation" where fireworks are concerned,' pounced Mrs Rudd. 'Last year when my husband and I went out into our garden there were seven expired rockets on our lawn. Are you claiming that they were aimed at us, which is what a "controlled situation" would suggest?'

'Of course I'm not, you can't say where a rocket is going to fall . . .'

'Which is my point exactly. There is no such thing as a controlled situation.'

Patterson rolled her eyes heavenwards. God, it was such a useless exercise even attempting to argue with this woman! 'But I'm not talking about rockets . . .' she began, exasperated.

Mrs Rudd moved in for the kill, triumph in her voice. 'Rockets,' she said, 'are fireworks.'

Patterson groaned. 'Yes,' she said, 'but . . .' She stopped. Was it really worth all the mental effort, the stress, just to win an argument with Mrs Rudd? Was this how wars started? The final exasperation when you realised that you could argue until you were blue in the face but that you might as well be talking to a brick wall for all the good it did.

'Well?' demanded Mrs Rudd, a smile appearing on her face as she sensed victory.

Patterson opened her mouth to utter just one word, very rude, that would wipe the smile off Mrs Rudd's face for good; but at that moment, and with exquisite timing, the bell went to mark the start of the school day.

'Saved by the bell,' declared Mrs Rudd triumphantly.

You certainly were, thought Patterson.

• • •

Beeston sat at his desk and contemplated the piles of papers that threatened to overflow the edges at any moment, most of them decorated with the logo of County Hall. The coat of arms on the County Hall letterheads, he had often reflected, was especially wrong. Instead of the present design, which appeared to depict a lion having sexual congress with a unicorn, a more fitting heraldic device would have been a dodo attempting to stick its beak up its own backside. And unsuccessfully at that.

'My God,' he said. 'Don't you think it is actually awe-inspiring, in its own horrific way?'

'What is?' asked Mrs Stone, still trying to balance the week's dinner monies and hoping that Mr Beeston wouldn't try to draw her into one of his long conversations. Actually, conversation was the wrong word: monologue was better.

'The sheer volume of paperwork that County Hall produces,' he said. He picked up one of the assortment of memos and scanned it quickly, then read through it again, more slowly this time. 'Good God, he said.

Mrs Stone sighed wearily and put down her pen. She knew she should have gone into her own office to deal with the dinner registers, but when she was handling money she preferred to keep it in the safety of Beeston's inner sanctum and thus out of the way of any small hands that might happen to be tempted by it. 'All right,' she said. 'I give up.'

Beeston looked at her. 'What?' he said.

'What are you going to tell me?'

'I wasn't going to tell you anything, I was just reading this.'

'Good,' she said, and picked up her pen again.

'But then I was going to tell you about it.'

Mrs Stone deliberated: would she be able to claim diminished responsibility for killing a headmaster? Surely no jury in the world with half a heart could find her guilty.

'When did this memo from County Hall come in?'

'Which one?' she asked. 'They come in on an almost hourly basis, it seems to me.'

'This one, with all these references on. CT, BLG, PBS, RT. God, all these people just to write one letter.'

Mrs Stone peered over his shoulder at it. 'I think that came in this morning,' she said. 'Yes, it did. I haven't had a chance to read it yet, with this rotten dinner money not balancing, so I put it on your desk. What does it say?'

'According to this we've got to invite every parent to a meeting with the School Governors. And we've got to do it immediately.'

'But why? We had a Governors' meeting just a few weeks ago, and most of the parent governors were there then.'

'Ah, but this is a special meeting,' said Beeston. 'According to this, we've got to arrange a meeting because the Education Minister tells us to.'

'The Education Minister? Not County Hall?'

'Well, yes, it is County Hall, but this time they're blaming the Minister of Education himself. And justifiably, in this case, which makes a change. Usually they cast the blame for their actions on the most unlikely organisations, like the local bus company or someone. This one is because the government is insisting that schools become responsible to the parents.'

'But surely we are already?'

'Not enough, apparently. The Minister wants the parents to run the school, to decide what is taught in the school, who teaches in the school, even down to what sort of kids are allowed to be taught in the school.'

'But only one or two parents will actually get involved, so if that happens then one or two parents will control the running of a school, and they'll organise the school for the sake of their own children first.'

'Obvious to you or I, Mrs Stone, but not to the alleged brains that run this country. However, this is the first step, and ours not to reason why, ours but to bash our head against the nearest wall when ordered to do so. The long and the short of it is we'd better fix a meeting a bit sharpish, and send a letter out today with every child, telling their parents about it.'

'Today?!'

'I'm sorry, but this memo stresses that the meetings have to be arranged by the schools as of today's date.'

'Well, really! As if I'm just sitting here with nothing to do, waiting to suddenly start producing 350 letters.'

'Ours not to reason why . . .'

'If you say that again I shall scream. I wouldn't mind, but it's all such a waste of time. All that work, printing the letters, sending then out, opening the school in the evening, when we've already seen the parents a week or so ago, and they'll be the same ones who will turn up?'

'That's a subversive statement, Mrs Stone. Careful or you'll have MI5 tapping your telephone.'

'I'm just stating the reality of the situation. After all, it's me who's got to spend valuable time preparing 350 letters, and I still haven't got this dinner money balanced.'

'Shall I help you with the dinner money?'

'No fear. The last time you did it I ended up 40 pence out and I finally put it in out of my own pocket.'

'You never told me.'

'From my point of view it was 40 pence well spent. Now, please, I must get on. Especially if I've got these 350 letters to produce.'

'Right,' said Beeston. 'I won't say another word.'

'One more thing,' said Mrs Stone. 'Before I get on with this.'

'Yes?'

'You know it's Fireworks Day soon . . .'

'Don't I just. Do you know . . .'

'You said you weren't going to say another word.'

'Yes, but then you started talking again.'

'Only to give you a reminder about something. I don't want another of your anecdotes, I haven't got the time. I just wanted to say, have you given a warning to the school about the dangers of fireworks?'

'Not yet. I'm going to.'

'Well you shouldn't leave it too long. It's a very dangerous time of year, not only for the children but for old people and pets as well. They need to be told.'

'Who, the pets?'

'Would you like these tins of dinner money emptied over your head?'

'Don't worry, I'll do a speech on "The Dangers of Fireworks" in assembly tomorrow.'

'Right.'

Beeston watched Mrs Stone return once more to the pile of open dinner registers. He waited until she had started adding the first column of figures before asking with mock innocence: 'Anything more before I'm allowed to talk again?'

She looked up at him, at the same time surveying her desk as if weighing up which would be the most suitable and cheapest object to throw at him. 'You're not allowed to talk again because you keep putting me off,' she said. 'And yes, there is, as you mention it. Don't forget to remind everyone about foot inspection.'

'That hasn't come round again, has it? The search for the missing verucca.'

'It's the last one we'll be having. With the new round of cuts, it'll be going the same way as the head inspections.'

'So from now on head lice and athletes foot can breed in abundance without official intervention?'

'Only up until tomorrow, when the nurse comes, so remind the teaching staff.'

'Right.' He waited. Nothing more seemed to be forthcoming. Mrs Stone seemed to be about to attempt to wrestle with the intricacies and mysteries of the dinner money once more. 'Is that it?' he asked. 'Can I start talking again yet?

'No,' she said without even looking up. 'And if you persist in talking, I shall commit serious damage on you.'

Beeston sighed. 'The trouble is my pearls of wisdom are just not fully appreciated in this school.'

'If you want my opinion,' said Mrs Stone, looking up at

him briefly from the registers, 'I think you ought to be on the radio.'

Good God, thought Beeston. Flattery from Mrs Stone. 'Why?' he asked, pleased. 'Do you think I'd make a good broadcaster?

'No,' she said, 'but at least I could switch you off easily.'

• • •

It was a quarter past ten at night when the phone rang in the Beeston household. Beeston and his wife, Ann, were in the middle of watching the news, and an item which consisted of 'experts in education' making statements concerning the Minister of Education's most recent pronouncements. It was all irritating Beeston immensely.

'You shouldn't let it get to you,' Ann said as Beeston gave a snort of disgust for the umpteenth time.

'No? Look at them! Most of these idiots wouldn't recognise a child if you tied one to their kneecap, and they get on the box and pontificate about what education needs. What education needs most is for cretins like that to be parcelled up in sacks and dropped in the middle of the Sargasso Sea.'

At this point the Minister himself came on the screen, smiling benignly, and the television set was only saved from actual harm from Beeston's foot by the ringing of the telephone.

Beeston and his wife looked at one another. 'I bet it's for you,' Ann said.

'Why?' asked Beeston.

'Because it usually is. It's either a parent, or a teacher . . .'

'It might be for you this time,' he countered.

'You can't mean you'd prefer to watch this instead,' she said, gesturing at the Minister on the screen, who was now in full flood as he condemned the rising tide of left-wing infiltration into Britain's schools.

'You're right,' said Beeston, and he went to answer the phone.

Fortunately, he reflected, the voice on the other end of

the line was unfamiliar. He always dreaded the phone calls from Mrs Rudd, which seemed to go on for ever. He had visions of hell consisting of endless phone calls from Mrs Rudd in the after-life.

'Mr Beeston?' said the voice, a man.

'Speaking.'

'This is the police station. I understand you're the headmaster of King Street Junior School.'

'Yes, that's right.' The police? An ominous cloud seemed to descend round the phone. Not another break-in? 'What's the trouble?'

'I'm afraid there's been a fire at your school.'

'A fire?!'

'Yes, and there's been some damage caused. I wonder if you could come over and . . .'

'I'll be there right away.'

Beeston slammed the phone down. A fire! Bloody November the Fifth was starting early this year.

• • •

By next morning rumour was rife among all the children going to King Street. The stories ranged from the aeroplane that had dropped on the school, the bomb that had exploded in it, the lightning that had struck it, the boiler that had leaked, the poltergeist who had set light to it, all the way to spontaneous combustion. However, on one thing all the children were agreed: the whole school had been burnt to the ground and they were just going to have a look at the cinders and the ashes before going back home. After all, they could hardly go to a school that no longer existed, could they?

In fact they were all unanimously disappointed to find, as they turned the final corner, that King Street Junior School was still standing. Only Mr Long's hut had been damaged, one of the end walls burned away completely, exposing the classroom like a cut-away drawing. A large sheet of polythene had been draped over the exposed end and nailed into place; but everyone could see that this was where the fire had been. At least, they said to themselves with some satisfaction, they were partly right, part of King Street had been burnt down. They were only disappointed that it hadn't been their classroom. Not because they wanted it to happen to them, they just wanted to share in some of the glory that was now surrounding Mr Long's pupils. These children were now the new heroes of the school: homeless, the survivors of the Big Blaze.

For the members of Mr Long's class this was no consolation. All they could think of was all their possessions, both school and personal, now made useless by fire and smoke. Mr Long was feeling equally bitter, and he was making his feelings known at the emergency staff meeting that Beeston had hastily cobbled together before school proper started.

In trying to calm his staff's fears about their own rooms, and to equip them with the real story of the fire, Mr Beeston's choice of words was perhaps somewhat unfortunate. 'It's not as bad as the kids are making out, and you need to stress this to them,' he had said. 'The only damage is to Mr Long's hut . . .'

At this Long nearly exploded. 'The *only* damage? My class has lost everything!'

'It could have been worse,' pointed out Patterson. 'It was only one room.'

'That is true,' added Miss Lewis.

Long was not appeased. 'You wouldn't be saying that if it was *your* classroom that had been burnt to the ground,' he said angrily.

'But it's not exactly to the ground, is it?' said Sims. 'In fact, most of it's still standing.'

Long didn't even bother to conceal his annoyance at this. 'Well I didn't exactly measure what percentage of it was still upright . . .' he began sarcastically.

At this point, Beeston decided he had better step in before it came to blows. God, he groaned, I hate staff meetings. Put any two of these people together and they'd find something to argue about.

'All right, all right,' he said, calling them to order. Long calmed down, but was still seething, just waiting for another chance to erupt.

'The fact is that Mr Long's hut has been badly damaged by fire and it will need replacing,' said Beeston.

'And where are his class going to go until it's replaced?' came a question.

Yvonne Patterson, thought Beeston. Trust her to ask the dodgy questions. 'For the moment,' said Beeston, 'they'll have to make do with the library. Just until we can get something sorted out.'

As Beeston expected this was the trigger for Long to erupt again.

'Can you imagine trying to teach in the library?' he demanded angrily of everyone. 'It's preposterous.'

Beeston was just about to tactfully change the subject, when Miss Lewis did it for him. 'How did the fire start?' she asked.

On this Beeston felt on safer ground. Surely here there was a topic which wouldn't set Long foaming at the mouth and trying to eat the furniture? 'The fire brigade and the police forensic department are going through the remains at the moment to try to find the cause.' There, he thought. A perfect politician's answer. Speak a lot and say nothing.

'Do they suspect arson?' asked Sims.

Beeston regarded him with a slight irritation. What an idiot. What did he think had caused it, Moses coming back to earth and trying a repeat of the burning bush? 'Frankly, it's difficult to think what else it could be,' Beeston answered.

'It could have been fireworks. Some kid letting one off wrongly and it landing on the hut,' suggested Holliday.

Here we go, groaned Beeston inwardly. Now we open up a whole catalogue of possibilities.

'I expect it was one of Mr Long's science experiments that he'd left on,' said Mrs Rudd sniffily. 'I've always had my doubts about the safety of his science exeriments.'

True to form, Long rose to the bait, this time almost getting out of his chair. 'That's the last thing I'd ever do, and I resent that,' he stormed.

Oh God, thought Beeston, this is all we need, the staff coming to blows. Aloud he said: 'Can we calm this down a bit? This is turning into some kind of World Boxing Match instead of an emergency staff meeting.'

'I'm sorry,' said Long gruffly after a meaningful look of daggers at Mrs Rudd. Beeston decided to plough on, otherwise the meeting would still be going on at home time.

'In case the police want to know, who was the last person here last night?' he asked.

There was a long pause while the staff looked around at each other. It was like one of those scenes in an old British murder mystery film, Beeston mused to himself, where all the suspects are gathered so that the Detective can reveal who really bumped off Uncle Arthur. 'Well?' he asked. 'Someone must have been here last?'

'I suppose I must have been,' offered Sims. 'My car was the last one in the car park.'

'Right,' said Beeston. 'That's answered that one.'

'Although I can't recall seeing anything suspicious.'

'That may have been because you weren't looking for it,' pointed out Miss Lewis.

'Yes, that's possible,' said Sims, a thoughtful expression now on his face.

Oh God, he's off again, thought Beeston. His short experience of Sims had shown him that when he got that thoughtful expression on his face it meant they were in for something like the complete history of arson throughout the ages. Before Sims could open his mouth to develop anything other than simple breathing, Beeston ploughed on: 'Also,' he said, 'just so that you all know, I intend to use the announcement about Mr Long's hut in assembly this morning to lead into a short talk about the dangers of fireworks.'

'Perhaps,' said Mrs Rudd with heavy sarcasm, 'if you'd given the talk earlier, then you wouldn't need to be talking about Mr Long's hut being burnt down.'

The thought occurred to Beeston, as it often did, that he must have been in a masochistic frame of mind when he took on the various members of his staff. He could not possibly believe that they had really changed so much since they started working at King Street. Mrs Rudd, particularly, had seemed so nice at her interview. A bit pushy, perhaps, but nice. Now any meeting with Mrs Rudd was like swimming in a small pool with a hungry piranha fish. What was it about teaching that did this to people? Whatever it was, it needed to be brought back into line every now and then before it took over the personalities completely and turned them into raving maniacs. Not that Mrs Rudd had far to go, in his opinion.

Beeston put on his 'polite but firm' voice and said pointedly: 'Although I accept that I should have given the talk earlier, Mrs Rudd, before you allocate blame, I think we'd better wait and see what the forensic people say *caused* the fire.

Fortunately for Beeston, before Mrs Rudd could come back with a pointed response to this, the bell went. 'Right,' said Beeston, 'there she blows.'

Like Pavlov's dogs the staff were already responding to the bell, each wondering what excuses they could find to delay going to their classrooms by a few seconds longer. The excuse was given to them by Beeston.

'By the way,' he said. 'Before you go, those of you with kids with feet, it's foot inspection day today. The nurse is coming in, so be prepared for interruptions. I'll see you in assembly.'

• • •

It had often struck Mrs Stone that people and their professions were often totally incongruous: plumbers whose houses were filled with leaking taps and radiators that didn't work, builders whose own houses seemed to be falling down, dress designers who appeared on TV chat shows apparently having dressed that day with a shovel. The woman now standing in her office seemed to be no exception to that rule. Nurse Jones from the County Health and Welfare Department seemed to be a residue of illnesses: running cold, sore throat, bad back.

'I shouldn't be here,' she said.

Privately Mrs Stone agreed that she shouldn't. If Nurse Jones was the best advert for the health service that could be found, then it might as well be done away with now.

'I should have been at St Andrews Infants,' clarified Nurse Jones.

'Ah,' said Mrs Stone, none the wiser.

Fortunately, before Nurse Jones could expand on why she should have been at St Andrews, the telephone rang. It was Mrs Wix, the parental plague of Mr Beeston's life, wanting to know what this sudden meeting of the parents was all about and why it was happening so soon after the last one.

'This is a complete and utter waste of ratepayers' money,' Mrs Wix pointed out.

Mrs Stone agreed that it was.

'I am a ratepayer,' Mrs Wix added, just in case the point had been lost on Mrs Stone.

'So am I,' said Mrs Stone, 'and I agree with you.'

'Good,' said Mrs Wix. 'Well you can tell Mr Beeston that I shall be there tomorrow night at this ridiculous and unnecessary meeting.'

'Right,' said Mrs Stone, and replaced the receiver. I'm sure, she thought, that Mr Beeston will be delighted. Usually just the mention of Mrs Wix's name was enough to make him go into hiding.

Mrs Stone turned back to Nurse Jones. She wondered how many germs Nurse Jones had already passed on to her in the short time she had been in the office. 'Now,' she said. 'I'd better find you a child to show you round the school.'

• • •

The saga of Nurse Jones trudging around the school, spreading germs and bacteria throughout King Street in her never-ending quest for veruccas, ingrowing toenails, bunions and corns continued on right through the school morning. At lunch time it was the main topic of conversation, especially for Mrs Rudd, who could hardly eat her dinner for indignation.

'Honestly,' fumed Mrs Rudd, 'I was in the middle of a music lesson when this woman came in and demanded to look at the children's feet! How can I be expected to form a proper school orchestra with that sort of thing going on?'

'We were warned that she was coming round,' pointed out Glenda Lewis, trying to calm Mrs Rudd down. She hated it when Mrs Rudd got angry at lunch time – she was likely to throw her arms out to emphasise a point and knock over the salt and pepper pots.

'That is not the point,' said Mrs Rudd, who was always very well aware of what any actual point was. 'She could have waited until they were in another lesson. I'm sure that when Sir Colin Davis is conducting he doesn't have someone interrupting him to look at the orchestra's feet.'

'She's not much of an advert for the Health Department, is she, breathing cold germs over everyone,' pointed out Mrs Patterson.

'I should think in her job having a blocked nose is an advantage,' commented Lewis with a grin. 'Especially with some of our kids.'

'Well, it's not good enough,' said Mrs Rudd. 'And if she comes round this afternoon when I've got the recorders, I shall tell her so.'

With that, and to emphasise the point, she thumped her fist down on the dining table, knocking the pepper pot over. Miss Lewis sighed.

• • •

For Beeston, visits by the police to his school usually meant that the Local Council were either suddenly having a blitz on road safety, or that one of his children had been caught doing something highly illegal. Today was not the case. Today, instead of the uniformed branch arriving and towering over everyone in sight, Detective Constable Arnott was visiting King Street to find out how and why the fire had started that had burnt half of Mr Long's hut.

Det-Con Arnott now knew what had caused the fire. 'Arson,' he said simply.

Beeston and Fred Holliday exchanged glances. It was as they'd both suspected, but no one likes to think of a pyromaniac roaming their premises and setting fire to them. It's like burglary, but more psychopathic. It's a terrifying invasion. It's deliberate.

'You're sure?' asked Beeston, but more out of politeness. They already had been sure before the forensic people had done their investigations.

'As sure as we can be after a first look,' said Arnott. 'It also fits a pattern with other fires we've had in this area.'

'Oh?' said Holliday. 'Other fires? That sounds sinister.'

'It is, but it may help us catch him. Or her.'

'Providing you know where they're going to strike next,' pointed out Beeston. 'And I didn't think the police employed full-time clairvoyants.'

Arnott didn't smile. Maybe he wasn't sure if Beeston was joking. 'I wonder if I might talk to the rest of your staff?' he asked. 'Maybe they might be able to throw some light on it.'

'In what way?' asked Holliday.

'Any way they can,' said Arnott. 'After all, if you're grasping at straws any old haystack will do.'

It crossed Beeston's mind to say: 'If you want an old haystack I'll get Mrs Rudd for you', but then he remembered that the detective didn't seem to have much of a sense of humour. Also, he wouldn't get the joke. You needed to work with Mrs Rudd to get it. 'You'd better start with Mr Long,' he said instead. 'After all, it was his hut.'

'Good idea. Where will I find him?'

'He should be in the dining hall having his lunch.'

Holliday shook his head. 'He must have finished,' he said. 'He was in the staff room when I last saw him, talking to Sims.'

'Sims, eh,' said Beeston. 'Good, that'll kill two birds with one stone.' In answer to the puzzled expression on the detective's face, he said: 'Mr Sims was the last one here last night. If you jog his memory he might be able to remember something. Follow me, and I'll show you where they are.'

• • •

For Long it was all too much. Here he was, half his classroom burnt to the ground, trying desperately to teach in what little space there was in the school library, and what did he get? Sympathy? Moral support from his teaching colleagues? No, all he got was feet. It had been bad enough trying to eat his lunch with the conversation turning on foot deformities, which was why he'd sought refuge in the staff room. But what did he get? Peace and quiet? No, he got Sims dropping into the chair beside him. That would have been all right if Sims had stopped to commiserate, offer some practical help, like offering to share his classroom now and then until his own class were rehoused. But what did he get? He got more feet!

'And then,' chuckled Sims, 'when Arnold took his shoes off, the smell was really quite incredible. I don't think he could have washed his feet for weeks. Months.'

It was too much. 'Frankly,' said Long sharply, 'I really cannot understand this sudden obsession with feet.'

'It's not an obsession,' defended Sims. 'I'm just telling you what happened when the nurse came into my class.'

'You and everyone else,' snorted Long. 'I even came down from lunch without having my pudding because just as I was about to dig into it, Yvonne Patterson starts on about her granny's feet and how many bunions there are on them per square centimetre.'

'Well it's natural, isn't it,' said Sims, 'with a foot inspection taking over the whole school.'

'I would have thought it was more natural,' pointed out Long, feeling very miffed, 'to be discussing the state of my hut.'

'It's been burnt', said Sims knowledgeably.

'I know that,' said Long, irritated, 'but do I get any sympathy over the fact that I'm trying to teach kids in between other kids coming in and borrowing library books? No, I do not.'

‘I suppose it’s because there’s so much else going on,’ suggested Sims, trying hopefully to ease the situation.

‘So much else?’ said Long indignantly. ‘What much else? There’s feet going on, and that’s it. Feet we can have 365 days a year . . .’

‘Not if you count school holidays.’

Long glared at him, weighing up whether physical violence between teaching staff might bring disrepute on the NAS. He decided to keep to dialogue. ‘Do you have to be so pedantic?’ he demanded. ‘In my opinion huts burning down is a different matter.’

‘A different matter from what?’

‘Feet, of course.’

‘Of course it is, I know that.’

‘Yes, but where’s all the discussion about who did it, that’s what I want to know?’

‘And why?’

‘And more to the point, what am I going to do with my class? We can’t stay in the library for ever.’

If he had been hoping that at this prompting Sims would leap in and offer to share his classroom, Long was disappointed. Any such hope evaporated as Beeston arrived, accompanied by the detective constable, hot on the trail of evidence.

‘Detective Constable Arnott,’ introduced Beeston. ‘Mr Long.’

The constable gave Long a polite and formal nod, to which Long responded with an equally polite and formal ‘Hello’. It crossed Beeston’s mind that the two had possibly met at some earlier time: Long demonstrating and the officer arresting. However, the introductions were equally formal when Beeston introduced Sims to the detective. He wondered if this was the detective’s technique: treat everyone as a possible suspect. Whatever it was, he decided it would be best to let the detective get on with it. He’d find out what had happened later. Word on the bush telegraph would soon get back. It always did. As his parting shot, Beeston said to the detective: ‘As I told you, Mr Sims was the last person to leave the premises yesterday after school.'

'That's right,' said Sims, adding: 'although as I said to Mr Beeston, I'm afraid I didn't see anything out of the ordinary.'

'No kids still hanging around?' asked Arnott, flicking his notebook open.

'Not that I noticed,' said Sims, feeling a bit of a failure as far as eyewitnesses went.

'Have you found any clues yet?' asked Long.

'Not yet,' said Arnott. 'We're still looking. One thing, though.'

'Yes?' asked Sims and Long together.

'It looks to us like the same method used in other school fires we've had in this area.'

Long and Sims exchanged puzzled glances. 'Other fires?' said Long.

'Yes,' said Arnott. 'Not as bad as this one, but it looks like the same people.'

'Which schools were these at?'

'St James in High Town.'

'Good heavens!' said Sims. 'Did you say St James?'

'That's right,' said Arnott.

'Well, that's a coincidence.'

'What is?' asked Arnott, and Long noticed that a pencil had appeared as if from nowhere and was now poised just above the pages of Arnott's notebook.

'I used to teach there on supply,' said Sims. 'In fact, I was up there just last week borrowing some fax sheets from their Resources Centre.'

Which day was this?' asked Arnott.

'Tuesday.'

There was a stage pause, before Arnott said casually, almost too casually, Long thought: 'The fire was last Wednesday.'

Sims either didn't notice this 'too casual' act by the policeman, or just took it as a sign of awkwardness in dealing with members of the public. He smiled and said cheerfully: 'Ah, that would account for the fact that I never saw any sign of it. What a coincidence, though.'

'Where were the others?' asked Long, keen to get his colleague off the suspicious list over the St James fire, resentment over the 'feet' business now nearly gone.

'One at Millbrook,' said Arnott, not needing to check in his book.

This time Sims came in cheerfully with: 'The Catholic school by the roundabout?'

Arnott gave Sims a curious look and said: 'That's the one.' He then added thoughtfully: 'You haven't been up there recently, have you?'

'No,' said Sims, 'although I did one day's supply teaching there about a year ago. I also go past it every day, on my way here, and then on my way home.'

'I see,' said Arnott. 'About what time would that be?'

'Eight o'clock in the morning, and then about five, depending on if I'm staying late here,' said Sims.

The detective turned back to some notes he had written earlier in his book, then looked directly at Sims. 'The fire was spotted at half past five,' he said.

'Good God!' said Sims, astonished. 'I see, and you're wondering if I might have seen anything.'

There was a pause before the detective answered. 'Well,' he said, 'that is one thought.'

'When was this fire at Millbrook?'

The detective looked at his notes again. 'Two weeks ago,' he said. 'Thursday the 17th.'

Sims's face creased into a frown as he racked his brains. Long gave an inward groan. 'The 17th,' mused Sims. He mused a bit more, finally coming up with: 'No, I didn't see anything suspicious. Mind, I wouldn't really have been looking.'

'I see,' said Arnott, although what he saw he wasn't going to say.' Tell me, Mr Sims, where is your classroom in relation to Mr Long's?'

Before Sims could answer the staff room door opened and Mrs Stone put her head in and called out: 'Is Detective Constable Arnott in here? His office wants him on the phone.'

Once Arnott had gone, after having made arrangements to see Sims after school, Long sat and stared incredulously at Sims. Sims looked back at Long, puzzled. 'What's the matter?' he asked.

'You,' said Long.

'What do you mean, me?' asked Sims, slightly indignant.

'What I mean,' said Long, spelling it out, 'is that it's a wonder he didn't arrest you on the spot.'

Sims frowned, baffled. 'Arrest me?' he said. 'Why should he arrest me? I don't get you.'

'Three fires. And the single uniting factor is, everywhere you've been, there's been a fire.'

The effect on Sims was as if someone had smacked him over the head with a wet fish. He stared at Long, stunned for moment, then said: 'Oh my God! No, that's ridiculous!'

'You think so?'

'But surely the police wouldn't think that *I* had anything to do with them?!'

'No? You were also the last person here last night. If this was Juliet Bravo, you'd be under lock and key right now.'

• • •

'Right, ready recorders?'

Mrs Rudd was in full control. It may not have been the Halle Orchestra, it may have only been Mrs Wilberforce's class, but it was music, the food of the Gods. Mrs Rudd struck the chord on her piano with a finesse that Mr Beeston had once likened (out of her hearing) to that of a pair of rivet hammers. The recorders took up their cue and gave forth an eerie noise, like a cross between a lovelorn seal and a faulty hot water system. It was at this point that the door of the music room opened and Nurse Jones looked in.

'Excuse me,' she queried, 'is this Mrs Wilberforce's class?'

'Recorders, stop!' called Mrs Rudd, and the eerie noise ground to a halt like an antique bellows winding down. Mrs Rudd glared at the offending intruder. 'I beg your pardon?' she demanded imperiously.

If Nurse Jones was meant to wilt under Mrs Rudd's glare, she showed no sign of doing so. 'Is this Mrs Wilberforce's class?' she repeated.

'Yes,' said Mrs Rudd, 'as it happens, it is.'

'Good,' said the nurse, 'I've got to examine their feet.' And with that she started to unpack the tools of her trade: a little medical chest with spatulas in it.

Mrs Rudd counted slowly to three, and then said with as much sweetness and politeness as she could muster: 'Well, if you wait for twenty minutes they will be back with Mrs Wilberforce and you can examine their feet then.'

'I'd rather do them now,' said the nurse, pulling on a pair of disposable gloves.

Mrs Rudd bridled. Really, couldn't this woman understand plain English? Still politely, but with the sweetness now gone, she said, '*I'd* rather you did them later.'

Nurse Jones was not so easily put off. 'I can't do them later. I'm doing them in numerical order. That way I can keep a check on who has been done and who hasn't.'

The children kept their mouths firmly shut, hardly daring to breathe, hoping that they wouldn't be noticed. This was good stuff, this was a battle of wills between Mrs Rudd and the nurse. This was something to talk about in the playground later. They had actually been there when it happened!

Mrs Rudd was fully aware of her young audience's expectations and had no intention of losing this match. 'I'm sure you consider that feet are of vital importance,' she said with as much dignity as she could muster, 'but I am trying to take a music lesson and we are at a very crucial stage with the recorder parts.'

Nurse Jones was also one who did not give up easily. Nurse Jones reached for her Big Guns. 'Mr Beeston assured me,' she retorted acidly, 'that I could receive full co-operation in carrying out the examinations.'

Grim-faced, she waited for Mrs Rudd to capitulate and throw in the towel. Mrs Wilberforce's class could have told her that she had used the wrong gambit. They knew that to flaunt Mr Beeston's authority on Mrs Rudd was like waving a red rag in front of a bull. Mrs Rudd drew herself up to her full sitting height at her piano stool and delivered her reply: 'And so you shall. In twenty minutes when I have finished.'

The children watched and waited. Stalemate. What would Nurse Jones's next move be? Nurse Jones deliberated briefly, and then produced her Biggest Gun of all: 'I shall have to report this to County Hall Health Department.'

Was this a hit? No! Mrs Rudd smiled, and to the children's delight her honeyed voice dripped pure acid as she replied: 'Do. The name is Rudd. R-U-D-D. Now, recorders, when you hear the chord . . .'

The children put their recorders back in their mouths and once again the eerie blowing noise filled the room, obliterating the sound of the door opening, and then slamming shut, as Nurse Jones made her exit.

• • •

'Right,' said Beeston, 'what response have we had from the parents so far?'

'Mrs Wix phoned,' said Mrs Stone.

'I guessed she would,' groaned Beeston. 'And?'

'That's it.'

There was a pause while this sank in, then Beeston queried, just to make sure he'd got it right. 'That's it? Just Mrs Wix?'

'Yes.'

'No other acknowledgements?'

'Not yet. Don't forget, the letters only went out yesterday.'

'Yes, but the meeting's tomorrow night. You did put a tear-off strip on the letter for them to send back, didn't you?'

'Of course I did,' said Mrs Stone indignantly. 'You saw the letter before it went out.'

'Yes,' said Beeston. He gave a sigh of resignation. 'Oh well, it'll be interesting if no-one turns up. That's the sort of parental consultation we could do with.'

'I think the problem is you didn't give them enough notice,' pointed out Mrs Stone. 'To send out a letter telling them about a meeting in two days time . . .'

'It wasn't my fault, that was all the notice County Hall gave me. "These meetings must be instigated by blah blah blah . . ."'

'Instigated isn't the same as having them. You could have instigated it for next half term.'

Beeston shook his head firmly. 'Not according to the wording from County Hall. 'Immediate parental consultation' were the words used, and when things go wrong with this new policy and the detritus starts hitting the proverbial fan, I want to know that we at King Street are well and truly covered.'

'With detritus?' enquired Mrs Stone with mock innocence.

Before Beeston could have the last word, the door to the office opened and Fred Holliday appeared, spotting Beeston.

'Ah' he said, 'there you are. Busy?'

'No,' said Beeston acidly, 'I just come to this school for a rest.'

'Oh that's all right then,' said Holliday, and with that he came in and shut the door.

Beeston was dumbfounded. What did he have to do to the staff at King Street to let them know that he was too busy to see them, apart from build a brick wall across his office door? 'Of course I'm busy,' he said irritably. 'I've got this foot woman causing minor bits of havoc throughout the school, and Long's burnt-out classroom causing major havoc. Like, where do I put them?'

Holliday cast a quick glance at Mrs Stone, now engrossed in sorting the requisitions into order, and said in a confidential tone: 'Funnily enough, that's why I wanted to see you.'

'You've got an idea where I can put them?'

'No,' said Holliday, 'about Long's classroom being burnt down.' And again he cast a glance at Mrs Stone, and then over his shoulder as if expecting to find someone behind him. 'Can we talk confidentially?'

Beeston looked at Holliday, baffled. What had happened? Had Fred finally flipped his lid? Maybe it was a desperate attempt to prove insanity as a way of persuading County Hall to give him early retirement. Mrs Stone had noticed it, too, and was now trying to pretend to concentrate even harder on the requisitions than normal. 'You'd better come into the inner sanctum,' said Beeston, wearily.

As they went into Beeston's office, Mrs Stone called after them: 'I'll see that you're not disturbed.'

As soon as they were in the office, Beeston decided to ask a point-blank question. He'd been in these 'confidential' situations before and he'd known them take half an hour before the person concerned finally came out with what they wanted. 'Right,' he said. 'What's all this cloak-and-dagger stuff in aid of?'

'The police think Sims did it,' said Holliday.

Beeston remained baffled. 'Did what?' he asked.

'Started the fire.'

There was a pause while this sank in, then Beeston looked at Holliday and laughed. 'What?!' he laughed. 'Sims?!'

'Ssssh!' urged Holliday. 'They do. Long was telling me.'

'Oh do me a favour, Fred,' said Beeston. 'The local plod may not be Maigret, but even they wouldn't go for anything as idiotic as that.'

'I don't know,' said Holliday. 'The other day he told me he thought that Guy Fawkes was framed.'

'Who did?'

'Sims.'

'So?'

'Well. Maybe it's symptomatic. Sympathy for fire-raisers and all that. After all, what do we know about him? He's new. And he has taught at all the schools that have been burnt. If you ask me, there's no smoke without fire.'

'Particularly in this case,' commented Beeston, adding:

'Don't be ridiculous, Fred. I know we've had all sorts here, but an arsonist?!'

All right,' said Holliday philosophically, 'but don't say I didn't warn you.'

Further discussion of the possibility of Sims being a fire-raiser vanished within the next few seconds as the sounds of raised voices from the outer office filtered through. Beeston and Holliday could just hear Mrs Stone's murmurs, but above everything was Nurse Jones, venting her full indignation.

'I really must complain to Mr Beeston. I've never been so humiliated,' they heard her say.

'More trouble,' groaned Beeston, and with that he opened the door. 'I heard my name,' he said. 'Is there a problem?'

'The nurse seems to be having a spot of bother,' explained Mrs Stone.

Nurse Jones decided her case would be better presented if she did her own explanations. 'It is a lot more than a spot of bother,' she raged. 'I was almost thrown out of a classroom.'

'Oh? Who by?' said Beeston, already mentally taking bets on the identity of the culprit.

'A woman playing the piano,' announced Nurse Jones. 'She said her name was Rudd.'

Right again, said Beeston's mental bookie.

'Did she?' he said aloud and with as much sympathy as he could bring himself to muster for this walking germ bank. 'Come into my office and we'll discuss it there.'

'We may talk about it, but I will not be fobbed off,' said Nurse Jones resolutely. 'I have my job to do, just like everyone else.'

'True,' said Beeston, and with that they both disappeared into his inner office.

• • •

By next morning the story of Mrs Rudd's battle with Nurse Jones had become a legend throughout the school. The staff were talking about it, the children were talking about it, everyone was talking about it.

Mrs Rudd was no exception, although she wasn't talking about it as a legendary battle, she was talking about it as an unwarranted interruption to her music lessons. And the person she was talking to about it, of course, was Beeston.

'All I'm saying,' said Mrs Rudd in a voice of many decibels, 'is that I object to my lessons being interrupted like that.'

Beeston growned. Every morning of late seemed to consist of himself being harangued by someone, and too often that someone was Mrs Rudd. 'And all *I'm* saying,' he replied with as much reason in his voice as he could force, 'is that this woman is here to inspect feet and inspect feet she is going to.'

'But why can't she choose another time to do it?' demanded Mrs Rudd.

'She has chosen other times,' snapped Beeston irritably, his long-suffering patience finally giving out. This discussion, if any sane person could call it that, seemed to have been going on for hours and he'd just about had enough. 'Nurse Jones has interrupted Mr Holliday's maths lesson, Mr Sims's history lessons, Miss Lewis's domestic science lessons, and can you imagine everyone taking off their shoes in the middle of *that*!'

'Well, I think it most disloyal of you to take the side of an outsider against your own staff,' snapped Mrs Rudd.

'I am not taking the side of an outsider, I am taking the side of the kids. Or, in this case, their feet and the need for those feet to be inspected.'

At this point the first of many school bells for the day sounded. Mrs Rudd glared at Beeston. 'You haven't heard the last of this,' she said as she left to prepare for assembly.

Beeston slumped against the door which she had just slammed shut. 'I don't doubt it,' he groaned to himself.

• • •

However, the real bombshell for Beeston was to come later that day and from a different direction entirely.

Sims had just finished trying to explain to his class the

rudiments of geometry, to nobody's satisfaction. Mercifully for everyone, this ordeal had been put to an end by the bell going for break. When the class were nearly all out, one little girl, Raza, stopped and said: 'Mr Sims, I heard a rumour about you last night.'

'Oh,' said Sims with an indulgent smile as he reflected that children were always making up the most amazing stories about teachers. 'What sort of rumour?'

Raza hesitated, then said: 'If I tell you, you promise me you won't shout at me?'

Sims didn't know whether to laugh out loud. Him? Shout? Mr Mild Manners himself? 'Why should I shout at you?' he asked gently.

'Because teachers shout when they get angry,' said Raza with great seriousness.

'Not all teachers,' said Sims. 'When have you ever heard me shout?'

Raza thought it over. 'When Gary threw that chalk at Asim.'

'Yes, well,' admitted Sims, grudgingly. After all, what was once in how many possible occasions? 'But that was just once, wasn't it? I wanted to make sure he didn't do it again.'

'And when the leg fell off your chair when you sat in it.'

'Yes, all right . . .' admitted Sims again.

'And then when . . .'

Sims was now beginning to feel as if he was the main participant in the Spanish Inquisition. 'Yes, all right,' he said, more than a little nettled now, 'but those are very rare occasions. Teachers aren't perfect, you know.'

'And you won't shout at me now?'

'Of course I won't,' he assured her. 'Now, what is this rumour about me that you heard?'

'Well,' she said, 'Some of the big boys say you set fire to Mr Long's hut.'

There was a momentary pause while Sims let this sink in. Raza watched him, waiting. He had gone very quiet. Had he heard? Then she saw his lips tighten, his nostrils flare out, his eyes narrow menacingly. He looked like her father after that man had said something rude about him. Warningly she said quickly: 'You said you wouldn't shout.'

Mr Sims nodded, but still he didn't speak. Finally he said: 'You're right. I won't shout. Who said that?'

'Some of the big boys.'

'And where did they get that ridiculous idea?'

'They heard Mr Holliday say it to Mr Beeston.'

'How?'

Raza weighed it up. On the one hand there were the Big Boys, who would be most upset if they found out it was her who told on them and how they knew everything. On the other hand there was Mr Sims, with his tight lips and his nostrils going in and out like an angry horse's. She weighed it up again. The Big Boys were far away, and they could always think it was someone else who had told on them. Mr Sims was here *now*. She would tell him. 'They were hiding outside Mr Beeston's window,' she said. 'They always hide outside Mr Beeston's window to hear what goes on.'

'Do they,' said Sims, now looking very grim. 'Right.' And then he was heading towards the classroom door. Raza wondered what Mr Sims was going to do. Was he going to hit the Big Boys? How could he when he didn't know which Big Boys it was?

'Where are you going, Mr Sims?' she called after him. 'Are you going to shout at someone?' But answer came there none, because Mr Sims had already gone. Raza reflected that whoever Mr Sims had gone to shout at, she felt sorry for them. She was glad it hadn't been her.

• • •

Beeston had been in his office when Sims had stormed in. Up until that moment Beeston had counted this as a lucky day. He had only had one encounter with Mrs Rudd (although another one was promised), and he had managed to avoid Nurse Jones. There was still the spectre of that night's parents' meeting hanging over him, where Mrs Wix would take total control over the school, but that was one of these occupational hazards that he was used to taking in his stride. The sudden appearance of Sims, bursting into his office like Clint Eastwood looking for someone to eat alive, took him completely by surprise. It took Beeston a good two minutes to work out what it was all about. Finally he managed to sort out, between Sims's voice going up and down irately, that he had heard about Mr Holliday's confidential visit. Good God, he thought, this office must be bugged.

Sims was still irate. 'I am absolutely furious!' he stormed, just in the case Beeston hadn't got the message clearly.

'Yes,' said Beeston, 'so I gather. Would you mind not kicking my chairs?'

'Frankly it's slander,' stormed Sims, now kicking the desk. 'How dare Mr Holliday say such a thing . . .'

'He didn't actually say that . . .' began Beeston.

'And now the whole school thinks I'm some kind of fire-raiser!'

'Of course they don't,' said Beeston soothingly, trying the softening approach.

'Oh yes they do, because you've got a telegraph service right outside your window.'

'What?'

'Some of the older boys sit out there and listen to everything that goes on in here.'

'The rotten little . . .' Beeston went over to the window, opened it and looked out. No one there. They'd obviously scarpered as soon as they heard him coming. The rotten little perishers! Well that had blown any chance of trying to kid Sims that no such conversation had taken place. As Sims said, it was probably all over the school by now. Might even find its way into the local paper. Beeston shut the window. 'There's no one there,' he said.

Sims wasn't going to let him get away with it as easily as that. 'There was earlier when Mr Holliday was accusing me . . .' he raged.

'He wasn't accusing you . . .' began Beeston.

'Then what was he doing?'

What? How to get out of this without making it worse

than it already was? Oh well, in the last resort, if all else fails, try the truth. 'He was just mentioning that Long had told him . . .'

Sims leapt upon this additional name like Inspector Clouseau after a clue. 'So!' he said triumphantly. 'Long was behind it!'

'No, he wasn't!' defended Beeston. Honestly, the man was impossible. It was like having a male clone of Mrs Rudd on the staff. 'For one thing there's nothing to be behind. You make it sound like a conspiracy! Long had mentioned to Holliday how you'd given that copper who came here the impression that everywhere you went there was a fire, and that's all. So, frankly, it's your fault.'

Sims looked baffled. 'My fault?'

'Well, who else's fault is it if every time you go somewhere it burns down?'

'That was not the impression I gave at all, and I think it most unethical of Mr Holliday . . .'

This last was too much for Beeston, who groaned audibly. 'Oh please,' he said, 'don't start on ethics, or we'll be here for weeks.' Luckily for Beeston, as so often happened at King Street, the bell went, forcing an early end to the contest before it got out of hand. 'There's the bell for the end of break,' said Beeston, in case Sims hadn't heard it. 'I think your class will be waiting for you.'

'Yes,' said Sims grimly. 'They'll be waiting for me to set fire to something.'

There didn't seem a lot more to say to that, and under the circumstances Beeston thought it prudent to let Sims have the last word. Maybe his honour would then be satisfied and he'd drop the matter. Then again, pigs might fly.

• • •

It was at lunch time that Fred Holliday heard the news. He was sitting with Long, Lewis and Patterson, and listening to Patterson trying to identify the meat that Mrs Purkiss, the notorious school cook, had dished out. She had gone through seven different types and finally settled on kangaroo meat ('one that had died of old age'), when

Holliday said: 'What's up with Sims today?'

'What do you mean?' asked Lewis.

'He's not talking to me,' said Holliday, 'I said Hello to him just now and he just stormed past me.'

'I know what that's about,' said Patterson, who had now changed her diagnosis of the remains on her plate to an old shoe. 'It's because of your accusations about him burning down Mr Long's hut.'

Holliday stared at her, stunned. 'Me? I never said any such thing.'

'You did according to the children in my class this morning,' said Patterson.

At this point, Mrs Rudd arrived at the table with her dinner, which gave Holliday a few seconds to sort out the confusion in his mind. Who had said such a thing? Only Beeston had been in the room when he mentioned it, and surely he'd never tell Sims. 'Well,' he said at last, when everyone had got settled down again. 'I think it's bit much the kids spreading stories like that.

'You can't blame the kids,' said Patterson. 'I overheard you saying the same thing to Mr Long yesterday.'

'That was in confidence,' protested Holliday. 'People shouldn't listen to things said in confidence.'

'There's nothing confidential at this school, you should know that,' commented Long. 'I'm not surprised he isn't talking to you.'

'That foot woman refused to talk to *me* today,' said Rudd.

Thinking it was a good time to change subjects before the salt and pepper pots started flying around all over the place again, Miss Lewis put in: 'Is anyone going to this parents' meeting tonight?'

There was one of those awkward silences when no one wants to admit that they're not volunteering. Finally Mrs Rudd said: 'Unfortunately I already have a prior engagement this evening. Mr Rudd and I are singing in the High Street.'

'And people say teachers are too well paid,' said Long acidly. 'You should write and tell the *Daily Mail* that.'

'For charity,' clarified Mrs Rudd.

'Oh,' said Long.

'What about you, Mr Holliday?' asked Lewis, desperate to try and bring some lightness back to the table.

Holliday pondered on it, finally saying: 'Depends. Is Sims going, does anyone know?'

'I don't know,' said Lewis. 'Why?'

'Only if he is I might as well give it a miss,' Holliday said gloomily. 'After all, if I want to spend an evening with someone sitting glaring silently at me I might as well stay at home.'

• • •

The parents' evening that night set a new record, not only for King Street but possibly for any school in the United Kingdom, if not the world. By ten past eight the meeting at the school consisted of Beeston, Sims, Holliday and Lewis. Not one parent had appeared. By twenty-five past eight, the silent consensus was that this meeting was a disaster of a kind rarely met with. By eight thirty, the four had reached the agreement that they might as well start the meeting (which had been due to start at eight o'clock), and get it over with. A brief vote was held, electing Beeston to chair the meeting, and then three pairs of eyes turned to him, waiting for him to declare the meeting over.

Beeston looked back at them and shrugged helplessly. 'Well,' he said, 'thank you all for coming to this meeting. I know it was short notice, which possibly accounts for the fact that no one's turned up.'

The Chairman had obviously got off to a bad start, judging by the reaction this remark caused.

'I'm here,' said Lewis.

'And I don't think I can be desribed as "no one",' said Holliday, adding: 'And Sims is here.'

'Yes, well, I hadn't got anywhere to burn down tonight,' said Sims with bitterness in his voice.

'Look, Sims, I didn't mean . . .' began Holliday. Goddamit, he had even tried to show there were no hard feelings a few seconds ago. What did the man want? Blood?

'Please,' said Beeston, 'can we get back to this meeting? I mean that no parents have turned up.'

'Not even Mrs Wix,' said Lewis, 'which is quite something.'

'Quite something of a relief,' added Beeston, feelingly. 'She phoned me at home and said that her husband had hurt his back and she had to stay and look after him.'

'If you want my opinion . . .' said Sims.

'This does relate to the meeting, does it?' asked Beeston warily. He didn't want the man suddenly leaping up and attacking Fred Holliday.

'Of course. I think you should have looked at the *Radio Times* before you fixed it for this evening and seen what was on the television tonight.'

The other three looked blankly at each other. It was Lewis who remembered. 'Oh, of course!' she said. 'It's the last part of that serial!'

'Which serial?' asked Holliday. 'I never watch anything these days.'

'The one with Sean Connery. What time is it?'

Beeston gave what he hoped would be his last sigh of the day. 'Oh well, that's it, then,' he said. 'The whole fate of the education system of this country, blown because of a television serial.'

'It's very good,' said Lewis. 'I'd forgotten it was tonight.'

'Right,' said Beeston. 'I declare this meeting over.'

It was at that moment that they heard it: the soft pad of footsteps coming slowly, but definitely, down the corridor towards them. They looked at each other. Miss Lewis was the first to speak. 'Perhaps if we turn out the lights we can pretend we've all gone home?' she suggested hopefully.

Her suggestion came too late. The door swung open, and . . . 'Ah, Mr Sangretti!' beamed Beeston jovially. 'Welcome! Come in and join us. Come in and find a chair.'

• • •

It was half past nine when the meeting finally ended, the last part of the serial on the television long since over. By nine thirty-two Beeston was alone, trudging to his car and cursing the government, County Hall, parents who didn't turn up, parents who did turn up, kids who listened outside windows, music teachers, young teachers, old teachers, middle-aged teachers, and nurses who looked after feet. He was just starting to lengthen his list by adding selected targets from the world outside education, when he saw someone walk through the school gates into the darkened playground. Not another vandal? Someone else come to set light to more buildings?

'Mr Beeston,' called a voice. It was Detective Constable Arnott. 'I phoned your home and your wife said you'd still be here. A parents' meeting, I understand.'

'A one-parent meeting, but it's finished now. Any luck with the investigation?'

'That's what I've called in to tell you,' said Arnott. 'We've caught them.'

'You have?' Praise be, at least something positive had happened today.

'They were trying the same thing tonight at another school. West View High. Someone spotted them and we were lucky, we got them.'

'Who were they?'

'Just two kids doing it for a laugh.'

Beeston gave an angry snort. A laugh?

'Exactly,' agreed Arnott. 'Some laugh it would have been if someone had died because of a fire they started.'

'How old were they?' asked Beeston.

'About eight or nine.'

'From around here?' Why didn't he ask it openly: are they from my school? Because he didn't want them to be. Not from King Street.

Arnott knew what he was really asking, and he shook his head. 'No,' he said, 'they're not from your school. Anyway, that's all I came to tell you. I'd better be off, I've got another case on. A series of muggings. Nine year olds again.'

'The victims?'

Arnott shook his head again. 'The criminals. Attacking old ladies and robbing them.'

'It's a rough life at street level,' commented Beeston. There didn't seem to be a lot more to say.

'For you and me both,' said Arnott. 'Good night, Mr Beeston.'

Then Arnott was gone as quickly as he came. Beeston continued on his way to his car. And curse nine-year-old muggers, he mentally added to his list.

CHAPTER THREE

THE SPIRIT OF CHRISTMAS

'While shepherds watched their flocks by night
All seated on the ground,
The angel of the Lord came down
And glory shone around.'

Beeston and Holliday stopped their ramble around the maze of the school's corridors to listen to the sound of children singing, coming from the hall, helped every now and then by an admonition from Mrs Rudd.

'Bit early for carols, isn't it, Fred?' asked Beeston. 'It's only the end of November.'

'You know what Mrs Rudd's like,' said Holliday. 'She wants them licked into shape by the carol concert.

'There speaks the spirit of Christmas,' said Beeston with a wry smile. The two men resumed their stroll around the school, checking the Repairs Necessary list for Country Hall.

'What I can't get over,' said Beeston, 'is how much earlier Christmas seems to pop up every year, particularly in the shops. Almost as soon as Easter's over and the stacks of chocolate eggs are gone, they're replaced by Santa's Grotto. And the price of the presents!'

'I know,' agreed Holliday. 'When I was a kid I was lucky if I got an apple and an orange. By the way, did you get the message about Marchant?'

'No?'

'He won't be in today, he's got a bug or something.'

'Always the way when we get near Christmas,' said Beeston philosophically, 'the staff start dropping like flies. It's the winter, it reduces their resistance.'

• • •

Someone else with the approach of Christmas on her mind was Miss Lewis. She was looking for Beeston, but in the maze had missed him. It was amazing, she thought, how two people could work in the same small place, yet contrive to miss each other all the time. It was because of the twists and turns in the corridors, and the classrooms with more than one door. She was surprised that no one had yet thought to stage a French farce in a school like this. Oh well, she thought, I'll try his office, see if he's returned.

He hadn't.

'He's walking around the school with Mr Holliday,' said Mrs Stone. 'They could be anywhere.'

'I know,' said Lewis. 'I thought I caught their tracks once or twice, but I seemed to keep missing them. I think they've been getting the caretaker to teach them how to become invisible.'

'Shall I give him a message?' asked Mrs Stone. 'He's supposed to be back here straight after break to go through the school insurance documents with me.'

Lewis shook her head. 'No, that's all right,' she said, 'I'll see him later. I just thought I'd grab him while my class are watching television with Mrs Wilberforce's. I wanted to tell him that I've got to go into hospital in a couple of weeks.'

'Oh dear,' said Mrs Stone, instantly sympathetic. 'What for?'

'Do you remember that accident I had with my big toe?'

Mrs Stone cast her memory back. 'That was about two years ago, wasn't it?'

'Yes,' said Lewis. 'Well it's taken this long before the hospital can finally fit me in to have the operation on it.'

'Two years?!' said Mrs Stone. 'Really, it's too bad.'

Lewis gave a philosophic shrug. 'There are others who've waited longer than me, so I suppose I can't really complain.'

'Still,' said Mrs Stone. 'Two years! And it's come at a very awkward time, hasn't it? So near to Christmas.'

'And that's really why I want to see Mr Beeston. Getting a supply in to cover my class may not be too difficult, but it's the Nativity play. I've done it for so many years now that it's difficult to know who to ask to do it.'

Mrs Stone chuckled. 'You weren't going to ask Mr Beeston to do it, were you?' she asked. 'Can you imagine what he'd make of it?'

'No,' said Lewis, 'but I thought he'd know who to ask to take it over.'

It was at that point in the conversation that Mrs Stone had what she took to be a brainwave. If she'd known the unrest her brainwave was going to cause, she would have kept it to herself. 'I've got a suggestion,' she said. 'Why not ask that new teacher to do it? Mr Sims. I've heard some very good reports of plays that he organised at one of the high schools he was on supply at. A neighbour of mine works there, and she said that he did a musical version of *Waiting for Godot* that was quite remarkable.'

'Yes,' said Lewis doubtfully, 'but this is only a first year production with the little ones. It's a far cry from Samuel Beckett.'

'You can only ask him,' said Mrs Stone. 'But personally speaking, I'm sure he'd jump at the chance, and I think he'd make a lovely job of it.'

• • •

If the Christmas spirit had entered some parts of King Street Junior, it had yet to make its appearance in the staff room. Mrs Rudd and Mr Long were taking opposite sides on the question of who should be taking the absent Marchant's class. For her part, Mrs Rudd was declaring that it was outrageous, and demanding why it was that someone else couldn't take them.

'Take what?' asked Mrs Patterson, appearing on the scene.

'I've got half of Mr Marchant's class after break, in addition to my own,' complained Mrs Rudd, keen to find a new ear to bend.

'I've got the other half,' said Long defensively.

'I am not concerned with you,' said Mrs Rudd. 'I had

planned to do quiet listening after break. How can I do quiet listening with forty-five children balanced on thirty chairs? And Mr Marchant's class this year are notorious for their awful behaviour.'

'What do you mean?' demanded Long indignantly. 'They were my class last year. There's nothing wrong with them.'

'That,' said Mrs Rudd pointedly, 'depends on your standards.'

Long glared at her, open-mouthed. He took a deep breath and was just about to start on a long and angry diatribe in retaliation, when Patterson cut in with: 'Talking of standards, can I interest either of you in this Christmas catalogue?'

With that, like a magician producing a rabbit from a top hat, Patterson pulled a Christmas catalogue out of her bag and opened it. Long turned on her, furious at being cut off before he could even get his tirade against Mrs Rudd under way.

'What's that got to do with standards?' he demanded angrily.

'Nothing, but I wanted to bring it into the conversation,' said Patterson with totally disarming candour. 'It's for the World Wildlife Fund which is a very good cause. Look . . .' And she started flicking through the brightly coloured pages like a double-glazing saleswoman showing off home improvements. It's got Christmas cards, wrapping paper, gifts, stocking fillers . . .'

Meanwhile, in another part of the staff room, Miss Lewis had cornered Sims and was sounding him out about his producing the King Street Junior Nativity play. 'Because I've done it every year for the last seven years, everyone expects me to do it again,' she said. 'But with this going into hospital it's impossible this year. So, I was wondering, would you fancy taking it on?'

Sims stopped with his tea cup halfway towards his mouth, flattered. 'Me?' he said.

'Yes,' said Lewis. 'Mrs Stone was telling me about some of the drama work you'd done at the high schools, and I've seen the assemblies your class have put on and I've been very impressed by them. I know the Nativity play is only the little ones, but they do so enjoy doing it . . .'

'I'd love to,' said Sims.

'You would?' smiled Lewis. 'Oh, that's wonderful. You're sure you don't mind?'

'Not at all,' said Sims enthusiastically. 'I'd be delighted. It will be quite a challenge. Maybe I could even try out a way of doing it a little differently.'

A little diffferently? Lewis's relief at having found a safe pair of hands for the Nativity play wavered a little. 'Well, you could,' she said, making sure the doubt was clear in her voice, 'but most people expect it the way it's always been done. Shepherds, wise men, kings, a manger, the baby Jesus.'

'Yes,' agreed Sims, 'but in a school like this, where there are more non-Christians than Christians, maybe we could do it in such a way that everyone gets something from it.'

Lewis was affronted, to say the least. So that *everyone* gets something from it, she thought. What a cheek. 'Well,' she said, holding back her indignation, 'they always seem to have got something from it in the past. I know I may not be Jonathan Miller . . .'

Whoops! thought Sims. 'Don't misunderstand me,' he said quickly, 'I'm not criticising, I'm just saying that maybe we could do something *different*.'

Something *different*? At that word Lewis's last vestiges of relief vanished like a popped bubble. Something different? She was responsible for the Nativity play and she had gone and handed it to someone who was going to do Heaven knows what with it. It would have been better if she'd given it to Mr Beeston to do, at least it would have looked roughly the same. There was no alternative, she'd have to say she'd changed her mind. 'Actually . . .' she began.

The bell went.

'No,' said Sims with a big smile. 'I want you to know that you've made my day by asking me. No, you've made my term. I'm going to do something with this play that no one will ever forget.' And with that he almost bounded out of the staff room, heading for his class. Lewis's heart finally sank. What could she say? Or, worse, what would everyone else say?

• • •

Sims started to sketch out his plans for a totally new Nativity play that very lunch time. What we want, he thought, is something that the kids can identify with, something radical. He was still feeling high on enthusiasm, sketching out roughs for costumes and scenery, when the door to his classroom opened and Mrs Patterson came in.

'There you are,' she said.

Sims regarded her with some puzzlement. From the tone of her voice it was obvious that something was wrong. And from the way she was looking at him, whatever was wrong concerned him. He racked his brain. What on earth could he have done to have offended her? Nothing that he could think of, he had hardly spoken to her. Maybe that was it? Maybe she thought he had been avoiding her over this Christmas catalogue that he'd seen her bearing down on people with. In which case, she was correct, he *had* been avoiding her – but only because he always avoided people he liked who were trying to sell him things. But even if she'd cottoned on to what was happening, that was hardly reason for her to glare in that way. He decided that a smile was the answer to defuse the problem, so he gave a wave and a cheery 'Hello.' It didn't work.

'Have you had the red crepe paper from the stock cupboard?' Patterson demanded, and the penny dropped. She needed red crepe paper, and he'd used the last of it. He'd heard about red crepe paper in junior schools, how using the end of it was almost a capital offence, but the situation had never arisen for him before. It was arising for him now. He tried his disarming smile again.

'Only some of it. We're making a big Father Christmas for our wall display. I even thought of putting a mini tape recorder inside his head so that he goes 'ho ho ho'. There it is,' and he pointed towards the outline of a Father Christmas, already with the red crepe paper on it, that was taking shape on the back wall of his classroom. 'What do you think?'

'Very nice,' said Patterson, her face and voice still menacing, 'but where did you put the rest of it?'

Sims tried a bluff. 'The rest of it?' he said. 'He's all there, though in bits. If you open that cupboard you'll find a cotton wool beard, black paper for his boots . . .'

'I'm talking about the rest of the red crepe paper,' said Patterson. 'Where did you put it after you'd finished with it? I can't find any in the stock cupboard.'

'Well,' said Sims, trapped, 'there wasn't any left . . .'

This was the confession that Patterson had been waiting for. 'You mean you used all of it?!' she exploded.

'I only used what was left on the roll,' said Sims defensively. 'And there was hardly any there to start with.'

'You used *all* of it?!' snarled Patterson.

Sims looked around for a way of escape in case she should get violent. It was no use, she had the door covered, and he doubted if he could reach the window in time. 'Will you stop repeating yourself,' he said, trying to move onto the offensive in this argument. 'No, I did not. I used what was left on the roll. The rest of the school and whoever had it before me used all of it.'

'But there is none left!'

Was it his imagination, or was Patterson's voice getting louder with each sentence?

'Well that's not my fault,' he said.

'Then whose fault is it, considering that you used it all up?'

'I did not use it all up,' Sims insisted. 'I used the end of it. And if you want my opinion it's the fault of whoever didn't order enough. They know everyone uses red crepe paper at Christmas.'

There, he thought, answer that. But Patterson moved

on to another line of argument, trying a question that put the onus back on Sims.

'Then you tell me,' she said, 'what am I going to do my Santa Claus in?'

Sims paused. This was a dangerous moment, the wrong answer and he felt his life could be in serious danger. 'Isn't there another colour near to red you could use?' he asked warily.

'There's tons of black,' snapped Patterson. 'Are you suggesting I use black and say he got that way coming down a chimney?'

'Well . . .' began Sims. He thought about it. The best thing, he decided, was silence. It was safer. He tried a smile and a helpless gesture with his hands. It worked in the films.

It didn't work here.

'I shall raise the matter,' said Patterson stiffly, 'at this afternoon's staff meeting.' And with that she opened his classroom door, and then slammed her way out.

Phew, thought Sims. So much for peace and goodwill to all men.

• • •

True to her word, no sooner had the staff meeting got under way, than Patterson spoke up; and although she didn't name names, she made it fairly clear who she was talking about by looking directly at Sims. 'Before this staff meeting gets fully under way,' she said, 'I wish to state that I think it most unfair that all the Christmas stock is being used up before everyone's had a chance to share it out.'

All eyes immediately followed the direction of Patterson's reproving glare, and came to rest on Sims. 'It was nothing to do with me,' Sims protested.

Hello, thought Beeston, personality differences here. Unless I move fast, this whole meeting is going to be shanghaied by Mrs Patterson for a slanging match. Aloud, he said: 'Point taken, Mrs Patterson, but I didn't really want this staff meeting to be about the Christmas festivities. After all, Christmas is still a few weeks away . . .'

Patterson was not to be that easily put off. 'Exactly,' she said. 'That is my point. Some people are starting to prepare for Christmas earlier and earlier. If we go on this way they'll start decorating their rooms for Christmas in September and there'll be no stock left at all. I think we ought to have a fairer division of Christmas stock, stuff like glitter and silver foil.'

'And red crepe paper,' joined in Mrs Rudd. 'There was none left when I went to get some earlier today.'

Despite Sims's desperate, if muted, appeal: 'As I keep saying, that was nothing to do with me,' Beeston could begin to hear the undercurrents of murmuring agreement amongst some other members of staff. Deciding that it was wisest to quash these stirrings of revolution now, he waved a silencing hand. 'All right,' he said, 'in future we'll have an allocation of Christmas materials for each class so that we don't get it happening again.'

'That's all very well for the future, but what about this year?' demanded Patterson stiffly.

'I'll see if I can get any more from County Supplies,' said Beeston. As the choruses of pleasure started to sound at this thought, he held up a warning hand. 'Though I wouldn't count on it,' he added hastily. 'Now, if we can get on to the main reason for this staff meeting: the new County-wide tests that are to be introduced for seven- and eleven-year-olds.' He looked around the staff, fully aware that this was the most contentious issue they'd had to deal with for ages. Staff were split on the whole idea, and to his mind, though not to Mrs Patterson's, the problems of red crepe paper paled into insignificance beside it.

Sims spoke up before Beeston had a chance to stop him. 'Surely it's just reintroducing the old eleven-plus under another name,' he pointed out, the note of objection clear in his voice.

Mrs Rudd gave him a look of triumph. 'And high time, too,' she said.

Sims shook his head. 'No, I totally disagree,' he said.

'Absolutely,' supported Long. 'In my opinion . . .'

Right, thought Beeston, I've given them their minute to air their opinions, now we can get on. He held up a silencing hand. 'If we can get to my main point,' he said, 'which is – whether we agree with it or not – we are going to have to carry it out.'

Mrs Rudd wasn't going to be stopped from airing her opinion as easily as that. 'Actually I think it totally wrong that we are discussing testing at this time of the year,' she stated. 'Christmas is coming, there is so much to do. There's the carol concert, decorating the rooms . . .'

'Well it's hardly my fault if County Hall choose now to send out this memo,' said Beeston, 'or "consultative document", as they prefer to call it.'

'We'll have a job decorating anyway, with no crepe paper,' said Patterson, determined not to let anyone forget.

Beeston ignored her remark and ploughed on. It was the only way to run a staff meeting at King Street. 'Now,' he said, 'County Hall want comments from all teaching staff about implementing these new tests, and they want them by next week. So, in order to meet their deadline, *I* need your comments by the end of this week. And no rude ones, please. Sensible comments only on what points should be tested. And that doesn't mean only subjects, it means levels of ability, understanding, Old Uncle Tom Cobbley and all . . .'

• • •

By the next morning the staff meeting was just a dim memory, one of at least a billion staff meetings, Beeston reflected, where any issue became a talking shop for theories of education. Personally he agreed with Sims and Long on the issued of testing. Invariably, all tests did was test the psychological state of the person being tested at the time of the test, and how they stood up to the stress of being tested. Continuous assessment was the only answer, but continuous assessment by whom? How did you cut out bias by the tester?

The way things were going, he sighed, achieving such a system was a long way off. On the plus side, however, it was ten o'clock and he'd survived the morning so far without anyone coming to register a complaint with him. Maybe no one was talking to him. Chance, he thought as he opened the door of the office, would be a fine thing.

Mrs Stone was hard at work typing a stencil. 'Good morning,' she greeted him cheerfully.

'Morning,' said Beeston. Another problem arising from the previous afternoon's staff meeting popped into his head, less serious than the tests, but still one which could turn out to be major. Mrs Stone might be able to throw some light on it. 'Here,' he said.

Mrs Stone stopped typing and looked around. 'Where?' she asked.

'Very funny,' said Beeston. 'Has Sims been nicking the red crepe paper?'

Mrs Stone looked at him, surprised. 'I think that unlikely,' she said. 'What makes you ask?'

'Because Mrs Patterson and Mrs Rudd were like the SS in the staff meeting, demanding that anyone who used the Christmas stock a day too soon should be hung, drawn and quartered. And poor old Sims kept hopping up and down protesting his innocence, which pointed the finger straight at him.'

'I can see their point of view,' said Mrs Stone. 'It is very annoying to go to the cupboard and find everything gone.'

'The Mother Hubbard syndrome,' quipped Beeston. 'A good description of the general state of educational finance today.'

Mrs Stone turned her attention back to the stencil in her typewriter. 'How did they react to the new tests?' she asked.

'How do you think?' said Beeston. 'Half of them bayed for the blood of the people in charge of education, and the 'bring back flogging' brigade thought the idea was wonderful.'

'Did Miss Lewis get a chance to speak to you?'

'Not likely,' said Beeston firmly. 'As soon as the staff meeting was over I was out of there like a rocket before Mrs Rudd could inflict grievious bodily harm upon my ear.'

'About what?'

'About anything. You name it, Mrs Rudd can complain about it. Why, what's Miss Lewis's problem? Not the red crepe paper?'

'No, the Nativity play.'

'That shouldn't be any problem for her,' said Beeston confidently. 'She's been doing a brilliant job on it for years now. She could do it with her eyes closed.'

'Yes, but she can't do it this year.'

'Eh? Why not?'

'She's got to go into hospital for an operation on her toe.'

'You mean they finally remembered she was on the waiting list?' commented Beeston sarcastically. That's taken its time, hasn't it? How long ago was it? Three years?''

'Two.'

'Still, long enough.'

'Absolutely,' agreed Mrs Stone. 'And some people have to wait even longer.'

'Huh!' snorted Beeston. 'I suppose they reckon if they leave people as long as possible, eventually most of them will die off and they won't need the operation.'

Mrs Stone stopped typing and turned to glare at Beeston, offended. 'That's a very nasty thing to say,' she said. 'There are some very dedicated people working in the Health Service. My sister's a nurse, and my nephew is studying to be a doctor.'

'I'm not saying there aren't,' countered Beeston. 'It's the same as teaching, I'd trust nearly everyone at the coal face. It's the people who allegedly run the systems that I'm suspicious of. Anyway, this is getting off the point. I'd better find someone to do the Nativity play in place of Miss Lewis.'

'There's no need,' said Mrs Stone, 'Miss Lewis has already arranged it.'

'Has she? Who's she got doing it?-'

'Mr Sims.'

Beeston chuckled. 'Good old Sims!' he said. 'Not only the Phantom of the Red Crepe Paper, but the Saviour of the Nativity Play as well.'

'Well actually, I'm not so sure about that,' admitted Mrs Stone doubtfully. 'Miss Lewis was talking to me about it this morning. She's worried about what Mr Sims is going to do with it.'

'What does she mean "Do with it"?' asked Beeston. 'There's not a lot he can do with it. Find a bunch of small kids, the ones who can hold sticks are shepherds, stick coloured flowerpots on some of the others and call 'em kings, chuck a bit of straw down around a manger, Hey Presto! Merry Christmas everybody, and off we go.'

'She seems to think he's going to try and do a different version,' said Mrs Stone, now looking worried.

Beeston laughed. 'But there is no different version,' he said. 'That is it: kings, shepherds, baby Jesus . . .' An awful thought suddenly struck him. 'Oh no, you don't reckon he's going to try some kind of religious experiment do you?'

'Such as?' frowned Mrs Stone.

'You know, an atheist Nativity with no baby Jesus, or some similar crackpot thing.'

'I don't know,' Mrs Stone shrugged helplessly, 'Miss Lewis just said . . .'

'Honestly, whatever possessed Miss Lewis to pass it on to Sims!' exploded Beeston.

'It was my fault, I suggested it,' said Mrs Stone, defending Miss Lewis.

'You should have known better,' snapped Beeston.

'But I'd heard such good reports of drama productions he'd put on at one of the high schools he worked at. Samuel Beckett, Shakespeare, even classical Greek plays.'

'That's different,' said Beeston dismissively. 'They're just literature. This is much more important, this is a

Nativity play.' He groaned. 'I'd better go and see him, see what he's up to.'

• • •

Fred Holliday was having a bad morning. For a start at eight o'clock there had been roadworks at the corner of the slip road that led to the bypass, and then when he'd actually got onto the bypass it was down to one lane of traffic. Then, when he'd gone to mark his class register he'd found his pen had leaked in the inside pocket of his jacket. Now, to cap it all he found himself on playground duty at morning break with Sims, who would insist on talking all the time. Actually it wasn't so much the talking, it was the fact that he kept looking at Holliday and wanting a response. At least with Mrs Rudd she just went on and on and on and never paused for breath long enough for anyone to be able to get a word in. Holliday had often thought that she could only achieve this feat by breathing through her ears. And Sims always chose such contentious subjects, either the theory of life or what was wrong with education. If you asked Holliday, one of the things that was wrong with education was that some teachers talked too much.

'In my opinion,' Sims was saying, 'the whole idea of testing is spurious. Most tests, after all, are very arbitrary.'

'Are they?' said Holliday flatly, not wanting to sound too enthusiastic. He didn't want to encourage the man.

'And this is not just me speaking,' Sims continued, warming to his theme.

Holliday looked at Sims bleakly. 'You mean there are more of you inside that suit?' he asked.

Sims looked at him, baffled for a second, then his face cleared as he saw that Holliday was joking. 'No,' he said, 'I mean other people's opinions based on extensive research.'

'Oh.'

'In my opinion, all a test tests is how the person being tested reacts to the test, not to the subject being tested.'

'Oh,' said Holliday again.

'What do you think?' asked Sims pointedly.

'I think that I wonder why I keep ending up doing playground duty with you,' said Holliday gloomily.

Then Beeston's voice was heard coming across the playground towards them. 'Mr Sims!' Beeston was calling.

Thank God, thought Holliday, the Seventh Cavalry to the rescue.

'Mr Sims,' said Beeston, 'have you got a minute?'

Sims looked at Holliday questioningly, then back at Beeston. 'Well,' he said, 'I'm on playground duty at the moment . . .'

'No, no, that's all right, you go,' said Holliday hastily. The chance to get rid of Sims's incessant talking for five minutes was too good to miss, even if it did mean doing playground duty on his own. 'I can manage.'

'Well,' said Sims doubtfully. After all, he didn't want to leave Holliday in the lurch. 'If you're sure.'

Beeston gave them no chance to spend a precious few minutes going through the 'After you, Claude; no, after you Cecil' routine that he feared this might develop into. 'Of course he's sure,' he said. Then he grabbed Sims's elbow and began to steer him towards the main building. Holliday could just hear Beeston's voice floating back to him as he said: 'I wanted to find out what your intentions are. About the Nativity play . . .'

• • •

Beeston stood in the corridor, leaning against a radiator, and listening with a large measure of disbelief as Sims enthusiastically outlined his plans for the Nativity play. Novel, it certainly was. To be honest, however, he wasn't sure that 'crackpot' wouldn't have been a better description . . .

'In other words,' enthused Sims, 'it is a Space Age Nativity for the Space Age.'

Beeston mulled it over, the doubt writ large on his face. Ought he to call the Health Service and have Sims committed now, he wondered, or wait until after the angry parents had torn him limb from limb? 'I see,' he said, in such a way as to let Sims know that he didn't really. 'But you will still have the Archangel in it and there will be a baby Jesus?'

'Oh yes,' nodded Sims. 'Except the whole setting will be in the future. I thought I'd set it on a remote Space Station. You know, Jesus sent to save the Galaxy.'

Beeston groaned inwardly. Should he just stop the thing here and now before it got out of hand? But say Sims was right, say the thing was an astounding success? Sims certainly seemed to think it would be, and he hated to block any teacher with creative ideas that would inspire children. 'Well,' he said tactfully, his face still showing his doubts, 'it's an interesting concept.'

Either Sims was too impressed with his own artistic vision to notice Beeston's reservations, or he deliberately didn't want to. 'I think the children will relate especially to it,' he said. 'After all, think how much of their viewing is space-related: *Star Wars*, *Star Trek*, *Dr Who* . . .'

'Yes,' said Beeston before Sims went through the whole catalogue of science fiction. 'However, I think it's only fair to warn you that there may be some – well – adverse reactions from some of the parents. Not to mention some of the staff. I can picture Marchant on the phone to his Church elders once he gets to hear about it, that's if his direct line to God's busy.'

Sims dismissed the idea of objections with a shrug. 'Oh I don't think so,' he said airily. 'Not once everyone's seen it. The important thing is *the message*.'

'I'm not so sure,' said Beeston, still trying to warn Sims. 'Junior schools are very different from high schools, believe me. To most parents the important thing is that their child is wearing a sack and minding a lump of carpet disguised as a sheep.' One look at Sims's face showed that he hadn't dissuaded him. Beeston shrugged. Oh well, if Sims thought he could pull it off . . . 'However,' he said, 'I wish you well with it, and I hope you know what you're doing.'

'Believe me,' said Sims, completely confident, 'I think everyone will be pleasantly surprised when the play is unveiled.'

More fool you, thought Beeston gloomily.

• • •

Three days later, and Mrs Patterson was still walking around badgering people with her Christmas catalogue. The pressure was on, she felt, if she was to get her order in by the deadline to make sure all the stuff came back. And the World Wildlife Fund was a good cause. She checked the list she'd written out: those who had definitely ordered something, those who had said they would let her know, and those who might have threatened to stuff her catalogue down her throat if they hadn't been so polite.

She looked at the second section of her list. Mrs Wilberforce she'd now seen and transferred to the third section. That left Mr Beeston, Mr Sims, and Mrs Stone. She checked her watch. Ten forty, she thought. Just time before break ends to grab the most possible of the three.

Mrs Stone was at her typewriter when Patterson walked in.

'Ah-ha, you're in,' said Patterson.

'If it's about the Christmas catalogue,' said Mrs Stone, 'I've put a note in your pigeonhole. I'll have one of the small packets of gift wrap. It'll do for last-minute presents.'

Patterson ticked it off on her list. 'Right,' she said. I'll get that put on the order. And, while I'm here, has the new consignment of crepe paper arrived yet?'

'It came in this morning,' said Mrs Stone. 'I've put it in the stock room.'

'Great!' said Patterson exultantly. 'I'll get there before anyone else does.'

'Every colour but red,' added Mrs Stone.

Patterson stared at her, unable to believe it. 'You're joking?!' she said.

Mrs Stone shook her head. 'I'm afraid I'm serious. There's lots of blue and yellow, though.'

Patterson kicked the leg of Beeston's desk savagely. 'Honestly,' she stormed, 'who wants blue and yellow at Christmas?'

'I've tried Supplies, and they're going to see if they can scrounge any,' said Mrs Stone. She looked past Patterson to check that no one was lurking outside the office, then added confidentially, 'If they do send some, I'll put it by for you.'

'You're a wonder,' said Patterson. 'I'm going to need it. Have you heard about the competition?'

Mrs Stone shook her head. 'No?' she said. 'What competition's that?'

'A prize for the classroom with the best Christmas decorations.'

'Oh? Whose idea was that?'

'Mr Beeston's.'

Mrs Stone's eyebrows went up. 'You do surprise me,' she said.

'It surprised us all with the way he's always complaining about Christmas,' admitted Patterson. 'By the way, I heard you want to see Miss Lewis last night. How is she?'

'Sitting up in bed, surrounded by books, and worried to death about what Mr Sims is doing with the Nativity play.'

'I don't blame her,' said Patterson, still not having forgiven him. 'A man who takes the last of the red crepe paper is capable of anything.'

• • •

Meanwhile in the staff room, as far as Long was concerned, Christmas decoration contests, Christmas catalogues, and even Nativity plays were taking second place to what he considered should have been the main topic of discussion, the proposed new tests for the children. 'These tests should not be allowed to take place,' he stated categorically.

Mrs Rudd shook her head for the umpteenth time. 'You are totally wrong, Mr Long,' she said. 'We *need* tests. Take the driving test, for example. If we didn't have a driving test, how would we know that the roads wouldn't be populated by people who couldn't drive?'

'The driving test is a good case in point,' argued Long. 'How many people who are wonderful drivers freeze up on the day of their driving test because they are petrified?'

'But we must have standards, otherwise we are faced with anarchy,' came back Mrs Rudd. 'I like to know that, if I go into hospital for an operation, the surgeon carrying it out has passed a test to prove that he or she is competent. The idea of having no tests at all means that anyone could just walk in off the street and operate on me.'

'Not at all, I'm not saying we shouldn't have assessment,' said Long. 'All I'm saying is it's wrong to determine someone's fate on the basis of what happens in a couple of hours on a particular day.'

'Ah!' said Mrs Rudd.

Long looked at her in surprise. 'What?' he asked.

'Mr Sims has just come in,' said Mrs Rudd. 'I must go and tell him off.'

'He hasn't taken more crepe paper, has he?' grinned Long.

'I am talking about this outrageous Nativity play he is attempting,' said Mrs Rudd. 'Someone needs to tell him.'

Sims, unaware of the impending doom heading towards him at full sail across the staff room, was just pouring himself a cup of tea. The Nativity play, although in its early stages, was going well, he thought. He wasn't sure about the space costumes for the futuristic shepherds, though, and the music he had on tape wasn't quite right, but he could look at that while his class did some silent maths work in the next lesson, then he would be all ready for the next rehearsal at lunch time.

He was just sorting around on the table to see if anyone had left a spare biscuit, when he became aware of Mrs Rudd at his elbow.

'Mr Sims,' she said, 'I wish to talk to you.'

Sims gave up his search for a spare biscuit and sipped at his tea instead. 'Will this take long?' he asked. 'Only I have some preparations to do for the Nativity play.'

'Which is precisely why I want to see you,' said Mrs Rudd.

It was obvious from her attitude that she hadn't come over to compliment him. Was she upset because he was using soundtracks of space effects for the music, instead of the traditional carols?

'If it's about the music . . .' he began.

'It is not about the music,' said Mrs Rudd stiffly. 'Rumour has it that you are planning a Star Wars version of the story of the Nativity.'

Sims smiled. 'Well, not Star Wars, more Arthur C. Clarke, really,' he said. 'The way I see it . . .' He didn't get a chance to tell her the way that he saw it.

'Mr Sims,' she said, 'drop it immediately.'

Sims stared at her, baffled. 'Drop what?' he said. Was there some dangerous insect on his tea cup that he couldn't see? He peered closer at his saucer, carefully in case it should leap at him and bite him. Whatever was the woman talking about? With her next words it all became clear to him. 'There is only one way to do a Nativity play, and that is the way it has always been done.'

So that was it!

'Oh, nonsense,' he scoffed.

Mrs Rudd bridled. 'Nonsense?' she demanded.

'If we all had that attitude then there would have been no progress,' said Sims. 'The wheel would never have been invented; the electric light, the internal combustion engine, manned flight, none of these would have come to fruition because they'd never been done before.'

'That is not the same at all,' snapped Mrs Rudd. 'We are talking here about matters of religious sensitivity. Christmas, Mr Sims, is a hallowed time, and it is hallowed because things have always been done in a certain way. And these do not include Joseph and Mary teleporting to Bethlehem.'

'Mrs Rudd,' said Sims patiently, 'whatever you may have heard about the Nativity play . . .'

'That is the point, Mr Sims,' sad Mrs Rudd, 'I have heard nothing. You seem to have enveloped the whole thing in a cloak of secrecy worthy of MI5.'

True, thought Sims. Acknowledging this, he said: 'There is a reason for that. It is because I don't wish people to attack this new concept while it is at a halfway stage in its preparation.'

'Better then than that they should attack it when it is finished,' said Mrs Rudd. 'You seem to forget, Mr Sims, that it will not only be you on trial when it is performed before the parents, the whole school will be held responsible.'

At that point the bell sounded for the end of break. Thank God, thought Sims. Escape! He gave Mrs Rudd a weak smile, put down his empty tea cup, tapped his watch by way of explanation, and headed for the door. However if he thought he was going to get away with it that easily, he was mistaken. Even as he left the staff room, Mrs Rudd's voice boomed after him: 'I will have more to say to you later!'

• • •

Mrs Stone's eye fell on her calendar. Friday, she thought. Glenda's having her operation today. I must phone the hospital when I get home and see how she got on. Glenda would appreciate that, she was sure, because she felt that it was unlikely that Glenda's mother would call at the hospital. One of the drawbacks to having no family ties, no partner or children, Mrs Stone reflected. When you're ill, there's no one to ask how you are. She was in the middle of these thoughts, when the door to her office opened, and Beeston looked cautiously in.

'Anyone else in here?' he asked mysteriously.

'No, only me.'

'No one hiding in my office?' he double-checked.

'No,' said Mrs Stone, still baffled as to what this was all about.

'Good,' said Beeston, and he slipped into the office and shut the door behind him, leaning against it like an escaped convict. 'I feel like Harry Lime today, with everyone hunting for me.'

'You're exaggerating as usual,' said Mrs Stone, and

opened the stock requisition book. If he was going to be melodramatic, she'd just ignore him and get on with her work. But today Beeston seemed determined he wasn't going to be ignored.

'I'm not exaggerating,' he insisted.

Wearily Mrs Stone gave him her full attention. 'All right,' she said, 'just who is after you?'

'Mrs Patterson, for one,' said Beeston. 'She's after me to complain for the umpteenth time about crepe paper and tinsel.'

'That's just one person,' said Mrs Stone dismissively.

'Mrs Rudd, and Messrs Wilberforce and Marchant from the God Squad are still after my blood because of Sims's Space Age Nativity play.'

'Yes, so I've heard.'

'And I daren't go anywhere near Mr Long because I get a harangue about the social inequalities of testing, as if I was personally responsible. Mrs Purkiss is after me because she says there won't be enough Christmas pudding. Every time I turn a corner some kid jumps out at me and wants me to hear them sing a Christmas carol. I thought this was supposed to be a time of peace and goodwill?'

Mrs Stone gave a small smile. 'Don't worry,' she said, 'it'll all be over in a week or two. Anyway, what's all this about a prize?'

Beeston frowned. 'What prize?' he asked.

'For the best Christmas decorations?'

'Oh, you've heard!' Beeston exclaimed, as her mention of it jogged his memory. An awful thought struck him. 'You're not thinking of going in for it as well, are you? I hope not, otherwise I won't be able to move in here. It's bad enough with your paper chains as it is.'

'No,' she said, 'but I would like to know what's brought on this sudden burst of Christmas spirit?'

'If you must know it was a ruse to stop myself being persecuted by everybody,' said Beeston. 'I thought that if I gave them something like that to keep them occupied they'd forget to chase me.'

'It didn't work, did it?' said Mrs Stone, amused by the whole thing.

'No it didn't,' admitted Beeston grimly.

A knock at the office door made him jump.

'Don't let them in!' he whispered hoarsely.

He was too late. The door opened and Holliday looked in, his face brightening when he saw Beeston.

'Ah, there you are,' he said. 'I've been looking for you.'

'Thank God it's you,' said Beeston. 'I thought it was someone come to have a go at me.'

'It is,' said Holliday. 'I've been looking at the Father Christmas outfit, and it's got holes in it.'

Beeston rolled his eyes to Heaven wearily. Honestly, as if he didn't have enough problems! 'That's your fault for smoking your pipe when you wear it,' he said. 'I expect you burnt it last year.'

'I certainly did not,' retorted Holliday indignantly. 'These are moth holes.'

'Then you should have put mothballs in it last year,' Beeston pointed out.

'And walk around smelling of them? I hate dressing up as Father Christmas as it is without smelling of mothballs into the bargain. And another thing.'

Not more, groaned Beeston to himself. Much more of this and he'd develop a persecution complex. 'Yes?'

'It's too small. It must have shrunk.'

'Or you're putting on weight,' suggested Beeston.

'Nonsense,' denied Holliday.

At her desk Mrs Stone hid a smile. Men were always complaining about women spending too much time talking about their weight, yet how vain men were about their figures.

'Anyway,' said Holliday, 'I think it's about time we had a new outfit.'

'All right,' said Beeston wearily. 'I'll see what we can do for next year.'

'Next year?!'

'Come off it, Fred, we're only a week away from Christmas and all the parties. You know what County Hall are like, if we send in a requisition for a new Santa Claus outfit now we'll be lucky to get it in time for Easter.'

'Oh well,' grumbled Holliday, 'I suppose I'll just have to put up with it. But I don't like doing it.'

'Stout man,' said Beeston, giving Holliday a grateful slap on the shoulder.

'Not that stout,' snapped Holliday quickly, still sensitive about Beeston's remark.

'No, no, of course not,' agreed Beeston. Anything for a quiet life . . .

'Oh, and Mr Marchant is looking for you.'

'See?' said Beeston to Mrs Stone. 'What did I tell you?'

'I heard,' admitted Mrs Stone drily.

Beeston turned back to Holliday. 'Let me guess, Sims's Christmas Star Trek Special?' he asked.

Holliday nodded. 'From what I can gather.'

'How is it going, does anyone know?'

'No idea. He's certainly keeping it close to his chest.'

'Which makes me dread the finished production more and more. Haven't we got any spies in his cast?'

Holliday shook his head. 'Not that I know of,' he said.

Beeston racked his brains. 'There must be someone who knows what form it's going to take,' he said. 'After all, it's only another four days to lift-off.'

'I'm sure he'll do a perfectly sound, if unconventional, job of it,' said Mrs Stone from her desk. 'I'm sure you've got no need to worry.'

'You're only saying that because you feel responsible for it,' pointed out Beeston. 'It was your suggestion that got us all in this mess in the first place. *How* unconventional, that's the problem?'

'You said he could do it,' said Holliday. 'If you didn't want him to you should have put your foot down earlier.'

'I know, I know,' said Beeston, now feeling more trapped than ever. 'I suppose all we can do is pray that no one religious turns up to see it.'

• • •

The twelve small children from Miss Lewis's and Mrs

Wilberforce's class watched Sims as he spun around the classroom, gesturing to show them where each new planet in this new version of the Nativity was. To be honest, they were a bit disappointed. Yes, it was all very exciting, especially for Mr Sims, but it wasn't how they'd thought it would be. It wasn't how it had been for their big brothers and sisters when they'd been in the Nativity play. Sundar had wanted to wear a crown like his big brother had done. Instead he was stuck with this plastic space helmet. He turned his attention back to Mr Sims, who had just switched on a tape recorder, and the sounds of eerie space music were now zapping around the room.

'Now when you robots, who are supposed to be the shepherds, hear that,' said Sims, 'you know that this is a message for you to go to the Space City.'

'Sir?' asked Sundar.

Sims switched the music off. 'Yes, Sundar?' he asked.

'Why can't we do it the old way?'

A few of the other children nodded in agreement. Sims looked at them, baffled.

'Do what the old way?' he asked.

'The play,' said Sundar.

Subi standing next to Sundar nodded, her little face serious. 'Yes, sir,' she said. 'We don't think anyone's going to get it.'

'Get what?' asked Sims.

'What it's about,' said Subi.

'What do you mean, what it's about?' said Sims, exasperated by all this quibbling. 'It's obvious. It's the Nativity play. We've been practising it now for over a week.'

'Yes, sir, we know that,' said Sundar, 'but will *they* know that?'

'What he means, sir,' explained Subi, 'is: won't they want the proper one?'

Sims looked around at the children who all seemed to be regarding him with the same doubtful expressions. Honestly, what on earth was up with these children? They should have been excited at doing the Nativity play this way instead of looking as if he'd just taken all their Christmas presents away from them.

'This *is* the proper one,' he said, 'it's just a modern way of doing it.'

One look at their faces told him that this argument had not convinced them. 'After all,' he pressed on, hammering his argument home, 'some of the old ways can be a bit boring. We want to interest people with what's happening *now*.' He threw in what he considered the clincher of the whole argument. 'After all, do *you* still ride on a donkey nowadays?'

As a clincher it was not very successful. The children were not impressed.

'My uncle does in Pakistan, sir,' said Ghazala.

'Yes, well, that's in Pakistan,' said Sims defensively.

'And Omar did when he was in Turkey,' said Subi.

Sims could feel his argument falling down about his ears. 'Look,' he said determinedly, 'this is getting off the point. What we are trying to do is make it *modern*. So that everyone enjoys it.'

The children looked at one another, unconvinced.

'Well?' he demanded.

From the children came a chorus of heartfelt sighs of resignation, and then they all said in unconvincing unison: 'Yes, sir.'

'Right,' said Sims grimly. 'Let's start again. Sundar, you're Space Messenger Gabriel and you have come to this woman on this Space Station with the Good News. Right. Go.'

Sundar took up his position, the plastic space helmet slipping sideways over one ear. 'Are you Mary, the wife of the Space Station carpenter?' he intoned in a monotone.

'I am,' said Subi, her tone suggesting that she was unimpressed by this vision from another dimension with the skewwhiff plastic helmet.

'Then I have a message for you,' announced Sundar, 'from across the Galaxy.'

• • •

The bell for the end of school rang just as Beeston was passing beneath it. He stood there, the ringing still going on inside his head, standing to one side as a sea of children surged out of their classrooms and headed towards the cloakrooms.

'Stop that running!' came Long's voice from just along the corridor, and Beeston groaned to himself. Maybe he hasn't seen me, he thought wishfully. With the Good Fairy obviously in temporary absence, his wish wasn't granted.

'Ah. Mr Beeston!' Long called.

'I'm just on my way home,' defended Beeston.

'So am I,' said Long, dismissing the excuse.

'Right, I'll see you in the morning,' said Beeston, thinking he'd got out of that one easily enough. He hadn't.

'Not so fast,' said Long. 'Look,' he appealed, 'can't we do something about these tests? You know they're wrong.'

Beeston sighed wearily. 'I don't know they're wrong,' he said. All right, he did, but he wasn't going to say that to Long otherwise Long would be quoting him in evidence and petitions to County Hall. 'You feel they're wrong, but other people feel they're the correct way to assess the children's progress. And as they're the people in power, there's not a lot you can do about it.'

'But it seems such a backward step.'

'To you,' said Beeston. 'Look, live with it. What else can you do? The kids will survive.'

Long scowled, totally dissatisfied. 'I'm still not going to let it rest just like that,' he warned as he traipsed off along the corridor.

No, I'm sure you won't, thought Beeston. Anyway, at least I can go home now, and that's one less obstacle. If I make a quick dash for it I might even make my car before Mrs Rudd or Mr Marchant or Mrs Patterson grab me. He turned the corner and came to face with the last person he expected to see, Miss Lewis. The sudden and unexpected meeting made them both jump.

'What on earth are you doing here?' Beeston demanded. 'Why aren't you lying in hospital with your toe in plaster? I was coming to see you this evening with some grapes.'

'I don't like grapes,' said Lewis.

'No, but I do,' said Beeston. 'But what happened? Why aren't you limping?'

'They needed the bed for an urgent case, so they discharged me,' said Lewis, and the disappointment was clear on her face.

Beeston gaped in astonishment. 'Discharged you?! Without doing the operation?' Really! he thought. That is going too far. To drag someone in, get them all ready for the operation, and then kick them out before they'd done it. What on earth was the Health Service coming to? He was sure it wouldn't be much longer before they issued patients with a Black and Decker kit and told them to carry out the operations on themselves!

'So,' said Miss Lewis unhappily, 'it's back on the waiting list again.'

Beeston was still stunned by the whole idea. 'You mean they kept you in for all that time, and then didn't do anything? My God, and we complain about the education system.' He shook his head. The sheer idiocy of it all. It just made him more than ever convinced that the lunatics had taken over the running of the asylum. 'Anyway, there was no need to come back this afternoon. I mean, I know you're dedicated, but . . .'

Lewis shook her head. 'To be honest, I wanted to get back to find out what's happening about the Nativity play,' she said. 'I keep hearing odd little rumours about it.'

'No problem,' said Beeston with a mask of confidence, 'Sims is totally in control.'

'What's he actually doing with it?' asked Lewis.

Beeston shrugged. 'No idea at all. He's keeping it a mystery.'

'Be serious,' said Lewis.

'I am being serious,' said Beeston. 'Apart from the fact

that it's set in the future, no one's got any idea what he's up to. For all I know he could be doing Joseph and Mary meet Darth Vader.'

'Oh God!' groaned Lewis.

'Cheer up,' said Beeston. 'You never know, God might like it. It'd be nice if someone does. Anyway,' he added, 'we'll all know what he's been keeping up his sleeve the day after tomorrow.'

• • •

At lunchtime on the fatal day, Sims rehearsed his tiny cast, still behind closed doors, adding more fuel to the speculation as to what shape the Nativity play was going to take. When asked point blank what he was going to do, and whether it would bring a horde of angry vicars in a deputation to the school, Sims just shook his head and said that no one would be offended, it would be very normal.

Normal? thought Beeston. What's normal about Jesus in a spaceship? However, he noticed that by the day of the performance, Mrs Rudd had toned down her complaints about Sims's production. In fact she wasn't complaining any more at all, which struck Beeston as very odd. The two were also seen conferring in the corridor by Holliday, their heads together over bits of paper, obviously script, said Holliday. Mrs Rudd, part of a Space Nativity? thought Beeston. Well, it was a start. Maybe he'd be able to get her sent up on the next space shot.

By two o'clock that afternoon the school had started to have a Christmassy feel about it, with parents walking around, nosing in and out of classrooms on their way to take their seats for the Nativity play. The decorations glittering and swinging everywhere, the fake snow spray and the paper snowflakes on threads of cotton turning in the draughts, Mrs Wilberforce's Christmas tree, the red and black cardboard pillar box with the imitation snow on the roof, the paper robins, the red beads on the green paper holly, it all added up to the realisation that Christmas was finally here, thought Beeston. Not six months away, as it is in the big department stores, but here. Or, at least, just a fortnight or so away. Only two weeks more, two weeks of Christmas carols, class parties, Mrs Purkiss ruining a bunch of turkeys, Fred Holliday walking around as Father Christmas doing his best to ho-ho-ho, and another year would be on its way out.

But first, he thought, to get this afternoon over. He took his place standing at the side of the school hall, next to Holliday and just behind Mrs Rudd, who was already fully armed at her piano. Every year this was his place. He had to be near enough to the front to step out and congratulate all those who had taken part, yet not near enough to get in the way. And so every year, he ended up standing rigidly against a wall, getting a sideways view of the play and cramp.

The whole school was crammed together, sitting cross-legged (or as near as some of them could get to sitting cross-legged) on the floor. Behind them, on hard wooden and creaky chairs, were the parents, eager to see how their child would perform. Miss Lewis was at one side, with her class, but not looking as worried as she had done the day before, thought Beeston. As for Mrs Rudd, she was positively beaming. Beeston felt a bit irked. What could Sims have said to reassure them, that he couldn't say to Beeston? After all, he was Head Teacher at this school. The overhead lights in the hall were turned off and the spotlight came on, picking out what looked to Beeston suspiciously like a bunch of shepherds dressed in the same old sacks as usual, with a bunch of old white carpets rolled up as sheep lying on the small stage beside them. From the far side of the stage Sundar suddenly appeared, wearing one of Mrs Holliday's old white dresses cut down and with a halo floating mysteriously above his head. Suddenly a small voice filled the hall:

'And lo – a angel of the Lord came down and said, "Get up from watching your sheep and go to Bethlehem".'

Beeston frowned, puzzled. What on earth had all the fuss been about, let alone the secrecy? Ten minutes later, as the cardboard donkey's head fell off a child and into the manger, Beeston whispered to Holliday: 'When's the space ship going to come in?'

'Don't ask me,' shrugged Holliday, equally baffled.

'As far as I can see it looks the same as it has every other year,' Beeston whispered again. 'Kids in sacks and cardboard crowns. The same bent walking sticks for staffs. Even that same old sewing box of Mrs Wilson's for the frankincense. If this is the future, it doesn't say much for it.'

'Sssh!' hissed Mrs Rudd at him out of the side of her mouth.

'I'm just wondering where all the Star Trek stuff is,' whispered Beeston.

'Well, don't,' whispered Mrs Rudd back. 'You're putting everyone off.'

'No, I'm not,' Beeston defended himself in a whisper.

'Yes, you are,' said Mrs Rudd. She nodded her head towards the audience. 'Everyone's looking at you.'

Beeston looked at the audience. Sure enough all heads, parents and children, staff, even the members of the cast on stage, were all turned towards them. Beeston looked guiltily around, and then the penny dropped.

'No they're not,' he whispered to Mrs Rudd. 'They're looking at you.'

'Me?' whispered back Mrs Rudd. 'Don't be ridiculous, why should they be looking at me.'

'I think they're waiting for you to play some music,' said Holliday in a low voice, still keeping up the whispering stakes. 'There's a bunch of kings waiting to walk in the back doors.'

Mrs Rudd looked, and sure enough, there they were, waiting for their musical cue to come on. Mrs Rudd went bright scarlet, composed herself, hissed at Beeston: 'This is all your fault for distracting me,' then hammered her hands down onto the piano keys. Immediately the Three Kings marched forward, balancing their crowns precariously on their heads and doing their best not to trip over their trailing robes.

It wasn't until after the play was over, the parents gone,

and Lewis and Mrs Rudd had swamped Sims with their congratulations on a 'truly wonderful traditional' Nativity play, that Beeston was able to get hold of Sims. Beeston fought his way past the shepherds, who all still smelt of sacking, and grabbed Sims and steered him to a quiet corner at one side of the stage.

'All right, Mr Sims,' he demanded. 'What happened to it?'

'What happened to what?'

'To the Nativity play? Where were the space ships, the little green men?'

'Oh,' said Sims glumly, 'you noticed.'

'It was difficult not to,' said Beeston. 'I thought to myself, either Flash Gordon's changed his image, or we're doing the old traditional version.'

'The kids didn't want to do a Space Age version, so we did this one instead,' said Sims simply. 'And that was all there was to it.'

'But why all the secrecy? All the fuss and bother?'

'Because I only decided to change it two days ago. At first the secrecy was because I thought people might interfere. After I'd changed back to the old style . . .' he shrugged, shamefaced, 'Well, I suppose I was too pig-headed to admit it openly after all the fuss over the Space version.'

'Oh well,' said Beeston. 'The main thing is, you did it very well. Miss Lewis was particularly relieved.'

'I still can't understand why they didn't want to do the modern version, though,' Sims complained. 'I would have preferred it.'

'Then you still have a lot to learn about small kids,' said Beeston. 'It's because kids are real conservatives at heart. With a small "c", I hasten to add. Maybe even a big "C". It's often occurred to me that kids start off as conservatives, become socialists when they're in their late teens, and then make that final decisive leap when they reach adulthood.'

'And what leap is that?' asked Sims.

'To political apathy,' said Beeston.

Sims looked at Beeston askance. 'That's a bit cynical,' he commented.

'Possibly,' admitted Beeston, 'but it's Christmas, I'm allowed to be cynical at Christmas. No, kids like tradition. They want to do what their big brothers and sisters did last year. And, considering that, you did what Miss Lewis has done every year before, and you did it very well indeed. You kept the spirit of Christmas. Well done, Mr Sims, and a Merry Christmas to you.'

CHAPTER FOUR

PRESSURE

The drilling was driving Mrs Stone mad. The road gang had arrived, complete with red and white cones, mechanical diggers, air compressors and pneumatic drills at eight o'clock; and by a quarter to nine the pneumatic drills were in full operation, and the patch of road just outside her window was turning into a series of huge great holes. It was now half past ten and the drills had been going for an hour and three quarters without a break. It was all right for the drillers, Mrs Stone thought bitterly, they had those huge great ear muffs on their heads to protect their ears. It wasn't too bad for some of the teachers, they were a bit further removed from the noise, but for her it was a hell on earth. She couldn't move her office, where could she go to? She needed to be near the telephone, she needed to be near the photocopier and the duplicating machine, she needed to be near her electric typewriter. None of these were small pieces of equipment that she could simply pick up and take to somewhere quieter. Where, in fact, was quieter? The sound of the drilling seemed to fill the whole school.

She slipped the sheet of paper she was typing out of the typewriter, and was just about to put it on the pile of letters for Beeston to sign, when she spotted a typing error, 'Dear Sot' instead of 'Dear Sir'. As the letter was to the Secretary of an Education Committee who was well known as a heavy drinker, Mrs Stone reflected that it was a particularly apt greeting. However it would not be welcomed. Normally she would have spotted it before she took it out of the typewriter, but with this damned drilling . . .!

At that point the telephone rang, and for the

umpteenth time that morning she picked the receiver up, knowing full well that she would not be able to hear what the caller was saying. Really, it was intolerable!

'King Street Junior . . .' The voice at the other end was barely distinguishable beneath the roar of the drill, which at that moment had seemed to increase in volume. 'What? I'm sorry, I can't hear you . . . I'm sorry, could you say that again, louder please . . .' Finally two or three words trickled through. 'Miss Marshall at Downside . . . Right, I'll tell Mrs Patterson . . . I said I'll tell her!'

Mrs Stone hung up and fed a fresh sheet of paper into the typewriter. Her head was starting to throb. That damned noise! She sensed, rather than heard, the door open as Beeston came in. He said something which she couldn't quite hear. 'What?' she called.

'I said: that bloody noise!' barked Beeston. 'Where have they come from? The Anti-Education Squad?'

'It's terrible,' said Mrs Stone. 'Absolutely terrible.

'Maybe they're the terrorist wing of the Noise Abatement Society,' snorted Beeston. 'Teaching is impossible under these conditions.'

'Why don't you stop them?'

'I tried,' said Beeston. 'I phoned the Council to find out what was going on, but was told it was for the good of the nation's roads. I said it certainly wasn't good for their hearing.'

'Isn't there another Department you could phone to get it stopped?'

Beeston shook his head. 'By the time they find out which Department has power over the Highways Department, and put me onto them, even the motorways will be mended.'

'If you were in here suffering it you'd be on the phone fast enough finding out who to moan at.'

'I tried,' defended Beeston, 'And anyway, even if I did get hold of them, I know what the reaction would be.'

Mrs Stone was not to be pacified. She gestured to the papers on her desk. 'I've got the exam figures to do,' she said.

'I know,' said Beeston.

'I've got the returns on the dinner figures. I've got the stock money to balance. I'm trying to type these letters to parents about the school trip. County Hall want the insurance figures this afternoon.' Her voice was now rising as the catalogue of pressures on her built up. 'I've got teachers coming in here with all manner of things to be done: photocopies to be made, work sheets to be run off, letters to type. The phone keeps going. And with that drilling going on right outside my window, I just cannot cope!'

'All right,' said Beeston soothingly. 'I'll phone them again and see what I can do.'

'When?' demanded Mrs Stone.

'As soon as I get a chance,' said Beeston. 'I'm covering for Fred Holliday at the moment. Remember, he's off sick today.' He made for the door. 'I'll phone them as soon as I get a minute,' he promised.

'You ought to do it *now*!' insisted Mrs Stone. 'Listen to that awful noise! I cannot cope with it.'

Too late, Beeston was gone. Mrs Stone sagged in her chair, letting the noise wash over her. 'Oh God!' she groaned. Then, resignedly, she pulled herself up and resumed typing. At that moment the phone rang again.

• • •

In Mr Sims's class the bell for morning break came as a merciful relief. The noise of the drilling, although distant, had been ever-present throughout the whole early part of the morning, making it almost impossible for either Sims or his class to concentrate. As the children scampered out of the room to the playground, and Sims gathered up his books, he became aware of tiny Chandra hovering by his elbow. 'Yes, Chandra?' he asked.

'Please, sir, Mr Sims,' said Chandra mournfully, 'Can I stay in? My leg hurts.'

A smile almost came to Sims's lips, but he held it back. Not again, he thought. 'Oh?' said Sims. 'What have you done to it?'

'I don't know, sir,' said Chandra. 'It just hurts. I must have hurt it coming to school.'

'And how did you hurt it?'

Chandra shook his head unhappily. 'I don't know, sir,' he said.

Sims sighed. This whole game had really gone on for long enough, it was really about time he put a stop to it. 'Look, Chandra,' he said, 'I might feel more inclined to believe that your leg hurts . . .'

'It does, sir.'

'. . . if you hadn't come to me yesterday at break time asking to stay in because you had a cold.'

'I did have a cold,' protested Chandra righteously.

'And the day before,' continued Sims, 'saying that you didn't feel well because of your head? Frankly, Chandra, it does look to me like you just don't want to go out.'

Chandra shook his head in vehement denial. 'No, sir . . .'

Sims held up his hand to stop Chandra's protestations, which he knew would be long and full of deep conviction. 'Go on,' he said, 'get your coat on and out you go. The fresh air will do you good.'

'But, sir . . .' said Chandra, and this time a note of desperation seemed to be creeping into his voice.

Sims pointed at the door. 'Out,' he said.

Chandra's face dropped, and for a second, seeing the misery on the boy's face, Sims was tempted to change his mind and let him stay in. But then what? The next break all his class would want to stay in.

'Yes, sir,' said Chandra in a voice low with misery. And he went.

• • •

Beeston stood in front of Holliday's class, watching their faces as he outlined The Mysteries of the Apostrophe to them. It was always in the eyes; either the sudden flash of connection as they realised what he was talking about, or that glazed look forming a mental barrier between their brain and his mouth. Fortunately today they seemed to be understanding what he was saying. He did sympathise with them – the rules of English grammar were often a mystery indeed. Spelling, for example. He remembered as a child being baffled how three different spellings could all sound the same, like threw, through and rue, and yet words that had the same spelling all sounded different, like through, rough and bough. That was the trouble with a language that had been constructed out of so many other languages, a bit of Latin, a bit of Saxon, a bit of Viking, a bit of French, a bit of Gaelic, a bit of everything. It was a miracle, really, that a language with such confusing grammatical rules had ended up being the second most widely spoken language in the world. It didn't say much for the others.

Beeston pointed to the example on the blackboard. 'So we use the apostrophe in the place of a missing letter,' he reiterated, 'and where else?' He looked around. Who to ask? Someone who wasn't terrified of getting it wrong, but not one of the show-offs who wanted their voice to be the only one that was ever heard. They were as bad as some teachers. 'Sundar?'

'To show that something belongs to someone, sir,' said Sundar.

'Good,' said Beeston. Then he stopped. That mark on his forehead hadn't been there before they went out to play, and it looked pretty ugly. What was it? Beeston came over to Sundar and looked closer at him.

'Yes, sir?' asked Sundar, wondering what was going on.

'How did you do that?' asked Beeston.

'Do what, sir?'

'That bruise on your forehead?'

'Oh, I fell over, sir.'

Fell over? And no marks anywhere else? Beeston frowned. It was possible, of course. Trip and fall against a wall. 'Where? asked Beeston.

'In the playground, sir.'

'When?' He knew it sounded like an inquisition but he had a feeling that Sundar wasn't telling him the whole truth. A hunch told him that it had been some kind of fight, but when? It couldn't have been just now because he had been on duty, and nothing like that had happened in the playground. That was one thing about a schoolyard fight, it was advertised in great shouts seconds after it had begun.

'At break time, sir,' said Sundar.

'Well, why didn't you come and tell me?' Beeston demanded. 'I was on playground duty.'

'I thought it would be all right, sir,' said Sundar.

'It is not all right.' Beeston turned so that his next remark was addressed to the whole class, making sure that everyone got the message. 'You must always tell a teacher if anyone falls over or has an accident. Right?'

Sundar nodded, eyes cast down in apology. 'Yes, sir. Sorry, Sir.'

'Don't apologise to me, it's your head,' said Beeston. 'This afternoon when Mrs Rogers comes in, go and show it to her.'

'Right, sir,' said Sundar.

Beeston wasn't convinced. There was something more. A scrap of some sort, he felt sure, but whatever it was, if it had been a bad one someone would have told him.

Beeston put down the piece of chalk and picked up the text book. 'Right,' he announced, 'back to the apostrophe. Open your books at page 17, exercise 2. There you will see a list of ten questions; each question has an apostrophe missing.'

• • •

Mrs Stone looked at her watch. A quarter to twelve, and the drilling was still going on. Her head was throbbing as if the drilling was going on in there. She'd taken two pain-killing tablets already, but they'd had no effect whatsoever. Whatever claims the adverts made for them, obviously no tests had included having a team of people armed with pneumatic drills tearing up the floor of the laboratory.

She picked up the requisition book and started sorting the carbon copies into three piles: yellow for her files, pink for County Hall, blue for the local Education Office. She looked at the reference numbers in the top right hand corners, and her eyes seemed to swim. Outside the drillers hammered relentlessly on. I can't cope, she muttered to herself. All she could think of was the incessant sound, drilling in through her skull, her ears, tearing up chunks of her brain.

She forced herself to look at the carbon copies again. '2987, 2988, 2989,' she muttered, gritting her teeth to force herself to concentrate.

Drill drill drill drill drill . . .

'2990 . . .'

The telephone rang.

'Oh no,' she groaned. 'I can't deal with that. I can't hear!'

Drill drill ring ring drill drill ring ring drill drill . . .

She made a decision, though later she couldn't have sworn that it was she herself who made the decision. It was more a decision made for her by the noises ringing and drilling and pounding inside her head.

She got up from her desk, walked past the ringing telephone, took her coat from its hook, opened the door of her office, and walked out into the corridor. As she did so she bumped into Mr Sims, obviously on his way in to see her.

'Ah' he said, 'Mrs Stone. I wanted to see Mr Beeston . . .'

'Well when you do, tell him I've had enough and I've gone home,' she said. And with that she walked out.

• • •

Beeston, meanwhile, was now fully in his stride on the finer points of the apostrophe, and luckily for him so were Holliday's class. 'Number seven,' he announced, tapping the open text book, 'the apostrophe is between John and the letter 's', showing that the book belongs to John. Any questions on that?'

One hand shot up. 'Yes, Jenny?'

'Please, sir,' asked Jenny. 'When are they going to stop the drilling?'

'I meant questions relating to the work you're doing,' said Beeston.

'Yes, sir,' complained Jenny, 'but it's giving me a headache.'

Adam's hand went up. 'And me, sir,' he said.

Neil's hand went up in sympathy, then Sarujeet's, and more voices joined in the general chorus to condemn the drilling going on outside.

'All right, all right,' said Beeston, 'hands down.' The chorus subsided, and the forest of hands descended back to desk level. 'The drilling will be dealt with later,' said Beeston. 'Right now let's get on with Question 8. Omar . . .?'

There was a knock at the classroom door. Beeston groaned. If it was the drillers come to ask for water to make a cup of tea . . . Aloud, he called: 'Come in!'

The door opened and Sims peered apprehensively in. 'Mr Beeston?' he said. 'Have you got a minute?'

'Is it urgent?' It was a silly question, Beeston reflected even as he asked it. The day a teacher admitted that the problem wasn't urgent the earth would stop spinning.

'I'm afraid it is,' said Sims.

Beeston sighed wearily. 'Right,' he said. And to the class: 'Carry on checking your work. I'll be back in a minute. And I'll be just outside that door, so no loud noises.' He joined Sims outside in the corridor, and as soon as the door was shut asked: 'Right. What's the emergency?'

'Mrs Stone has just walked out,' said Sims.

Beeston stared at him, dumbstruck. 'What?!' he said. 'Where?'

Inside the class the children strained their ears to hear what was going on. They could tell by the expression on Beeston's face through the glass panels in the door that it was pretty bad, whatever it was. Was someone injured? Or even dead?

'Home,' said Sims. 'She said she's had enough.'

'But . . .' said Beeston, lost. This had never happened before in all Mrs Stone's years at King Street.

'I think it's the drilling that's done it,' said Sims. 'I didn't want to interrupt your lesson, but I thought you ought to know as soon as possible.'

'Absolutely,' said Beeston, still dazed by the news. 'Thank you, Mr Sims.'

'What are you going to do?' asked Sims, wondering if there was anything he could do to help.

'Without Mrs Stone?' shrugged Beeston. 'There's only one thing I can do.'

'What's that?'

'Panic.'

• • •

At lunch time in the packed and as always raucously noisy school dining hall, the major topics of conversation were the continuous drilling and Mrs Stone's walk-out.

'And then she just walked out,' said Sims, who found himself in the spotlight as the only eye-witness of the event.

'I know the feeling,' said Lewis. 'I felt like walking out myself with that terrible drilling going on in the background. It's like being at the dentists for days on end.'

'I couldn't agree more,' chimed in Mrs Rudd.

'The trouble is it was happening right outside her office,' said Sims. 'She was the one getting the full effect of it.'

'And, as always, Mr Beeston had done absolutely nothing about it,' pointed out Mrs Rudd.

Sims looked at her, puzzled. 'But I don't see what he can do about it,' he said. 'After all, the roads have to be mended.'

'It's all right for you, Mr Sims,' snapped back Mrs Rudd, 'but my music room is right by where those dreadful road menders are working. I can hardly hear myself play the piano.'

'Oh, it's not all bad news then,' cracked Long.

Mrs Rudd regarded him as if he were a bad smell. 'You may take it lightly, Mr Long,' she said in her most superior voice, 'but then you are not inconvenienced as I am.'

‘Oh no?’ said Long. ‘I can hear it too, you know.’

‘I’ve a good mind to go and tell them off myself,’ Mrs Rudd continued, grim-faced.

‘You’ll have a job,’ commented Long, ‘they’ve packed up and gone off for lunch.’

‘In that case,’ said Mrs Rudd, pushing her empty pudding plate aside, ‘I shall go to my music room. While there is a bit of peace at least I can hear to sort out my instruments.’

They watched her go, and then returned to dissecting Mrs Purkiss’s imitation of a treacle tart. For Sims, another problem apart from the drilling was still nagging at his thoughts, a nagging suspicion that had been there ever since seeing Chandra’s face fall so desperately earlier that morning. Yes, of course all children wanted to stay in, he thought, but there had been something more than that, he was sure. He looked at Lewis and Long, both tucking into their pudding and getting their teeth stuck together. He wondered if they had noticed anything out of the ordinary lately with their children? ‘By the way,’ he said airily, just to introduce the new subject into the conversation.

‘Here it comes,’ said Long.

‘What?’ said Sims.

‘Whenever you say “by the way”, watch out.’

‘Not at all,’ said Sims defensively. ‘I was going to ask if either of you have had problems with your kids not wanting to go out at break time lately?’

‘We always have problems with that,’ said Long dismissively.

‘That’s true,’ agreed Lewis. ‘Kids love staying in, especially when they know they’re not supposed to.’

‘And when everyone else has to go out,’ added Long.

‘Yes, but have you?’ insisted Sims.

Lewis stopped eating and thought it over. ‘Yes,’ she said. ‘Now you come to mention it, I have. Why?’

‘Beause it’s been happening quite a lot lately in my class with certain children, and I wondered if anything was going on?’

‘What sort of thing?’ asked Long.

Before Sims had a chance to answer, a small girl suddenly appeared at Lewis's side. 'Please, Miss Lewis?' she said.

Lewis looked around at her. 'Yes, Roisin?' she asked.

'There's a woman come to see you. Angela de Souza's mum. She's waiting outside your classroom. Mr Beeston told me to come and tell you.'

'Right,' nodded Lewis. 'Tell her I'll be right there.' Roisin did a small bob that was almost a curtsey, and then trotted off to relay her message.

'What does Mrs de Souza want?' asked Long.

'She's worried that Angela isn't reading as well as the other children in my class. I think she wants to know what I'm going to do about it.'

'I get that as well,' said Sims. 'There's a huge amount of competition amongst the parents, isn't there?'

'Competition that isn't easily dealt with,' added Lewis. 'I'll see you both later.'

After she had gone, Sims turned back to the problem that had been buzzing around in his mind. He thought he might have a glimmer of the answer, but it was a pure guess. Still, at the moment it was all he had to go on. He pushed aside his plate, and turned to Long. 'By the way . . .' he said, trying to appear casual.

'There you go again,' observed Long.

Sims laughed briefly at his own obviousness, and then came to the point.

'How's your new boy settling down in your class? What's his name?'

'Carlos?' answered Long. 'Fine. No problem. A bit noisy, but aren't they all?' He put the last piece of treacle tart in his mouth. 'I don't think he'll cause any trouble.'

• • •

If Long could have seen Carlos at that moment, he wouldn't have been so confident. And if Sims and Beeston had known what was going on, then the questions in their minds concerning Chandra and Sundar would have been answered.

Carlos Costa was small for his age and, as Long said, noisy. But overriding the noise was a determination that wherever he was, he, Carlos, ruled. That had been the way at his last school, that was the way it was going to be here at King Street. He had only been here four days, but already he'd established his rules. Carlos's rules.

The first thing he'd done on arriving at the school was to find out who the chief bully was, and then threaten him in the toilets with a water pistol that he'd said was filled with acid. The boy had believed him. It had been as simple as that. They were babies here, Carlos had sneered to himself. Once he had the chief bully working for him, the rest had been simple. In the last three days he'd built up an army. The Big Boys. And with that army Carlos now ruled. Not only the playground but the streets around King Street as well.

The important thing was not to leave marks. Frighten his victims, but don't leave marks. Marks meant questions. They had been unlucky with Sundar that morning, falling like that, and he'd warned Rashid it must never happen again. Too many marks on too many kids and the whole thing could be blown. He had a good little racket going here and he didn't want it destroyed because some little kid's mother came up to the school complaining.

Not that the kids would talk, they were too frightened. And it was important to keep them frightened to keep them on their toes.

It was at that point in his thoughts that he saw Chandra in Mr Sims's class walking across the playground near the music room. How dare he! He'd told him the rules. Well he wasn't going to let the little toerag walk over him just like that! Who did he think he was! Make an example of him, that was the answer. Let him know that he, Carlos, wasn't to be ignored. If he said something then he meant it.

'Here!' he called savagely. 'You!'

Chandra stopped, already quaking.

'Come here!' yelled Carlos.

Chandra looked around for a teacher, or a dinner lady,

but there was no one around. Terrified, he walked slowly over to where Carlos was standing. That's the way, thought Carlos, make them come to you. Make them see who's boss.

'I told you yesterday I didn't want to see you in this part of the playground,' Carlos snarled.

Chandra was nearly in tears. 'But Mrs Rudd said . . .' he began, holding his hands up to his face to ward off the blows that might come.

'Don't argue with me,' snapped Carlos. 'Do you want my boys to hit you?'

Chandra shook his head.

'Because you broke the rule,' said Carlos, 'I want fifty pence from you tomorrow. Plus another fifty pence for arguing. And if you don't pay, you're dead. Now get lost.' He watched Chandra shuffle away. He could tell that the kid was almost wetting himself with fear. Should he call him back and make him do something like stand to attention, just so he could watch the kid pee in his trousers? Carlos smirked at the thought, then shrugged it aside. No, he thought, he was too busy. He had other kids to see, other money to collect. He'd make that kid pee himself tomorrow. It would be fun.

• • •

For her part, Miss Lewis was having a difficult job explaining to Mrs de Souza that every child was an individual who progressed academically at a different rate. As she sat in her classroom with Angela's mother, she almost wished that the road crew's dinner hour would end and the drilling would start up again. At least that would be a good reason to bring this argument, which seemed to be going round in circles, to a speedy close, however temporary.

'I do understand how concerned you are, Mrs de Souza . . .' she said for what sounded to her like the umpteenth time.

'I am,' nodded Mrs de Souza. 'Our next door neighbour's child, who's exactly the same age as Angela, is already reading books on her own.'

‘I know,’ said Lewis, ‘and Angela will be reading books on her own as well.’

‘But when?’ demanded Mrs de Souza. And this was the 64 thousand dollar question. ‘Surely she should be reading them now.’

‘Not necessarily. It’s a question of readiness.’

‘Ready for what? What me and her father want to know is, is she lazy or is she backward?’

Inwardly Miss Lewis groaned. There had to be a simple answer. And one answer, not a complex mixture of answers. One answer which would mean one simple solution, and then Mr and Mrs de Souza, and every other parent like them, would be satisfied. But wasn’t that the way it was nowadays? World famine? One simple answer was all that was required. Unemployment? One simple answer, that answer varying depending on which political party was giving it. No one liked to admit that there might be more than one problem at the root of any apparently single issue. But how do you say that to people who watch television drama shows where every major problem is neatly solved in thirty minutes? Lewis tried.

‘Look, Mrs de Souza,’ she said patiently, ‘not every child does everything at the same age. Children develop at their own speeds. Some children walk at six months, some children walk when they’re a year old. Some don’t walk until even later.’

‘I don’t see what that’s got to do with reading,’ said Mrs de Souza stiffly. ‘After all, when they’re babies they’re in different homes. Here she’s in the same class with other children who are already reading better than her.’

‘Believe me, Mrs de Souza,’ Lewis persisted, ‘even in the same families, children develop different skills at different speeds.’

It was obvious from Mrs de Souza’s next question that she hadn’t taken any of this on board. ‘What we want to know is, is she backward?’ she asked bluntly. ‘After all, I could read when I was five, and her father was reading when he was six. And Angela’s seven.’

Lewis did her best to keep down the irritation that she

was feeling. 'No, she is not backward,' she said firmly. 'As I said before, it's a question of readiness. She'll be reading fluently when she's ready.'

'But can't you get her to read quicker?' persisted Mrs de Souza.

Here we go, thought Lewis. The extra lessons, the cramming in the evenings. The flashcards every morning before breakfast. The refusal to allow Angela to watch her favourite television programme until she's read at least two pages 'all on her own'. The constant reading tests, where in the end Angela would end up knowing the tests by heart, and knowing nothing about reading. The reading and the re-reading of pages which would mean as much to the girl as if they were in Latin. 'Well if I pressurised her,' said Lewis, 'it may appear to make her read earlier . . .'

Mrs de Souza obviously missed the word 'appear' in Lewis's answer, because she smiled, satisfied that at last they were getting somewhere.

'But in the long run,' added Lewis, 'it could have the opposite effect.'

The smile slowly disappeared from Mrs de Souza's face. It seemed to Mrs de Souza that Miss Lewis was offering up the answer, and then snatching it away again 'How do you mean?' she demanded.

'It could put her off reading altogether. You see, a child has got to *want* to learn.'

Again, Mrs de Souza rejected any thinking along those lines. 'That's all very well,' she said dismissively, 'but she's losing time. We don't want her to grow up dim.'

Again, Lewis sighed silently to herself. 'She is not dim,' she said. She decided to try another tack. 'Look, cast your mind back to when you were at school, and all the things that you were put off . . .'

• • •

Beeston looked at his watch. One forty-five. Surely all of County Hall couldn't still be at lunch? He called 'Hello? Hello' into the receiver, then blew into it. He felt like adding 'Testing, testing', but refrained. Outside his window the drilling had started up again five minutes ago, and was now continuing at full volume. He put a hand over his other ear to try to shut out the sound, just as someone at the other end of the line said a tentative 'Hello?'

'Hello,' barked Beeston. 'Which Department am I talking to?' He'd asked for the Highways Department, but experience had shown him that he couldn't assume that was who he had been put through to. The switchboard operator at County Hall seemed to use a system for plugging in calls loosely based on Russian roulette, and whoever you spoke to depended on where the plug had gone in. Because of the noise of the drilling outside he thought the person at the other end of the line said 'Traffic Engineers', but he couldn't be sure. He weighed his choices up. He could either ask to be transferred to the Highways Department, and then sit holding an empty telephone until eventually someone like the Catering Department answered, or he could hang up and start all over again. Neither of these was satisfactory because he had Fred Holliday's class sitting in their room without a teacher, hopefully reading silently, although he doubted it. He made a decision.

'Look,' he said to the poor unfortunate with whom fate had connected him, 'this may be nothing to do with you, but Traffic Engineers sounds like something to do with digging up roads so don't try to pass me on to another department. I've told my story twice already since I've been on this phone, and frankly, I don't fancy going through it all again with you for a third time if I've then got to tell it to someone else for a fourth time.'

A squawking noise at the other end of the phone that he could dimly hear through the drilling sounded to him as if the person was asking who he was. Whether that was what they wanted to know or not, he told them.

'My name is Beeston . . . that's right, Beeston, and I'm the headmaster at King Street Junior school, and I don't know if you can hear it or not but right outside my window there is one of your men tearing up whatever is left of the road with the noisiest pneumatic drill ever invented.'

The person at the other end of the line started to say something. Beeston guessed it was the usual disclaimer about not being their department, but before they could, Beeston cut them off. 'No,' he said, 'don't talk, it's a waste of time because I can't hear a word you're saying because of this drilling, just listen. Because of this infernal row, my School Secretary has been forced out and most of my staff are planning to join her.'

Beeston thought the person said something about the Education Department, but he carried on, riding straight over that. 'In short,' Beeston continued, now speaking very loudly indeed, 'it is impossible to run this school with that noise going on. . . . What? . . . Say that again . . .'

The person at the other end was muttering something about the necessity of mending the roads, but what exactly Beeston couldn't quite hear. Good God, no wonder Mrs Stone had gone home. He'd have gone home too, if he'd been her.

'Listen,' said Beeston, 'I don't care if all the roads in the United Kingdom have got little holes in them, are you suggesting I send the kids home and tell the parents and the Education Committee that it's your fault?'

At last he heard some words clearly from the other end of the line. 'But the roads have got to be done,' said the voice defensively. 'When do you suggest we do them?'

Good, thought Beeston. Such a statement could only come from someone whose responsibility this drilling was. 'Do it at the weekend,' said Beeston. 'Or in the school holidays.'

'We can't do that,' said the voice at the other end indignantly. 'And I would have thought a man in your position would have known that.'

'Really,' said Beeston, now fuming noisily. 'Well I'll tell you what this man in my position is going to do. If you don't stop those men outside my window from drilling, I shall walk all my pupils, *and* their parents, down to your office, and you can explain to them all why we're going to have to close the school and why they can't have any education. Right?'

A squeak of protest started to come from the other end of the line, but was drowned out by a sudden surge in the drilling.

'I can't hear you!' bellowed Beeston, and he put the phone down. He sat, looking at it for a moment. His reputation at County Hall, he reflected, was now even further down than it always had been. Bang go my pension rights, he muttered to himself. A knock on the door made him look up. 'Come in!' he called.

It was Sims. What had happened? Was he coming to report that Holliday's class were on the rampage? 'Mr Beeston,' said Sims, 'can I see you a moment?'

Do I have a choice? thought Beeston. 'Haven't you got a class?' he asked.

'At the moment they're having music with Mrs Rudd,' said Sims. 'This is my marking period.'

'Well I've got Holliday's class,' said Beeston, 'who are undoubtedly killing each other at this very moment.'

'It won't take a second,' said Sims, 'and it is very important.'

Beeston sighed. 'All right,' he said, 'but make it quick.'

Sims weighed up his words, then said: 'Mr Beeston, I think there's something going on.'

'God, thought Beeston, we're not going to have one of Sims's major insights into the education system, are we? Aloud he said irritably: 'Of course there's something going on, there's this rotten drilling. Holliday's class are without a teacher. Mrs Stone's gone off . . .'

'No,' said Sims quickly, 'I mean something . . . unpleasant.'

Unpleasant? This brought Beeston up short. He looked at Sims. The man was obviously worried over something. 'What sort of unpleasantness?' he asked, and he felt a feeling of apprehension. Unpleasantness involving children was always bad news.

'For the past couple of days children in my class haven't wanted to go out into the playground at break,' said Sims.

The feeling of apprehension started to evaporate. If that's all Sims was bothered with, he thought, there's nothing to worry about. 'That's understandable,' said Beeston. 'I was the same at their age, there's something great about staying in when everyone else is out.'

'Yes, that's what everyone says,' said Sims, 'but in this case I think there's more to it than that. And the same has happened in some other classes.'

Suddenly Beeston saw what Sims was getting at.

'In my opinion I'd say it was more an atmosphere of, well, fear I'd call it, rather than some kids just wanting to be one up on everyone else,' Sims continued.

'Which children do you think are affected?' asked Beeston.

'Well, Chandra in my class certainly,' said Sims. 'And Asam. And Ghazala. And Ruby.'

And Sundar, Beeston added to himself. Yes, it was all adding up now, and he could kick himself for not having spotted it himself before.

'I think there may be some bullying going on out in the playground, and that's why they're frightened to go out,' Sims finished.

Beeston nodded. 'The same thought is occurring to me now,' he said. 'In fact it would have occurred to me earlier if it hadn't been for this damned drilling. Who? Any ideas?'

'No,' said Sims. 'I wondered if you had?' That wasn't strictly true, thought Sims, but he didn't want to reveal what was just a hunch until he had something to back it up.

Beeston thought it over. 'See if you can make some discreet enquiries,' he said. 'And I do mean discreet. Where bullies are concerned the whole thing's on a knife edge. The victims don't talk easily.'

'I was intending to do that, anyway,' said Sims.

'Good,' said Beeston. 'In the meantime I'll alert the staff to keep their eyes and ears discreetly open. If that damned drilling permits us all to, of course. However,' Beeston got up, 'right now I'd better get back to Mr

Holliday's class and hope it's still in one piece. But well done, Mr Sims. Thanks for spotting it. Let's just hope we can stop it before it spreads too widely.'

• • •

Ten to four. With a bit of luck, thought Rajnesh as he slipped out of the back gate of the school, Carlos and the Big Boys will have all gone home now. But they may be waiting to beat me up as I walk home along Dane Road, so if I go round by Stuart Street and through the back alley instead I will miss them. It will take me longer, but I will tell my mother I had to help another boy carry something home. A rabbit he brought into school. Yes, that is it. She won't mind that, she will think I have been a good boy because I helped another boy carry a rabbit home.

'Hello, Rajnesh.'

They were waiting for him by the corner of Dane Road. They must have guessed that he would try and go the other way when they saw that he hadn't come out of the main gate. There were three of them, two of the Big Boys and Carlos, crowding around him now, making sure that he couldn't run. He couldn't have run anyway, he was shaking so much. Could they see how much he was shaking?

'Trying to go home a different way tonight?' said Carlos.

'No,' Rajnesh lied desperately, almost begging them to believe him, 'I have to go and see my uncle . . .'

Carlos smiled. He knew that Rajnesh was lying and he wanted to make it worse for him, make him grovel, make him beg. Carlos grinned at the Big Boys with him. 'Well we'll walk along with you, shall we, Rajnesh? Make sure you get there all right?'

'He . . . he may not be in yet,' stammered Rajnesh, terrified.

Carlos nodded to one of the Big Boys, Simon, who moved round and placed himself now directly behind Rajnesh.

'We were worried that you might be trying to avoid us, Rajnesh,' said Carlos, faking a sympathetic expression.

Rajnesh shook his head in violent denial. 'No no,' he said. 'I wouldn't do that. I have to see my uncle . . .'

Carlos wasn't listening. 'Trying to avoid us is against the rules,' he said with a little smile.

'I wasn't trying to avoid you . . .' begged Rajnesh.

Carlos gave a little nod, and a vicious punch hit Rajnesh in the small of the back, making him feel sick, pain coursing through his kidneys.

'So is answering back,' said Carlos, and now the smile had gone and was replaced by a vicious snarl. 'We're going to have to fine you.'

'But . . .' begged Rajnesh, and he was praying silently, please don't let them hit me again, please don't let them hit me again.

'Bring in a pound tomorrow,' ordered Carlos.

A pound?! Where could he possibly get a pound from?!

'But I do not have any money,' he begged.

'Then get it,' said Carlos flatly.

'Where from?'

Carlos looked at the Big Boys on either side of him, and then looked back at Rajnesh and shrugged. 'That's not our problem,' he said. 'You owe us the money, so it's down to you to get it. Otherwise,' and again he nodded at Simon, 'you'll get more of this.'

This time it was a kick on the back of the leg, and Rajnesh nearly fell down with the pain, but he knew that if he did they would possibly all start to kick him once he was on the floor. He must stay upright!

Carlos smiled. 'We'll see you tomorrow, Rajnesh,' he said. 'At break time. And make sure you've got the money.'

Rajnesh cringed, waiting for a final punch from Simon, but it never came. Instead Carlos and the Big Boys turned and ambled off, totally confident in their own invulnerability.

• • •

Mrs Stone sat in her kitchen looking into her coffee cup. How could she? she thought. In all her years at King

Street she'd never done anything like that. To walk out! Whatever would they think of her? The drilling had seemed so bad at the time, yet now it seemed so small, so petty. She shook her head. No, it hadn't been petty. It had been impossible! What with that, and everything else . . .

The doorbell ringing made her look up. Who could that be at this time? She expected it was the Jehovah's Witnesses again. They'd called earlier, but when she'd told them she was busy, instead of taking the hint they'd said they'd call back later. She remembered talking about them to Mr Beeston once, and he'd said he always got rid of them by telling them he was a Jehovah's Bystander. 'It's like a Witness, only I don't like to get involved.'

She sighed. She wondered what Mr Beeston would be saying about her now? She should at least have told him she was going face to face, but she couldn't. All she'd wanted to do was get away from that awful noise.

She opened the door, and there on the doorstep was Beeston, carrying a large bunch of flowers, and wearing a silly smile on his face.

'Hello,' he said meekly. 'Can I come in?'

• • •

Beeston nibbled at his second biscuit. The flowers, he thought to himself, had been a nice touch, and they looked good in the vase where Mrs Stone had put them. Mrs Stone put his coffee down in front of him, still a bit bewildered by his sudden appearance.

'The point is,' he said dramatically, 'can you forgive me for not going out there and removing that pneumatic drill from that man? I am really so sorry.'

'You're sorry?' she said. 'I'm the one who's sorry, walking out like that. And once I was home here, I felt such a fool.'

'Nonsense,' said Beeston, at the same time thinking, I wonder if I could sneak another biscuit?

'I did,' said Mrs Stone. 'All I could think of was: how on earth can I go back and face everybody now I've done that?'

'Easy,' said Beeston, and another biscuit disappeared from the plate.

'No it isn't. To be honest, I thought I'd have to resign. If you must know, I'm still thinking about it.'

Beeston stopped with the biscuit halfway to his mouth, and stared at her. 'Resign?!' he said, shocked. 'Resign?! Oh come now . . .'

'Yes,' insisted Mrs Stone, still obviously upset. 'Don't you understand how I felt, and afterwards how I felt it must have looked to everyone else at King Street?'

Beeston put down his biscuit and looked at her sternly. 'If you even think of resigning,' he said firmly, 'I shall refuse to accept it. And if you try and get it past me to the Chief Education Officer, I shall steal it back from his office.'

Mrs Stone gestured helplessly, still at a bit of a loss. 'But . . .' she began.

'Mrs Stone, this was once in how many years? Hundreds!'

'Not that many,' Mrs Stone replied, somewhat irritated by Beeston's choice of words. 'I'm not Methusaleh, you know.'

'Well, a long time. Look at Mrs Rudd. She storms out on a daily basis. And she never resigns. Worse luck.'

'This was different . . .'

'Yes, this was a more deserved going home. You went home with a headache because of the drilling, and that's that. Staff do it all the time.'

'But . . .'

'Please, no buts,' said Beeston. 'The school needs you. Goddammit,' he exploded, '*I* need you.'

Mrs Stone smiled for the first time since his arrival. 'I shouldn't let my husband hear you say that,' she said.

'I expect he knows it already,' said Beeston.

'The problem is,' she said, 'will I be able to cope with the drilling tomorrow? Who's to say the same thing won't happen again? What do I do, keep storming off every day?'

'If the drilling's still going on, by all means.'

Mrs Stone looked at him, puzzled. 'What do you mean, if it's still going on? I've never known the Council to finish mending a road in just one day.'

'Let's just say I've tried a bit of a bluff,' said Beeston. 'If it's worked, with luck the drillers will have packed up for a bit while they decide what to do. If, on the other hand, they call my bluff and the drilling's going on . . . Well,' he shrugged, 'we're going to have a very large school outing.'

• • •

The next day found the hole in the road outside King Street Junior deserted. The compressors were still there, the warning cones were still there, and the hole was still there, but of the workmen there was no sign. Everyone agreed that whatever Mr Beeston had said to the Council, it had worked. Even Mrs Rudd was charitable in her praise of him, saying that, for once, he must have done something right. The big question was, how had he done it? What did he know about someone high-up in County Hall that had put a stop to it, however temporary that stop was? What was it the Mafia said? If you want to succeed in your rival's business, know where the bodies are buried. Whose bodies did Beeston know the whereabouts of? Which skeletons in whose cupboard had he rattled? Whoever he had got a hold on, everyone thanked God that something had been done.

Sims had other things on his mind. He knew he had to do something about the bullying he believed was going on in the school, and morning break found him in his class with Chandra, instead of expressing relief about the lack of drilling with the rest of the staff.

He had kept Chandra in because he felt the boy was the weakest link in the bullying chain. He hated to put pressure on him, but unless he did the situation would get out of hand, if it wasn't already. Sims smiled, hoping that a smile would put the boy at ease. Chandra, though, knew that something was up, knew what he was about to be asked, and was ready. He was not going to talk easily, the fear of whoever was bullying him was too great.

'Chandra,' Sims said gently, 'I know you're being frightened out in the playground . . .'

Immediately Chandra defended. 'I'm not!' he protested.

'I know you are,' said Sims, still talking gently, but with a firm conviction in his voice that he wouldn't allow Chandra to deny, 'because it happened to me when I was your age.'

Chandra looked at Sims, puzzled. To Mr Sims? But Mr Sims was so big. Mr Sims was huge!

Sims took advantage of Chandra's sudden silence, talking on, his voice knowing, putting into words all that Chandra had experienced over the past few days, those terrible experiences. 'The bigger boys who would punch you if you didn't do what they said,' continued Sims. 'Who'd wait for you outside the school gates, and follow you home.'

'They did that to *you*?' said Chandra, astonished.

'Yes,' said Sims. 'The same as they're doing it to you.'

'No,' said Chandra quickly, fear in his eyes.

'Chandra,' said Sims, his voice soft, knowing. 'I *know* they are.'

There was a long pause. Chandra dropped his head, lowered his gaze. How could Mr Sims know? How could he?

'I know,' said Sims again.

A tear trickled out of the corner of Chandra's eye. 'Yes,' he said, so quietly it was almost a whisper.

'It happens at break times, doesn't it?'

'And dinner times,' he said, tears now running down his miserable lowered face.

'And home times as well, yes?'

Chandra nodded. 'Yes,' he said, crying quietly, 'so I go home the long way to avoid them, and then my mother is upset because I am home late from school.'

'And who is it who's doing it?'

For a second the tears stopped, and there was a long pause, before Chandra said: 'I do not know.'

Don't lose him now, thought Sims. Don't lose him on

this question, this is the important one. 'Come on, Chandra,' he said, his voice still low, still gentle. 'Of course you know them. Who's class are they in? Our class?'

Chandra looked up at this and shook his head emphatically. 'Oh no, sir!' he said, shocked at the idea.

'Mr Holliday's? Mrs Wilberforce's?' Sims watched Chandra closely as he threw in the next name, already sure in his own mind that it was the answer. 'Mr Long's?'

Chandra dropped his head and the tears started again.

'Mr Long's class,' nodded Sims. 'It's Carlos, isn't it? The new boy.'

'No sir,' sobbed Chandra.

Sims leaned back and sighed regretfully. 'Very well,' he said, 'if you won't tell me, then I'll have to speak to Mr Long . . .'

Chandra sat bolt upright, sheer terror now on his face. 'No, sir!' he begged. 'He'll think I said.'

Got him! thought Sims. 'Look, Chandra, it's got to be stopped, and if you won't tell me then I'll have to do it another way. We can't let it go on. You don't want to be hit all the time, do you?'

Chandra shook his head. 'He doesn't hit me, sir.'

'Then what does he do?'

'He . . . he gets the other boys to do it.'

'In Mr Long's class?'

'Yes, sir.'

'And how many other children do they do this to?'

'Lots, sir.'

'And what exactly happens?'

'He . . . he gets us and says that the bigger boys will do us unless we do what he says. So we do what he says.'

'What sort of things?'

'Sometimes we just run around when he tells us to. Or we give him things.'

'What kind of things?'

'Our sandwiches. Our sweets. Money.'

Sims surveyed the sad little boy in front of him. Sad wasn't the word, destroyed would be a more accurate description. Anyway he'd be able to put a stop to Carlos's activities now. Or could he? Chandra would deny everything for fear of reprisals from Carlos and the other boys, and without that admission, what case did he have? Suspicion wasn't enough, he needed evidence. Exasperated, he asked: 'Why didn't you tell me about this before? Or Mr Long?'

'Because he says he will do us properly if we tell,' said Chandra simply, and then he began to cry again. 'If he finds out I've told you, he will do me.'

Sims shook his head and patted Chandra reassuringly on the shoulder. 'No he won't,' he said. 'Leave it to me. He won't know that anyone's told me anything. And don't worry, I'll be watching out for you. He won't touch you again.'

• • •

For Mrs Stone the day was a complete relief. She'd expected at worse the drilling to be continuing, and at best people to avoid her. Neither was the case. In fact people had bent over backwards to come in and to ask after her health. Mr Sims, Mrs Wilberforce, Mrs Patterson, Mr Long, all of them had poked their heads around the door. And no drilling! She still couldn't quite believe it.

'Morning.' It was Miss Lewis now appearing. 'Or rather, afternoon, as it's lunchtime. How's the head?'

'Mine?' asked Mrs Stone, 'or do you mean Mr Beeston?'

'Yours. We all know how *he* is.'

'I tell you, I'm so relieved they've stopped that drilling,' said Mrs Stone.

'Yes. I wish I knew how he'd done it, I could use it when they're digging up my road while I'm trying to watch Wimbledon.'

Meanwhile, for Carlos's victims out in the playground at lunch time, there was no such air of relief. For Rajnesh it was the moment he'd been dreading. He'd persuaded his mother that he had been ill in the morning, but she'd insisted that he was all right to go to school in the afternoon, and she had even brought him to the school so that there had been no escape for him. Now he was trapped in a corner of the playground at the back of the library, ordered there by Carlos, away from the eyes of the teacher on duty. Carlos didn't even bother to have his Big Boys as back-up, he didn't need it. The fact that he, Carlos, said anything was enough.

'Where's my money, Rajnesh?' he demanded.

'I couldn't get it,' Rajnesh blurted out all in a rush. 'I asked my Mum but she didn't have any change. I'll get it for you tomorrow, I promise.'

Carlos sneered. 'Well promises just ain't good enough. I told you to pay me today.'

'Please,' begged Rajnesh, 'I tried . . .'

'I didn't tell you to try, I told you to get it.'

'But she didn't have change . . .' pleaded Rajnesh, nearly in tears now.

'Then you should have taken what she did have,' snarled Carlos, now getting impatient. Who did these kids think they were to try this rubbish on with Carlos?

'But I can't take it from her purse,' begged Rajnesh. 'I've never done anything like that.'

'Are you arguing with me?' demanded Carlos, moving in closer, his fists bunched tight.

Rajnesh felt that he was going to be sick. 'No, Carlos . . .' he began helplessly.

'*Mr* Carlos! snapped Carlos. 'I'm going to have to teach you a lesson in manners . . .'

'That's enough!' came a voice from behind him.

Carlos whirled round, startled. Mr Sims was just coming out of the library. What was he doing here? How much had he heard? 'Yes' he said, quickly dropping back into his innocent schoolchild persona.

'You're coming with me to see Mr Beeston,' said Sims grimly.

Carlos looked at Sims, baffled. 'What for, sir?' he said, doing his best to look open and honest. It usually worked for him with adults, he reflected. 'I haven't done anything.'

'Threatening people and demanding money from them,' said Sims.

Carlos looked at Sims, then at Rajnesh, then back at Sims again, and then broke into laughter. 'Oh that,' he laughed. 'No, sir, it was just a game. We were playing crooks. Weren't we, Rajnesh?'

Sims looked enquiringly at Rajnesh, who swallowed hard, and then said helplessly: 'Yes, sir. We were just playing.'

'Rajnesh is my friend,' grinned Carlos, and he put one arm around Rajnesh's shoulders and gave him an affectionate squeeze.

Sims didn't alter his expression at all as he regarded Carlos. 'It didn't sound like that from where I was,' he said.

Carlos shrugged, but carried on grinning broadly, supremely confident. He held all the aces. Rajnesh wasn't going to say anything. None of his victims would say a thing, and he knew that. Even if Sims was suspicious, what could he prove without evidence? Nothing. He, Carlos, was safe. Absolutely safe. 'That's how we play, sir,' he said, now openly cocky. 'Like they do on the telly.'

Sims nodded thoughtfully, his expression still not altering as he watched Carlos with a fixed grim stare. 'That's interesting, Carlos,' he said, 'because some of your gang have told me differently.'

Carlos looked back at him, looking puzzled. 'What gang, sir?' he asked.

'They've told me how you ordered them to beat up the smaller children.'

'That's a lie!' stormed Carlos.

For the first time Sims smiled, and the sight of his smile suddenly put a chill that ran right through Carlos. Maybe Sims did have something after all? Not all his gang were as tough as he was, this school was made up of babies, he'd always said it. A bit of pressure and they'd crack. He could tell by the smile on Sims's face, not only did Sims know, he had proof from one of them!

'Is it?' smiled Sims. 'Well, we'll soon find out when we

bring your parents up to the school and see what they've got to say.'

Carlos felt his heart sinking. His mother. He'd always been able to keep his mother away from school. He'd never been in trouble, he'd always been too careful. 'My parents?' he repeated. 'Why do you want to see my parents?'

'So that they can tell us where you've been getting all this money.'

'What money?' It was a desperate throw by Carlos, he knew he was losing his grip on this one. It was all his gang's fault. One of them had gone weak and grassed. Sims was moving towards him, hand outstretched.

'Save it for Mr Beeston, Carlos,' he was saying.

Carlos backed away. 'You're not taking me to see him,' he said. He knew what would happen, Beeston would call his mother, and she'd go for him. She'd kill him. He turned and made a run for it, but too late, he'd let Sims get too near! The next second Sims had him tight, both arms up behind his back. Desperately Carlos kicked out, screaming and yelling, the commotion bringing other children rushing from the other parts of the playground to see what was going on.

'I ain't going to see him!' sobbed Carlos, wriggling desperately in Sims grip, fighting hopelessly to get away. 'I want to go home!'

'And that is precisely where you're going,' snapped Sims with grim satisfaction. 'With Mr Beeston for company.'

'No,' begged Carlos, now distraught, and all the children watching from a safe distance felt revenge and exultation as they heard his sob, watched him beg, as his voice yelled: 'I didn't do nothing! They gave me the money, I didn't ask them for it! Please don't tell my Mum! She's not well! Please!'

• • •

By half past twelve Carlos had been deposited with Mr Beeston, still desperately trying to deny that any money he had ever taken had been by force. By twelve thirty-five the rest of his gang had been rounded up and had confessed everything to Mr Beeston. By twelve forty Beeston had contacted Mrs Costa, who had shrieked over the telephone, and was now on her way to the school in a state of fury, with Carlos, with the school, with Sims, with everybody.

By twelve forty-five the story of the breaking-up of Carlos's gang was all over the whole school and the children began to follow Sims with their eyes as he walked across the playground as if he was walking on water. However, if Sims thought he was everybody's hero, he was mistaken. While Mrs Costa was in Beeston's office, screaming at Carlos, then at Beeston, and threatening to sue Sims and the school for assaulting her son, Sims was about to run into trouble in the staff room.

Sims was just making himself a cup of tea, relieved that Carlos was now removed, and that Carlos's victims were safe, when Long stormed in.

'So!' he said grimly.

'Hello,' said Sims. 'I imagine you've heard.'

'Yes,' snapped Long. 'But not from you.'

'I was coming to see you . . .'

'When?' demanded Long sarcastically, and there was no mistake at all about his anger.

Sims was taken aback. He hadn't expected to be received as the Saviour of the School by everyone, but he hadn't expected this.

'I don't understand,' he said, bewildered. 'I thought you'd be pleased. After all, he was in your class.'

'Exactly, snapped Long. 'So I'd have thought you'd have done me the courtesy of coming to see me first before you started going out arresting people.'

'I wasn't arresting anyone,' defended Sims. 'And anyway, what could I have said? I didn't have any proof.'

'I don't care if you had proof or not, he's in my class. I should have been told what was going on instead of you sneaking around setting traps like you were someone out of MI5.'

'I wasn't sneaking around,' said Sims. 'Look . . .'

Long didn't give Sims a chance to continue his defence. 'If you want my opinion,' said Long, tight-lipped, 'it was very unprofessional.'

Unprofessional, be damned, fumed Sims, his initial feelings of sympathy for Long's point of view now fast fading. What about the kids who had been at risk from Carlos? 'I caught him, didn't I?' Sims said simply, not bothering to conceal his irritation with Long's attitude.

'*I* would have caught him if I'd been told,' retorted Long indignantly. 'How would you like it if I started interfering in your class's affairs without consulting you?'

'It was something that was affecting my class. In fact it was affecting the whole school.'

'Which is why I should have been consulted instead of you bulldozing your way in,' stormed Long. 'I think you owe me an apology.

Sims stared at him open-mouthed. An apology? For stopping a child from terrorising the whole school, for saving children from being forced to steal from their families, for saving children from having to live their school lives in terror? An apology?

'Well?' said Long stiffly. 'I'm waiting.'

'Then you can bloody well wait a long time,' snarled Sims, and with that he stormed out of the staff room, slamming the door behind him.

• • •

As he was leaving the school that evening, still fuming over Long's reaction, Sims bumped into Beeston. 'I suppose,' Sims said pointedly, 'that Mr Long has been to see you?'

'Everyone's been to see me,' said Beeston wearily, 'including the whole of the Costa family, the families of the rest of the gang, and last but not least Mr Long. The only good thing that's happened is that the drillers haven't returned, although on points I'm not sure I wouldn't have preferred them to Mrs Costa.'

'Mr Long's not happy about what I did,' said Sims.

'Yes,' agreed Beeston, 'that was the impression I got as well.'

'But I did it because it was the right thing to do.'

Beeston winced. 'You sound just like John Wayne,' he said.

'I didn't mean . . .' began Sims.

'I shouldn't let it worry you, he'll get over it,' said Beeston, clapping Sims sympathetically on the shoulder. You'd have felt the same if it had been someone in your class.'

'I suppose so,' Sims admitted grudgingly.

'The main thing is, you stopped it before it spread. Only I would suggest, next time try a bit more consultation, eh. It makes things easier all round.'

'But I didn't have any proof!' protested Sims. 'As it was I had to bluff Carlos into admitting he was doing it.'

'Maybe if you'd talked to Mr Long, we'd have got the proof,' suggested Beeston tactfully.

Sims bridled slightly. Was Beeston also saying that he was wrong? 'All right,' he said defensively. 'But I had to do something.'

'I know, and it worked. So well done. All I'm saying is . . .'

'In the future, more consultation,' finished Sims.

Beeston nodded.

'Let's just hope it doesn't happen in the future,' said Sims.

'Oh it will, most certainly,' said Beeston ruefully. 'Not from Carlos. I put the fear of God into the little swine, and his cronies. Believe me, none of them will do that again while they're at this school. But there'll be others. There always are.'

Sims thought that over. Yes, he was sure Beeston was right, that was what made it so sad. 'I suppose so,' he said. 'But what causes it?'

'You're the history expert, Mr Sims. You tell me,' answered Beeston. 'What causes alleged humanity to commit the same atrocities and the same errors over and over again since time began? The Carloses of this world are just part of that.'

'That's very pessimistic.'

'It's just life, Mr Sims,' said Beeston philosophically. 'All we can do is hope we keep catching them before they do any damage. And if we can't, pick up the pieces afterwards.' From the office Beeston could hear the phone going. Mrs Costa again? Or another member of the Costa clan phoning to cry all down British Telecom's precious lines over their poor misunderstood child? 'I'd better go, Mr Sims,' he said. 'The telephone calleth me.'

'Right,' said Sims. 'I'll see Mr Long tomorrow and sort it out with him.'

'Don't worry,' said Beeston. 'He'll be all right by the morning.'

He watched Sims leave. A good teacher, he thought, but he still had a lot to learn about dealing with other members of staff. Still, he'd rather have someone like that than someone who was a whizz with other staff members and as useless as a brick with the kids.

The telephone was still ringing. Oh well, he supposed he'd better grab it. After all, it might even turn out to be important. He pushed open the door of the office and picked up the receiver. 'King Street Junior School,' he said.

'Is Mr Beeston there?' demanded a voice.

Something about the voice made Beeston cautious. 'Who's calling?' he asked.

'Mr Johnson, Head of County Highway department. Tell him it concerns a complaint about road mending outside the school.'

Oh, did it. Well Beeston was pretty sure of one thing: whoever this Mr Johnson was, from the tone of his voice he was not a fan of Beeston's and this did not promise to be a friendly phone call. After a day like he'd had, this was one call he could definitely do without. He had been right to be cautious.

'I'm afraid Mr Beeston's gone home,' he lied. 'And I'm afraid I can't really help you with this. I'm just one of the staff. I suggest you call him tomorrow.'

He smiled to himself as he replaced the receiver.

Cowardly? Yes. Petty? Definitely. But every victory over County Hall, no matter how petty or small, was a great leap forward for mankind. Not quite Neil Armstrong, but he was quite sure that if he ever met the astronaut, they'd agree that the sentiment was the same.

CHAPTER FIVE

THE FACTS OF LIFE

'Right,' said Beeston, 'that's the repairs to the minibus dealt with. Anything more on the minibus before we move on?' Fortunately there was nothing more to add. And thank God for that, thought Beeston. That was one of the advantages of having staff meetings in the lunch hour, there was a definite cut-off point when the bell sounded, which meant it sharpened up everyone's thoughts. Now, before they said anything, they looked at their watches. When staff meetings were held after school they could, and often did, go on for hours, with all manner of oddball points being raised and debated. Those staff meetings had often resembled the House of Lords in one of its more lunatic debates. He remembered one famous occasion when Fred Holliday and Mrs Rudd had kept a discussion on the numbers of sticks of chalk each classroom should be allocated going for over twenty minutes, and if Mr Long hadn't fallen asleep in the middle of it and snored, the discussion would have gone on for another twenty.

Beeston checked the notes he'd written down. 'Next item on the agenda,' he announced, 'rude words on the boys' lavatory walls.'

This caused a few raised eyebrows amongst some of the more 'delicate' members of the staff, who felt that such things should not be discussed openly.'

Mr Long was not one of those delicate souls. 'Have you noticed, as the writing gets higher the spelling gets better?' he joked.

'I don't think that's very funny, Mr Long,' sniffed Mrs Rudd unappreciatively.

'No,' said Long. 'I didn't think you would.'

Beeston opened his mouth to make his comment on the matter, but before he could, as always, Mrs Rudd was faster.

'These rude words are a symptom of the whole lowering of standards in this school,' she announced.

This brought a chorus of disapproval from what Beeston thought of as the more 'liberal' faction.

'Oh, come on,' protested Sims, but quietly and with moderation, thought Beeston, as befitted what he suspected to be Sims's middle-ground politics. 'I hardly think that's the case. People have been writing rude words on lavatory walls since the beginning of time.'

'Speak for yourself, Mr Sims,' retorted Mrs Rudd pointedly.

'Has the caretaker been complaining, then?' asked Holliday.

'I'm sure he would if I could find him, but as usual he hasn't been seen,' said Beeston. 'No, a parent reported it. Mr Asam.'

'What was Mr Asam doing in the children's toilets?' asked Lewis.

Beeston kept back the answer that sprang to his mind and instead said: 'He didn't actually go in them, his son came home and told him about the words. Mr Asam doesn't like them.'

'Quite right too,' said Mrs Rudd approvingly. 'He has my wholehearted support.'

'I'm sure he'll be delighted to know that,' said Beeston. 'So, if you can all have a word with the boys in your class and warn whoever's doing it that they will be in big trouble if it carries on.'

This was met by general murmurs of assent and agreement in differing volumes. Beeston knew precisely what would happen: Lewis and Long would talk to their classes about self-discipline, Sims would give his class a long lecture on caring for society, the anti-social nature of writing on walls, how the toilet walls were owned by the community as a whole and how the desecration of them affected everyone. Holliday would simply march into his classroom and announce: 'Someone's writing on the toilet walls. Whoever it is, stop it.'

'I wonder if we can't do more?' said Mrs Rudd.

Beeston groaned inwardly. Please don't let her choose this subject to start a campaign on. 'What do you suggest, apart from demolishing the toilets?' he asked.

'I'm talking about inculcating some morality into the children,' she said stiffly. 'In my opinion . . .'

The rest of the staff started looking at their watches. If Mrs Rudd got into her stride this could be a long haul. Beeston stepped in to cut her off before she got under way. 'Absolutely,' he said swiftly, 'but can we leave that subject for the moment? It's twenty past one and I want to get on to the main item on the agenda before the bell goes.'

'Well . . .' said Mrs Rudd, not at all happy to leave the subject.

Beeston gave her no chance. 'Now,' he said firmly, 'as you may or may not know, County Hall have apparently suddenly discovered sex, and according to a new directive from them, we now have to have a proper system of sex education.'

'We already do have,' pointed out Yvonne Patterson.

'Yes,' agreed Beeston, 'but they want it less *ad hoc* and more structured.'

'That's the trouble with sex,' said Long. 'When the bureaucrats want to get in on the act, you know the fun's over.'

'What about the Muslim parents? Won't they have any objections?' This last from Sims. He's worried about the Muslims, thought Beeston. He should think about the trouble we're going to get from the Exclusive Brethren and the fundamentalists.

'I've already thought of that,' said Beeston. 'We're going to have two groups on Friday mornings: fourth-year girls go to Mrs Patterson, and fourth-year boys go to Mr Holliday, and together they'll tell them everything they need to know.'

'With kids today, I expect they'll be able to tell me,' commented Holliday ruefully.

'Actually,' said Mrs Rudd, 'I may be considered old-fashioned . . .'

Here we go again, groaned Beeston. Add on half an hour for the thoughts of Mrs Rudd. Will we get this all in before the bell goes, or will we have to continue it tomorrow? I really should make sure she's locked in the toilets before these staff meetings begin.

'But I am not convinced,' Mrs Rudd continued, 'that school is the right place to teach children about sex.'

'Then where is?' asked Patterson.

'The home, of course. Sex is a private matter, and I think it debases it to bring it into the classroom.'

'Nonsense,' said Patterson tersely. 'What about those homes where the parents are inadequate, or too embarrassed to talk about it?'

'Can we move on?' asked Beeston, and proceeded to do so before everyone could object. 'Right, last item: this year's educational visit, or school holiday. This year we have space for thirty children; and from the replies that I've had so far from the fourth-year parents, it looks as if roughly five girls and twenty-five boys want to go, which means three male teachers and one female teacher. So, the names of the staff I've got down are Mr Holliday, Mrs Patterson, Mr Long and Mr Sims.'

'Why?' asked Mrs Rudd.

My God she's on form today, thought Beeston. 'Why what?' he asked.

'Why have you got those names down?'

'Because they are the people who volunteered to go.'

'But . . .' began Mrs Rudd. At which point the bell went for the start of afternoon school. Just done it! thought Beeston.

However, if Beeston thought he'd escaped the wrath of Mrs Rudd, on this particular occasion he was wrong. He was just heading back towards his office, the staff meeting safely (and, as far as he was concerned, successfully) behind him, when he became aware of footsteps hurrying after him.

'Mr Beeston!' came Mrs Rudd's plaintive cry.

Beeston hesitated. Could he pretend he hadn't heard her, make a sudden dash for his office and bury himself beneath a mound of County Hall paperwork? Too late, before he could move she was on him, cornering him against the door of the stock cupboard.

'Mr Beeston,' she said, 'I wish to see you.'

It never failed to astonish Beeston how Mrs Rudd could make a big production number out of stating the obvious.

'Haven't you got a class?' he asked hopefully.

'I have, but they can wait a moment. I wish to complain about the staffing arrangements for the school trip. You only ever ask certain people. It is blatant favouritism.'

'But you never want to go,' pointed out Beeston. 'I asked you one year and you said you would never ever go inside a tent.'

'That is not the point. For all you know I may have changed my attitude towards camping.'

'Have you?'

'How do I know if I am never given the opportunity? As it happens, this year I would have quite liked to have gone.'

'All right,' said Beeston resignedy, 'if anyone drops out . . .'

'That is not the point,' said Mrs Rudd firmly. 'It is not good enough. I will see you later about it.'

And then she was gone to wreak havoc on the school piano. Beeston sagged against the wall for a moment, reeling. What did I ever do to deserve this? he asked. Job had boils, I've got Mrs Rudd.

Mrs Stone was looking up as he slumped into the office. 'What was all that about?' she asked.

'Didn't you hear it?' asked Beeston. 'I thought most of the northern hemisphere would have heard it.'

'Only the tone of voice. It sounded like Mrs Rudd on the warpath.'

'That's a fairly safe assumption whenever you hear a raised voice in this school. Yes, it was Mrs Rudd on the warpath.'

'What did she want?'

'To go on the school trip,' said Beeston gloomily.

'That's good of her,' said Mrs Stone perkily.

Beeston looked his secretary with distaste. How easily even people he regarded as sane were taken in by Mrs Rudd. He attemped to put the record straight on Mrs Rudd's obviously (to him) dubious motives. 'Of course it isn't good of her. She's only saying it because she wants to have a go at me. Actually show her a tent and she'd run a mile.'

'I don't know,' said Mrs Stone. 'I think you're being a little harsh on her.'

Not as harsh as I'd like to be, thought Beeston vengefully. Boiling in oil sounds a healthy proposition.

'Oh, before I forget,' said Mrs Stone, picking up a list of messages that looked ominously long from where Beeston stood.

'Yes?'

'Mrs Purkiss came in looking for you.'

'That was a close shave. What does she want, apart from cooking lessons?'

'She came in to complain about a small drip in the kitchen.'

'That'll be Mrs McCarthy. What does she want me to do about her?'

Mrs Stone rolled her eyes in exasperation. 'Be serious,' she said. 'One of the radiators has a slight leak.'

'Oh,' said Beeston. 'That sort of drip.'

'She's been looking for the caretaker, but can't find him.'

The caretaker! There was another thorn in Beeston's side, though completely different from Mrs Rudd. If Mrs Rudd was like a limpet who leapt upon him at every move he made, the caretaker was like the invisible man. It had often crossed Beeston's mind that the caretaker at King Street didn't actually exist, and that someone just came in when no one was looking and rearranged the brown overall hanging on the peg by the caretaker's door.

'She wants you to do something about it,' added Mrs Stone.

'Right,' said Beeston, 'I'll get on to County Hall, Engineers and Plumbers Department. I think I've got a couple of days free to spend on the phone. Anything else?'

'Yes,' said Mrs Stone, checking her list again. 'While you're on to County Hall, you can tell them I'm still waiting for a new Stock Requisition Order Book.'

'Right.'

'And we still haven't had the new canteen figures yet, and they were promised for last week.'

'Right.' Beeston hesitated before making for the safety of his office. Was that it? Had Mrs Stone got to the end of her list? No, she hadn't. She ticked off another item and said: 'Mrs Rogers is still waiting for her disposable gloves.'

'I wish I hadn't asked if there was anything else now,' Beeston complained. 'I didn't expect something as long as the passenger list on the Queen Mary. Anyway, what does Mrs Rogers want more disposable gloves for? She has hundreds in her cupboard. What does she do with them?'

'Disposes of them, of course. That's why they're called disposable gloves. Remember that new ruling from County Hall? Every case of illness involving excreted bodily fluids . . .'

Beeston shuddered. 'Do you have to, I've not long had breakfast.'

'The point is, it means she must use gloves.'

'I should hope so. Frankly I doubt if I'd want to attack some of our kid's hygiene problems without a complete radiation suit for protection.'

'And,' continued Mrs Stone, 'the only problem was they only sent one packet of gloves, and when we had that epidemic of gastro-enteritis last week, she used them all up in two days.'

'Typical of County Hall's Forward Planning Policy,' said Beeston. 'Okay, I'll see what I can do. Is that it?'

Mrs Stone checked her list again, and then nodded. 'For the moment,' she said.

'Good,' said Beeston. 'Well I've got one for you.'

'Oh? What is it this time?'

'The new sex education policy. Fred Holliday's and Yvonne Patterson's lessons will start next week. We need to advise all the parents of the children involved, so we'd better send a letter out with the kids concerned.'

'That's all the fourth-year children?'

'Right.'

Mrs Stone gave a warning sigh. 'It'll cause trouble among some parents,' she said. 'You'll see. I can feel it in my bones.'

'Name me something in this school that doesn't,' said Beeston. 'Right, well I'm off.'

'Where to, in case anyone wants you?'

'Shangri-La.'

'Oh?'

'Yes, it's the only place left that I haven't looked for our alleged caretaker.'

• • •

It had been a good lesson, thought Sims. Not one of his best, but a good lesson nevertheless. Creative writing, getting the flow of inspiration going. Although it had been tough at first. Frankly, with some of the kids in his class, getting even a trickle of inspiration flowing was a bit of a miracle.

As the class surged out for morning break, Gary Wright came up to Sims. Poor Gary, thought Sims. His had been the hardest flow of creativity to get going. Less a flow, more a stagnation. Gary's creative surge had consisted of him chewing as much of his pencil as he could without keeling over from instant lead poisoning, poking the boy next to him, and finally writing the words 'My name is Gary'. End, as the Americans say, of story.

'Sir?' said Gary.

'Yes, Gary?' said Sims.

'Is it very wrong to tell lies?'

Sims heaved a secret sigh of relief. Thank God it was an easy one. For a moment he'd thought it was going to be something like 'Is there a God?' or 'How much do you get paid?'

'Of course it is,' said Sims. 'You know that.'

'I see,' said Gary, and there was no mistaking the deep misery this answer brought upon him. Gary gave a heavy sigh that Mr Beeston would have been proud of, and headed with bowed head for the door. Sims frowned. He didn't need to be the Brain of Britain to know that there was something troubling Gary.

'Wait!' he called, and Gary stopped. 'Why? Has someone you know been lying?'

Gary shook his head convincingly.

'Have you been lying?'

Another shake of Gary's head, even firmer this time.

'Good,' said Sims, still not entirely sure what was going on. 'Then what made you ask?'

There was a long pause while Gary pondered how to answer this question. Being unused to philosophical problems like these, his brain took what seemed like an eternity to come to a decision; and Sims could see his break-time cup of tea vanishing. However, pastoral care came first.

'Well?' he prompted.

'It's these new reports,' said Gary at last.

'Which ones?'

'The new ones you're going to do, telling our parents about us.'

Sims looked at Gary, slightly baffled by this. 'But we're not doing them for ages,' he said.

'But you will do.'

Sims gave Gary what he hoped the boy would take for a confident smile of reassurance. 'Yes,' he said airily, 'but you've got nothing to fear from that, Gary. All I'll be saying is the truth, that you're well behaved, honest, and that you try very hard indeed. Your parents will be proud of you.'

Gary didn't appear to be convinced by this. 'Yeah, but I ain't very clever.'

That was possibly understating the case, thought Sims, but he didn't want to hurt Gary's feelings by saying so out loud. 'It depends what you mean by "clever",' he said diplomatically.

Gary had obviously seen too many politicians ease their way off an interviewer's hook on television to be put off by this ploy. 'When you come to put down how many marks I get in the exams,' he explained. 'It'll show then that I ain't very clever.'

'You don't know that,' said Sims with all the false reassurance he could muster into his voice.

'I do,' said Gary. 'I try very hard, but I never do well in tests. I get all confused, and I get them all wrong.'

This was not going the way Sims had hoped. He'd thought a few reassuring noises and that would be that. Instead here he was spending his precious tea break being subjected to an inquisition by this small boy. 'We all get confused when we're taking tests,' said Sims. 'I remember when I was doing my driving test . . .'

Gary was not to be diverted. 'I always come bottom,' he said.

Oh well, thought Sims. If lies won't work, try the truth. 'Look, Gary,' he explained, 'unfortunately tests don't really test people. All they test is what they're like when they're taking the test.'

'Yeah, but I look stupid in tests. And then my dad'll hit me,'

'Hit you?' Sims looked at Gary in a new light. No wonder the boy was so concerned over the answer to his question.

'Whenever I come bottom in a test he hits me,' said Gary. The fact that made Sims feel particular chilled was that Gary was talking so dispassionately about it. Not fearful, just as someone who was fed up with being hit. 'So I was wondering,' the boy added, 'would you say this time I did better than I did?'

Sims was completely taken aback. 'Well . . .' he began, momentarily lost for words.

'It'll stop me being hit,' said Gary.

'Well . . .' said Sims again, still baffled as to what to say.

'I mean, it can't be wrong if it stops me being hit, can it? And you only have to do it this once. And I won't tell no one. It's just, I get fed up with being hit.'

Sims just stared at Gary, feeling completely inadequate and helpless. 'Yes' he said, trying to appear to be still in control of the conversation, but feeling completely out of his depth, 'I can see that you would. Well . . .' Well . . . What? He tried a last argument that he knew to sound utterly feeble, but what else could he say? 'We have to tell the truth, Gary. If we didn't tell the truth, who'd trust us?'

'I'd trust you.'

And to that, Sims reflected, there was little that he could answer.

• • •

By the next morning Sims had decided the best way to deal with Gary's problem was to take advice from someone who'd been at the school longer than he had. That meant every other member of the staff. The question was, which one? However the question of Gary was momentarily pushed out of his consciousness by another topic of staff room discussion, exemplified by Mrs Rudd's voice rising above any other attempts at conversation as she let the world know that she thought that it was disgraceful.

'Let me guess,' said Mrs Patterson. 'You're talking about the sex education lessons.'

'No, of course not,' snapped back Mrs Rudd, 'although I believe they are dubious. I'm talking about this forthcoming school trip. I don't wish to accuse you of currying favouritism, Mrs Patterson . . .'

Yvonne Patterson could already feel her hackles rising. 'Oh no?' she said, ready to do battle.

The potential battle, however, was defused by Fred Holliday's appearance, and his rather morose: 'What's this about curry? We're not having that again, are we?'

'I'm talking about the school trip,' said Mrs Rudd.

On the other side of the staff room Sims was trying, with little obvious success, to pump Long about what actually happened on the school holiday.

'Careful with that word "holiday",' cautioned Long. 'It may be a holiday for the kids, it's hard work for us. We're on duty 24 hours a day, don't forget.'

'Yes, I know,' persisted Sims, 'but what actually do we *do*?'

'Didn't Beeston tell you what you were letting yourself in for when you volunteered?'

'Not exactly,' said Sims. 'He came up to me and asked me if I'd been a Boy Scout. I said no, but I was in the Wolf Cubs, and he said that would do, and did I fancy a week's camping holiday at the school's expense. I said it sounded a nice idea, and then the bell went, and next thing I knew I was volunteered.'

Long gave a sly little chuckle. 'Beeston missed his vocation when he went into teaching,' he grinned. 'He should have been a double glazing salesman.'

'But what actually goes on?' asked Sims for the third time, desperation now beginning to creep into his voice. 'I asked Mr Holliday what everyone did for the week, and he just said "suffered".'

'All right,' said Long, 'if you insist. Well, we travel down in a coach: you, me, Yvonne, and the thirty kids. Fred goes down in the minibus taking the luggage and odds and ends.'

'Right,' nodded Sims, making mental notes.

'Then we put them five in a tent, and then we all start praying.'

Sims looked at him, baffled. 'Praying?' he said. 'What for?'

'That it doesn't rain.'

Sims groaned audibly, almost drowning out Mrs Rudd. 'Why won't anyone give me a serious answer around here?' he demanded, pained.

• • •

In his office Beeston was having his own problems with a morning caller. It was now ten past ten, and Mrs Carioni sat stiff-backed in the chair on the other side of his desk, hesitant, fidgeting with her handbag for comfort, unsure how to say what she had come in to say.

'Yes?' prompted Beeston gently.

'It's . . .' And Mrs Carioni paused. Oh no, groaned Beeston inwardly, at this rate we'll be here for ever. She looked up at him, now firm in her resolve. 'It's this sex education business,' she said.

'Oh?'

'I'm not happy about it, Mr Beeston,' she said. 'Nor is Mr Carioni.'

Well, thought Beeston, at least she's come in to see me instead of rushing around the parents getting a petition up about it.

'Which particular part of it aren't you happy about?' he asked.

She hesitated again, fiddling with her handbag, thinking it over, and then said: 'Well, it's the things we read about in the papers. You know, things that teachers are teaching children about sex. Homosexuality and things. And abortion. I'm not happy about it.'

With some parents Beeston would have just laughed and got them to laugh with him, but not with Mrs Carioni. Mrs Carioni was obviously sincerely concerned. The papers said it was happening so it must be true, and as far as she was concerned her daughter was at risk. Curse all gutter press leader writers, thought Beeston. Aloud, he said: 'Mrs Carioni, just because it's in the newspapers doesn't mean it's true. Frankly I wouldn't believe anything I read in any newspaper, except the date. And with some newspapers I'd have second thoughts about that.'

'Yes,' and there was no mistaking the concern in her voice and on her face, 'but you know what they say, there's no smoke without fire.'

'Let me reassure you,' said Beeston in his most comforting voice, 'this is just a straightforward biological scientific explanation of how babies are conceived and born, and that's all there is to it. I promise you.'

'No word of marriage?' asked Mrs Carioni.

Beeston was taken aback. Marriage? Oh yes, of course, the Catholic view.

'Well, we thought one step at a time . . .' he began helplessly, aware as he said it what a useless answer it was. Fortunately Mrs Carioni was moving on with her arguments. Though they weren't really what he would call arguments, they were concerns, and Beeston could understand them. How to allay them? That was the problem.

'It all seems a bit soon,' Mrs Carioni was saying. 'They're only eleven, after all. Children.'

'But some children are mothers at twelve,' Beeston gently pointed out. 'How would you feel if Julietta came home and told you she was pregnant?'

'That's what we're trying to avoid. It's a hard world, Mr Beeston.'

'I know, and we're doing our best to prepare them for it. And sex education is part of that preparation.'

Mrs Carioni dropped her gaze away from him and back to her handbag again. 'I don't know,' she said after a long pause. 'We're not happy about it. I think we'll leave it for the moment.'

Beeston frowned, puzzled. 'Leave it?'

'Yes,' said Mrs Carioni. 'We'd prefer it if Julietta doesn't go to these sex lessons.'

As with so many times in his teaching career, Beeston felt a sad sense of defeat. 'You mean you're going to tell her yourself?' he said, knowing full well that the answer would be 'No' in some form or other.

'When the time comes.' Mrs Carioni looked up at him again. 'When she's ready. It's too early yet.' And then she got up, still nervous at having been so bold as to raise the subject. 'Anyway, I've got to go. Thank you for seeing me, Mr Beeston.'

Beeston repressed the sigh he wanted to make, and instead got to his feet and went to the door of his office to open it for her. 'Thank you for coming in, Mrs Carioni,' he said, and added with as much emphasis as he could without making Mrs Carioni feel that he was getting at her: 'but I do wish, for Julietta's sake, that you'd reconsider.'

'Later, perhaps. When she's ready.'

'But she's eleven,' said Beeston, hanging onto his argument with a quiet desperation, but not wanting to frighten Mrs Carioni away from his point of view. 'Nearly twelve.' He was on a loser and he knew it. He could tell by her face that she'd just shut out any other point of view than her own.

'She'll know soon enough,' she said simply. 'I must go.' And with that she went, out through Mrs Stone's office, and out into the school.

Beeston gave the heartfelt weary sigh he'd been holding in during the latter part of her visit.

'Problems?' enquired Mrs Stone, sympathetically.

'Yes and no,' said Beeston glumly. 'Problems for Julietta, certainly. When she's ready to be told about sex, she says. When will that be? When Julietta's fourteen, three months pregnant and it's too late for her to have an abortion?'

'Not all girls get pregnant that early,' countered Mrs Stone.

'A lot more do than most people realise,' Beeston pointed out. 'And what do we get then? The abandoned baby dead in the phone booth. A thirteen-year-old dying because she tried to give herself an abortion?'

Mrs Stone turned back to the letter she was typing. 'You'll make yourself depressed if you start thinking about it like that,' she commented.

'What other way is there to think about it?' said Beeston.

'Maybe Mrs Carioni feels she's doing the best for her daughter,' said Stone. 'She's doing it with a good heart.'

'I know she is,' groaned Beeston. 'That's what makes it so depressing.'

At that point the door to the office opened and Miss Lewis put her head round. 'Hello,' she said.' Am I interrupting anything?'

'No,' said Beeston, still sounding as miserable as he looked. 'Come in, Miss Lewis, and make my day.'

'He needs cheering up,' said Stone.

'Oh dear,' said Lewis. 'In that case I'm afraid I'm the wrong person.'

Beeston could feel his heart fall. Another major problem coming, he could sense it. 'What's happened?' he asked.

'I've got domestic science this afternoon and the cooker's packed up.'

Beeston groaned aloud. There was always something! 'Can't you do something else?' he begged. 'Make a salad, or something?'

Miss Lewis shook her head. 'No,' she said. 'We've spent before break preparing the food in our classroom and we'd planned to put it in the oven in our cooking lesson after break.'

It was always the hardware that broke down, Beeston reflected. Teachers went on and on, even if bits were falling off them. Or some of them did. Mrs Wilberforce was the exception, of course. Show her a germ and she immediately took three days off. Beeston gestured resignedly at Miss Lewis. What could he do? 'I'll look for the caretaker,' he said without much conviction, 'but I can't see him getting it fixed before break finishes. To be honest, I doubt if I'll even *find* him before break finishes.'

'I know,' said Lewis, 'so I've swapped lessons with Mrs Wilberforce, so that we can have the domestic science room in her period this afternoon. But I need it working by then.'

Beeston nodded. What else could he do but nod and sound sympathetic? He remembered the days when there was more money around and Head Teachers could actually do something about problems. 'All right, Miss Lewis,' he said. 'Leave it to me. I'll go and find Mr Therm.'

• • •

Sims walked back through the corridor after break, the problem of what to do about Gary still resounding in his head. He'd thought of mentioning it to Mr Marchant, whose class Gary had been in the previous year; but every time he tried to get near Marchant the man was haranguing somebody about the implications of sex education in schools and threatening dire consequences of sin and damnation. Hardly someone who would be sympathetic to the idea of fiddling a child's report form, Sims thought.

He became aware of a child's footsteps scampering

after him along the corridor, and a voice calling: 'Mr Sims! Mr Sims!'

'What is it, Omar?' asked Sims. And, as Omar skidded to a halt, Sims added the belated admonition: 'And don't run in the corridor.'

'No, sir,' said Omar, brushing this last aside. 'Sir, it's this sex education.'

'Yes,' said Sims. 'What about it?'

'Well my brother's in the fourth year, so I mean he's getting it, right?'

Sims thought this over. From what he'd seen of Omar's rather large elder brother, it wouldn't surprise him. However, assuming that Omar was referring to the sex education lessons, Sims gave a careful: 'Er – yes.'

'Well what I want to know is, why can't we have it in the third year?' said Omar, coming straight to the point. 'I mean, I know as much as my brother.'

Then God help your parents, thought Sims.

'I mean, it ain't fair, is it,' said Omar, hammering home his point.

'Well, when you say it like that,' admitted Sims, 'No, I suppose it isn't.'

'I mean, we all got to learn how to do it, ain't we? So what I mean is, can we have them as well?'

Sims was caught. What could he say? He stared blankly at the wall of the corridor for inspiration, and inspiration amazingly came. The first rule when presented with difficult problems in teaching: when trapped, refer responsibility to a higher authority. 'I'll speak to Mr Beeston about it,' said Sims. 'I'm sure he'll be sympathetic.'

• • •

If Sims had seen Beeston at that moment in time he would not have been so confident about the amount of sympathy that the Head would have shown. Back in his office Beeston was ruefully reflecting that the sex education programme might be a good thing, but in its wake it certainly brought its problems. First Mrs Carioni, now the angry personage of Mr Higgs putting his opposition, and in a much firmer way than Mrs Carioni had done. No fiddling with handbags for him, no averted eyes for Mr Higgs. He had come in determined not to 'beat about the bush', and beat about the bush he wasn't going to.

'I'll come straight to the point,' he had said, and he duly had. 'It's about this proposed sex education. I don't want it for Anthony.'

Fair enough, thought Beeston. Aloud, he said: 'Is there any particular reason why not?'

Higgs gave him a curious look as if Beeston was being deliberately obtuse. 'Surely it's obvious,' he said stiffly.

'Not immediately, no,' said Beeston, reflecting that there could be any of a hundred reasons why Mr Higgs didn't want his son to receive sex education. He was curious to know what Mr Higgs's particular objection was. When it came it surprised him.

'AIDS,' said Mr Higgs sternly, and with a contemptuous curl to his lip as he said it, suggesting that to his way of thinking even mentioning the word was a way of catching the disease.

Beeston looked at Higgs, baffled. 'AIDS?' he repeated.

'Yes,' said Higgs. 'I'm told there are only two ways he can get it. Well, I don't want him encouraged.'

What on earth did this man think they were going to teach his son, thought Beeston incredulously. 'I'm sorry, Mr Higgs,' he said, 'you've lost me. Are you saying that the sex education that Anthony receives at this school will lead him to get AIDS?'

'It will make him think about it. Sex, I mean. It's only one step on from there.'

'I think it's a bit more than one step,' said Beeston. 'I would have said more like a quantum leap. Mr Higgs, surely . . .'

Higgs didn't let him finish. 'It's easy for you to say that, Mr Beeston, because Anthony's not your son.'

Got to tread carefully here, thought Beeston. Higgs has obviously got a huge bee in his bonnet over this. The 'kid glove – let's discuss this' approach will be the best here. 'I respect that, Mr Higgs,' he said, 'but surely just because we teach him the facts of life of how babies are born he's not going to go out and become a Casanova. That's a bit like saying we mustn't teach children about Henry VIII because they'll want to cut people's heads off.'

As a 'softly softly' approach it failed miserably, because Higgs unmistakeably bridled. 'That is a totally different subject,' he rebuked Beeston, 'and I object to you making fun of me.'

'I am not making fun of you, I'm just trying to explain to you . . .' began Beeston.

Once again, Higgs never let him reach the end of his sentence. 'There are some of us left with morals,' he said, emphasising 'some' in such a way as to let Beeston know that Higgs did not include King Street's Headmaster in that select list, 'no matter how much modern society tries to undermine us.'

'I am not trying to undermine . . .'

It was a waste of breath, Higgs was not to be stopped in his lecture. 'Temptation is all around them enough as it is, Mr Beeston. On television. In magazines. Books. Filth. Our children should at least be safe from it in schools.'

For Beeston, this last was going too far. 'Mr Higgs,' he said, and there was no mistaking the annoyance in his voice, 'I can assure you that there is no 'filth' as you call it anywhere in the teaching in this school.'

'No?' said Higgs in deliberately obvious disbelief. This time Beeston did not give Higgs time to start his lecture again. 'If you wish Anthony to be withdrawn from sex education, then that is your prerogative,' he said, 'and I'm sure the fact that I consider you to be wrong, you will consider to be irrelevant.'

Higgs, determined not to give Beeston the last word on this subject, gave the Headmaster a look of moral superiority. 'No, Mr Beeston,' he said disdainfully, 'I do not consider it irrelevant. I just consider it another example of the general lowering of standards. Now, if you'll excuse me, I'll say goodbye.' And with that he made what he intended to be a dignified exit, marred only by the fact that he knocked a pile of paper off Beeston's filing cabinet as he swept righteously out.

'Well that put me in my place,' muttered Beeston as he wandered into the outer office.

'Mr Higgs giving you trouble?' asked Mrs Stone.

'Everyone's giving me trouble,' Beeston grumbled. 'It was this sex education thing again. To hear Higgs talk you'd think we were about to open another branch of Sodom and Gomorrah.'

'It was much easier in the days when you just told them how plants did it,' said Mrs Stone with a smile.

'Don't you believe it,' said Beeston ruefully. 'We'd still have had parents like Mr Higgs in, worried that their children were going to catch greenfly!'

• • •

It never fails to amaze me, thought Sims, that small children can make so much noise while eating. Was he the only one who was aware of the noise level in the dining hall at lunch time? Had the rest of the staff's ears become so accustomed to it that they no longer noticed it? True, every now and then one of them did bellow the occasional 'Shut up!', whereupon the decibel rating would drop from 1,000 to 900 for a few seconds; but generally lunch time at King Street was like eating in the middle of the Charge of the Light Brigade. What with all that, and the problem of Gary, it was all rather hard to concentrate on what Mrs Rudd was going on about at the other side of the table.

'The point I'm making, Mr Sims,' continued Mrs Rudd, 'is that if your face fits then anything is possible.'

'Yes,' said Sims absently, wondering who to talk to about Gary. What about Mrs Patterson? She must have had him at some time or other in her remedial group.

'And obviously my face does not fit,' said Mrs Rudd.

'True,' said Sims, not really listening.

Mrs Rudd looked at him, fork halfway to her mouth, surprised. This was not the right answer. 'I beg your pardon?' she said.

'Do you know Gary Wright in my class?' asked Sims.

This new turn in the conversation, if one could have called it a conversation, seemed to surprise Mrs Rudd. 'Gary?' she said. 'Yes?'

'What's his background? What are his parents like?'

Mrs Rudd put down her fork. 'Mr Sims,' she said with quiet menace, 'I think you're missing the point, I'm talking about not being wanted.'

'Yes,' said Sims, thinking aloud, 'I think I may be as well.'

Further along the table Beeston was filling Holliday in on the day's visits from the anti-sex education lobby. 'Then after her came Mr Higgs,' he told him, 'worried that after listening to you for half an hour, his Anthony is going to become a sex maniac.'

Fred Holliday nodded sagely. 'They're just the tip of the iceberg, you know,' he said. 'Don't forget: the Silent Majority.'

'I'll say one thing for the Silent Majority,' said Beeston, 'thank God they're silent. The last thing I want is them coming up here bashing my earhole like Mr Higgs and Mrs Carioni.'

A shadow looming over his plate made him turn round, to come face to face with Mrs Purkiss. 'I've been looking for you, Mr Beeston,' she said.

I knew I should have gone to a cafe, groaned Beeston silently. Aloud he said jovially: 'Yes, Mrs Purkiss, what can I do for you?'

'I've been trying to see you about the leaks.'

Fred Holliday looked suspiciously down at his plate. 'Are these leeks?' he said. 'I thought it was cauliflower.'

'She means the leaks in her radiators,' explained Beeston. 'Yes, Mrs Stone told me, but I thought there was only one?

Mrs Purkiss shook her head. 'There's two now,' she said. 'It's coming out both ends.'

'That's what Mrs Rogers was saying all last week,' said Holliday, still not convinced about the identity of the vegetables on his plate. 'Remember?'

Mrs Purkiss was not to be put off with reminiscences

about Mrs Rogers's hygiene problems. Her kitchen, her territory was In Trouble. 'What are you going to do about it?' she demanded. 'I can't have leaking radiators. Not in a kitchen.'

'No, very true,' agreed Beeston, hoping to pacify her. He was just wondering what sort of answer would make her go away so that he could finish his dinner in peace when the voice of Miss Lewis came at him from the other side.

'There you are,' said Lewis. 'Is the cooker working yet?'

Mrs Purkiss looked at Miss Lewis suspiciously. 'Which cooker?' she demanded, immediately leaping to the protection of Her Kitchen And All Things In It.

'Don't worry, Mrs Purkiss,' said Beeston, 'she doesn't mean your cookers. We know they're working.' Pity we can't find a cook that is, he added mentally. He turned to Miss Lewis: 'No, Miss Lewis, I haven't been able to find the caretaker yet . . .' The look of disappointment on Miss Lewis's face as he said this was so deep that, before he could stop himself, he added generously: 'But Mr Holliday and I were just on our way to take a look at it.'

Holliday stared at him. 'We were?' he said.

Beeston ignored him. 'I'll send a child to find you when it's fixed,' he said to Miss Lewis with a reassuring smile. Miss Lewis had been working for Beeston too long to be convinced by this, but knew that at this stage it was the best she could hope for.

'Right,' she said. 'I do hope you can get it working.'

Holliday watched her walk safely out of earshot before turning back to Beeston. 'Send a child to find her when we've fixed it?' he said sarcastically. 'With what you and I know about cookers, by the time we get it fixed most of the children will be in the high school.'

'And,' added Mrs Purkiss, just to let Beeston know that she was still around and wasn't going to go away, 'I hope you haven't forgotten my leaks.'

• • •

Beeston and Holliday stood in the domestic science room, looking at the small unworking cooker with the same degree of comprehension they would have shown if it had been a small metal alien from another planet. They had tapped it, peered at it, poked it, knocked it, but all to no avail. It still refused to function.

'What do you reckon this thing does?' asked Beeston, touching a small black knob on the side of the cooker that seemed to serve no obvious purpose.

'No idea,' said Holliday helpfully. 'I wouldn't touch it, though. You might electrocute yourself.'

'If only I knew where that caretaker hides,' Beeston grumbled.

The sound of the door opening made them both look round. Sims peered in. 'Ah, there you are, Mr Beeston,' he said. 'I've been looking for you.'

Automatically Beeston looked around for a way of escape, but Sims had the only exit, the door, covered. Holliday returned to poking at the cooker with the stem of his pipe. Beeston sighed wearily. His whole time these days seemed to be made up of interruptions. 'Well?' he said, 'What is it?'

Sims hesitated. Which one should he choose. Gary, or . . .? He looked at Holliday, now peering into the depths of the cooker as if he was trying to conjure up a picture on it, and decided to leave the question about Gary unasked for the moment. It wasn't the sort of problem he wanted to raise in front of too big an audience. 'It's the sex education lessons,' he said.

As expected, Beeston gave one of his groans. 'You haven't come to complain as well, have you?' Beeston sighed.

Complain? Sims shook his head. 'No no, he said, 'I think they're a splendid idea.'

'You don't have to give them,' came Holliday's voice morosely from behind the dead cooker.

'All right,' said Beeston, 'I'll buy it. What about the sex education lessons?'

'One of the children stopped me just now and asked me why the third years can't be included.'

'The third years?' echoed Beeston, blanching slightly.

'Yes,' continued Sims, now feeling more confident in raising the subject. 'After all, sex is a very natural thing and I believe we could be creating unnecessary tension by keeping it under some kind of cloak of secrecy until a finite age.' He was now aware that both Beeston and Holliday had totally forgotten about the dead cooker and were standing regarding him with a blankness that didn't bode well. What had gone wrong? Surely his argument was totally sound? He pressed on. 'By limiting it to the older age groups, surely we are encouraging the myth that sex is somehow "dirty".'

Before Sims could enlarge on his argument any further, Beeston held up his hand. 'Mr Sims,' he said, 'what you say may very well be true. But, and it is a big but, I've got enough trouble with parents believing we're corrupting their children because we're giving sex education to the fourth years.'

Sims gave a scornful laugh. 'Surely they're just a handful . . .'

Beeston didn't give him a chance to say exactly what Sims thought they were a handful of. 'They may be a handful to you, Mr Sims,' he said, 'but if we start on the third years we'll have them coming round accusing us of all sorts of things. We'll have *The Sun* doing an exposé on us. I can almost see the headline: "Loony Teachers in Porn Kids Scandal".'

Sims mulled it over, thought obviously not happy about it. 'Yes,' he said grudgingly, 'I suppose that's possible.'

'Possible? It's a cert.'

'Absolutely,' agreed Holliday.

'I must admit I hadn't thought of it like that,' admitted Sims. 'I see what you mean. I was only trying to be helpful, though.'

Beeston relented slightly. After all, he would have possibly been bearing the same kind of message at Sims's age. And with the same results. 'If you really want to be helpful,' he said hopefully, 'are you any good at mending cookers?'

'No,' said Sims.

'Nor are we,' said Holliday, giving the cooker one last kick. 'If you ask me, we're wasting our time. I, for one, am going. I've got stuff to prepare for this afternoon.'

'Traitor!' Beeston muttered as Holliday went out.

Beeston returned to studying the small cooker. Maybe it was something really simple? What about the switch at the wall? No, that looked all right. He groaned. There was only one real answer: a series of long and involved phone calls with County Hall Engineers Department, and then perhaps in two years the small cooker would work again. Perhaps. However, determined not to give up so easily and subject Miss Lewis's hard-done cooking to the dustbin, Beeston lifted an electric plate. 'Let's see what this wire here does . . .' he muttered.

'By the way, Mr Beeston . . .' came Sims's voice.

Beeston's heart sank. God, was he still here. He thought he'd gone. And that phrase 'By the way'. Beeston now knew from bitter experience that whenever Sims casually said 'By the way', he was about to unleash some fairly major topic with momentous consequences.

'I thought you'd gone,' he said.

'It's about Gary Wright,' said Sims.

So far so good, thought Beeston. At least it's not about another member of the staff, or a complete rescheduling of the timetable. 'What about him?'

'I don't know what to do about his attainment result on his report.'

Beeston looked at Sims, baffled. Was the man serious? Interrupting him in the middle of trying to get this cooker working, to ask about reports? 'But the reports don't have to be done for ages yet,' he said.

'No,' agreed Sims, 'but I'm thinking about it now. Should I mark him up and say he's done better than he really has?'

Again, Beeston regarded Sims quizzically. What was he on about? Had the man been drinking at lunchtime? 'Why on earth should you do that?' Beeston asked.

'Because his dad hits him when he gets low marks.'

The penny dropped. 'I see,' said Beeston.

'So, I thought,' went on Sims hurriedly, now having committed himself to raising the matter, 'that maybe for this one year, I could make his results look a little better, if they're bad. He deserves a better result, he tries very hard indeed.'

'Then give him a good effort mark,' said Beeston.

'But that's not the same, is it,' Sims countered. 'Parents like his don't look at the effort mark, they look to see what he's scored.'

'And you want to exaggerate that? Make it look good for him?'

Sims shrugged non-committally, but the answer was obvious. 'I was considering it, yes,' he admitted carefully, adding quickly: 'Only I'm not sure. I know it's wrong, but in this case it seemed like maybe the lesser of two evils, if you know what I mean.'

'And you want my advice,' said Beeston. It wasn't a question, they were now down to the stating of facts.

'Yes,' said Sims.

Beeston paused a moment to let the full implication of what Sims was saying settle, then threw the question back at the younger teacher. 'If you mark him up, what happens next year?'

Sims frowned, unsure what Beeston meant by the question. 'What do you mean?'

'Say he's at the bottom again?' said Beeston. 'Do his parents thump him a bit harder because he will have actually gone back down, according to his test marks?'

Sims frowned. 'Well,' he said awkwardly, 'yes, that is a possibility . . .'

'Or will he persuade his next teacher to fiddle the books for him, so he learns that you don't work to get rewards, you fiddle?' threw in Beeston.

'But he does work,' defended Sims. 'He works very hard indeed. He just doesn't achieve.'

'The story of the majority of people, Mr Sims. How many people actually do achieve the ambitions that other people set for them?'

'Yes, but not every child gets beaten because they don't.'

Beeston nodded in agreement. 'All right, 'he said, 'so you do it for Gary. What about the next child who comes along and asks you to do the same for them because it will please their Mum, who's been having a bad time lately.'

'I'm not talking about other children,' said Sims, now very much on the defensive.

'But you have to. What about another child who works very hard, as hard as Gary, and does achieve a good result? Isn't that result and hard work devalued because you've fiddled Gary's mark?'

'No one will know.'

'Gary will know. The others will soon know. And where is your credibility in the eyes of the other children then?'

There was a long pause while Sims weighed it up, and didn't like what he saw. None of us do, thought Beeston.

'All right, I accept all that,' said Sims, and now there was a hint of desperation on his voice, 'but if it stops Gary being hit for this one year . . .'

'Will it?' Beeston stopped him. 'With some parents any excuse will suffice. If it wasn't his test result it would be the way he eats, or the fact he hasn't combed his hair.'

'Then shouldn't we do something to protect him?' demanded Sims. 'Isn't he a battered child?'

Beeston shook his head. 'No, Mr Brown. If he was, we could deal with it. Gary is just a child who gets hit now and then, and there is a major difference. Parental chastisement. As you may have noticed, the current social climate actually supports it.'

Sims fell silent for a moment, then he said bitterly, almost accusingly: 'I see. So, Gary loses.'

Beeston shrugged helplessly. 'Whatever you do, Mr Sims, Gary loses. The big question is, who else loses as well?'

'So,' said Sims, now very tight-lipped and angry, 'I leave things as they are.'

'I don't like it any more than you do, Mr Sims,' said

Beeston. 'Personally I'm against these tests, but we don't make the rules.'

'No,' said Sims accusingly, 'we just carry them out.'

'Someone has to.'

'For a moment Beeston thought that Sims was going to come back with some cutting remark, about having consciences that could be bought or similar, but then Sims obviously thought better of it because he just shrugged and said simply: 'Well, that's it, then.'

As Sims opened the door to leave, Beeston remembered the cooker, and the fact that Miss Lewis wanted it working, and he called out: 'If you see the caretaker . . .'

'Yes?' asked Sims.

Beeston hesitated, then shook his head. 'Forget it,' he said, 'it doesn't matter.'

Sims nodded, then left. Beeston looked at the small cooker and sighed. We should be mending kids, not cookers, he said to himself bitterly. He gave the cooker a last small pat on its top, and then followed Sims. He had phone calls to make. Mrs Purkiss's radiator and Mrs Rogers's disposable gloves.

• • •

Twenty minutes later, just as the bell went for afternoon school, Beeston put down the receiver of his phone, and looked at this office wall and contemplated going across to it and banging his head against it. Fifteen minutes of hanging on the phone since he'd got back to his office, and all he'd been able to do was occasionally call into the void with a helpless 'Hello, is anyone there?'

Finally County Hall's switchboard operator had come back on the line for the umpteenth time, only this time instead of saying 'Sorry to keep you waiting' in an irritating sing-song voice, she'd announced that the Engineers Department was closed for the day due to 'staff training.' What in? thought Beeston.

He sat there, looking in deep despair at the phone, and cursing everyone from Alexander Graham Bell onwards. The realisation had just occurred to him that he'd better go and see Miss Lewis and tell her that the small cooker wasn't working, when there was a knock at his door.

'Come in!' he called wearily.

It was Yvonne Patterson. 'Have you got a minute?' she asked.

'Not really, no,' he said. 'I've got to go and see Miss Lewis before she takes her class to the domestic science room. The small cooker still isn't working.'

'Oh don't worry about that,' Patterson said airily. 'I've fixed it.'

Beeston sat staring at her. 'Fixed what?' he asked.

'The cooker. I saw Fred Holliday and he told me it wasn't working, so I had a quick look at it.'

'You?' said Beeston, still trying to grasp the fact that the hideous device that had ruined his lunch hour had been fixed with such apparent ease by Patterson.

'Yes,' said Patterson, 'I had one like that years ago, and it kept packing up as well. A design fault, the manufacturers said. Anyway, I guessed what it might have been, and it was. So Miss Lewis is all systems go.'

'Yvonne,' said Beeston, 'you are a marvel! That is the best bit of news I've had all day. In fact, it's the only bit of good news I've had all day. All the rest of it has been terrible.'

'Oh dear,' said Patterson cautiously. 'In that case, this is going to be par for the course.'

'What is?' said Beeston. 'There's nothing even worse happened to the cooker, is there?'

'No, the cooker's fine.'

'That's all right, then.'

'But I'm afraid *I've* got some bad news for you.'

The feeling of elation, almost happiness, that had filled Beeston a few seconds earlier when he'd heard the news about the repaired cooker, vanished like a punctured balloon. 'What sort of bad news?' he asked, feeling once more as if he was made of lead, and that banging his head against the wall was the best idea he'd had all day.

'My brother is coming back from America for a visit for just a week. He's actually coming on business, but he wants to take the time to see all the family. Well, as many as he can in a week.'

Beeston frowned, puzzled. 'That sounds like good news to me,' he said. 'Or don't you and your brother get on?'

'Nothing like that,' said Patterson. 'I'm really looking forward to seeing him. The trouble is, it's the same week as the school trip.'

'Ah,' said Beeston. 'I see.'

'I'm sorry, especially after all the arrangements have been made . . .'

Beeston shook his head. 'Don't worry, Mrs Patterson,' he said. 'Family comes first. Leave it to me, I'll sort it out.'

Patterson smiled. 'Thanks,' she said. 'If there was any way out of it . . .'

Beeston shook his head again, and got up to open the door for her. 'A woman who can fix the cooker and make Miss Lewis happy can be forgiven anything,' he said.

He gave her a cheery smile as she went off. Then he closed his door, walked over to the wall and was just about to tap his head gently against it (after all, he didn't want to damage County property), when he stopped. An idea came into his head which filled him with a happiness that he hadn't known in ages. 'I'm saved,' he muttered joyfully to himself. 'There *is* a Father Christmas, even at this time of the year!'

• • •

'Well I think it's a bit much,' said Long.

'What is?' asked Patterson.

'This emergency staff meeting he's called. We're almost having staff meetings on a daily basis.'

'Oh, shut up complaining and pass the sugar.'

In another corner of the staff room Mrs Rudd was heard demanding loudly 'Does anyone know what it's about? And will it take long? I promised the recorders I'd listen to them this lunch time.'

Sims stood alone, sipping his tea and wondering if Beeston had called the staff meeting as a result of his talking to him about Gary. Was Beeston going to announced that there should be no fixing of reports?

At that moment the staff room door opened and Beeston entered with a crisp: 'Right, let's get started. I've called this emergency staff meeting,' he announced, 'because of the school trip.'

Puzzled glances were exchanged. Surely it was all settled? No one noticed the small sigh of relief given by Sims.

'Unfortunately, Mrs Patterson can't go after all . . .' He held up his hand to stifle the immediate chorus of sympathetic murmurings that arose. 'And she will tell you about that in her own good time. However, in the light of recent criticism expressed over the choosing of the staff to go on the trip . . .'

'If that is aimed at me . . .' bridled Mrs Rudd.

'. . . I thought it best to call this meeting,' Beeston finished. He looked at Mrs Rudd and gave her a friendly smile. 'Now I had promised Mrs Rudd first chance if anyone dropped out. I know she's very keen to go. Aren't you?'

There was a sudden silence in the staff room as all eyes turned on Mrs Rudd, and if anyone had dropped a pin it would have sounded like a 20-megaton explosion. Mrs Rudd looked around her. What could she say? She looked at her watch as if there was a way out there, but today even her watch wasn't helping her.

'Well, actually . . .' she started to say.

Beeston didn't give her any time in which to wriggle out, he'd waited too long for this moment to arrive to lose it that easily. 'You did say how much you wanted to go,' he said in his friendliest voice.

'Yes, but . . .' faltered Mrs Rudd. 'But . . . if any of the rest of the staff would prefer to go, I can understand. I don't want to stop anyone else.'

'No, no, of course not,' beamed Beeston. 'But it has to be a *female* member of staff.'

'Of course,' said Mrs Rudd. There was another painful silence. Mrs Rudd looked about her at her female colleagues in quiet desperation. 'Miss Lewis?' she asked hopefully, 'what about you?'

Lewis shook her head with a rueful grin. 'No thank you,' she said. 'I've been before.

Mrs Rudd cast her net wider, now no longer smiling. 'Mrs Wilberforce?' she asked helplessly.

Mrs Wilberforce averted her eyes, and Mrs Rudd felt the ultimate betrayal. If she couldn't count on Mrs Wilberforce, what hope was there?

Beeston smiled broadly. Revenge, he mused, is better than sweet. 'No other takers?' he enquired genially. 'Well, then that's it, Mrs Rudd goes, along with Mr Holliday, Mr Sims and Mr Long. And I'm sure it'll be lots of fun.'

• • •

Holliday was still fuming as he and Beeston walked across the playground to check on the progress of the kitchen radiators. Beeston, on the other hand, was feeling light as air and had to resist the temptation to break into a sudden dance. 'Did you see her face, Fred?' he crowed.

'Did you see mine?' snorted Holliday indignantly.

'Well, you've always got on with her, haven't you,' grinned Beeston.

Holliday was not to be placated. 'I wish you'd talked to me about it first.'

Beeston couldn't be contained, he was like a child who had just found a new toy to play with. 'Mrs Rudd under canvas,' he chortled. 'I hope it pours.'

'I'm going as well,' pointed out Holliday, pained.

'So you are,' said Beeston, suddenly apologetic. 'I hope it only rains on her.'

A sudden noise from the entrance to the school made him look round, and the next second he had almost fallen. Holliday looked down at Beeston as he grabbed at his sleeve.

'Heart attack,' said Holliday. 'Serves you right for fixing me up for a week with Mrs Rudd.'

'No,' croaked Beeston. 'Look!'

Holliday looked. And there, an unbelievable sight. Just walking in through the school gates was the vaguely remembered figure of the caretaker.

Beeston shook his head in amazement. 'This,' he said, 'is doubly a day to remember.'

CHAPTER SIX

UNDER CANVAS

Beeston stood at his office window looking out at the hordes of kids scrambling aboard the coach. Actually there were only thirty children, but it looked like hordes. In fact, as far as he was concerned, just two very active children could look like a horde. He sighed deeply. 'Look at them,' he said.

Mrs Stone looked up from a final check of the parental consent forms. 'Who?' she asked.

'The school trip getting on the coach,' said Beeston. 'It's like one of these documentary films about the fall of Saigon. It's like a riot out there, even with the parents watching.'

'Don't worry,' said Mrs Stone, turning back to the forms. 'Mr Holliday will deal with it.'

Beeston peered out at the milling throng. 'I can't see him,' he said.

'He's there somewhere.'

'Maybe one of the kids has eaten him,' said Beeston. 'The only ones I can see are Sims and Long. I'd better go out there.'

Mrs Stone shot him a warning glance. 'Oh no you don't,' she said, her tone threatening. 'I want you to check that all the paperwork is completed before the coach sets off. We don't want to find we've got a parental permission form missing *after* they've left.'

Good God! Beeston suddenly saw a movement that brought out the disciplinarian teacher in him. That rotten Richards kid! 'Did you see that?' he demanded.

'I'm too busy to look,' said Mrs Stone, now moving on to the completed equipment lists.

'That Richards kid made a rude gesture behind Sim's back.'

'You make rude gestures behind Mrs Rudd's,' pointed out Mrs Stone.

'Yes, but I'm allowed to, I'm the Headmaster,' Beeston defended. 'By the way, where is Mrs Rudd? She should be out there. She'd soon frighten them into submission. The Frankenstein of King Street.'

As if on cue, the door of the office opened and Mrs Rudd swept in. 'Mr Beeston . . .' she began.

'Ah, Mrs Rudd,' beamed Beeston, 'we were just talking about you.'

'Have all the forms been checked? We're nearly ready to go.'

Beeston nodded. 'Nearly finished, Mrs Rudd, I was just double-checking them.'

'We don't want to be late leaving. We're due at the camp site by noon.'

Beeston nodded again. 'Right,' he said.

As soon as Mrs Rudd had gone and the door shut, Mrs Stone snapped accusingly at Beeston: 'Liar. You haven't even started checking the papers for the trip.'

'Oh yes I have,' said Beeston. 'I checked them yesterday afternoon.'

Mrs Stone was taken aback. 'Oh,' she said. 'I apologise.'

'Though I must admit it was by accident,' Beeston confessed. 'I thought I was checking a different pile of papers. Honestly, with all the paperwork that County Hall produces, it's a wonder there are any trees left in the world.

'But they are all there?'

'Yes. Parental permission forms. Insurance forms. Emergency contact forms. Illness and allergy forms. You name it, we've got a form for it.'

The door opened again. This time it was Fred Holliday, unlit pipe clenched firmly in his teeth.

'Ah, there you are, Fred,' greeted Beeston.

Mrs Stone gave a small smile. 'He thought you'd been eaten.'

Holliday looked at her and Beeston, baffled. 'Eton?' he said. 'We're not going to Eton.'

'Not Eton, eaten,' explained Beeston. As the expression on Holliday's face startled to become even more baffled, he sighed and said: 'Never mind.'

Holliday shrugged it aside. One of Beeston's jokes, he supposed. Funny sense of humour the man had. Still, that was the way it sent you, becoming a Head Teacher. He got on to the main purpose of his call. 'I've been going through the route with the coach driver,' Holliday announced. 'After all, as I'm driving the minibus with all the equipment, I won't be on hand to navigate him.'

'No, that's true,' agreed Beeston, and groaned inwardly. He wasn't going to be subjected to one of Holliday's famous monologues which required the name and number of every road in the United Kingdom, was he? He was.

'Anyway, I've told him,' said Holliday, 'up the A10 until you get to where it joins the B1039 . . .'

'Yes, yes, I'm sure you have,' said Beeston hastily, cutting Holliday off before he could get into his stride. 'The minibus is all right, is it?'

Holliday frowned at this sudden change of subject. The minibus? 'Why?' he asked. 'Has anyone reported anything wrong with it?'

'No, no, just thought I'd make sure everything was okay,' said Beeston. 'Have you got everything? Medicines, contact numbers, pocket money . . .'

'And don't forget the accident book,' Mrs Stone reminded him sternly.

'Don't worry, I've got them all,' Holliday reassured her.

Beeston looked again out of the window. The kids seemed to have settled down now, and many of the parents had drifted away, off to work now that they were sure their offspring were firmly on the road to the countryside and out of their hair for a whole week. Beeston smiled at the memory of some of the school camping trips he'd been on. A week away from the city. Everything seemed different, more relaxed. He turned to Holliday. 'You know,' he said, 'I almost envy you, Fred. A week in the country, living close to nature, under canvas, all that fresh air.'

Holliday was not impressed by Beeston's vision. 'You can take my place if you like,' he offered.

The reality of it came back to Beeston in a flash, the toilets, the rain, being on duty 24 hours a day . . . He shook his head. 'No, no,' he said, 'someone's got to slave away here.'

'I assume you are coming down to see us during the week?' asked Holliday.

'Oh yes, of course,' said Beeston, sounding enthusiastic. 'I wouldn't miss it for the world. I thought Wednesday afternoon.'

'Right. You can count the survivors.' With that he went out to the minibus to make his final check that all the luggage was securely on board.

'Right,' said Beeston. 'Well, if everything's ready, I think I'll go out and see them off.'

'That's a nice thought,' said Mrs Stone.

'Not really,' Beeston admitted, 'I just want to make sure that Mrs Rudd really is on that coach when it leaves.'

Outside the gates, Long got off the coach and leant against it. 'Right,' he said to Sims, 'that's the third time I've counted them, and I've finally made it thirty.'

'It's that Osmond girl,' said Sims. 'She keeps moving her seat to wave goodbye to her mother.'

'I'll wave at her with something if she moves again,' Long muttered vengefully. 'Maybe I'd better count them again, just to be on the safe side.'

'No need,' said Sims. 'I've counted them three times as well.'

'And how many did you make it?'

'Twenty-nine the first time, thirty-one the second, and thirty the third.'

'Here I am,' announced Mrs Rudd, arriving with a regal swirl of her coat. 'Has anyone counted the children yet?'

'No,' said Long, all innocence. 'We thought you'd like to do it.'

'Honestly,' sniffed Mrs Rudd in annoyance, 'it seems I

have to do everything.' With that she boarded the coach, and they could hear her moving down the aisle counting loudly: 'One – two – three . . .'

'What do you reckon she'll make it?' asked Long.

'Twenty-eight,' said Sims.

'I bet twenty-seven,' said Long.

Any attempts to make the bet final by putting money on it evaporated as Beeston appeared. 'All ready?' he asked.

'As ready as we'll ever be,' replied Long.

Beeston looked around carefully. 'Where's Mrs Rudd?' he asked.

'On the coach,' answered Sims.

'Don't let her get off,' said Beeston.

At that moment Mrs Rudd returned and descended from the coach. 'Thirty,' she said.

'And you don't look a day over twenty-one,' Beeston cracked.

Mrs Rudd was not amused.

'I am referring to the children,' she said. 'They're all here.'

Long and Sims exchanged glances. They had both been wrong.

Beeston watched as Sims, Long and Mrs Rudd climbed on board and took their places. Various children pressed their faces against the windows of the coach mouthing goodbye to him, making some of them even uglier than usual, a feat that Beeston would have thought impossible. The coach driver put the huge noisy vehicle into gear, let out the clutch, and with a roar and a cloud of diesel fumes and dark smoke, the coach moved off. Beeston waved them all goodbye. A safe journey and good luck, he thought.

• • •

Sims paused from hammering in a tent peg and stood looking around the large flat field at Long and Mrs Rudd, besieged by children hurrying from tent to tent like worker ants. It had been an uneventful coach trip down, just three children sick enough to warrant plastic bags. So far all the omens for the week were favourable. The sun was shining, the grass was green, the air smelt fresh and good.

The field was at the back of a farm, and all around the camping field were more fields, fenced off and with firm orders from the farmer to make sure that no children trampled over them. At the bottom of the field ran a small stream, a perfect spot for nature work, thought Sims.

The organisation of the children's tents he'd left to Long, who had been on these school trips many times before. Long had soon got the place looking like a proper camp, with six large tents accommodating five children in each; four smaller tents, one for each of the staff; a large marquee tent for dinner, if it rained; a largish tent that could be used as a First Aid tent or a common room for the teachers; and latrine tents at a hygienic distance from the main camp. Sims was impressed, and wondered where Long had learnt to put up such a well organised camp.

He turned back to hammering in another peg. 'We've got our stuff in the tent, Mr Sims,' said a child's voice from behind him. 'What shall I do now?'

Sims looked around the field. He was an organiser, it was up to him to organise. The trouble was, he was frankly unsure what was going on, except for what he was doing.

'Go and see if Mr Long wants a hand with the food stores,' he said.

'Don't you want a hand putting up that pole?' asked the child hopefully.

'No thanks, I can manage,' said Sims.

The child disappeared to go and get in Long's way. Sims returned to hammering the tent pegs.

'Mr Sims, there's no sign of Mr Holliday yet.' Mrs Rudd had appeared, scanning the distant horizon with her hand shielding her eyes from the sun. It was a point which Sims had observed too. It was unlike Mr Holliday to be late, and he'd seen the minibus starting up as the coach had left the school. He wondered if something had happened to the minibus on the way? A breakdown, or something? However, he didn't want to start a panic. He returned to pushing in another tent peg.

'I'm sure he'll be here soon,' he said to reassure her. From the expression on her face, Mrs Rudd was obviously worrying about Holliday's safety. She shifted her position to try and scan the distant road a little better.

'I do hope nothing's happened to Mr Holliday and the minibus,' she said. 'He's got my suitcase with him.'

The shadow of the pole that Sims was putting up fell across her. Lucky it's only the shadow, thought Sims.

'I wouldn't stand there if I were you,' he said tactfully.

'Why not?' Mrs Rudd demanded, her tones suggesting that she did not like being ordered about by new teachers.

Sims gestured at the pole at it wobbled in the slight breeze. 'This pole isn't quite stable yet and it might fall on you,' he said.

Mrs Rudd glared at the pole indignantly, the expression on her face challenging it to dare to do such an outrageous thing. 'It had better not,' she said. She looked at it, puzzled. 'What is it for?'

Sims stood up and regarded it with a touch of pride. 'It's a flagpole,' he told her. 'I thought the children could make a flag while we're here and put it up to show that it's our camp.'

Mrs Rudd sniffed to show that she was not impressed. 'Well, if you must be ostentatious,' she commented, disapprovingly.

The sound of the minibus approaching at long last made them both look round. 'Ah, there he is,' said Mrs Rudd. 'I must go and get my suitcase.'

With that she turned away, pulled out one of the tent pegs holding up the flagpole, and moved swiftly off towards the arriving minibus. Sims's prospective flagpole wobbled, swayed visibly, then fell over with a dull thud on the grass. Sims gave a weary sigh. Oh well, he thought, back to the drawing board.

Holliday drew the minibus to a halt and got out, his face like thunder as most of the children came running up to give him a cheering welcome. Holliday didn't appear to be impressed.

'What happened to you?' asked Long.

'Did you see those roadworks?' Holliday demanded.

'Which roadworks?' Long asked.

'On the A414.'

'No.'

Holliday ignored Long's ignorance. 'Well I thought that it might be quicker in that case to follow the A1169 and go round using the B194,' he said, 'but just as I reached the B181 . . .'

'You got lost.'

Holliday bridled at this suggestion. 'No I did not,' he snorted indignantly. Some idiot had switched the signpost round and I went fifteen miles out of my way.'

'There you are,' said Mrs Rudd, arriving on the scene. 'Do you know where my suitcase is?'

'Give me a chance,' said the irritated Holliday. 'I've barely had time to get the ignition key out.'

'I need it because I put my handkerchiefs in there,' Mrs Rudd explained, eager to hurry him along with the unpacking.

'Do you want to borrow a tissue?' asked Long.

Mrs Rudd regarded Long with disgust. 'Certainly not,' she rebuked him.

A child suddenly appeared, popping her head up almost through Long's arm. How do they do it? thought Long. I'm sure that you could be in the Sahara Desert, miles from anywhere, and a child would suddenly appear and stand on the very spot you are standing on.

'Please, sir,' said the child. 'That big pole that Mr Sims was putting up has fallen down.'

Mrs Rudd gave one of her impatient snorts. Really, why do children feel it necessary to tell the whole world everything, whether it concerns them or not? she thought. Aloud she said: 'Don't bother us with it, child, go and tell Mr Sims.'

'He already knows, Miss,' said the child. 'It hit him on the head and he's lying on the ground.'

The three teachers spun round. Sure enough, there was Sims, lying flat out on the ground, and next to him on the grass was the prospective flagpole.

'Oh my God!' exclaimed Long.

Holliday wearily started to climb back into the minibus. 'Where's that accident book?' he said.

• • •

It was ten o'clock that night before the teachers had got the children settled down enough in their tents to be able to relax in the large communal tent. If 'settled down' was the right word to describe some of the noises to be heard. Long opened the flap of the large tent, stepped out into the night air, and yelled out 'Stop that noise!' Immediately the noises subsided to just a buzz of whisperings, as all the guilty parties felt he was shouting just at them.

Inside the large tent, by the light of the camping lamp, Holliday sucked on his pipe and opened up the Camp Log and the Accident Book.

Monday, he wrote, and then read aloud with relish as he made the entry: *Prospective flagpole collapsed, striking Mr Sims on the shoulder. No apparent injury.*

'I slipped,' said Sims defensively. 'I was just trying to dodge out of its way.'

All this gave Mrs Rudd her cue to open up the subject again, just as Holliday had mischievously hoped. 'Well if you want my opinion it was such a thoughtless thing to do,' she said. 'When I saw you lying there . . .'

'It's really not worth all this fuss,' said Sims. 'I wasn't hurt.'

'Not now, maybe,' observed Holliday sagely, 'but in thirty years time when that shoulder of yours starts aching, and you want to sue somebody, you'll need evidence, so it's got to go in the book.'

'Not that anyone'll be able to find the book,' commented Long.

'True,' admitted Holliday, 'but it's the principle of the thing.'

In the distance one of the tents had obviously forgotten about the momentarily repressive shout from Long, because the sound of childish yells and shrieks erupted and floated over to them.

'Shut up!' yelled Long again.

As the shrieking died down to a more acceptable level, Sims asked: 'Which tent was it?'

'One of Mrs Rudd's, I expect,' said Long.

Mrs Rudd bridled, but decided against giving Long the satisfaction of rising to his obvious bait, keen to show that he was beneath her contempt. The time had come, she decided, to Get Things Organised; and as Mr Holliday was obviously in no hurry to start organising, despite his being Team Leader, it looked as if it would have to be up to her.

'I suggest we begin by organising the things to do on this trip, and who does them,' she announced. 'Is everyone in agreement?' She looked around at the other three for their reactions.

'Good idea,' agreed Sims. Personally, after his first day at the camp he was ready for an early night, but if the others were in the mood to sort things out, fair enough. He looked at Holliday, who nodded, almost showing enthusiasm for the first time that day, having spent most of it still fuming over the villain who'd switched the sign-post around.

'Agreed,' said Holliday. 'And I think the first thing to get sorted out is the pub rota.'

He looked at the other three for their agreement. Long nodded enthusiastically. 'An excellent idea,' he beamed.

Mrs Rudd looked at both of them, her face registering bafflement. 'The pub rota?' she echoed.

Sims, like Mrs Rudd also on a King Street camping trip for the first time, was equally bewildered. 'What's the pub rota?' he asked.

Long smiled at his innocence. 'It's a way of making sure we all get a chance to go down the pub in the evenings,' he said.

'Essential after a day with this lot,' nodded Holliday.

If he had seen Mrs Rudd's face, her expression hidden in the shadows, he would not have been so sure that she would have agreed with him that 'essential' was the right word. To Sims, however, it seemed like an impressive piece of forward planning on the part of Long and Holliday. 'It sounds like a good idea to me,' he said. 'How does it work?'

Fred'll explain it,' said Long. 'He's good at working these things out.'

Holliday pulled a piece of paper from his pocket and tapped it with his pipe. 'I was working it out on the way down here,' he said. He looked at his plan for the rota. 'I suggest that tonight Long and I go, tomorrow night Sims and Mrs Rudd, then me and Sims, then Mrs Rudd and Long, and then, well, then it'll be time to go back to school.'

He sat back, pleased with himself, and waited for their appreciative reactions. When Mrs Rudd's reaction came it was far from appreciative.

'I think,' she said, tight-lipped, 'that is disgraceful!'

Holliday looked at her, surprised. Oh well, he thought, you can't please everybody. 'All right,' he said, 'you and Sims can go tonight, then Long and I can go tomorrow . . .'

Mrs Rudd cut him off before he could outline it further. 'No, I think the whole idea of going to the pub is disgraceful. I insist that we all stay here and do something constructive in the evenings. I, for one, have a book with me.'

The other three looked at her, astonished. Holliday stared, first at her, then at his piece of paper, then back at her again. 'A book?' he said, incredulous.

'Yes,' said Mrs Rudd firmly, adding with pointed sarcasm: 'You do know what a book is?'

'Of course I know what a book is,' snapped back Holliday, irritated, 'but what's the point?'

'Well, for one thing,' said Mrs Rudd piously, 'there are the children.'

'But the children will all be in bed asleep,' Long pointed out.

'But we are responsible for them,' countered Mrs Rudd.

Sims sat and watched in silence. Were these camping trips always like this? My God, no wonder no one volunteered for them. It was bad enough when arguments broke out in the staff room, but at least there you could always disappear quietly and let the combatants slug it out. Here, in a field miles from anywhere, there was no escape.

'We are being responsible,' Holliday stated, not wanting to lose this argument. 'There'll always be two of us here on duty.'

'Yes, but what sort of example is that to set the children? Their teachers rolling back to camp drunk?' demanded Mrs Rudd.

'I'm not suggesting we roll back to camp drunk,' said Holliday.

'Though you can if you feel like it, Mrs Rudd,' joked Long. The joke did not go down well, to judge from the expression on Mrs Rudd's face.

'All we're saying,' stated Holliday clearly, 'is that we could do with a break from the kids. What do you think, Sims?'

Immediately three pairs of eyes turned towards Sims. This is it, he gulped. I should have known this would happen. We're taking sides already. 'Well,' he said, firmly, 'I agree.'

This answer apparently didn't satisfy any of the other three, because Mrs Rudd asked: 'Who with?'

'The idea of going to the pub,' said Sims. 'We don't have to drink, but it would be good to take a break.'

Mrs Rudd shook her head firmly. 'I totally disagree,' she said resolutely.

'You can disagree all you want, but I for one am not spending my whole week stuck here every evening,' snorted Holliday. 'And as you're outvoted three to one, that's it.'

'There can be no voting on such an issue as this,' said Mrs Rudd. 'And if you insist on going, then I will have no alternative but to report it to the authorities when we get back.'

The other three stared at her.

'Which authorities?' demanded Holliday.

'County Hall, of course.'

The snort of contempt showed just what Holliday thought about County Hall. 'I couldn't care if you reported it to the United Nations,' he exploded, 'I am not . . .'

Long held up a silencing hand, hoping to try and effect a compromise before too much blood was drawn. It was going to be hard enough trying to survive a week with both of them, but if they got off to this terrible start the week would be unendurable. 'Wait, wait,' he urged. 'If Mrs Rudd feels so strongly on this point . . .'

'I do,' affirmed Mrs Rudd.

'Then maybe we could leave it for tonight and let her see that the children do settle in all right, and then we'll review it tomorrow.'

Holliday fell silent and clenched his pipe between his teeth. For a minute Sims thought that he was going to bite right through it. He deliberated on it for a minute, glaring at Mrs Rudd, before finally saying in a disgruntled growl: 'All right. But we'll review it tomorrow.'

At that moment the unmistakeable sound of a fight was heard coming from one of the tents, the raised voices obviously belonging to two of the girls.

'I believe there's a fight going on in one of your tents, Mrs Rudd,' said Sims, in case she hadn't heard it. Mrs Rudd had, and she smiled triumphantly at Holliday as she declaimed: 'See, and what if this had happened while you were in the pub, Mr Holliday? How would you have felt then?' With that she swept out of the tent to restore peace and order, calling out as she went: 'Children! Stop that!'

Holliday glared after her and sucked on his pipe. 'If I'd been in the pub I'd have felt a lot happier,' he said pointedly.

• • •

The next day the sun wasn't so evident. There was also a distinct chill between Holliday and Mrs Rudd, causing excited little whispers behind the backs of little hands as the children watched them studiously ignore one another. However, things calmed down as the morning wore on, and by lunch time everyone's attention was too taken up with the food prepared by the Food Detail, presided over by Sims.

'I never thought anyone but Mrs Purkiss could ruin boiled potatoes,' commented Long as he poked his fork suspiciously at them.

'Everyone's eating them,' Sims pointed out, looking around the tables that had been set out in the field.

'In emergencies people will eat each other to survive,' said Long, rather obscurely Sims thought.

After lunch the camp divided into two parties: those who were going on a water nature study group under the leadership of Sims and Long; and those who were going nature watching in the fields for birds and animals, led by Holliday and Mrs Rudd. The fact that the majority of the children volunteered to go on this latter suggested that either most children were interested in birds and tiny mammals, or that they were interested in watching two full-grown mammals, namely Rudd and Holliday, restart their battle. In the final event two equal-sized groups were formed, and the two parties set off. An hour later found Mrs Rudd, Holliday and fifteen children sitting silently in a small wooden copse at the edge of a field. Mrs Rudd looked at her watch. They had been sitting silently ever since she had sneezed, which was at least half an hour ago. Really, she thought this is intolerable behaviour from a grown man, and unless something is done about it, it will get worse.

She reached over and tapped Holliday on the arm. He looked around at her, still saying nothing. Mrs Rudd looked around at the children, also sitting silently, but aware that their ears were trained like radar on both her and Holliday. However, in her view the man had left her with no alternative, and she was only going to say what he was forcing her to say. Holliday raised a questioning eyebrow at her, wondering what was up. She leaned closer to him. After all, it had to be said, and better now rather than leading to another argument that evening in the tent.

'There is no need to sulk at me, Mr Holliday,' she whispered, 'just because I prevented you from going to the pub last night.'

Holliday glared at her, looked around at the children ostentatiously 'not listening', and whispered back fiercely: 'I am not sulking. And you did not prevent me. I stopped going on my own accord.'

'Well you look like you're sulking,' said Mrs Rudd. 'You hardly spoke to me this morning, and now you haven't spoken to me for the hour that we've been here.'

'That is because we are supposed to be observing wildlife,' said Holliday, his voice still low, 'and if we make any noises it'll frighten them off. If you wanted to talk, you should have gone with Sims and Long looking at plant life by the river. So shush.'

Mrs Rudd bridled. 'Don't you shush me,' she said.

One of the children, Sundeep, leaned forward. He didn't like to break things up at this crucial point, but they were supposed to be on a nature watch, and he had a book to fill in of Things He'd Seen.

'Mr Holliday,' he asked, 'what's that bird there?'

Holliday looked. 'It's a chaffinch,' he said. And then he saw something moving in the field very near to them. 'Look over there,' he said, hardly daring to raise his voice above the slightest whisper. 'I'm sure I saw something move in that grass.'

Mrs Rudd looked up at the sky. 'I felt a drop of rain,' she said.

Holliday felt irritated. Honestly, how was anyone expected to watch out for wildlife with this woman prattling on? 'Water vapour from the river,' he whispered tersely.

'Coming downwards?' queried Mrs Rudd archly.

'Atmospheric pressure,' said Holliday. He strained his eyes, trying to see whatever it was that was moving ever so slightly in the grass. Mrs Rudd looked up at the sky again, holding out her hand now. 'I just felt another one,' she said.

'I didn't feel anything,' said Holliday.

'I did, sir,' piped up Rajnesh. Honestly, didn't these people realise they were frightening the animals away?

'Sssh,' urged Holliday. It was no use.

'My Mum said it was going to rain,' added Miriam. 'She said her foot was hurting, that's how she knew.'

Holliday turned on Miriam and the other prophets of weather doom. 'I checked all the weather forecasts before I set off, both long range and short range,' he whispered fiercely, 'and you can tell your mother's foot when you get home that it was wrong.'

'Yes, sir,' agreed Miriam.

'Well *I* think it's going to rain,' Mrs Rudd said, not to be defeated so simply.

'Sssh,' whispered Holliday in quiet desperation. 'I think we have a shrew here.'

Mrs Rudd glared at him, offended. 'Really, Mr Holliday . . .' she began, and at that there was a little rustle in the grass, and the tiny mammal made a run for it.

Meanwhile, down by the stream, Sims and Long were just finishing sorting through the children's collections of water plants. Sims looked up. That sky, he thought, looks ominously like rain. He mentioned his fears to Long, who dismissed them confidently.

'Never,' he said.

'It looks like it,' insisted Sims. 'Look at those clouds.'

'Those are fair weather cumulus clouds,' said Long knowledgeably. 'They may look threatening, but they pass straight over.' He gave an immodest shrug. 'One of the advantages of being in charge of science.'

Sims was not convinced. 'It still looks pretty gloomy, though,' he said doubtfully.

'A temporary phase,' explained Long confidently. 'Any minute now those clouds'll clear and the sun'll be out again.'

There was a sudden rumble of thunder from overhead

and the whole party looked up. The next second they all became aware of raindrops falling, slowly at first, almost individually, then getting heavier, and heavier. As the rain now started to run down his hair and into his eyes, Sims glared at Long challengingly.

'One of the advantages of being in charge of science?' he demanded.

This theme was immediately taken up by the children. 'Mr Long was wrong when he said it wasn't going to rain, wasn't he, sir,' said a wet but gleeful Wayne. 'My Dad says that teachers should never be wrong.'

Long turned on Wayne. 'Does he?' he scowled. 'Well you can tell your Dad . . .'

They never found out what information it was that Long wanted Wayne to impart to his parent, because at that moment Alice Reardon came running over to them in tears.

'Sir! Sir!' she cried. 'My hat's fallen in the water!' Immediately there was a surge of children heading for the edge of the stream, all shouting 'I'll get it! I'll get it!'

'Stay away from that edge, all of you!' ordered Sims, and miraculously all the children skidded to a halt before they could topple in. 'Can't you see that the grass on the bank is wet and slippery? When it's like that, it's easy to fall in. I'll get Alice's hat.'

'It's all right,' said Long, obviously determined to do something to make up for being shown up as an inadequate weather forecaster, 'I'm nearer, I'll get it.' The children watched as Long grabbed up a long piece of broken branch and stretched out with it across the water, towards Alice's floating hat.

Wayne turned to Sims, his face serious. 'I don't think he's balanced properly,' he commented. 'My Dad says . . .'

'Don't worry,' said Sims. 'Mr Long knows what he's doing . . .'

A cry from Long at the edge of the stream belied Sim's words. Before everyone's astonished eyes, Long's feet slipped on the wet grass. He flailed his arms wildly for a few seconds, like an erratic crooked windmill, before toppling face forwards into the water, both he and Alice's hat disappearing from view.

'Oh my God!' said Sims.

'My hat!' wailed Alice.

• • •

That night in the large tent, the four teachers sat listening to the sound of the rain as it drummed relentlessly on the canvas. It had been raining without let-up from that very first raindrop. However, thought Sims, at least Long had saved Alice's hat.

Holliday opened up the Camp Log and Accident Book, and made another entry, announcing it as he did so: *Tuesday. Mr Long fell into the river and banged his head against a floating tree.*

In his corner of the tent, glaring up at the roof as the rain hammered down, Long scowled. 'That tree had no right to be in that river,' he snapped. 'Trees ought to be on land. And if it hadn't been for that sudden downpour making the grass all wet . . .'

'No visible damage,' said Holliday aloud as he wrote it down.

Long glared at him indignantly. 'What do you mean, "no visible damage"?' he demanded. 'I've got a bump on my head.'

'Yes, but we can't see it,' Holliday pointed out.

'Only because it's under my hair,' countered Long. 'If I was bald you could see it.'

Holliday shrugged. 'All right,' he said philosophically, and he turned back to the open book. 'Due to lack of baldness, Mr Long's bump was not visible.'

Long stared at him incredulously. 'You're not really writing that down?' he demanded.

Holliday put the top back on his pen and replaced it in his pocket. 'Of course I'm not,' he said. 'I've written "contusion to side of head".'

'It's at the back,' grumbled Long, keen to make sure that everything was correct and that justice was done.

'Too late,' said Holliday, unimpressed. 'I've written it, so it's at the side now.'

'It's my head,' Long complained.

'It's my accident book,' responded Holliday.

'It's the *school's* accident book,' Rudd corrected him, looking up from her book.

'But I'm in charge of it,' pointed out Holliday.

My God, thought Sims, doing his best to appear to be immersed in an out-of-date newspaper, they're worse than the children!

For a while silence reigned again. If it could be called silence, with the noise of the rain coming down as if Noah was due for a repeat performance. Finally Mrs Rudd broke the silence, with an annoyed: 'Really, this rain is intolerable. It's typical of Mr Beeston.'

Sims looked up from his newspaper, bewildered. Surely, even by Mrs Rudd's standards, this was a tenuous apportioning of blame? 'You're not blaming Mr Beeston because it's raining, are you?' he asked.

'Not because it's raining, but because we are under canvas,' expounded Mrs Rudd. 'Anybody with a grain of sense would know that it always rains at this time of the year.'

'But it's the Summer,' pointed out Sims.

'Exactly. By now I would have thought we would have graduated to a more civilised form of school trip. Namely: indoors.'

'If you'd listened to my suggestion we'd be indoors right now,' commented Holliday, looking up from the log.

'Don't be obtuse, Mr Holliday,' reprimanded Mrs Rudd. 'I am not referring to a public house.'

Sims thought it was about time he stepped in and defended the weather, otherwise this week would be a complete washout in more ways than one. Be more positive, that was the answer. What was it he'd read once in a book written by a survivor of a notorious jail? 'Change your attitude and you change your happiness.' He addressed them all, positive conviction in his voice. 'Well,' he announced, 'I for one don't mind the rain.'

They looked back at him, all three of them eyeing him oddly. 'You don't?' said Long acidly. 'You sure that flagpole didn't hit you on the head?'

Sims gave a light laugh. 'All right,' he admitted, 'I'd prefer it if it was good weather, but just think of the challenge for the children. Camping in the countryside in the rain. How often will they get the opportunity to do that?'

'Not often, providing they're sane,' commented Holliday drily. He looked intently at Sims. 'Sims, are you serious?'

Sims nodded. 'They'll get to see a different countryside in the rain,' he said. 'It has a special beauty all its own.'

Mrs Rudd sniffed, unconvinced. 'Well, that's one way of looking at it, I suppose,' she said.

Sims got up and stretched, then reached for his coat. With luck, he thought, they'll all feel better about the weather now, although right at this moment he couldn't see any signs of it. 'I'd better get off and do the rounds of the tents,' he said. 'Make sure that everyone's all right.'

They watched Sims as he opened the tent flap, then squelched his way out. They could hear the rain thudding down on him, and hear his boots squelching through the mud as he set off on his duty rounds. Holliday tapped his pipe stem against his forehead. 'I think the man's barmy,' he said.

• • •

By the next morning, Wednesday, the rain had stopped, but the damage had been done. The campsite was a quagmire. The part that had been grass was now swamp; the part that had previously been bare earth was now a mudbath. Wellington boots became the regulation footwear. Any pretence at being out in the wonderful countryside was abandoned, and the morning was spent inside the large marquee, doing lessons. To ease the boredom, Sims offered to take a small group out to examine the mud in greater detail and do a mud study, something which again had Holliday tapping his forehead with the stem of his pipe in comment on Sim's mental state. So, early that afternoon, Sims and his party of seven set off, armed with plastic buckets and trowels, to collect different samples of mud from the surrounding fields. Thus Sims wasn't around when Beeston's car pulled up on the track at the entrance to the muddy field, come to pay his dutiful visit.

My God, it's the Somme revisited, thought Beeston. He looked at Holliday's face as his Deputy approached him, squelching through the mud. Lucky I brought my boots, thought Beeston gratefully. That was one of the advantages of being a veteran of these kind of things, you were prepared for every possibility. 'How's it going?' Beeston asked. 'Having fun?'

The look on Holliday's face was answer enough, but just in case Beeston missed it, Holliday barked: 'Ha!'

'Things going wrong?' Beeston asked sympathetically.

'Apart from the weather, you mean?' gritted Holliday.

'Yes, it has been a bit wet lately, hasn't it?' said Beeston. He looked around him at the swamp. 'It's certainly a bit muddy here.'

'Are you trying to be funny?' said Holliday.

'Good heavens, no,' said Beeston. It seemed like a good time for him to change the subject. 'How's everyone else getting on? Mrs Rudd?' Again, his deputy's face darkened, and again came the monosyllable that said it all: 'Ha!'

'I see,' said Beeston, though frankly he didn't, he could only imagine. 'What's she been up to?'

'The woman's a menace!'

Beeston smirked. 'I've been telling you that for years,' he said. 'Anyway, by the look of things nothing too drastic's happened so she can't have been up to too much. No accidents or anything?'

'Two.'

Beeston felt an icy hand clutching at his heart. Two accidents? Who to? Why hadn't he been informed? Holliday's next words, however, removed the fingers from the icy clutch. 'Sims and Long. Nothing serious, though.'

'But the kids are okay?' Beeston wanted it clarified, just to make sure.

Holliday nodded. 'Yes, it's only members of staff who've been injured.' And he added darkly, 'Not the right member of staff, though.'

Beeston chuckled. 'Fred, this is most unlike you,' he grinned. Then realisation dawned. 'I know, she's refused to go on the pub rota.'

Holliday snorted, touched to the quick. 'If you ask me,' he said, 'the woman's just plain anti-social.' Suddenly he saw Mrs Rudd approaching out of the corner of his eye. 'Here she comes,' he said. 'Right, that does it. I'm off.'

'What . . .' said Beeston. Too late, he was talking to empty air. God, he thought, it's astonishing how fast Fred can move through mud. Beeston didn't have long to marvel at this miracle of mobility. The next second Mrs Rudd was by his side, encased below the ankles, as far as he could tell, in mud.

'There you are,' she said, stating the obvious as was her custom.

'Yes,' said Beeston jovially, 'come to lend my support, as I promised. How's it going?'

'Have you seen this mud?' Mrs Rudd demanded accusingly.

It's hard not to, he thought. For some odd reason Beeston felt that he was being blamed for it. However Mrs Rudd was capable of blaming him for the fact that the sun set every evening. 'Yes,' he said. 'A lot of it, isn't there?' There didn't really seem much else to say on the subject.

'And another thing,' she said. 'Did you notice what happened just now?'

'Notice what?' said Beeston. 'I've only just got here.'

'Mr Holliday,' said Mrs Rudd. 'The way he went off when he saw me coming.'

'Did he?' said Beeston, feigning innocence.

'As you know,' continued Mrs Rudd, 'I am not one to tell tales, but there are things happening here that cause me some disquiet.' Good grief, thought Beeston, it's just like being back at King Street. I've only been here three minutes and already I'm being complained at by Mrs Rudd.

Mrs Rudd was now continuing, adding little confidential facial gestures when she felt they were necessary, so that Beeston would not miss any of the points she was trying to make.'I do not wish to detract from Mr Holliday's reputation, but as Team Leader I feel he leaves a lot to be desired. Now there are still two and a half days left, and I feel it is not too late for a new Team Leader to be appointed. Someone more . . . co-operative.'

Beeston nodded. 'Like Mr Long,' he said.

'Mr Long?' she echoed, offended. 'Certainly not. No, what I have in mind . . '

Beeston was only too well aware of what Mrs Rudd had in mind. 'Yes,' he said, grabbing her elbow and steering her towards the camp proper. 'Can you tell me as we walk? I would like to say hello to everyone else in the camp as well.' Together they squelched through the mud, with Beeston chattering brightly, rubbing salt in the wounds: 'How have you been enjoying the weather? It's been quite sunny back home.'

• • •

Meanwhile Sims and his mud squad were admiring mud of different colours and dumping trowelfuls of it into the plastic buckets. They had also discovered hundreds of worms of various sizes, which had started a competition amongst the children as to who could find the biggest worm. So far, miraculously, no one had yet fallen completely in the mud, though Sims felt it was just a matter of time.

Sims knelt down with three of the children and helped them dig, uncovering bits of shiny rock quartz. The children exchanged meaningful glances. They weren't so much interested in the mysteries of minerals as what was going to happen between Mr Holliday and Mrs Rudd. Sarujeet and Omar nodded furiously at Wayne, urging him to get on with it and ask Mr Sims. After all, Mr Sims would know, he was a teacher.

'Here, Mr Sims,' said Wayne suddenly.

Sims stopped digging. 'Yes, Wayne?' he asked, prepared for questions on What was the Point in Being a Worm. Instead he got: 'D'you reckon they're gonna have a fight?'

Startled Sims looked round, searching for potential combatants amongst his group of seven children. It all seemed fairly peaceful as far as he could see. He turned back to Wayne, puzzled. 'Who?'

'Mr Holliday and Mrs Rudd.'

Sims smothered a smile. 'Certainly not,' he said, putting on an indignant front. 'Whatever gives you that idea?'

'The way Mr Holliday bites his pipe whenever she talks to him. I keep waiting for him to bite it in half.'

Sarujeet and Omar kept their heads and eyes down, listening intently.

'You're imagining things,' said Sims simply.

It wasn't the end of it. Wayne let a full half a minute go before saying: 'You know what it is, don't you. It's 'cos she won't let him go down the pub.'

This, Sims realised, was going too far, even though he knew he'd be thinking the same in Wayne's place. Goddammit, he was thinking the same in his own place! 'Look, shut up about Mr Holliday, or I'll tell him you're talking about him behind his back,' said Sims sternly.

Wayne looked suitably disappointed. 'All right, sir,' he said glumly. They all went back to digging at the mud. But not for long. Less than a minute later the garrulous Wayne was piping up again: 'Do you reckon there are maniacs around here?'

Sims gave him a stern look. 'I should warn you,' he said, 'that if you're still talking about Mrs Rudd and Mr Holliday . . .'

'No, I mean serious maniacs,' protested Wayne. 'Like in them films.'

'What films?'

'*Friday the Thirteenth. The Nightmare.*'

My God, thought Sims. What sort of parents do these

kids have, allowing them to watch films like that? And where do they watch them? Even I get frightened by them. 'Children your age shouldn't be watching films like that,' he told them. 'Even I don't watch them.'

'That's 'cos you're a teacher,' said Wayne. 'Teachers never watch anything interesting. Anyway, they're always set in a place like this. A campsite in the country miles from anywhere. And there's always a maniac who lives in the bushes who creeps in and cuts 'em up while they're asleep.'

'Sounds delightful,' said Sims sarcastically. He glanced at Omar and Sarujeet, both listening intently to Wayne. What a pain Wayne was, thought Sims. No wonder his mother was so insistent on him going on this trip. 'Look,' he said, 'I don't want you talking like this to any of the other children, you might frighten some of the more impressionable ones.'

'Yeah, but . . .'

'No "buts",' said Sims firmly. 'Why don't you talk about nice films for a change. A Walt Disney, or something.'

Wayne thought about this suggestion for a moment, his face screwed up in deep concentration. Then he said: 'You mean like *Snow White*?'

At last, thought Sims, I'm getting through to him. 'Exactly.'

Wayne sat back on his haunches, remembering the Disney classic with obvious pleasure.

'Did you like *Snow White*?' Sims asked the other two children.

Omar and Sarujeet both nodded.

'D'you know the bit I liked best?' Wayne asked rhetorically. 'It's where the witch killed her with the apple. Good, that was. I liked the witch. And when she went all evil and frightening . . .'

Sims groaned. 'Wayne,' he said, 'shut up or I shall chuck this bucket of mud over you.'

• • •

By Thursday the tensions in the camp between Holliday and Mrs Rudd were beginning to tell on Sims's nerves. If he talked to one, then the other assumed that he was on 'that woman's' or 'that man's' side. Long did his best to keep out of it by volunteering for all the domestic details, which gave Sims a chance to make sarcastic comments about Long's cooking for a change. However, his heart wasn't really in it, all he wanted was one evening without a verbal gun battle breaking out, or the tension of enforced silence, which was even worse.

That evening, as the four of them sat in the communal tent, he tried to brighten up their last evening. 'Beautiful weather today,' he said. 'After all that rain, it was just what we needed. I think it's wonderful to see the countryside after a heavy rainfall, when the sun's bringing everything back to life again.' He waited, but no one picked up the conversation. He tried again. 'The smell of grass. The sounds of the birds. I think it's wonderful.'

'Has anyone got anything to read?' asked Mrs Rudd.

'I thought you'd brought a book along,' snapped Holliday.

'I did. I've finished it.'

'Must have been a short book,' Holliday commented tersely, throwing aspersions on Mrs Rudd's reading habits now that everything else had been used up.

'Because it was so interesting I read it quickly,' snapped back Mrs Rudd. 'It was on Bach.'

Long looked at her in surprise. 'What, the stuff on trees?'

'Bach the composer.'

'Oh.'

'I've got Monday's paper, if you like,' Sims offered helpfully.

'Thank you, but as it's Thursday that's hardly very useful,' said Mrs Rudd sarcastically.

Sims was irritated. That's what he got for trying to be helpful and bring sunshine and goodness into people's lives. 'I haven't exactly had much chance to get into town to buy another, have I?' he pointed out with icy politeness.

Then he mentally slapped himself over the wrist. Careful, he said, or you'll end up like them.

'None of us have got into town,' yawned Long. 'I've begun to forget what civilisation looks like.'

'Considering some of your attitudes, Mr Long,' said Mrs Rudd, 'I'm not sure if you ever knew what civilisation was like in the first place.'

Oh oh, thought Sims. Here we go. Now they'll all be involved and pretty soon it'll be a verbal version of Gunfight at the OK Corral. If only they'd all go into town . . . The thought was so obvious, he wondered why it hadn't struck him before. 'I've got a good idea,' he announced.

The other three looked at him balefully. 'If it's that we all go outside and admire the beauty of the countryside in all this damp and cold and darkness, then you're a bigger idiot than I thought,' said Holliday.

'No, I was going to suggest that the three of you went into town, while I stayed here.'

There was a pause while they looked at him, letting this sink in.

'What?' asked Holliday, baffled.

'Why?' asked Mrs Rudd, suspicious.

Sims shrugged. 'Well . . .' he began.

'I'm nearly out of tobacco,' Holliday mused to himself. 'If we go into town, I could get some.'

'And I could phone my wife and make sure everything's all right at home,' said Long.

'I would quite like to telephone Mr Rudd and make sure that everything is all right at *my* home,' admitted Mrs Rudd. 'But surely we cannot all go, can we? I mean, three of us.'

'I don't mind,' said Sims magnanimously. 'After all, it's our last night here.'

'Right,' said Long, needing no second bidding, 'let's get that minibus started.'

'I don't know,' said Mrs Rudd, still caught by both her conscience and her statements at the start of the week. 'It only leaves one of us on duty.'

'You can stay behind if you like,' said Holliday, getting up and pulling his coat on.

'Well, as Mr Sims insists,' said Mrs Rudd, and she too got up and went to get her coat.

'You sure you'll be all right?' asked Long.

Sims nodded, relieved to be free of them. 'Absolutely,' he said. 'Nothing's likely to happen on our last night, is it?'

'Come on,' said Holliday, now pulling on his boots, 'we're wasting valuable time. And thanks, Sims. I won't forget this.'

'I'll bring you back a pint,' promised Long gratefully. 'Two pints.'

'And I'll lend you my book on Bach to entertain you,' said Mrs Rudd, now ready and raring to go. 'You'll find it fascinating, I'm sure.'

• • •

Sims looked at his watch. Ten past midnight. Strange, he frowned. He had expected them back much earlier than this. He cocked an ear, listening out for the sound of the minibus engine approaching. Nothing. Only the sounds of the night outside the tent. He shrugged. He supposed they had decided to stay on and have more than just a few drinks after all. Still, it was a relief after all the bickering to have one evening to himself. In fact, this sudden mood of relaxation made him feel quite tired; and what with that and Mrs Rudd's book on Bach he had been ready to go to sleep an hour ago.

A noise outside the tent made him sit up. A footstep, surely! He approached the tent flap cautiously, although he knew it wasn't necessary. After all, who else could be in the camp but someone who should have been? He supposed they'd parked the minibus somewhere far away and walked the last bit. But why?

Sims opened the tent flap, and leapt back as he came face to face with Wayne. 'What on earth are you doing out at this time?' he demanded. 'It's gone midnight.'

'I wanted to go to the toilet, and when I came back I saw

the minibus wasn't there, so I wondered if all the teachers had gone,' said Wayne.

'We're hardly likely to do that, are we?' said Sims feeling a little shaken up at seeing Wayne. Goddamit, the child should have been alseep ages ago. 'No, Mr Holliday, Mr Long and Mrs Rudd had to pop out.' He could almost feel his nose growing, Pinocchio style.

Wayne frowned. 'They're late back, ain't they? The pubs shut hours ago.'

Sims glared at Wayne, but not too harshly, he didn't want to send him to bed frightened. Although he doubted if anything could frighten Wayne. 'Just because they're out it doesn't mean . . .' he began.

'Do you reckon the maniac's got them?' asked Wayne.

Now it was Sim's turn to frown. 'The maniac?' he asked, puzzled.

'Like in *Friday the Thirteenth*,' said Wayne. 'Maybe they're out there now, buried somewhere in the woods.'

Really! thought Sims. Whatever next!

'Go back to bed,' he said sternly, and pointed firmly towards Wayne's tent.

'All right,' said Wayne. 'But I'd keep a look-out if I was you. If there is a maniac he'll be after you next.'

Sims watched Wayne trudge back the few yards to his tent. Then he went back inside his own tent and picked up Mrs Rudd's book on Bach. Honestly, he thought, 'the maniac'. That was the trouble with children watching films like that, it got their imagination working overtime. If Wayne starts waking up the other children and frightening them as well . . . thought Sims vengefully. Still, he admitted, it *is* a bit late., They should have been back well before now. I wonder what's happened to them?

He put the book down and listened. Nothing. He checked his watch again. Twenty past midnight. It shouldn't have taken them that long to get back from the village, even if they'd walked it! They must have gone somewhere else instead, somewhere much farther away. Yes, he relaxed, that was it. He picked the book up again, and then stopped. No they wouldn't do that. Long might, but not Mrs Rudd or Holliday, they were both too much sticklers for the rules. Then what had happened to them?

Perhaps I ought to go outside, he thought. Check that everything's all right in the camp. But why shouldn't everything be all right in the camp? Shut up, he told himself. That's that idiot Wayne, talking about 'the maniac'. They don't have maniacs liked that in rural England. Oh yes they do, an inner voice told him; and he remembered all those tales of lonely people found murdered in their beds in country houses. Witchcraft covens. Campers mysteriously battered to death.

Oh, this is ridiculous, he said to himself. Just because they're a little late back! A little late back? A lot late back! I'd definitely better check outside, he urged himself. Make sure the children are all right.

He put on his coat and boots, stepped cautiously out through the tent flap, and then stood there in the cold night air, straining his ears, listening. There was no sound that could in any way be that of a car engine of any sort, let alone the minibus. He moved forward, walking as quietly as he could in the mud towards the children's tents, still listening. Nothing. Not even an owl hoot.

And then he heard it. A definite movement in the field at the back of the camp. He stood stock still, his heart thumping. Imagination, surely. What could it be? A cow? There were no cows in that field, there were no animals of any sort in the surrounding fields. Not large ones, anyway. Maybe it was a deer?

He listened, straining to hear, trying to see. Yes, there was definitely something moving there, approaching the camp, he was sure! In the darkness he could just make out bushes jerking and moving. Whoever it was was keeping under cover. There was no doubt in his mind, ridiculous though it may have seemed, there was someone moving stealthily towards him! Towards the camp!

Whoever it was, his best move was attack. Frighten them off. Let them know they'd been seen, then maybe they'd just run away. Providing they weren't armed, of course. That was a chance he had to take. He swallowed, then advanced across the mud towards the bushes, and called out suddenly: 'All right! Hold it right there! I warn you, I am a blue belt in karate!'

Echoing back to him through the darkness came Long's voice, fed up, and now also baffled: 'Eh? What's that got to do with anything?'

It was Long! Thank Heavens, thought Sims. He hurried forward, and saw Long emerge from the bushes and into the camping field, covered in mud from head to toe. 'It's you,' he said, relieved.

'Of course it's me,' said Long, fed up. 'Who else do you think it would be, staggering around the woods at this time of night?'

'Er,' stumbled Sims, searching for a reasonable excuse. 'I thought you were a deer.'

'A deer?' said Long. 'And you were going to challenge it to a karate contest?'

Time to move on to a less awkward topic of conversation, thought Sims. 'What's happened to you?' he asked. 'Where are the others?'

It obviously wasn't a maniac, that much was obvious, otherwise Long would be in more of a state than he was. At the moment he just looked like a mud man. However, it had been the right topic to divert Long away from further questions about Sims's karate prowess.

'The minibus broke down halfway back,' said Long, now knocking bits of mud off himself. 'The other two are staying with it, waiting for the AA to arrive. I came back on foot to tell you what had happened in case you were worried, and I tell you walking through that lot in the dark was no joke. It's like a quagmire. I'm covered in mud. And I couldn't see where I was going, so I've fallen over twice.'

The voice of Wayne suddenly was heard coming from the nearest tent. 'Sir?' he called. 'Is it a maniac, sir?'

'I will be in a minute.' Long called back at him, but not loud enough to wake the other children. 'Go back to bed.'

'Yes, sir,' said Wayne, disappointed, and went back to bed.

'And on top of all that,' growled Long, trudging towards the large tent, 'I went and left your beer in the minibus.'

• • •

The morning after the night before was spent avoiding talking about it. Not because Sims didn't want to but because Holliday and Mrs Rudd studiously avoided mentioning it. The memory was obviously too close and painful to be discussed easily by them, and the last thing they wanted was to talk about it in front of an audience of thirty pairs of tiny ears who were all eager to know what had gone on.

It wasn't until they were in the coach, on the way back to school, with the children at the back safely singing, that Sims was able to get the whole story from Long, and even then he dwelt mostly on his nightmare trek back to the camp across the muddy fields.

The minibus had broken down, and Holliday had banged his head on the underside of the bonnet as he tried to get the engine going in the darkness. Holliday had staggered back, clutching his head, and trodden on Mrs Rudd's toe, ruining her shoe. She, in turn, had fallen over and grazed her knee, which was why he, Long, had volunteered to do the walk back to the camp.

'After all, there they were, the two invalids. What else could I do?' said Long. He mused thoughtfully on the memory. 'Mind you,' he said, 'if I'd known just how muddy it was going to be, I'd have let you sit there and worry. If you even were worried, that is. I bet you were having a quiet snooze before I arrived, without a care in the world.'

Little do you know, thought Sims. Maniac, huh! You'd have to be a maniac to go trudging around the countryside in conditions like that. 'So,' he said, 'we ended up with four accidents after all for the book. You in the water, me with the falling pole, Holliday's head, and Mrs Rudd's knee.'

'Sssh,' hissed Long, looking round. 'Don't let them hear you, they're both still very sensitive about it.'

A little voice at Sim's elbow made him look round to the seats behind. 'Please, sir,' said Omar.

'Yes? What is it?'

'I think I left a sock behind at the camp. Can I ask the driver to turn round for it?'

Long raised his eyes to Heaven. Sims groaned. 'Well as we're about fifteen miles away from it, I wouldn't if I were you,' he said.

'We told you to check you had everything before we left,' said Long.

'Yes, sir,' said Omar unhappily, and settled back in his seat to worry about his missing sock.

'At least one missing sock isn't too much damage,' said Sims philosophically. 'Apart from that and our accidents, it's been quite a good week, hasn't it?'

Long looked at him. Was the man mad? He'd been soaked, bashed on the head, and spent last night looking like a mud man from a horror film. A good week?!

Sims caught Long's expression of disbelief. 'Well, an interesting week,' he amended.

'Interesting's one word for it,' Long said. 'But would you go through it again?'

Sims shook his head with a wry grin. 'Not on your life,' he said.

CHAPTER SEVEN

SPECIAL NEEDS

Beeston quickly checked the details he'd jotted down on the pad in front of him, then he looked up at the two parents sitting opposite him and smiled. 'Well,' he said, 'that seems to be almost everything. And now, Sharon's age?'

'She's eight,' said Mr Stevens.

'She was eight on 23 February,' Mrs Stevens added.

Beeston jotted that down on to his list as well. 'Right,' he said. 'Got that.'

Mrs Stevens was talking again, pleased that Beeston was being so co-operative, eager to talk about the problems they'd had concerning Sharon's education. 'We'd heard so many good things about this school,' she said.

'From a neighbour of ours whose son is deaf,' added Mr Stevens. 'He came here . . .' He stopped, searching in his memory for the year, he and his wife looking at each other, trying to remember. Beeston checked their address on his notes.

'Wallace Avenue,' he noted, and the address jogged his own memory. 'Not Edward Jarvis?'

Mrs Stevens nodded, pleased. 'That's him.'

'Good heavens,' said Beeston nostalgically, 'that takes me back. How is Edward these days?'

'Doing very well, so Mrs Jarvis says,' said Mrs Stevens.

'He must be about eighteen now,' said Beeston. 'My God, doesn't time fly? One minute they're six years old, the next they're towering about six feet above you. Anyway, we're getting off the subject. Your Sharon.'

'Yes, well,' said Mr Stevens, 'as Mrs Jarvis said that Edward did so well here, we thought it showed that you might have the right sort of attitude towards Sharon.'

'There's no problem with regard to attitude at all,' Beeston reassured them.

The couple exchanged relieved smiles.

'However,' added Beeston, 'there is a major problem as far as Sharon's handicap is concerned. Edward was just deaf. In Sharon's case, she is in a wheelchair and unfortunately this school is just not properly equipped for it.' And that, he thought, is the nub of the whole problem. Again the couple exchanged looks. They were concerned, but used to this, Beeston could tell. They must have come up against this wall throughout all of Sharon's eight years.

'But when we contacted the Education Office to ask about the possibility of Sharon going to a normal school, they said that integration was a part of their policy,' Mr Stevens pointed out.

Beeston nodded in agreement. 'A part of their policy, I'll grant you,' he said. 'Unfortunately their policy doesn't extend to paying for the things that need to be done to achieve it, things like ramps, refitted bannisters, lower light switches, proper toilet facilities . . .'

'But they told us that they plan to do it.'

'That's what they told me as well, five years ago,' Beeston told them ruefully, 'and to date they're *still* planning to. "When" is another matter. Look, in all seriousness, have you fully examined the other options? The school at Ashfield is a very good school indeed . . .' As he said it, he could tell by the expressions on their faces that it was a waste of breath. The very mention of Ashfield, and they had closed up, closed ranks. Not aggressively, but firmly.

'We've never felt that Ashfield isn't a good school,' said Mr Stevens. 'We know it is. It's just that there's nothing really wrong with Sharon's brain, and we want her intellectual abilities to be extended as far as they can be.'

'And a lot of the class she'd be in with at Ashfield are mentally handicapped,' added Mrs Stevens.

They had a good team going, thought Beeston. With most couples who came to see him he could spot areas of disagreement: one parent would be concerned mainly about academic achievements at the school, the other's main preoccupation might be sporting activities. Or one would do all the talking, while the other would just sit there silently, often appearing to Beeston to be bored by the whole proceedings and giving the impression that they'd just come along to make up numbers and because it looked good. The Stevenses, on the other hand, were a team, interchangeable, and strong against all outside forces. It was interesting, thought Beeston, the way having a handicapped child affected couples. It usually had one of two effects: either it broke them up because the relationship couldn't stand the strain, or it drove them into being an even stronger union.

'Actually,' he pointed out, 'most mentally handicapped children in this area go to Walton Hill.'

'Yes,' countered Mrs Stevens, 'but there's this grey area as far as the Education Authority are concerned: when is it a mental handicap and when is it physical handicap?'

'When it's a bit of both they don't know how to classify them,' Mr Stevens added.

Beeston nodded sympathetically. How true, he reflected. He had often thought that if the civil servants had their way they'd prefer the children to be measured for handicap, 40% mentally handicapped, 60% physically; 51% mentally, 49% physically, and so on, so that they could allocate them. In the meantime it was a simple case of Pot Luck meets Red Tape, which meant Tough Luck for the children and their families.

'The thing is, Mr Beeston, we'd like to give it a try,' said Mrs Stevens.

'If it doesn't work out, well, all right, she can go to Ashfield,' Mr Stevens conceded, obviously speaking for both of them. 'But, for her sake, we want her to be with ordinary children if possible.'

'After all, inside she's ordinary,' pointed out Mrs Stevens. 'Just because she's in a wheelchair it shouldn't make her that much different.'

Beeston nodded. What else could he do? The Stevenses

were firm in their resolve and he couldn't blame them for that. The County had decided on an integration policy, although, as most teachers were only too well aware, it wasn't done from the altruistic motives of having the children's welfare at heart, it was done because it was cheaper to put handicapped children into mainstream schools than pay the high pupil-teacher/nursing ratios in special schools. 'All right. Leave it to me,' said Beeston with a smile. 'I'll see what we can arrange as far as getting ramps made up and toilet facilities altered. Although there we're dealing with County Hall Engineers, and that's like getting blood out of a stone.'

The Stevenses grinned ruefully. This was obviously not a new problem for them. 'That's why we thought we'd come in and discuss it now,' said Mrs Stevens, 'to see if it was possible and to iron out any problems well in advance.'

'Possible it certainly is,' said Beeston. 'The reality of it, we'll just have to see. But rest assured, we shall do our best.'

After they had gone Beeston ambled into Mrs Stone's outer office and peered over her shoulder at what she was typing. It was a habit of his that never failed to irritate her.

'Go away,' she said. 'You put me off.'

'Just making sure that you're happy in your work,' he said.

'I'd be even happier if you went away,' she said. 'Was that Mr and Mrs Stevens?'

'Yes,' Beeston nodded.' Nice people. They want Sharon to come here, starting in September.'

'Why not Ashfield?'

'Because, understandably, they want her to have a normal social life,' observed Beeston, 'and all these politicians in education getting up and talking about "integrating the handicapped" makes it sound to the parents like the Promised Land.'

'If only they'd give us the facilities and the staff so that we could do it,' Mrs Stone commented drily, still typing.

'Still,' said Beeston philosophically, 'all we can do is

our best. Anyway, what has happened in this Great Wide World while I was closeted with the Stevens? Anything urgent? I thought I heard the phone go.'

'Just Mrs Wix confirming the next PTA Meeting, and was the Summer Fete on the agenda.'

Mrs Wix was the one parent that Beeston couldn't stand. No, he thought, let's be fair, there are lots of parents I can't stand, but very few on the scale of Mrs Wix. Mrs Wix didn't just want to run the PTA, she also wanted to run the school, and, if possible, the Universe as well. 'I hope you told her: No it isn't,' said Beeston, 'and we've moved the next PTA meeting to Australia.'

'I know she gets you down, but she means well,' said Mrs Stone. 'She's got a good heart.'

'She's also got a big mouth,' said Beeston moodily. 'Oh well, if that's all, I think I'll go and irritate Mrs Rudd.'

Mrs Stone finished the letter she was typing and removed it from the typewriter. 'Don't you dare,' she said warningly. 'By the way, what's happened to Mr Holliday?'

The question surprised Beeston. As far as he knew nothing had happened to his Deputy Head, although events at King Street Junior moved in their own mysterious ways, most of which he couldn't fathom. 'Fred?' he said. 'Nothing that I know of. Why, he hasn't disappeared, has he?'

'No, he just seems full of the joys of Spring.'

Understanding dawned. 'Oh, that,' said Beeston dismissively. 'That's because of this speech of his.'

Mrs Stone frowned, puzzled. 'Speech? What speech?'

'To his Round Table. The day after tomorrow. Every year they have this dinner and they invite somone special along to give a talk.'

Mrs Stone was impressed. 'And they invited Mr Holliday to do it?' she asked, admiringly. 'That is quite an honour. Mr Holliday, the celebrity.'

'Well not exactly,' said Beeston. 'They had invited someone from the CEGB, but he was double-booked and had to cancel at the last minute. So yesterday they asked

Fred if he'd do it. It's made his day. He's been angling to give a talk to them for years.'

'What's he going to talk about?'

'Transport, past and present,' he grinned. 'That should have 'em queuing up to go in.'

• • •

The staff room at morning break time was its usual hubbub of noise, quite a lot of it coming from Mrs Rudd, who was agitating around the room searching for her missing cup. Miss Lewis was complaining that for the first four minutes of the television programme her class had watched that morning, they had been tuned into the wrong channel.

'You ought to have videoed it,' said Long.

'I would still have videoed the wrong channel,' said Lewis, exasperated.

'By the way,' said Sims, sipping at his tea, 'does anyone know what nits look like?'

It was one of those conversation-stopping phrases, and it successfully stopped Lewis and Long in their tracks. 'Nits?' asked Long. 'What sort of nits?'

'You know, head lice type nits.'

'Be specific, head lice or nits?'

'What's the difference?'

'Lice are the actual parasites and they tend to crawl about the scalp,' explained Lewis. 'Nits are the eggs and they stick to the hair.'

Just at that moment, Mrs Rudd came past, having just found her cup, and picked up the conversation. 'Do we have to have this kind of conversation at break time?' she asked, obviously pained. 'Some people are about to eat a biscuit.'

'It's just that I think Edwina in my class has got them,' Sims told her. 'It could be just crumbs in her hair, but I don't know. That's why I wondered if anyone would recognise them?'

'Well I certainly would not, Mr Sims,' said Mrs Rudd, outraged by the suggestion. 'I am scrupulously clean.'

'They go for clean hair,' said Long. 'I'd watch out if I were you, Mrs Rudd.'

Mrs Rudd ignored, or pretended to ignore, this observation, and nibbled at her biscuit.

'If you're worried, I'll have a look at her,' Lewis offered. 'Four years ago there was a plague of them in this school, and six of my class got them.'

'What surprises me is that they should still be around in this day and age in a so-called modern civilisation,' said Sims.

'You shouldn't let that surprise you even after the short time you've been teaching at King Street,' commented Long. 'In fact I'm only surprised there haven't been more.'

'Oh?' asked Sims. 'Why?'

'Well, since they stopped the head inspections as part of the cuts there have been no checks,' said Lewis.

'Right,' agreed Long. 'We may have laughed at Nitty Nora, but at least with her coming round every few months, if lice did occur we could control them. Now, with no checks, there's no way of knowing what the kids are carrying around on them.'

This last was too much for Mrs Rudd. 'Really, Mr Long,' she said, 'I hardly think this is a fitting conversation for this time of day. I shall take my tea elsewhere.'

'Well it's a point!' Long called after her, not to be dismissed so easily.

'I must admit I wondered when we were going to have an inspection,' said Sims. 'They seemed to happen all the time when I was at school.'

'I'll pop into your classroom straight after break and have a look. I've got a free period,' said Lewis. She looked at her watch. 'Actually, I'd better go to the stock room now. I need some paper for fourth period.'

'I'll come with you,' said Long, 'I need three rulers.'

Sims watched them go, then wandered towards his locker, intent on seeing if he had any more biscuits left. He was feeling quite peckish although after all this talk about nits he didn't fancy anything with currants in. He never made it to his locker.

'Ah, there you are, Sims!' called a voice, genially. 'I've been looking for you.'

It was Mr Holliday, and Sims's heart sank. Whenever Holliday cornered him it was usually to talk about his journey home, and the intricacies of all the various permutations, which seemed to involve lists of road numbers which left Sims's brain in a complete tangle. It had taken him long enough to work out where the A1 was, let alone the B352 and the A1046, or whatever they were called.

'You're an honest chap,' beamed Holliday, now cornering him between the wall and the table with the kettle so that there was no escape.

'That's very nice of you to say so,' said Sims warily.

'The sort who'll be straight if you ask them an opinion, especially if it's important.'

Sims now felt totally on his guard. He hated being asked his opinion on something by anyone at King Street, because it usually meant that two people were rowing about something and they wanted him to act as independent judge. All that usually happened was that both parties ended up hating him. 'Well,' he said warily, 'I suppose so, but it depends on what it is.'

'I'll tell you,' said Holliday. 'My speech.'

Sims looked at him, slightly puzzled. 'Your speech?' he asked.

'Yes,' nodded Holliday.

Sims felt an immediate sense of relief. At least he was on safe ground here. 'If you're worried about your speech,' he said, 'I can tell you now, it's perfect.'

Holliday looked back at him, bafflement appearing on his face. 'What?' he said. 'How do you know?'

'Just by listening to you,' said Sims. 'As I say, if you're worried about any impediment or anything, there's none there. I've always thought that your clarity was one of the good things about you as a teacher. When you're doing Assembly, even those at the back of the Hall can hear you perfectly.'

'Not that sort of speech,' said Holliday, irritated.

'Oh?'

'No. I'm giving a speech to my Round Table the evening after tomorrow.'

'Oh,' said Sims, now understanding, and the shadow of apprehension seemed to close up again around him. He guessed what was coming next, and he dreaded this almost as much as he dreaded being asked to give an opinion in an argument.

'Normally they like you to talk about your work,' said Holliday, now jovial again, 'but four of them have already given speeches on teaching, and I think enough is enough.'

Sims nodded in enthusiastic agreement. 'Oh, absolutely.'

'Not that any of them knew anything about it, of course.'

'Right.'

'So I've chosen transport through the ages. It's something I've always been keen on.'

Sims was only too well aware of this. He wondered if he could make a break for it before Holliday got to the crucial question? It was only a question of squeezing past the kettle . . .

'I'm sure it will go down well,' continued Holliday, 'but just to make sure I thought I'd like to try it on someone before I air it in public.'

Here it comes, thought Sims. 'Well' he said, 'I'm no expert on transport. Perhaps Mr Beeston . . .'

Holliday shook his head. 'No, no,' he said. 'He never has the time to listen. And most of the others wouldn't give me an honest opinion, they'd just say it was fine whether they meant it or not.'

'Oh, I don't know . . .' said Sims, casting his eyes vainly around the room to see who he could pass the job on to. He was out of luck, Holliday didn't want any other candidates offered, he had already chosen his sounding board.

'But you,' he said, 'you'd take it in, mull it over, and give an honest opinion.'

'Well, if I could . . .' said Sims helplessly, wondering how it was that other people got out of these things so easily. Mrs Rudd, for example. She'd just say No, and that would be that.

'Good man,' said Holliday, pleased. 'I knew I could count on you.'

'I'm very tied up right now, though,' said Sims. 'I've got a problem with nits.'

Holliday gave him a look of surprise. 'Oh?' he said, taken aback. 'Where did you catch those from? The kids, I suppose.'

'No, not me,' said Sims. 'Edwina in my class.'

'Well I wasn't suggesting right at this immediate moment, we don't have much time at break,' agreed Holliday, and Sims's spirits started to rise a little. 'I'll catch you at lunch time,' Holliday finished, and Sims's spirits sank again.

• • •

Mr Sims sent Edwina along to see Miss Lewis in the stock room at one minute past eleven, ostensibly with a note asking a routine question about the numbers of blackboard rubbers in her classroom. At three minutes past eleven Edwina returned, accompanied by Miss Lewis, who slipped a note to Sims. Sims read it, and then asked Miss Lewis if she would mind staying with his class for a moment while he went to see Mr Beeston. Miss Lewis said 'Not at all', and five minutes later Sims was in Beeston's office, and definitely feeling his head itching.

Beeston looked at Sims with suspicion. Whenever Sims appeared in his office during teaching time, it meant Something Was Up, and whatever was Up was going to be bad news for Beeston, he could bet on it. 'Yes, Mr Sims,' he asked, 'What can I do for you that's so urgent?'

'It's about nits,' said Sims.

'Any particular nits?'

'Hair nits.'

'Oh,' said Beeston, 'Those. I thought you might be talking about the nits at County Hall or something. Yes, right, nits. What about them?'

'Edwina Harris in my class has got them.'

I bet it's just breadcrumbs, thought Beeston. Or salt or something. If I had a penny for every teacher who's come rushing here in demanding the whole school be fumigated because some child has rubbed a sandwich through its hair, I'd be rich beyond my wildest dreams. Aloud, he said: 'How do you know it's nits?'

'Miss Lewis identified them,' said Sims. 'She didn't see any lice, but she definitely spotted the eggs. It doesn't mean the lice aren't there, of course. They could be hiding in her scalp. After all Edwina has got very thick hair . . .'

'Yes, thank you,' said Beeston hurriedly, eager to cut off this flow of description about human parasites. He could feel himself itching already.

'What I want to know is, what do I do?'

'What you do is send Edwina to the medical room, and I'll phone her Mum and get her taken home.

'Right,' nodded Sims.

'We still need it officially confirmed of course,' warned Beeston, dreading the thought of phoning Mrs Harris and bringing her all the way in, only to find out it was something completely innocuous.

'But Miss Lewis says . . .' Sims protested.

'I know what Miss Lewis says, but we still need the Health Officer to come in. So I'll get on to County Hall and arrange it.'

'Right,' nodded Sims again.

'We'll also need the whole school to be checked,' said Beeston, groaning inwardly at the thought.

'Yes, I imagined that you would,' said Sims, apparently unaffected by the thought of the furore it would create in the school. This irritated Beeston not a little. The man creates havoc and just stands there, calm, he thought. Doesn't he realise what it means to try and telephone County Hall? It's at least a two-hour job, and that's on a good day. Determined not to let Sims get away with his conscience unmarked, Beeston said: 'So, once again your class seems to have stirred up a hornets' nest in the school.'

Sims obviously missed the point that Beeston was trying to make, because he had the audacity to smile.

'More a nest of lice, really,' he said. 'Can you imagine, having them crawling through your hair . . .'

Urgh, Beeston could feel himself itching again. 'Yes, yes, thank you. Mrs Sims,' he said. 'By the way . . .'

'Yes?'

'Talking of Miss Lewis, according to the timetable she's got a free period right now.'

'Yes, that's right, she's looking after my class while I came to see you.'

'Well, ask her to come and see me, will you,' said Beeston. 'I've got something I want to talk over with her.'

• • •

Miss Lewis sat across the desk from Beeston and thought over what he'd just told her. The idea of having Sharon Stevens in her class appealed to her. It would certainly be a challenge, but a challenge with positive rewards all round, providing . . .

'Sharon's also about the right age for your class,' Beeston finished off. 'The question is, will you be able to handle the situation?'

'It depends how you mean "handle" it,' said Lewis. 'Educationally, yes. I've worked with handicapped children before when I did my training. But physically, that's another matter.'

'You mean lifting her, and things?'

'Not just that, there's the problem of Sharon negotiating the desks with her wheelchair. In special schools you only have so many tables. In our classrooms, with the desks all crammed together even the able-bodied have difficulty getting around.'

Beeston nodded; these were among the practical problems that he had foreseen himself. 'I agree,' he said, 'so what I want you to do is start to make a list of all the problems that you can see cropping up, and we'll see if we can sort them out before they occur. We've got a few months, after all.'

'It's not very long,' Lewis pointed out.

'Certainly not when County Hall are involved,' agreed

Beeston. 'I don't know about Rome not being built in a day, if County Hall had been in charge of it they'd still be doing the foundations now.' He suddenly frowned as a thought struck him. 'On a totally different subject,' he said.

'Yes?' said Lewis.

'How come you're such an expert on nits?'

• • •

That lunch time, the main topic of conversation among the children in the playground was that of nits. Despite the attempts by Sims and Lewis to keep quiet about the fact that Edwina Harris had them, they might as well have written it on the school wall. Wherever anyone went, the phrase being bandied around was: 'Did you hear that Edwina Harris has got nits?'

'Urgh!' was the comment from a member of one group, a boy called Warren who had a particularly vivid imagination. 'Fancy having a great horrible insect crawling all over your head, laying eggs all over it. Urgh!'

'They ain't that big,' said another child. 'My sister had 'em. You can hardly see 'em.'

'Your sister? Urgh! Did you get 'em?'

'No, they caught 'em before they got to me.'

'What, caught 'em in a box?' demanded another child.

'No, they killed 'em. They put this stuff on her head and it killed 'em.'

'Did she have to have her hair cut off?' asked another child, hoping for some particularly gruesome details.

'No,' said the child whose sister had been affected.

All the listeners were disappointed by this answer. They had wanted mutilation and disgrace. One boy in particular was crushed. All his hopes and aspirations had just vanished in that one word.

'I was going to tell 'em I had nits and get a skinhead haircut for nothing,' he said in bitter disappointment.

For the staff still eating their lunch in the packed dining hall, the main topic of conversation was the entry of Sharon Stevens onto the school roll.

'Rather you than me,' said Long firmly, and he did his best to cut up the mysterious piece of meat on his plate. Wherever did Mrs Purkiss buy her food from, the butcher or the mortuary?

Sims was surprised. 'I would have thought it was a challenge,' he said.

'A challenge is one thing, but not having the right facilities is another,' said Long. 'For example, what about toileting?'

Sims looked around. Fortunately for Long, Mrs Rudd was having her dinner out of earshot or there would have been another broadside of protest about The Right Place For That Sort of Conversation.

'What about it?' Sims asked.

'Well, at special schools every class has a nursery nurse to help in situations like that,' said Long. 'And also the class sizes are smaller so you can give more help to those who need it. What do you do if Sharon needs extra help? Leave the rest of the class on their own?'

'Surely it's no different to if I have to leave my class because a child had an accident,' said Lewis defensively.

'There's a big difference,' said Long. 'No child is going to be having the same accident every day.'

Sims was beginning to feel a little indignant about Long's attitude. 'So are you saying that we shouldn't help children like this girl . . .?'

'Sharon,' prompted Lewis.

'Are you saying we shouldn't help children like Sharon?' Sims challenged.

'No, of course I'm not,' said Long. 'All I'm saying is enthusiasm is one thing, the reality of it is another. It's all very well having a keen and enthusiastic surgeon to take out your appendix, but speaking for myself I'd prefer to have it done with the proper equipment in an operating theatre rather than with a hacksaw in a garage. And compared to what special schools have got, we're the garage.'

'I still think we can't turn our back on the situation as easily as that,' said Sims. 'From the parent's point of view it must be really distressing to think of your child locked away from ordinary children. Having the handicap is bad enough, but there's no need for them to be additionally punished by being kept out of society because of it.'

'I agree,' defended Long, 'but . . .'

'The money,' finished Lewis.

Long nodded. 'Exactly.'

"But it's not the whole answer, is it?' said Sims, still feeling indignant. He wanted to say, what about people's feelings? How can you put a price on them?

Almost as if reading Sims's thoughts, Long said: 'It's a big part of the answer when they really start integrating. How are we going to cope with deaf-blind and paralysed mentally handicapped children without special facilities? And special facilities cost money.'

'But we're not talking about extreme cases,' protested Sims, 'we're talking about one child.'

'The thin end of the wedge,' warned Long.

Lewis looked at both of them, apparently unphased by Long's arguments. 'Well as Sharon is down to me,' she said simply, '*I* think I can cope.'

'And if you want any extra help with her, then please call on me,' said Sims.

Long gave a sigh. Honestly, he thought, to hear Sims go on you'd think I was Sweeny Todd or Bluebeard or someone. 'Look,' he defended himself, 'I'm not the big bad ogre you both think I am. All I'm saying is, do it, but we need better facilities, otherwise it's the children themselves who'll suffer. We're pushed enough as it is.'

The argument would undoubtedly have raged on throughout the unidentifiable pudding, if a shadow hadn't suddenly fallen over the table. 'Ah, Sims,' said Holliday genially. 'There you are. Finished your dinner?'

Long and Lewis looked at Sims curiously. What was going on? Sims, meanwhile, was racking his brains for some excuse to get out of listening to Holliday's speech. It wasn't so much listening to it that he dreaded, it was having to give an opinion. Say, as he expected, the speech was dreadful?

'Er . . .' he began helplessly.

Holliday smiled and clapped him on the shoulder. 'Fine,' he said. 'I'll see you in my room in five minutes. Don't rush your meal, but as soon as you're ready.'

• • •

Beeston, meanwhile, was having his own problems with unwanted confrontations. In his case it was Mrs Rudd, who had erupted into his office like hurricane Edna, and accused him in ringing tones: 'So you're hiding in here, are you.'

'As this happens to be my office, I hardly think it qualifies for the description "hiding",' Beeston defended himself.

'I looked for you in the dining hall but I couldn't see you,' accused Mrs Rudd.

'No,' said Beeston, 'I couldn't face Mrs Purkiss's dinner, not after Sims's gratuitous descriptions of head lice at play.'

Mrs Rudd nodded. 'That is what I want to see you about. What, precisely, are you doing about it?'

'Under the circumstances I'm doing all I can,' he answered diplomatically. 'I've sent Edwina home, and I've contacted the Health Department at County Hall. Steps are in motion.'

Mrs Rudd thought his answers over. Nothing wrong there, if the steps were necessary, but one question remained unanswered to her satisfaction. 'Are we quite sure that the . . . animal in question was . . .' she paused, then added with distaste, 'a louse?'

Beeston nodded. 'Yes,' he said. 'Miss Lewis has identified it positively; and if anyone should know, she should, after the plague her lot got four years ago. I'd quite forgotten about it until she said. Anyway,' and he regarded Mrs Rudd with a certain suspicion, 'why all the interest?'

'Because,' stated Mrs Rudd primly, 'my sister is coming to see me at the weekend, and I don't know whether to put her off.'

Beeston was none the wiser for this information. What on earth did Mrs Rudd's sister have to do with it? Did she suffer from some rare tropical disease that meant the mere sight of a nit could sent her into a narcoleptic trance or something? 'Why?' he asked.

Mrs Rudd looked at him as if he was an imbecile, a look that she often bestowed upon him. 'Can you imagine how I would feel if one of these creatures should jump from a child onto my clothing, and then on to my sister's?' she demanded. 'I would be so embarrassed!'

'I wouldn't think your sister would be too pleased, either,' commented Beeston. 'Frankly, Mrs Rudd, there's not a lot more I can do. All I can suggest is, when Nitty Nora arrives tomorrow, let her have a look at your head as well.'

'I will do no such thing!'

'Why ever not? You were saying how worried you were a minute ago.'

'I said that I was worried that one might jump on my clothing.'

'They don't live on clothing, they need blood from your scalp to survive,' pointed out Beeston. 'Although you can take your clothes off and get her to look through them, if it'll make you happier. It'll certainly give everyone else something to look at to take their mind off it.'

Mrs Rudd glared at him, unamused. 'You really are a most distasteful man,' she snapped. 'Sometimes I wish I didn't have to talk to you.'

And with that she went. Funnily enough, mused Beeston, the same thought has often occurred to me.

• • •

Sims had realised that it was going to be a long session when he heard Holliday's opening preamble before he started on his actual speech.

'Originally,' he said, 'I thought I'd start with the wheel, but then I thought it was worth making the point that transport as such started a long way before that. However, it then occurred to me that if I went back as far as the foot, it would miss the point I'm trying to make about modern transport systems.'

The foot?! Sims groaned. My God, he thought, if he's starting with the foot I'm going to be here for ever.

'So, what I thought I'd do,' said Holliday, '– and this was quite a radical idea – was start with the Romans.'

The Romans! Sims's mind boggled. I don't know how long the Round Table think he's going to be talking for tomorrow night, he thought, but I hope they've booked breakfast.

That had been at a quarter to one. Sims sneaked a glance at his watch. Five past one? Impossible, his watch must have stopped. They'd been right through every mechanical form of transport known in history; surely it must be at least twenty-five past?

Holliday turned over yet another page, blissfully oblivious of Sim's restlessness. 'However,' he read, 'the stagecoach, which had been a major cause of traffic jams in the early nineteenth century, was coming to the end of its reign. Little did it know, in 1829, that within a few years . . .'

Sims frowned. 'Shouldn't that be "the owners"?' he asked.

Holliday stopped, bewildered at being stopped in mid-sentence. 'What should?' he asked, nonplussed and obviously irritated.

'Well,' said Sims defensively, 'a stagecoach, not having consciousness, wouldn't actually "know" anything would it? It would be the owners of the stagecoach who "wouldn't know".'

Holliday was definitely put out by this unseemly interruption, just when he was getting into his stride. 'Well, if you want to be pedantic about it . . .' he said heavily.

'I wasn't being pedantic, I just thought . . .' said Sims.

'Yes, yes, all right. No need to go on,' said Holliday grumpily. He thought about it for a moment, then asked: 'You don't think they might take it as poetic licence?'

'Take what as poetic licence?'

'A stagecoach thinking.'

Only if they were absolutely plastered, thought Sims. And as this is an after-dinner speech, and if it goes on as long as it already has done, and they've got any sense, they'll be so plastered they'll take anything as poetic licence. Aloud, he said: 'Well, it's possible.'

'After all,' pointed out Holliday logically, 'no one questions Thomas the Tank Engine talking.'

To which, thought Sims, there is no answer.

• • •

The rest of the day passed peacefully, although Sims had recurring daymares during the afternoon with stage-coaches trundling after Roman foot soldiers, all being pursued by George Stephenson on a hobby horse bicycle.

For Beeston, a miracle had happened. Only twenty minutes on the telephone, and he had got through to the right department at County Hall. After he'd put the phone down he nearly picked it up again and phoned up the *Guinness Book of Records* to ask if it qualified, but then he wondered if it would mean anything to them. They'd possibly think he was saying that twenty minutes was a record of length rather than a record of brevity. The main thing was, he'd got through, and the Health Department had promised an inspection for the next day. A twenty-minute phone call, and the promise of action the very next day. It was all too much for Beeston, who left his office as the final bell went convinced that the lack of even Mrs Purkiss's dinner was bringing on hallucinations.

He was nearly at his car when Miss Lewis caught up with him. 'Mr Beeston!' she called. 'Have you got a minute?'

'Certainly,' said Beeston. 'What can I do for you? If it's about the nit nurse,' he announced with a sense of triumph, 'she's coming tomorrow.'

'No, said Lewis, 'it's about the new girl, Sharon Stevens.'

'Oh?'

'I've worked out that if County Hall can't make a

permanent ramp, we can have a portable wooden ramp by the two stairs down from my room.'

'Oh, good,' said Beeston. 'Well done. Where will we get it?'

'I'll make it.'

Beeston regarded her with eyes anew. His staff were constantly surprising him with their talents. He'd find out next that she could translate Serbo-Croat, or something. 'You?' he said, pleasantly surprised. It was the wrong thing to say.

'I can handle a saw and screwdriver, you know,' Lewis said, insulted.

'Oh, of course,' Beeston said, letting an appeasing note of apology work its way into his voice. Just to make sure she got the message, he added: 'I can't.'

Lewis, however, had moved on. 'And if I put one of my cupboards out in the corridor, that should give me the space I need for her to manoeuvre within the class.'

Beeston was impressed, and said so. 'Considering I only mentioned it to you a couple of hours ago, well done,' he said. 'And if I can help in any way, let me know.'

'Don't worry,' she said, 'I will.'

Beeston watched her walk over to her car. What a dedicated teacher, he thought admiringly. The sort who never makes a noise, never makes a fuss, and will never get their due reward because the system favours the egotist and the ruthless. What was it someone had once said to him? The education system is like a stagnant pond, the scum always rises to the top. Mind you, he reflected, he hoped they hadn't been including Head Teachers in that category.

'Ah!' called Holliday's voice. 'I hoped I'd catch you before you left.'

'Me, leave?' joked Beeston. 'No, I live here. What is it?' He almost preened himself. 'If you want to know about the nit nurse . . .'

'No,' said Holliday.

Beeston was put out. Didn't anyone want to know about his triumph with the Health Department and the nit nurse?

'I wanted to know if you had one or two jokes I could use,' said Holliday.

'Jokes?' said Beeston, baffled.

'Yes. You know, in this speech of mine,' said Holliday. 'You've done these speeches, you know how a joke or two always helps it go down well. I tried it on Sims and I felt that he enjoyed it, but I felt that he might have enjoyed it more if I'd thrown in the odd joke or two.'

Beeston groaned. He was obviously going to get lumbered with hearing Fred's speech after all. 'All right,' he said wearily. 'Let's hear the speech.'

'Well,' said Holliday, 'if you're sure you want to'. And before Beeston could say another word, Holliday produced a wad of paper from his inside pocket. 'You'll like this,' he promised.

• • •

It was five to nine the next morning when Beeston finally got his chance to announce his success in getting a nurse from the Health Department to come to the school to search for nits. He swept into the staff room when he was sure that everyone was there, determined that no-one was going to miss out on his announcement. 'Right,' he said, 'I thought this was an opportune time to grab you all, before school actually starts.'

As if on cue the door to the staff room opened and Long walked in. Long took one look at Beeston, at the rest of the staff standing in silence with their tea cups in their hands, and looked at his watch. It was still only five to nine, surely? 'I didn't know there was a staff meeting this morning,' he complained. 'No one told me. There was no notice up.'

Beeston waved a hand to shut him up. 'It's not official,' he said. Trust someone to upstage him the only time he'd ever had a successful phone battle with County Hall. He turned back to address all the members of staff. 'I just wanted to fill you all in on what is happening as far as the nit situation is concerned. Yesterday I persuaded County Hall's Health Department that they had to send round a nurse today.'

He paused, waiting for everybody to be suitably impressed by this announcement.

'She should have been yesterday,' commented Mrs Rudd pointedly.

Oh well, thought Beeston. If people don't want to be impressed. 'The nurse has already been round this morning to see Edwina Harris at home,' he continued, 'and confirmed that she has indeed got head lice and nits.'

'I'd already confirmed that yesterday,' pointed out Lewis, slightly peeved.

'Yes,' said Beeston, 'but you're not official, Miss Lewis, it's not a nit until the Health Department say it is. Anyway, Edwina has now been officially excluded, and the hunt is on to see who else is affected. The nurse will be coming round to each class in turn, and with a bit of luck she'll have everyone done by lunch time.'

'I suppose she'll be starting with my class first, as the first definite sighting was in there,' said Sims.

The first definite sighting? Anyone would think it was a UFO. 'No, Mr Sims,' said Beeston.

Sims looked baffled. 'What? But I'd have thought . . .'

'So would we all, Mr Sims,' Beeston agreed, 'but her orders are apparently to work through every class in numerical order.'

Sims gave a short laugh of derision. 'But surely that's not very sensible. After all, we *know* they're in my class.'

'Ours not to reason why. If, by the time she arrives at you, the whole of your class have been consumed by head lice, it's not our fault, it's the fault of the Health Department.'

'Well, really,' muttered Mrs Rudd, expressing her distaste at Beeston's description.

At that point the bell sounded for the start of school, and Beeston clapped his hands together. 'There she blows!' he said. 'And let's hope Nitty Nora doesn't find too many.'

• • •

For the rest of the day the visit of the nurse from the

Health Department dominated King Street. Wherever one went in the school, groups of children could be found examining each other's heads. If two children passed in a corridor, one invariably asked the other 'Did she find any on you?'

Morning break found Mrs Rudd on duty on the playground and eyeing each child suspiciously. Had they been checked? she found herself asking, as yet another child passed dangerously close to her.

'Please, Miss!'

The voice behind her made her jump. She looked around, and observed the tiny figures of Warren and Sarah from Mrs Wilberforce's class looking up at her.

'We was wondering, Miss,' piped Warren.

'About the nits,' added Sarah in her small husky voice.

Was there no peace from them? groaned Mrs Rudd. 'What about them?' she asked.

'Will they have to shave the children's heads who've got 'em?' asked Warren.

Mrs Rudd bridled at the thought of working in a school with children with shaved heads – it would be positively mediaeval. 'Certainly not,' she said. 'Why?'

The two children looked at one another. 'Then how we gonna know who's got them?' asked Warren. 'I mean, if they had a shaved head we'd know who to stay away from.'

'Yeah,' husked Sarah. 'If everyone keeps their hair, *anyone* could have them.'

'If anyone is found to have parasites then they will be sent home,' Mrs Rudd told them.

'Does that include the teachers, Miss?' asked Sarah hopefully.

Inside the school, in the staff room, nits were also dominating the conversation among the staff.

'How did you get on?' Sims asked Lewis. 'Did Nitty Nora find any in your class?'

'None, thank goodness,' grinned Lewis, 'otherwise I'd still be scratching. Mind you, Mrs Wilberforce hasn't been so lucky, two of hers had them.'

'Which two?' asked Long.

'Ranjit and Tommy.'

'Tommy Watson, Edwina Harris's cousin?' asked Sims.

'Yes,' nodded Lewis.

Sims groaned. 'I bet I end up with hundreds in my class,' he complained.

'Think yourself lucky if you do,' said Long, 'they'll all have to be sent home.'

Sims thought about it, and smiled. 'Yes,' he admitted, 'there is that to it.'

The only person who wasn't thinking about nits in the school appeared in the group at that point and tapped Sims on the elbow. 'Ah, Sims,' Holliday said, his voice low and confidential. 'I wonder if you've got a minute?'

Taking his hint, Lewis and Long drifted away with little smiles. The last thing they wanted was to be caught up in Fred Holliday's rehearsals for his speech. It's also the last thing I want to get caught up in again, thought Sims.

'Well I'm really busy at the moment,' he said, more in hope than conviction, 'my class is due for nit inspection next, and I've got to go out at lunch time . . .'

'That doesn't matter,' said Holliday, not at all put off, 'I can do this now.'

Sims' face fell. Holliday gave Sims a beam, and then a firm look as if he was about to tell him something momentous. 'Do you mind if I tell you a joke?' he announced.

Sims was taken aback. 'A joke?' he asked, baffled. He'd thought it was going to be yet another trial run for bits of Holliday's speech, the continuing history of people riding in carts.

'Yes,' said Holliday. 'It's the humorous touch to lighten up the speech a little. Mr Beeston told it to me. See what you think.'

He had been right, Sims reflected gloomily. 'Oh,' he said. 'Right.'

'I told it to my wife last night but she was . . . well, she thought I ought to have a second opinion.'

But why did it have to be him? Sims thought. The

trouble is I'm not forceful enough. No, the truth was, he didn't like to hurt other people's feelings. He was too kind. Still, it was worth brownie points when it came to getting in to Heaven. When he got to the Golden Gates and St Peter asked him, what good had he done, he'd say 'I listened to other people's jokes', and St Peter would say 'In you come.' 'Is it a very long one?' he asked cautiously. 'Only the bell's about to go any minute?'

'No no,' said Holliday. 'Quite short. A man is driving along the motorway at night when a police car overtakes him and flags him down. "Yes, officer," he says. "Excuse me, sir," says the policeman – and here I thought I might do an accent – '

'Oh, very good,' said Sims, to let Holliday know that he was listening, and that he had his support. Holliday didn't seem to be impressed with this observation. He hesitated a moment, then continued as if Sims hadn't said anything: '"Excuse me, sir, but your offside rear light isn't working." So the man goes to the rear of his car, and kicks it, and the offside light comes on. "There," says the man. "Very good, sir," says the officer, having walked around the man's car to inspect it . . .'

'Is that the accent you're going to do?' asked Sims, to show interest.

Again, Holliday didn't seem happy about Sims's very supportive question. In fact he seemed distinctly unhappy about it. 'I'm working on it.' he said flatly. 'Look, Sims, can I tell you this joke or not?'

'Of course,' said Sims.

'Having walked around the man's car to inspect it . . .'

At that moment the bell went for the end of break. 'Oh blast!' snapped Holliday irritated almost beyond words. 'Anyway,' he continued, any pretext at humour now having vanished from his face and voice, 'the officer says "In that case, sir, perhaps you'd like to kick the front and and see if your tax comes up".'

'Oh, very good,' smiled Sims, forcing a little light laugh. He must have heard that joke about a hundred times.

'Meaning that the man's tax disc has expired,' explained Holliday, as if talking to an idiot.

'Yes, I see,' nodded Sims, still smiling.

Holliday wasn't convinced. 'Maybe I haven't got the accent right yet,' he grumbled as he moved off.

• • •

Throughout the morning, the search for the infamous nits continued; and by lunchtime the whole school had been completely examined. Six children had been found to be affected – two in Mrs Wilberforce's class, two in Sims's, and two in Holliday's.

In the staff room at lunchtime, the other teachers were all heaving sighs of relief, but many were still taking no chances. As Mrs Rudd came in from the dining hall she found the nurse now examining Long's hair.

'If you find any money in there, nurse, it's mine,' said Long.

Really, thought, Mrs Rudd. Such a lowering of standards. When I first entered teaching no one would have considered that a teacher was the class of person who could have caught nits, regardless of what had happened to Mrs Partridge a few years ago. But then Mrs Rudd had always considered that Mrs Partridge leaned too close to the children. One got what one deserved, that was her opinion.

The nurse finished examining Long. 'Right,' she announced, 'You're clear.'

'Thank heavens for that,' said Long, getting up. 'What about you, Miss Lewis?'

'I was one of the first to be checked,' said Lewis confidently. 'I'm clear.'

Long looked around the staff room to see if there were any other potential victims. 'What about you, Mrs Rudd?' he asked, grinning broadly.

'Thank you,' said Mrs Rudd primly, 'but I have no intention of having my hair examined. And if I ever did, it would be in the privacy of my own doctor's surgery. I do not hold with people making public exhibitions of themselves.'

'That's the point!' Holliday stormed. 'That's how it all started!'

Beeston and Stone looked at him, baffled. 'What do you mean?' asked Beeston.

'The culprit. It was that Singh child in my class. I was doing a lesson on transport with them, and I'd brought in one of those old motoring caps to show them. He put it on wrongly, so I put it on afterwards to show him how it ought to go.'

'And poor old Singh now turns out to be one of the nit carriers,' nodded Beeston. 'Yes, the nurse told me.'

'I'll poor old Singh him!' Holliday fumed. 'What am I going to do about my speech?'

'You could always just turn up and not tell them,' suggested Mrs Stone.

'And take the chance of spreading them among the Round Table?!' said Holliday, outraged. 'Why that's . . .' A thought crossed his mind, and the heavy scowl on his face suddenly faded, and he smiled. '. . . brilliant! Well done, Mrs Stone. And thanks to these little parasites, I'll have tomorrow off to finish my speech as well.'

'Oh come on,' laughed Sims, 'it's not really an intimate sort of examination, is it?'

'You may not consider it so, Mr Sims,' said Mrs Rudd. 'I do.'

'That's a point,' said Lewis, 'I haven't seen you have yours done yet.'

Sims shook his head. 'I had mine done with my class,' he said.

Mrs Rudd stared at him, horrified. 'What, in front of the children?'

'Yes, of course.'

'Really, have you no respect for the dignity of the profession?'

'I wanted to show them that it wouldn't hurt them,' Sims explained.

'It's a good idea to be looked at while she's here, Mrs Rudd.' prompted Lewis, joining in on the side of the persuaders. 'Remember Mrs Partridge three years ago, how she caught them.'

'Caught what?' asked Holliday, just having walked in.

'Miss Lewis was just trying to persuade Mrs Rudd to have her head examined for nits,' said Sims.

'Yes, Mrs Rudd?' asked the nurse.

'Certainly not,' snorted Mrs Rudd. 'Has Mr Holliday had his head examined?'

'No, but I sometimes think I need to, working in a place like this,' said Holliday wearily.

'Well there you are, then,' said Mrs Rudd firmly. 'If Mr Holliday hasn't, I'm certainly not going to.'

All eyes not turned to Holliday. 'Come on, Fred,' said Lewis coaxingly, 'just to persuade Mrs Rudd into doing it. If she sees you having it done . . .'

Holliday rolled his eyes to heaven. Honestly, the things one did! It hardly went with the image of the profession he'd had when he first qualified. 'All right,' he said, 'though after all these years of teaching I can't see the point, we older ones build up an immunity system to 'em.'

Mrs Rudd was not mollified. As the nurse approached

Holliday, who had inclined his head slightly for her to get a better look, Mrs Rudd continued to be on the defensive. 'Well, I don't care if Mr Holliday does want to make a fool of himself,' she said. Then she looked around the room at her colleagues, and sighed. 'Oh very well,' she said stiffly, 'if it will please you and stop you all harrassing me so, and as there does seem to be an epidemic going round . . .'

• • •

The news that a member of the staff had actually caught nits went around the school like wildfire. For the children it was the best news they could ever have had, one of Them had been caught. For the more sensitive children in the school it was a matter of horror, a Teacher had got nits?! What was the world coming to?

When Beeston heard the news he was both astonished and amused, especially when he heard who it was who was affected.

'I don't believe it! Of all the members of the staff to be affected!' he chuckled to Mrs Stone.

'Don't be rotten,' chided Mrs Stone. 'You wouldn't like it if it happened to you.'

'Poor old Fred!' chortled Beeston. 'Frankly I didn't realise he had enough hair for a nit to get onto!'

The door opened and the subject of the conversation came in, furious. 'Have you heard?!' Holliday demanded angrily.

'Stay away from me' said Beeston, moving away. 'If you want to cry on anyone's shoulder, use Mrs Stone's.'

'Thank you,' said Mrs Stone sarcastically.

'It's no laughing matter,' Holliday stormed. 'I've got to give a speech tomorrow night and I'm supposed to put this horrible stinking shampoo all over my hair and leave it on! Can you imagine what the Round Table would say if I turned up with that plastered all over my hair?'

Beeston did his best not to smile at the image that Holliday's words conjured up. 'You could always wear a crash helmet over it and say it's a visual aid to your speech,' he suggested.

LUST'S LABOUR WON

Other books by Blue Moon *Authors*

RICHARD MANTON

DREAM BOAT
LA VIE PARISIENNE
SWEET DREAMS
LOVE LESSONS
BELLE SAUVAGE
PEARLS OF THE ORIENT
BOMBAY BOUND

DANIEL VIAN

BLUE TANGO
SABINE
CAROUSEL
ADAGIO
BERLIN 1923

AKAHIGE NAMBAN

CHRYSANTHEMUM, ROSE, AND THE SAMURAI
SHOGUN'S AGENTS
WOMEN OF THE MOUNTAIN
WARRIORS OF THE TOWN
WOMEN OF GION

The Victorian Era

LUST'S LABOUR WON

Anonymous

BLUE MOON BOOKS, INC. NEW YORK

First Blue Moon Edition 1990
First Printing 1990

ISBN 0-929654-77-3

Manufactured in the United States of America.

Published by Blue Moon Books, Inc.
61 Fourth Avenue
New York, New York 10003

CHAPTER ONE

Phillip Mansfield's Day-Book

Where there is silence there is pain; where there is music there is often pain; where there is absence there is pain. And sometimes all these congregate, even in the presence of the once-beloved, becoming like a veil across the eyes, a tight band round the forehead, so that the pain obtains the greyness of an early-evening mist, obscuring the thoughts, the words, to which the mind would otherwise give birth.

In such moments, clamped within my own being, and feeling that the very spaces around me (those spaces between the furniture and the walls such as encroach on one in moments of *douleur* more than do the physical objects themselves) are areas of the alien, of foreignness, even though lived in, walked in, day by day—yes, in such moments I am drawn into a dullness, an unspeaking, a sense of being separated from myself and from all others.

It is because, I am told, I live too much in my mind, when in fact I would that I could live in others' minds—for I, the real Phillip (seemingly unknown to those I hold most dear) have sat and held his once-beloved's hand, discoursing with her in the manner of a flowing stream and pausing only at the stones and bridges of her words, absorbing and enfolding them to show my true identity with her. Ah, how often—how often—did I clamp my lips upon my wife's (aware that my own were too wet and too loose sometimes) and swear to her that in my love for her I would *become* her, dissolve and disappear in her, and know our souls to be united.

'They cannot be', she would say and turn her face. Downstairs a piano might be tinkling—its notes wounding with their brittle, careless sounds. Then would come a silence and my wife would stir. The bed must be smoothed, she would say, or the maid would see, and this despite my protestations that we had not made love, nor I as much as flirted a hand beneath her skirt.

'Even so, Phillip, even so', she always murmured and would pat her hair with that distracted air of a woman who is not appeased or, if she is, has her mind elsewhere, though she will not acknowledge it.

'I cannot be other than myself any more than you can be other than yourself', she often said.

'And thus there is a vacuum where love should be', said I.

'No vacuum, Phillip, but rather an enclave of desire that will renew itself. I cannot help myself if love between my legs enchants me more than is in my head'.

'Impure!', I cried, but said it only in my head.

The words we spoke grew rougher through the years, the intervals between our kisses longer. Hiding our deceptions as we might before the children, we could never quite dissemble them. Words of parting rose, and Amy cried, clung to her mother. Richard, whose nineteen years I then relied upon to make him manly, would not speak to either of us, yet I saw him in the last week of their abiding here kiss his mother thrice, and once in fullness on her lips, whereat she threw her head back, stroked his hair.

I could not shout at them to stop. Such is the guile of circumstance that I would have been accused by her of 'being miserable'. Pretending not to see, I turned away. The hour was late. Amy and Sylvia were both in bed. Passing straight-backed, straight-legged, out of the room, I heard a succulence of mouths, yet chided myself and not them for impure thoughts. 'Darling', she called him, though had never called me more than 'dear'.

A whole hour passed before she came to bed that night, her nipples stiff. I saw them as she dropped her camisole. I wished to ask why she had stayed so late downstairs, but could not bring myself to ask. The bows of her drawers were all untied already, and they fell down loose, at which she turned towards the bed wherein I lay and asked, 'Do you not like me thus—not like me thus?'

Her bottom cheeks were pink as though they had been clutched. There were fingermarks upon her bottom cheeks, I swear.

The lamp was on. One does not look between a woman's legs in light. I had not stirred nor answered her. She heeled the drawers off nimbly and I saw a damp stain there, down at the crotch.

'I am so moist there—put it in', she said. Her face was flushed from drinking too much wine—the red that brings a flush into her cheeks. Richard ascended from the drawing room where they had been. He passed our door on tiptoe and closed his own as though he feared the noise to sound.

'Do not speak so', I said. I would not look. She frequently had such a lewdness on her in her words.

There was a silence then—that silence of foreboding such as when a house stands dark and empty on a moor and the first snow falls upon the silent eaves.

'You do not want to—will not challenge *your* cock to my nest?', she asked, and laughed a scornful laugh that hurt my mind. 'If you believe your sinful thoughts of me, then sinful I may be, just to fulfill the image in your mind, Phillip. Come—challenge!—take me under you and I will tell you *very* naughty things. I only have my stockings on. You like to feel my stockings, do you not?'

Ah, wheedling voice, and yet I did not speak. That was the voice of sin and not of love. I felt her kneel up on the bed and knew her legs to be apart. I strained away. Her hand touched at my shoulder and then fell. It was the breaking point perhaps. I knew it to be so but could not help myself.

'Then I shall sleep elsewhere', I heard her say.

O utter loneliness of that wide bed when the door opened, closed, and she had gone! Her long, frilled nightgown lay still on the bed. I heard the slither of her stockinged feet. All night, it seemed, moans sounded in my ears. One cannot write of such, cannot. No words were spoken at the breakfast table. Amy and Sylvia were mute and hushed. Richard took coffee in his room. Within an hour the bags were all brought down. Solemnity fell upon us like a pall.

To Liverpool, she said—told Sylvia, not me. Dear Sylvia, she did not wish to leave. Or not as yet, she said, or not as yet. Her mother kissed her fondly, then was gone with Amy and Richard silent in her train.

Perhaps I should have spoken, said, asked, pleaded. No—I would not plead. I had trodden once too often on that stony ground, watching my words fly beyond her ears—not wholly disregarded, so I like to think, but such curt phrases as she often uttered blew my quieter words away. I have no mere words to utter to her—I have none. The bed in which she had slept that night was ruffled and I feared the maid would see, both pillows used where she perhaps had rolled. Too many purple and impassioned things she often said at nights that frayed my mind with their wild, wicked urges, things that should not be spoken of, and that I cannot bring myself to pen.

Thoughts of that night grow dark and dreary in my mind. I fear for what I think of that stained, twisted sheet, and must not think. I shall pray for her deliverance, and mine, though we may never meet again.

Sylvia played upon the garden swing today. Her sixteenth birthday is upon us soon. Our maid, Rose, should not push her quite so high. I saw above her stocking tops. Someone should speak to her of that, for I cannot. Such subjects are improper—thorn the tongue and prick the lips.

'You look sad, Papa', she laughed. I turned away. I am

often told such when in truth I feel but serious. Such innocence becomes the young who feel no pain from silence, music, absence, but ever turn their minds towards some other thing.

Sylvia Mansfield's Day-Book

I did not wish to side with anyone, but neither did I wish to go to Liverpool. Mama, I'm sure, forgives me that. I shall visit them at Christmas, anyway. Perhaps she did not understand that Papa needs quietness to pursue his work. His desk is all about with pages of his novel. I am sure his writing was the cause of it, because he wished for quietness, but Mama was hardly ever that. Richard was always kissing her of late. I wonder why. Perhaps he has long wanted to go to Liverpool, for he prefers a city life, and so I expect him to be pleased. I asked Mama is it nice to kiss, and she laughed and said 'Of course it is', but would not tell me any more until my birthday, so she said.

I do not think Mama and Papa had very much in common, and I hope that is not a horrid thing to say.

Papa says he will buy me a pony for my birthday. He must have thought of it of a sudden. Perhaps he saw a picture in a book, for I had not dared ask for one. I sometimes think of things that way, by looking in a book. I was undressing when he came up to my room. How awful—oh—my drawers were off and I had one leg raised upon my bed to peel my stockings down! Oh, I *did* blush!

Papa said 'Oh!' and shut the door again. I knew that he felt awful, just like me. He did not go away, and then I heard him call, 'It is about your birthday, Sylvia. Would you like a pony?'

'Yes!', I called and tumbled on my nightdress quickly lest he come within again. I waited, but he did not come. 'Thank you, Papa', I called.

'I will tell you in the morning', he replied, though he already had.

My thing has lots of curls around it now. I brush them with my fingers when I am in bed. Perhaps I should not. I wonder if it's wrong?

Mama said naughty things to Richard sometimes, he told me, but would not say what she had said. He was horrid and I think he made it up. He had his trousers open, but I would not look.

Phillip's Day-Book

I grow uneasy at the thought that I have perhaps proposed a pony where Sylvia would better have a true companion. I asked her so. '*Who*, Papa?', she replied and looked a little puzzled at my seriousness. 'I am perfectly all right, Papa, I really am', she said, and played with Rose again upon the swing. The two are very close, it seems to me. The servant should be at her work, but again I feel powerless—selfish even—to intrude, and would be better at my work than thinking of such things.

My novel, however, is like unto a carriage wheel to which the brake has locked itself. My thoughts stir much like porridge when they should really be ethereal. Of men I write well, for they say the proper things that I myself would say. As to women, I find it difficult to describe such thoughts as they may have. Their conversations are thus stilted, and not what I would have them say at all. The image of my once-beloved floats ever in my head. Alas, I see her with her nipples stiff, her drawers already untied beneath her dress. I should scourge myself upon such thoughts as my old tutor used to tell me to.

It is notable, however—and I must somehow convey this with such clarity as I can muster—that the thoughts we least would have are those which fight with tooth and claw against suppression. Clearly, such is the devil's work. Temptation it is called, and is only with ardent will to be put down. Thus would I not listen to her when she used crude words, however warm her breath against my mouth, however luring were her fingertips. The act of love should be performed in silence and be quickly done. It is deemed for procreation, not for pleasure, so I often said to her.

'Why, there is naught but paper in your mind sometimes. Someone should light it with a match', said she, and fell to musing who might do it best, just to annoy me and to try and make my mind a whirlpool of unthought-of things.

'You are not so much interested in the content of your writing as in the act of working with your pen, Phillip. Yet contrariwise, you are not so much interested in the act of love as in the abstract content of it', once she chided me.

That is not true, of course—that is not true. The irritation in remembering such words robs me of concentration. Half an hour ago I chanced to look out on the garden scene and saw that Sylvia has white drawers on and summer-thin. I must move the swing to face the other way, or else tell Rose to push her not so high.

Jane Mansfield's Day-Book

It was hardly surprising to learn that Deirdre has at last left Phillip. It was an uneasy marriage from the very start. Fire and water, as is the saying, and Deirdre, bless her, having all the heat.

I am glad I did not marry, just as Muriel is. Sisters are best together, and what lovely times we have! It is indiscreet to write of them, perhaps, but when I say so Muriel laughs and tells me not to spare a word of it.

There was such a pretty girl at the Fortescues' last night. I will write of her another time, for have not time today. We are to keep an eye on Sylvia, Deirdre asks in her brief note that reads as breathlessly as she makes love (I do believe). In what wise she did not say. The bolder that her education be, the better it will be for Sylvia, I think. In any case, the two cannot live all alone. We are resolved to visit Phillip. After all, he is our brother, though I believe he thinks our ways are rather strange.

We should settle for a fortnight at the least, says Muriel, and are resolved to take the coach tomorrow to his home. It is a whole year since we visited. How glum he looked then, but how bright was Deirdre! Really I believe she would have slept between us if he had not been there.

Deirdre Mansfield's Day-Book

Richard is sweet. They both like the new house. How smoky all is—yet in winter it will be even cosier when the fog envelops all the windows and the fires are lit. I must write to Sylvia tomorrow. *He* does not deserve a word, nor any man who scorns the amourous comfort of his wife and will forever dribble of his love but scarcely ever put the poker in to stir my fire.

'You are becoming a bad girl', Mama said to me years and years ago, but hugged and kissed me as she spoke. There was at least complicity in her reproof, whereas with Phillip all was dullness and unknowing in his very soul. To speak of naughtiness to him was counted as a sin, and yet I cannot find in it anything but an affirmation of desire which, if it is cloaked, will only spread its roots down more.

There is love when a tongue between my lips sweeps round my own—love when my breasts are burnished and my nipples stiffened by a fondling hand.

Last night I sat with Richard on the couch. He kissed my lips; his hand roamed to my breasts and felt their weight and their protuberance. In a moment he had sleeked that self-same hand beneath my skirt and murmured at the plumpness of my thighs.

I am in sin. Is it better than to be frustrated? I have been lax with him before. That last night at the house before we left, I let him kiss me with abandon, permitted him to loose my drawers till I thrust him up and took myself up to my ever-hopeful marriage bed, there to be scorned—indeed, almost reviled. Have I in truth what Phillip called a 'coarse, lewd tongue' when a fever of desire is in my veins? Should I be as marble, quiet as a church crypt? Never was I chided in my youth for saying naughty things in bed, or in the hayloft, in the summerhouse. There were sparklings then of love and lust combined, and sweet they were and heady as an old champagne. My cousin, Edward, had my sister, Adelaide, upon the lawn, and dusk it was, and we were seen; I had no doubt that we were seen by eyes that peered out from the house. And then it was I who fell and had my drawers pulled down by one who had waited on a moment such as that. Adelaide's eyes enchanted mine as we both came, and drew the sperm into our willing quims.

'You have been educated', Mama said that night, though she pretended not to know what had passed upon the summer grass.

Phillip has no mind for such. I never should have told him all my tales.

'There were lovings, Phillip', I explained. He would not listen, though, and turned away. His cock was stiff sometimes when thus I spoke, but was not always so, and that amazed me truly. Was he jealous of my fondlings, pumpings, in my early years? I think not, no. His marbled, cold ideas of purity came in long strides before that sweet emotion could take flower.

The night was broken on his 'shame' of me—I who would have sported with him as he wished and paid my wifely homage to his bed. I blundered out, left him to his dry dreams, and naked to my stockings made to sleep in an adjoining guest room where a bed is ever ready for a visitor. Alas for my would-be fealty, I blundered into Richard in the dark, he with his nightgown on—and he whose hands had so impulsively sought to caress my bottom cheeks downstairs.

It was an accident, perhaps, that his out-reaching hand should brush my bush. Upon such small things are new destinies contrived. I choked an exclamation back, went past him quivering from that faint touch and entered the dark room. He followed me. I dared not squeal or raise my voice—or so I told myself who sought to argue with the hypocrite in me. Or nay, I say the hypocrites in *all* of us. I jerked, I strained at Richard who had raised his nightgown as we fell in silent struggle on the bed, he fearing me to cry out, and I him to groan out too loud in the pleasures of forbidden fruit. Long did I struggle. Did I struggle long? I felt like the rebellious schoolgirl that I once had been who had to take the birch across her bottom first before she offered up her bottom sobbingly and took the mastering prick within her nest.

A score of times I must have whispered, 'Richard—no!', but oh, far-faint, mouth kissed, I then succumbed. I hear our nostrils hissing still as there we threshed, his legs between my own—an unreality at first, and yet spell-binding were the jets of come that then extolled my own fine spurts of love till we lay lax, tongues circling, coiling, twirling in the weak, soft aftermath that sweeps aside all barriers of guilt and makes the loins to work in sweet reprise.

How strangely silent were we that first time, save for our gentle, hungry moans, and how my toes curled as he came!

'Go from me, Richard, go', I breathed. I wanted to run into that small room that bears the name Remorse, and yet I knew it would not welcome me, for it had never done before. Upon my second threading in the summer-house when I was seventeen, my aunt held me, rained kisses on my lips while the big penis worked its will and flooded me with warm, thick, gruelly sperm.

'You raised your legs up at the last and curled your toes when he was coming in your quim', she smiled. He rose, I saw that long, thick penis drooling, soapy at the head.

'Now kiss me once again. I'll make you come anew', she said. She smacked my thighs to keep them open while he looked, but then he went lest Mama came. 'There is no sin of it, my pet, provided that you like it', so she said.

I wonder now, but cannot help myself no more than I could then.

'You are much loved', she said. 'Now you have taken his big cock a second time, you will again'.

I spoke of it with Adelaide. We rubbed our nipples as we spoke. How sweet the boldness that was on us then! Should I return to it? Last night with Richard on the couch, I heard my aunt's words once again that she had uttered in the hayloft the first time, when I had needed to be held.

'Please, don't! You can't! It's naughty—oh!', I squealed the while the swollen crest sheathed itself into my squeezing slit. I kicked. My legs were raised, beat ever feebly on his back. Remorselessly the pulsing peg sank in until his balls hung down beneath my orb. 'I'll tell Mama!', I moaned, though it was to be my last cry of any comprehensibility. Thereafter for a moment I was dulled, was slowly lulled though by the motions of his prick, and finally grew passionate for more.

But in that cry I heard my aunt say as my bottom squirmed, 'Shush, darling, sin is half the salt of it'.

Sin is . . . love is . . . I do no longer know. The sofa creaked last night. Did Amy hear? I closed my eyes, dreamed Richard other then he was, or made myself to think so, but he cannot be. O fervency of Youth's desire that he could sperm my cunny twice without withdrawing, as he did. I mewed. My naked bottom slurred on the brocade, cupped on his firmly gripping hands.

'Again!', I moaned and heard my voice as if from far away and long ago.

CHAPTER TWO

Muriel Mansfield's Day-Book

We are to Phillip's then, and I look forward to it. He must be got out of his strange ways. He is, and always was, too quiet and taut, and lives too much within himself. Dear Deirdre, one cannot blame her for her flight, and Sylvia we wish to see again; she is such a darling little thing.

I shall be thirty-four soon. Am I getting old? I wish I were Jane, and two years younger. If we had been twins . . . 'But you look scarcely thirty', she reassures me constantly. My bottom has got fatter. I keep looking at it. Jane says it is 'firmly plump' and feels exactly as a woman's should. I hope that is a compliment. Neither of us have had a man for several weeks now, and quite yearn for it.

'We shall have to go without it, too, in the next two weeks', I said to her. 'Perhaps!', she said and wrinkled up her nose, crinkled her eyes and laughed her wicked laugh.

Phillip we will surprise at least, and Sylvia, too. I mean to kiss her much, and so does Jane. We cannot help our fondness for young girls. Had we not been made tongue-ready and cock-ready when we both ourselves were young . . . But still, it's lovely, and I won't complain of it.

Phillip's Day-Book

Am I never to be left alone? The descending of my sisters startled me, but was greeted with much joy by Sylvia, which underlined my sense of guilt that she is too much now alone, though Rose is often at her side and in her room. I am not sure of that relationship and said as much to Muriel last night.

'Two pretty girls together make for pleasure, dear', she answered. Often she seems to have a double meaning in her words that I dislike.

'They play games, I expect', I said.—'I'm *sure* they do', she answered back. She is a trifle plumper round the hips. I could not help but notice that. Her dresses, just as Deirdre's were, are far too tight for decency.

'Would you rather that I took it off?', she asked when I remarked upon the low cut of her dress, the sweeping tightness of the lower half.

'Not, I would NOT', I said and went up to my room, feeling an angry flush about my ears. There was propriety at home when we were young. She never seemed to learn, nor Jane. I have closed my ears to scandals of the pair in which Deirdre seemed to revel. Mother was outraged once when she discovered Jane and Muriel undertaking 'Nature study' with Papa, and having little other than chemises on. He, I am sure, was as embarrassed as I would have been to have them in his room like that, he having wished to show them only his rare butterflies but for a moment, as he told Mama. Both Jane and Muriel ran then into the bathroom, saying that they wished to bathe. Poor Papa's face was quite suffused, for I know well how a man can blush in anger in such a fell circumstance. He had merely tried to educate them, as I told Mama. I had to interfere, for Papa would not answer her—had too much pride; I understood. A man must guard his morals often with a silent tongue lest he be not properly understood.

Sylvia shows herself to be more forward with her aunts now here. She enjoys her pony and insists on riding it with legs astride the saddle, though I have told her it is quite unladylike. She does not seem to realise that when she mounts and dismounts, one can see her drawers. She lets Rose ride the creature also. Gazing idly through the window, as I oftimes do, I was horrified to see that Rose wears no drawers, for she cocks her leg up high in getting on the pony.

'You must speak to her, or Muriel must', I said to Jane.

'No, dear, you are the master of the house. You cannot choose your duties, no more than a woman can. I will send her into you', she said, and smirked. I quite distinctly saw her smirk.

Then Rose appeared, I knew not what to say. I could not bring myself to use the word 'drawers' and so contented myself with 'insufficient clothing'. To my astonishment the girl replied, 'Oh, sir, it is the custom in the summer. We both leaves them off sometimes. The saddle is nice and smooth, besides. It does not scour our bottoms, sir, at all'.

The girl looked straight at me as she replied.

'It is not what I prefer', said I, whereat my daughter rushed within and said, 'Oh, Rose, come quickly! Aunty Muriel is riding now!'

'Wait, Sylvia', I said. I meant to speak with her in turn. She did not hear me and rushed out again. I drew apart the curtains, made to call to Muriel. In that instant she had one foot in the stirrup and the other raised high up. She, too, did not wear that garment of the greatest intimacy that every lady should. I saw that which no gentleman should see and found myself to be as deeply flushed as Papa was that far-off day.

I shall pray for them, and in the morning I shall speak to them. I must summon up the courage so to do.

Alas, I must add a footnote here which follows on a restless night. I spoke to Muriel first. The others seemed evasive, as I thought.

'As to your attire beneath your clothes', I said. Before I could say more, she tipped her head back and she laughed.

'Why, have you looked, you naughty man?', she asked, and then flounced out. And I am senior to her by six years!

I trust they will not stay beyond a week.

Jane's Day-Book

Oh-la-la! Phillip has seen dear Muriel's bottom now—as also Rose's and Sylvia's white drawers. I have told her it is too warm to wear such things. She did not mind my saying that and left them off today.

I meant to write, though, of the girl at the Fortescues'—lest I forget. Oh, such a slender, pretty thing she was. People were kissing, fondling, everywhere, at which she seemed bemused and shy and stood alone, hands at the wall, gazed from one couple to another, and was flushed.

I drew her quietly out into the morning room by dint of saying it was quieter there. Indeed, we were alone. I closed the door and, once within, embraced her and began to kiss her lips. How moist and smooth and velvety they were!

'No, do not, oh!', she gasped, for I had pressed her up against the wall and urged my breasts and thighs against her own. She is about twenty, I surmise, and so quivery did her tummy feel that I guessed she had not been mounted yet, which for a girl of that age is extremely rare.

'How pretty you are, dear', I murmured on and on, her mouth constantly escaping mine but ever then recaptured. Then light flooded in the darkened room. Our host appeared and cast his arms around both, saying that it was truly the most enticing thing to see two women kissing as we were. Thereat he raised both her gown and mine and, to her horror, felt around our knickered cheeks. She uttered a soft shriek—something that Muriel and I had never done when we were much below her age. 'Do not!', she moaned which made me all the more determined that she should.

'Hold her shoulders!', I instructed him, for in such moments etiquette is flown.

'No, no—no, don't!', she whined. He had her fast, I falling to my knees and eager for the feast. Soft words of reassurance came from him, though in his lust to see more of her thighs at least, he held one arm across her throat and gripped her chin. I heard her spluttering beneath his lips, hoisted her dress completely and took down her drawers which proved to be of the finest silk.

'You shame me! Oh, my god!', she cried. Ignoring her, I pinched her thighs to bring them more apart and licked my tongue beneath her well-plumped quim, and tasted nectar.

'Give me a moment at her slit', I breathed. I held her bottom cheeks apart, for such a hold secures a maiden well. Her rosehole came then to my fingertips. I soothed the tight and wrinkled aperture, at which she jerked and thus allowed my tongue to play the more beneath her cunnylips.

"I will fuck her in a moment; bring her on', said Norman Fortescue, at which she screeched a louder, wilder cry.

'How horrid! Oh, please, no—oh, let me go!'

I licked the more and felt her cunny open like a flower to my intruding tongue. Her bottom wriggled, bumped—her breath hissed out. Her musky saltiness was on my lips. The taste enrages with desire.

'Come—get her on the floor. You hold her shoulders, I her legs', said Fortescue with all the delicacy of an awoken male. Yet even so I did not mind his words. I had been taken thus myself at first and never had regretted it. Some women like a roughness—some do not. I had not needed to be held, yet much enjoyed to be so, with a hand upon my mouth lest I should squeal and lest Mama should hear. Dark was the dining room that night; a single candle burned—but I must not divert. I wished to make her spurt before he probed her nest, but of a sudden the door opened once again and—of all people—our hostess appeared, her unexpected entry being such that the girl was loosed and sprang away, legs twisting in her knickers as she did.

'No, Norman, no—it is too soon for Ethel yet', exclaimed his wife, though in a tone of one who bears a mite of news rather than a stern reproach. 'Help me pull her drawers up, Jane. You are really very naughty, both of you.'

The distraught girl (or so she made to be) cried out, but we restored her modesty, I believing—as I still do—she would have been better to be spermed, for her quim was moist and ready for the manly tool. Her modesty thus veiled again, she rushed out into the drawing room—no doubt to the surprised amusement of the guests, or such as were not fully occupied.

'Really, Norman, I thought that I had told you', his wife said. Rather sheepishly he made to grab at her, but—being repulsed—made haste to hide his rigid prick which in the heated moments he had fingered out. Thereat, and in the manner of a mournful confidence, Patricia Fortescue explained to me that Ethel was 'reserved', which was to say that she was not to be threaded until the day, a few months hence, when she reached her majority when several cocks that had waited long their chance would spout their pleasure up into her nest.

'I have never heard of such a thing', I said.

'Nor I, my dear—it is a family thing. I know not why and do not care so long as she remains intact till then. I gave my word upon the thing'.

'Why is she here?', I asked. Patricia shrugged.

'To tickle her imagination, I suppose', said she. Norman snorted, said it was a nonsense, then he ambled out, leaving the tingling taste of Ethel on my tongue.

'At least it is *piquant*', Patricia said and laughed. I thought it a bizarre event, and wonder if the truth was told—if I were being made a market of, though that I doubt.

Encountering Ethel in the drawing room, once again, I remarked quickly to her, 'What a dear, sweet thing you are'. She looked astounded. I believe my words had as

Sylvia's Day-Book

Phillip's Day-Book

Muriel asked me after dinner whether I am 'moral' in my tales. I answered her abruptly. Sylvia was there.

'Do not be too much so, Phillip', she replied, and winked at me as a loose woman might.

'We had best talk about that in my study', I declared, having nothing else to say upon the subject before Sylvia.

'Yes, we would both like that', said Jane. I thought them serious and so acceded to her wish. They read part of my manuscript, and Muriel had the effrontery to say that it was 'stuffy'. I hated her for that and always will. A childishness in me, perhaps, but I cannot help the quick reactions that my sisters both arouse in me.

'You would have me write of other things?', I asked as stiffly as I could. One does not accede to women in such things.

'You should write of passion and of love requited. Never do your couples kiss', said Jane to my profound astonishment. I rose in anger but they bade me sit again, said I was in a huffy mood, the which of course I hastened to deny. At that moment Sylvia entered to say goodnight. She kissed her aunts. I rose and kissed her cheek. I could not fail to notice they had kissed her on the mouth, but could not bring myself to say.

'You do not kiss her properly on the mouth?', asked Jane.

'Good heavens, let us have no more of this', I remonstrated. Sylvia had gone to bed. I found myself ensconced with them. Their breasts are always half-bared by their evening gowns. I pointedly avoid not looking there.

'Uncle Reggie always used to kiss us lovingly upon the lips. You never saw him kiss us lovingly and long upon the lips?', came then from Muriel who was clearly trying to provoke.

'Frankly your salacity is such that I do not wish to listen, Muriel. Uncle Reggie was a man of pious ways, just as Papa was. Neither would have entertained such, such...' I could not find the word I wished to say.

'Oh, *innocence*! Or do you blind yourself, Phillip? Are you a mole beneath the earth of life? Neither was so pious as you think. At least they did not neglect their women, as you do'. And this from Jane who glared at me.

'This interview is at an end', I said, whereat both laughed in scorn at me and made me flush exactly as Papa had done upon the afternoon of which I spoke and of which I still have tightlipped memories.

'Is it, indeed? I was not aware that interviews took place between close kin. Phillip, you will accompany us tomorrow. We will show you proof. Yes, proof, my dear—and do not sit there like some stupid owl. Oh, do not fear. We shall not say a word to Sylvia—unless you mean to show your stubbornness', said Muriel, and then stood up, and Jane did, too. I feared—yes feared—what they might do. The urge to tell them to leave my house was on my lips. Instead of that I shamelessly was dumb. Often enough such females make one fight for the appropriate words that only come after they have left. Besides, they were clearly bluffing. Uncle Reggie and our parents sadly were no more.

'You may show me what you will', I said, 'Then I will know your lies for what they are'.

'Oho, we are come to bitterness, and even about a lovesome thing, are we? We have both thrown the gauntlet down, Phillip. We shall all go into town straight after lunch', Muriel threw at me and then to my relief they both went out and left me trembling in a quiet rage.

Sylvia's Day-Book

Sometimes I lie down on my bed with Rose. I do not think she should be a servant, and I told her so. She told me about poor people, though, and how there was no room for her at home. That made me very sad. I wanted to give her money from my purse. She would not take it. Often we cuddle, and sometimes we kiss. I like to feel her mouth. She likes mine, too. We put our skirts up with our legs together, just a little bit. 'It's nice', she says, and wanted to kiss my titties through my dress, and so I let her. Oh, they tingled when she did! I felt so funny that I let her do it more. She undid my dress. I said, 'Oh, Rose!' She said, 'Come on, Miss, it feels nice'. I let her and she sucked my nipples until they were stiff and I felt funny, faint. I have told her she could call me by my Christian name when we're alone. She looked so happy when I told her that. She licked my breasts and said she would be a servant to me all my life.

CHAPTER THREE

Phillip's Day-Book

I was reluctant to accompany them today upon this so-called visit, but they had remarked to Sylvia that we were going out, and hence I could not find excuse to her to change my mind. In any case, I wished to purchase writing paper in the town. The stationery shop there is a favourite haunt, as is the bookshop where the stock is good, though the owner is not what I would term a scholar's man. He entertains some customers sometimes in a room behind the premises. I know not why, unless they too are in the trade. They do not seem to buy books from the shop, though often carry parcels out on re-appearing from behind his private door. It is not my business. One does not enquire.

'Whence are we going?', I asked Muriel. She replied that I would 'see', and had the carriage stop behind the smaller of the two hotels, for 'that was what we used to do', she said, and made great mystery of that which I felt was intended to arouse a curiousity in me I did not really feel. Then down the High Street was I led and into a small street beside that rejoices in the name of Cobbler's Way.

At a small house halfway we stopped. The door was grimy and the paint was peeled. I had no desire to go within, but Jane was behind me, Muriel in front. The bell was pulled.

'What is the purpose of this?', I enquired. Neither replied, and then a woman in an apron let us in. The hall was carpeted but frosty. Cheap prints hung upon the walls. A staircase loomed ahead of us.

'There's three of you?', the woman asked, presumably to show that she could count.

'You remember us?', asked Muriel. The woman frowned and cocked her head, then Muriel took her bonnet off and shook her hair down and bent and murmured something in her ear.

'Oh, Miss, it's you again! Five years it's bin at least, and this is your sister, too. Leastways, and with your pardon, Miss, I always thought you was', she said to Jane.

'And the gentleman who always came with us? Do you remember him?', asked Muriel. The door was closed. We edged within. I felt my neck flush and was uncomfortable.

'Oh, I dunno, Miss. Men, they comes and goes. Now, let me think. He had a black beard—did he?—yes, I'm sure he did. Real toff 'e was, just as your gentleman is now', the woman said to my distinct disdain as she looked at me.

'Do you remember flowers?', asked Jane whose hand uncomfortably pressed at my back.

'Flowers? Oh gawd, yes, I remembers now! A posy 'e always give me. What a gentleman 'e was! No one ever give me posies, Miss, before or since. I got it now—you always came on Thursdays, didn't you? Bottles of wine you brought, and give me money to buy glasses. Basket on your arm you 'ad. A real nice wicker one, it was. You left it 'ere the last time. I still got it, if you want. Used it a bit, Miss—hoped you wouldn't mind'.

All this I heard, my mind somewhat a-reel. Thursdays—a basket—I remembered that. It was six years now since Uncle Reggie passed away. He was the youngest of our mother's brothers. Died of cholera, poor chap. We could never understand where he got that.

'I remember something, too', said Jane. We had moved while speaking into a small front room of incredibly small proportions, and so much cluttered we could scarcely move.

'What's that, Miss, eh?' The woman looked anxious for a moment, but my sister smiled.

'The wallpaper just behind the bed upstairs had wine thrown on it once. Oh, not by us, as you well know, but I remember that it left a stain. Is it still there?'

'Yes, Miss, it is. I meant to cover it, I never did. Won't put you out, will it?' A wrinkling of her brow again.

'It never did. Now, let me see', said Jane with deliberate slowness and glanced at me, then added to the woman, 'Four shillings you charged him for two hours. I think that's right?'

'Two hours, Miss, always. Prompt you were. Well, nearly always. Once or twice it turned out to be almost three. Your gentleman always paid me for that, though. Give me an extra bob or two sometimes as well. You don't meet many like that, Miss. I've know 'em argue for an extra 'alf an hour sometimes. Got bleedin' cheek they 'ave—begging your pardon, sir', she said to me, then added to my horror, 'Two hours now you'll want, for old times sake, Miss?'

'Not today, but may we peep? Just to revive old memories. Here's half-a-crown for your trouble. We'll be no more than ten minutes, then won't bother you'.

'No bother, Miss. It's nice to see old customers return. Begging your pardon, I mean guests'.

'Of course you do', said Muriel and laughed. 'Come, *dear*', she then said to me in a rather biting tone and we turned about like mussels in the self-same shell.

I had no wish to ascend the narrow stairs, but "Thank you, Miss, for the money', the woman said and closed her door.

'I have no wish to go up', I then hissed. Jane got again behind me, prodded me. I was distinctly worried they would make a row and let the woman hear.

'You will, though', Muriel said and bustled up, her bottom large before my face. On the small landing she stopped and pointed to a door. 'There is a basin in there where we used to wash and tidy up ourselves, Phillip. This is the bedroom here. The other one we never entered into.

It's the woman's. Come! Remember what I said about the stain?'

She preceded me. I had no choice. Jane had the impudence to punch my back. The door opened and I saw a large, iron bed with brass rails at both ends, brass knobs on top. a mirrored stand and two old chairs were facing it against the further wall. The stain was there upon old, faded paper of quite hideous flowers that twined among a painted trellis of a sort. The floor was black and there were threadbare rugs.

'The brass knob on the end, it used to rattle. Listen', Muriel said and shook the rail a little bit. The knob tinkled till she took her hand away.

'I do not wish to know', I said. I had too many bitter thoughts. I pushed past Jane and ascended as quietly as I could. My sisters stayed for a moment. I could hear them whispering. Jane giggled—so did Muriel. Then to my utter alarm the woman appeared, wiping her hands upon her apron still.

'Nice gals they are. You don't wish to stay?', she asked. I felt disdainful of her horrid leer and shook my head.

'They are not girls, but ladies', I replied at last, but forced the words.

'Didn't mean no *imprudeness*, sir', she said, when she obviously meant 'impertinence'.

My sisters then came rustling down. They'd heard what I had said and laughed.

'He is jealous, Mrs. White', said Muriel, and thereat, in a rage, I strode to the door and went beyond.

"'Ow nice, 'ow lovely! Still, you'll come back, won't you? You've already paid your first hour', the woman called, but I already striding up the street and was full ashamed that such words should be spoke. Indeed in my anger I hailed a cab and then remembered that our carriage waited, so I turned towards the old hotel, the cabby calling something after me such as I could not lower myself to answer.

I reached it a full minute before my sisters did, was minded not to wait, but then regretfully decided that I must. They entered at last without a word and sat quite silent as I hoped they would.

'Oh, *you* remember, Phillip, well enough', said Jane as the carriage turned into the High Street once again.

'You will both leave my house tonight', I said and stared away from them and pursed my lips.

'We never travel by night, my dear', said Muriel and yawned infuriatingly, for I knew it was not real. They knew I had no power to throw them out, for Sylvia would know, or worse—if she did not—they would say that it was my fault and might say—as often had my once-beloved—that I was moody, dull, and quarrelsome. Moreover, in the cunning way of women they had guessed that I remembered certain things. Thursdays had always been their 'visiting day', they'd said, and Uncle Reggie was their so-called chaperone. They took—in the very basket I recalled—both cakes and wine 'for the poor cottagers', and frequently did not return till dusk. Several times Mama had wished to accompany them, but always they said that it would bore her. Yes—the memories came back and were as bitter aloes in my mouth.

The silence in the carriage was alarming, but I would not break it. For a half an hour we rode, and Muriel sometimes hummed just to infuriate me more. 'You are horrible—are wanton', I wished to shout, but somehow kept my tongue. I sensed the sarcastic answers that I would receive, and that they would not further my cause. I went up to my room and stayed. I heard them laughing downstairs with Sylvia. I fear from hour to hour what they might say to lay a blight upon her innocence.

Amy Mansfield's Day-Book

I saw Richard kissing Mama today. She had her skirt up and his hand was on her leg. I shall not speak to them for weeks. I don't like Liverpool so much as I first did. I want to go back home. Mama said no. I would write to

Papa and tell him, but I know that I cannot. Mama asked me why I was so quiet. I wouldn't tell her, but she kept on and on until I did not know what to say. It was because of Liverpool, I said. 'No, no, there's something else', she said, and then I blurted out that I saw Richard scratch her leg. I did not know what else to say. 'Oh, I had a gnat bite there, and he came in. He was being silly, Amy, scratching it for me. I pushed him off. Some boys are silly somctimes, don't you know', she said. I told her I was sorry then, but I didn't see her push him off. I didn't say that *last* bit, though. I'm glad I didn't write to Papa after all. Mama says she writes all our news, but I never see her take a letter to the post.

Deirdre's Day-Book

I trust that Amy is not becoming sly. I must confess I felt myself infused with guilt at what she told me yesterday, but then curiously enough my emotions altered. In order to have seen she must have peeped through the crack between the door frame and the door instead—as one might have supposed—of simply walking in the drawing room. I have told Richard he will have no more cuddles (a euphemism for naughtiness that both of us employ). He looked most glum. Amy had witnessed that which she should not have done, I said. It mollified my statement, as I thought, but did not stop him brooding all the day, and I felt glum myself in different ways.

A diversion occurred, though, yesterday, I having become acquainted with a gentleman of good address who helped me when I slipped upon the cobblestones. Indeed, he saved me from a fall, and then accompanied me to a coffee house, inviting me to drink to calm my shock.

I find him most *simpatico* indeed. He shares my own age and is robust in his frame. He had lately read Mr. Carroll's charming work and vaunted his idea of speaking freely for 'cabbages and kings', said the gentleman, meant that all topics should be free. I acquiesced in that, to his delight, while expressing apologies as to any forwardness that I might show in choosing terms that ladies do not use.

'That is precisely what I seek, my dear', he uttered and looked quite enchanted, praised my face and figure, and my dress. 'I confess to you, Madame', he continued in all seriousness, 'that my dear wife and I are what we call Libertarians and have gathered a few like-minded gentlefolk around us to the ends of—may I say it?—pleasure such as prim Society abhors, or I would rather say, pretends to, since so many lack but opportunity. May I invite you to meet my lady? You may discuss such even more freely with her than you can with me'.

'Oh, I am not a loose woman! Neither, of course, can she be. We shall only talk', said I, though my heart was quite a-flutter at the thought of finding those of my own turns of mind.

'Let us away then', he uttered to my astonishment, whereupon, despite some gentle protests on my part, I found myself whisked off in a cab to his residence which was not far away. And there I was greeted by the most delightful lady by the name of Eveline.

'Another convert, my dear', her husband said when introducing us.

'Oh, as to that, I do not know', I laughed, but such immediacy of friendliness there was that I was soon uncoated, gloves and bonnet off and invited to take sherry with the two.

Eveline has an hourglass figure despite having two daughters and a son. Her hair is invariably combed up high which leaves her swanlike neck in all its glory to be seen. Her breasts are weighty and her bottom full. Maurice, the husband, had as she said engaged her attention first in Rome the year before. Both their partners being deceased, they took to one another amourously and were soon wed. Maurice has a son and daughter of his own.

'I gained heaven when I married her', he said, and perched upon the side support of her armchair—he bent her head back and kissed her fully on the mouth. Had Phillip ever done that to me in front of others, oh how pleased I would have been! I have a penchant to be *watched* sometimes when an amourous mood is on me.

'A heaven with several mansions, dear', his wife said and then she laughed. I clearly was meant to raise my eyebrows in enquiry, and I did. My third glass of sherry was at hand. I felt emboldened.

'In what way?', I asked, and felt my question foolish and naive, but evidently it pleased them both. Eveline rose and walked across to me. I somehow knew the manner of that walk and placed my glass down on a table near my chair. She then bent over me and placed a hand beneath my chin. My eyes melted into hers. I saw a twinkle there.

'Come again tomorrow afternoon and you will see', she said, then asked in a much softer voice, 'May I kiss you to set the seal thereon?'

I knew that she would kiss my mouth while Maurice watched. He had the hawklike eagerness. To taunt her a little I did not reply, but parted my lips in readiness. O sweet and soft her mouth! Our lips met, tongues touched, I felt her gathering up my dress but swiftly pushed her hand away even as she bared my knees.

'No! Please, not yet', I said, my face averted. A small silence fell and then she took her hand away, unbent and soothed my dress back down.

'Tomorrow afternoon at three?', she asked.

I rose unsteadily, and Maurice smiled. 'Kiss her again', he urged. His eyes were bright—not illumined solely, though, by lust, but by a seeming fondness for us both.

'I shall tomorrow; she knows that', I said, and Eveline clapped her hands and laughed, said, 'Oh, I like you *very* much! You will come, won't you? Yes, I know you will. Maurice will fetch you in our carriage, if you wish'.

'No, I shall bring my own', I said. I had no wish to be dependent on them so, however agreeable might their company be. Besides, I then could leave at such hour as I wished.

Maurice escorted me into the hall. 'She will have your

drawers down if you come', he said, but put no lechery into his tone.

'If I stay long enough for that', I taunted him. The atmosphere was warm and free. I felt no fretful urgings on their part such as I had had sometimes in youth when jovial lusty males made free with me, whether I wanted them to or not.

'Our carriage will take you home, my dear', said he, and courteously escorted me to it.

Had Phillip only been thus too, what a wondrous marriage we might have had!

Richard's Day-Book

Mama came home yesterday in a most curious mood and would not say where she had been. She hummed and sang, but much avoided me. Amy was spiteful to me all the day and had her nose up in the air. I care not what she thinks in any case. I pleaded with Mama to let me kiss her, but she would not do, and said we should not do it any more. I ruffled her and she got quite fierce and in a paddy.

'May I not cuddle you tonight', I asked.—'No, you may not, dear Richard, no. There must come an end to naughtiness', she said. I was quite bereft and wished we had a pretty maid whom I could tumble, but the only one we have is dry and plain. I have a plan though for tonight. I only wish to kiss my dear Mama, but she will not believe that that is all I intend. I knelt and kissed her legs.

'Oh, Richard, please don't press me, dear', she said and went upstairs and locked her door.

If I carry out my plan, I'm sure she will.

CHAPTER FOUR

Muriel's Day-Book

Poor Phillip—I feel almost guilty that we have so confounded him, but it is time he learned the truth about the world.

'What is the trouble with Papa?', asked Sylvia, for he would not speak to anyone and took his meal upstairs, which did not please the serving maid at all. He grumbled at her that the food was cold, which it was not.

I said to Sylvia that men had moods upon them often when they could not get what they wanted.—'What does Papa want?', she asked innocently, but was pleased that we allowed her wine, which Phillip will not let her drink.

'Oh his winky-wink is not being exercised', laughed Jane. She goes beyond herself sometimes, and Sylvia of course asked what that was.

'His business *thing*', I said, which was in part the truth, and Sylvia took on an air of lovely innocence.—'I don't know what that is', she said, and added in quite a grown-up manner for her age, 'I think I will go and talk to him'. I believe the wine had gone a little to her head. We did not dissuade her. It could do no harm, and might indeed have brought Phillip back downstairs. She came down looking mournful, though, and said he would not let her sit upon his lap, or not for long, for she had tried.

'What a bad man he is', said I, though in as light a

manner as I could. We retired then to the drawing room, and Jane said she would go and see if Phillip wanted anything.

'I wouldn't talk to him if I were you', said Sylvia. She had also had a sweet liqueur and was bolder with her tongue than I had known her. This did not displease me, though, for she was even more receptive to a cuddle then. I had her on the sofa in my arms. Jane looked at us and went upstairs.

'You have a sweetness on your tongue. May I not suck it off?', I asked our niece.

'It's nice', she said and pouted and was clearly in a frisky mood, a trifle flirtatious even. Some girls *are* at that age, both with men and women, which I like.

'Let me share the sweetness, then'. I tickled her and bore her back upon the chaise longue, lifting up her legs so that she reclined full length, I saying that she should be kissed like a Princess and she asking, all a-giggling, when her Prince would come.—'Do not be so much concerned with gender as desire', I said, and asked, 'Now, shall I kiss your upper or your lower mouth?'

The minx divined what I was at, I'm sure, but pretended innocence and said she had no lower mouth. In a moment I had demonstrated otherwise and plunged my face between her silky thighs, and to such astonishment on her part that she did not resist. O sweet-lipped haven that I found! I burrowed in my tongue; she moaned and flailed her legs; I thrust both back and held them so and licked around and within her furrow all the time until I heard such whimpering noises as one loves to hear. Her bottom bucked. I cupped it on my palms and tickled up her darling spot.

'What are you, what are you, what are you d . . . d . . . d . . . ?', she choked all in one breath.

'Pleasuring you, my sweet, for the first time. You will remember long this day. Hold your legs back—let me lick it up and down'.

'Goo-goo!', she gasped, and was clearly coming on to heat. The lips were puffy where my tongue had licked—

her little, bursting bud erect.—'I f. . . f. . . feel oh funny, aunty! What is happening to me? Aaaah!' And then she sprinkled with a sharp, fine salty rain as my tongue worked the more and brought her on. I heard her moan, hiss in her breath, her knees bent over my shoulders, her heels kicked and then were still, my lips all rimmed with creaminess of her.

I rose and cast myself upon her then. Her hands clutched at my arms—she gazed in trembling wonder deep into my eyes.

'You came, my pet, you have expended your first juice of love, and will the more under my tutelage. Now, slip your tongue into my mouth and let me feel it work about my own. There . . . good!' Her tits had hardened—both her nipples stiff. I worked the buttons loose and slipped my hand within the while our lips were meshed together, warm and moist. She bleated, sobbed into my mouth.

'Do you want to come again?', I asked. I leaned up and rubbed her sticky fur. Her legs lay straight, quicsccntly apart. There was adoration in her eyes.

'It's n . . . n . . . naughty, isn't it?', she asked. Her tongue denied that which her lips spoke.

'*Very*, darling, that is why it is so nice', I told her, but decided then to tease and simply caressed her stockinged legs and lay beside her and once again, drawing up my own gown as I did so, our bellies pressed their shimmering surfaces together while my nest brushed all around her plump young mount.

'Papa may come', she murmured wonderingly.

'Then he will see our bottoms, pet, and much besides', I replied to her great wonderment. I eased a finger underneath her cunny lips and made her quiver while I spoke. 'Put your finger in between my legs in the same way. Come, I will teach you love, and so will Jane. Then we will have much more fun, all three of us.' How small her slim form felt! I caressed the pert, tight bottom cheeks that, lying face to face with me, she could not help but proffer to my other hand. 'Now rub', I said. She breathed into my mouth, was all a-daze. I rolled upon her, urged my lovelips to her own and moved my belly suavely over hers, telling her to wrap her legs up round my hips, the which she did and clung beneath.—'So many cocks this little cunt of yours will have', I said. I could not help myself—the words flew loose.

'Huh? Wha . . . aaart?', she moaned. I did not think she heard me clear. I had her bottom cheeks again and pried the springy halves apart. Our mouths were liquid fire, tongues lashed. I sucked upon the tip of hers and felt her tummy ripple under mine. Her head hung back; her mouth was open wide.—'Ha! Hooo! Woh-woh!', she sobbed, and then we spent love's juices in a mingling flow that made our cunny lips rub the more together, smooth as silk, all puffy at the rims, filled with delight.

I sank upon her. Both her legs had slipped, were splayed, heels dug into the couch's red brocade. We trickled, moaned together, and were done. I held her down, my weight upon her own. Then Jane's voice sounded, 'Oh! What have we here?'

Sylvia cried out. I clamped her mouth beneath my palm. Her eyes bulged and tried to close her legs, but could not for my own were deep between.

'The little darling! Has she come?', Jane asked. She perched beside us, smacked my naked bottom, fondled it, felt for my bottomhole and tickled round the rim.

'Twice, dear, and will again'. I eased my palm away. I feared a squeal. Instead, Sylvia stared at both of us, most of her slim form hidden under mine. She bit her lip, blushed red, and turned her face into the wall.

'You had best take her up', I said. I knew that lantern gleam in Jane's dear eyes, but cautiously drew Sylvia's gown down as I rose, fluffed out my own and drew the flushed girl up, she rising awkwardly and shy.

'It is nice to be kissed. I always think it is', Jane told her disarmingly, and murmured to her, 'Shall we go upstairs?' Sylvia nodded, was embraced, and leaned her head coltishly into Jane's shoulder. At the door, Jane turned and winked at me and tossed me something which I caught. It was a key. Had she dared what I though she might have done? I let her and Sylvia disappear into Jane's room and then ventured quietly up. As I suspected, Phillip's door was closed. I turned the handle gently. It was locked. I knew that the fact that Jane had given me the key meant that I was to enter.

On doing so, I found Phillip huddled up on his black couch along the wall beside his desk. He had his back to me and faced the wall, was curled up like a child.

'What are you at?', I asked as brashly as I could, and closed the door and turned the key again. He did not answer me. I bent and touched him on the shoulder. He appeared to me asleep at first and wished to give that impression, I am sure.

'Phillip?', I asked again. For a moment I felt a tremor of anxiety, then pressed upon his shoulder to make him turn. He would not do so. 'What?', I asked as foolishly as one does in such silent situations. Bending over him more and placing one knee just behind his hips, I noticed that his trousers were undone and that the knob of his prick was peeping out. Then of a sudden he began to cry in huge sobs like a child. No tears, just sobs. I turned him on his back and sat beside him and said sharply, 'Phillip!'

'Go away. Oh, my god, go away!', he moaned, but I sensed no real strength in his tone and so, plumping my bottom on the edge of the couch, I forced him over to look up at me, at which he made a feeble move to cover up his Peeping Tom.

'You naughty boy, what are you at?', I asked. I had no doubt that Jane's hand had preceded mine and that hers indeed had forced open the gap by guile, persuasiveness or coaxing.

'Mummy cuddle Phillip?', I asked. I know not why such words came to my lips, but they seemed to suit his mournful look and the situation which hung rather upon my acts than any that he might intend.

I thrust my legs up on to the couch and lay alongside him with my knees to his.

'Has naughty Jane been teasing you?', I wheedled. A tremendous gasp came from him as I palmed his prick and drew it from its hiding place, then plunged my tongue into his flaccid mouth. He jerked just as a girl does. 'Muriel play with it?', I breathed into his lips.

'I hate you—hate you both', he moaned.

'Of course you do, of course you do. Oh my, it's getting big now, isn't it?'

His cock indeed began to swell. His mouth was open to my tongue. He gurgled, but his arms lay limp. He clearly knew not whether he was in Hell or Paradise.

'Come on, come on, you naughty boy', I urged. The swollen rod pulsed more within my hand. I moved my fingers lightly up and down its girth and felt the veins all starting up. 'Muriel is going to make it nice', I said. I knew it not at the time, but I had chanced exactly on the words that fitted his dark mood—such inner longings as he has. He choked his sobs the more and worked his mouth to the sensuous encouragement of mine.

'No, no!', he gurgled as I felt him pulse the more. The night was lost for Phillip, though. I inched my gown up, brought my stockinged knee beneath his balls which I had wheedled out. My tongue worked more deeply in his mouth.—'I c . . . c . . . can't', he sobbed.

'You can—you must. Be a good boy and let it come', I said. Our noses rubbed, his loins were all a-twitch. —'Put your hand up between my legs', I whispered.

'Oh god, no! How wicked! Stop, I beg you stop—you must!', he groaned, but I—impatient—seized his limp right hand and brought it high beneath my skirt where he could feel my thighs above my stocking tops. 'Oh, sin!', came his weak moan.

'Feel Muriel's naughty thing, you silly boy', said I. I had seduced a few young boys more easily than I could my older brother—felt amusement and excitement both at once. I made his fingertips brush underneath my furry quim. He felt its stickiness, the parted lips, his face a mask of sensual agony.—'Come, darling—Uncle Reggie always used to come with both of us', I murmured, 'Do it, Phillip—do it in your sister's hand'.

'Gar-ah!', he choked. He seized my neck and brought

my mouth down savagely on his, sobbing the while in long and breathless gasps, and then he spouted in a fine, long arc. I raised my face to see. The long, thick strings of sperm shot in the air and splashed down on my wrist.

'Oh, my lovely boy! How nice it is to do it, is it not? Think of Uncle Reggie doing it in both our nests', I said.

'No, no! My god! Ah-OOOH!' He spouted then again—thrice more his jets arced out and then the weakening flood laid more cream on the cuff of my blue dress. I rolled upon him then and pinned him down, feeling his cock a-throb against my bush.

'There, there, good Phillip—what a lovely lot you did! Now you go sleepy-byes, my pet, and Muriel will do it to you in the morning, if you're good'.

'We are in sin!', he moaned.

My patience almost broke at that. I worked myself up from him, tickled his thick, sticky worm, then wiped my wrist upon his trouser leg and slipped without, leaving the key this time within the lock. Going to my room, I removed my dress, chemise and shoes, tightened my stockings and took myself on tiptoe to Jane's room. As I expected, the two lay naked in the bed.

'Is she not lovely? I have made her come again', said Jane. The two lay breasts to breasts. Sylvia quivered in her grasp and closed her eyes. I climbed in on the other side of our dear niece and sandwiched her between us.

'Put the tip of your finger in her bottomhole. She needs it there', said Jane.

'I d . . . d . . . don't!', squealed Sylvia. Her rose was moist between her tight, pert cheeks. I rubbed my finger round the crinkled orifice.

'You are going to learn to have to have it there', said I. Jane lifted up Sylvia's upper leg and brought it over her own hip. I urged my finger in a little bit and felt her squeeze on it protectively. Jane fingered Sylvia's oily honeypot. The dear child whimpered, came again—then I knelt over her and made her lick my cunny which she did quiescently until I sprinkled her with dew.

Richard pumped me last night, all against my will—O wicked boy. He hid beneath my dressing table where the covers drape! I did not see nor hear him and undressed, believing him to be abed. Naked I was when he sprang out unclothed, and I with my back to him and seeking out my nightdress from beneath my pillows. I screeched in my surprise, and surely Amy must have heard.—'No, Richard, no!', I pleaded softly, fearing she would come. He had me tumbled down upon the bed, my bottom up against his throbbing tool.

'Be quiet, Mama, I beg you—let me put it in', he choked.

How long we wrestled, fought, I do not know, I weakening all the time to feel his cock all rigid up against my flesh. I cried. He kissed my tears away, forced me upon my back and lay upon my belly, pleading on and on till I succumbed, O shamefully succumbed, and let the knob slip up between my lips. One urging thrust and it was in. My feet hung down upon the floor, I breathing broken sobs into his mouth.

Slowly he did it to me—long, slow strokes while I exerted suction on his prick, moaning my little moans of pleasure that I did not wish to feel. He sucked my nipples, spread my legs more, coaxed me on with devilish whispers of desire until I clasped him, fell headlong into the spell of it, working my bottom to his eager thrusts.

'Don't come too soon', I murmured all despite myself. Oh that my tongue should run away with me! We are possessed who cannot help ourselves. He pressed his cheek against my own, panted and worked his loins more slowly back and forth, holding his spermatic impulse back as best he could.

'You wanted me to do it to you, did you not', he husked into my ear. His balls slapped at my bottom as he jerked—slap-smack of flesh, the creaking of the bed. I answered him by raising up my legs and wound them tight about his waist. Our breathing sounded coarsely. Thrice I wet his balls. I would not speak, though, any more, would not. I was both witness and participant—lay under him and yet gazed at the same time down at both of us, the twitching of his buttocks, the slow gliding of his cock, his balls that gently slapped against my bottom's cleft. I looked amazed at what I saw—knew myself to be cloaked both in sin and at the same time in the freedom of delight. One wrestles endlessly with both, yet reaches out a weak hand to the latter all the time.

'Coming!', I heard him choke and squeezed the tighter on his pulsing tool.

How simple are the acts of love, yet how we clothe them in complexity by thinking all about and here and there as to what we should do and should not!

I would soon as listen to the 'shoulds' as to the 'nots'. It is Phillip, and others such as he, who crucify themselves upon the negative. Perhaps in sin I seek revenge for the hurts to my over-eager soul that I endured in a dry marriage bed.

At least my cunny was plump with sperm last night. Ah, should I weep therefor? I do not know.

CHAPTER FIVE

Phillip's Day-Book

Wretched was the day around me when I woke and heard the early chattering of voices down below. Such dreams of sin I had as should not come to any man who seeks to dust his soul with piety. I would remain here in my room forever, locked away from such temptations as beset me now, but I cannot. The innocence of Sylvia calls. I am her guardian angel—the lone one who can protect her now.

I dreamed of Uncle Reggie, too—that tawdry bedroom in that mean, small house.

'Do not imagine that you can see into the hearts and minds of those whom you hold dear, for you cannot', I recall that he once said to me.

His words are iron flakes upon my tongue, and should have been on his. There are stains upon my trousers; I will never get them off. I have hidden them away, tight-folded up, will never wear them any more. I shall keep cakes and biscuits in my desk that I may not have to go down too often. Alas, though, for the accidents, the incidents, of daily life. No sooner had I vowed this than Sylvia came running up, and I in my study lurking. Or, at least, I felt I lurked.

'Papa, you are late for breakfast. Shall you not come down?', she asked. I sat upon the couch that I now call

'Despair', and winsomely she sat upon my lap and coiled her sweet arms round me lovingly, the lower part of her person plump and pressing down where now both of my sinful sisters have exposed me to their view.

'In a moment I shall come down', I said, and felt discomforted, at a complete loss. She wriggles much when talking thus, does Sylvia. To my horror I felt a stirring underneath her lower part—a stirring on my part, I mean, for which I blamed both Muriel and Jane.

'Yes, do, Papa. The kidneys and the bacon are delicious—really nice. Oh, your beard is rough', she laughed and took her cheek from mine.

'My pet, I have not shaved as yet. I shall—that is to say—I shall. . . .'

I had risen with her and was conscious, hideously, of an erection in my private parts the which I prayed devoutly that she would not see, though in her innocence, as I told myself, she could not know the nature of it. Indeed, I thought her eyes dropped for a moment, then she looked away. Her lips were slightly parted. How demure she looks in such a winsome pose! Such fresh young lips, such pearly teeth. I pray they retain their purity.

'Aunt Muriel says she will purchase me a new dress today, Papa, and a new bonnet, too. She said that you will buy me stockings, if she does. Will you? I know not whether to have white or pink or blue, or even black. Aunt Jane says that darker colours are the more becoming', Sylvia chattered, leading me downstairs although I did not really wish to go.

My sisters both awaited me. I feared they would. No sooner had we entered the dining room than both sprang up and kissed me, to the great delight of Sylvia and yet to my confusion, for both called me 'dear' and insisted on my sitting down before they did. Jane unrolled my napkin and insisted on laying it across my lap, her fingers passing as she did across the slight protruberance I had.

'Oho, what have we here!', she laughed.

Sylvia looked up from sipping tea and wondered at Jane's words. As for myself I flushed. Jane's fingers lingered, though being beneath the tablecloth could not be seen. Rose entered then with a tureen which she placed down as usual on the sideboard. As she did, Jane deliberately swept the napkin to the floor and quickly sat.

'Oh, Rose, dear, will you pick up the Master's napkin?', she asked.

It had fallen forward underneath the table's edge. I blurted out that I would pick it up, but the wretched maid insisted on doing it and sprang forward like a young gazelle. I made to grab it from her fingers, but then stayed myself. To do so in front of Sylvia would have looked absurd, for I have always insisted that the maid do such. Alas, to my supreme horror Rose's hand encountered that which Jane had left more stiff. She had the grace to blush—at her young age she would—and said 'Oh, sir!' and rushed from out the room.

'What is to do?', asked Sylvia and then called, 'Rose!', and ran out after her, not asking me if she might leave the table as she ordinarily does.

'My god, what have you done—on top of all?', I asked of Muriel and Jane.

I had not meant to speak to them, but knew I must find voice at this.

'The male displays himself, my dear. It is very proper so to do in his own abode where surely he is king?', said Jane. I seared her with my eyes; she did not blink. Outside the door were whisperings.

'For god's sake fetch Sylvia back', said I, unable to get up myself in my ill-wished condition and fretful as to what things might be said by Rose whom I determined to dismiss.

'If you so wish, sir', Muriel said sarcastically, but ambled slowly out, opened the door and left it just ajar, and I forced to listen to the whisperings.

'You may *both* have to', I heard Muriel say. There was a squeak from Sylvia then. Unable to restrain myself, I bellowed out her name and she ran in.

'Finish your meal. Do not get up again until I tell you

to', I said, though scolded myself for the severity of my tone which brought a glint of tears into her eyes.

'You would do better to kiss her more often than to scold her, Phillip', Muriel said.

'Be quiet!', I said, but mollified my tone, the which astounded me. I felt uneasy and could scarcely eat. The ghost of Uncle Reggie smiled at me again.

'When your Papa was naughty', said Muriel across the table to Sylvia, 'Mama used to lock him in a cupboard until he atoned for his sins. Shall we lock him in a cupboard now?'

'Muriel, do not be ridiculous', I said. I made to push my chair back, which was fatal, for the pair rose up and seized my arms. Sylvia bit her lip and stared at us, but clearly thought it a game and smiled. Thus was I slyly placed once more in a situation I could not escape without venturing into violence, for they held my arms quite tight and pulled me up. Dear Sylvia knew not whether to smile or to look serious, but in the end her aunts' smiles won, as I feared they would.

'Naughty, naughty Phillip—come', said Jane and tugged on me and Muriel did so, too, I haplessly repeating my original words.

'Open the cupboard, Sylvia—oh, what a lovely game to start the day!', was said.

'No, Sylvia', I wished to say, but that would have dismayed her more. I forced a smile—a mirth I did not feel. Seeing me grimace so, Sylvia laughed in turn and opened up the corner cupboard from which shelves had been long removed. I had meant to have the cupboard, too, removed, and thought it an encumbrance in the room. In a moment I was turned and pushed inside. The cupboard, having double doors and being narrow, I was pressed between the sides, facing to the right. The door closed. There was darkness.

'You may atone by kissing Sylvia instead of scolding her. A proper kiss though, mind', called Muriel and therewith one door opened and with a squeal Sylvia was thrust against me, and the darkness came again.

'Oh, Papa, they are being silly. Really, though, I do not mind', said Sylvia whose lissome form was pressed too closely against mine. Indeed, she could not help but feel the eruption in my trousers to her belly pressed.

'Open the doors!', I called, thereby unwittingly dismaying Sylvia who was convinced I did not wish to kiss her.

'No! We are leaning to it', Jane called back, and indeed I felt their backs thump at the doors while Sylvia's legs quivered to mine, her forehead down against my chest as though dismayed by my refusal to 'obey'.

'You may kiss me if you want, Papa', she murmured and then raised her face. I felt the motion for I could not see. Her nose brushed underneath my chin. The honeysuckle of her breath came up to mine.

'Properly, Phillip! No pecks on the cheek', called Muriel.

'It is silly, but honestly I do not mind, Papa', whispered Sylvia. Her tummy could not help but press against that which it found below. The cupboard, being airless, both my hands were moist. I knew not where to put them, yet could scarcely move my arms in any case. I inclined my head. Our noses touched and faces blindly sought when they should not have done. O honey-sweet her lips, and moist! Boldly she merged them into mine. I held my breath. They lingered, slipped away.

'Well—has he kissed you yet?', called Jane.

'I have indeed—now let us out', I said, wherewith light shone upon us full and Sylvia fell sideways into Muriel's arms, clearly not knowing whether to stay or run away.—'She wishes to go into the garden', I said, effecting as I thought was her release. Indeed, dear Sylvia gave me a thankful glance and ran. They did not impede her. Both looked down at my unwanted display of that which they think of as manliness.

'She brought you up the more', said Jane, and with the effrontery of that remark both turned and hurried out, most craftily calling after Sylvia to wait for them.

Thus am I harried, made a joke of—worse, indeed.

For an hour or so after this ridiculous event that was no doubt meant to shame me in some way, I encountered Sylvia coming up the stairs. She was flushed and looked excited, so I thought.

'You do not have to kiss me, Papa, if you do not want', she said, and then ran in her room and locked her door.

I wished to call out that I did, in my paternalistic way, but knew that in that utterance I would be trapped by Muriel and Jane again who I was sure had put her up to say that very thing just to confuse. I am caught between she-devils and pure innocence.

Would that my once-beloved were here! I know that she would handle this. It needs another woman to outwit the pair. I cannot dismiss Rose, either, for I have no reason to offer up to Sylvia save one that would be impossible to express. Without much thought at first, but in some recompense to Sylvia, I took a ten-pound note from my wallet and slipped it underneath her door.

'That is for your clothes', I called.

There was a moment's silence, then I heard it rustle as she picked it up.

'Thank you, Papa', she called. Her tone was cool. I thought it so, but possibly my nerves were bad.

I will not have Muriel or Jane buy her anything. At least I have that one small victory, though on reflection it may not be so small, for Sylvia will know who guards her best.

Amy's Day-Book

I know they were doing something last night. I heard noises in Mama's room, and I heard Richard groan, as well. He had not been to bed—I peeped into his room. I thought I heard him say 'Coming', but that makes no sense. Perhaps he said 'Mummy', for he sometimes does, so childishly, instead of just 'Mama', which is more proper for his age.

Mama wore a lacy peignoir at breakfast. I could see her breasts, and so could he. I thought it very rude. She had pink garters on. They also showed. Her thighs are so much plumper than my own. I'm glad my own are not. I read my prayers this morning in my room. I wish that I had stayed with dear Papa.

CHAPTER SIX

Deirdre's Day-Book

A most unexpected afternoon at the home of Maurice and Eveline. Or at least, one frequently thinks such, yet upon reflection has no idea of what one's expectations were.

Eveline and I were alone for the first hour and discoursed much—and very warmly—on the philosophy of love. Such she at least calls it; I have no name for it save pleasure even though at times my conscience strikes me. Her elder daughter, Maude, joined us. She is a striking image of her mother and is twenty now. I expected, upon her appearance, for the conversation to turn and change. Maude gave all appearance, after all, of being quiet and prim, and I had no wish to tantalise the girl with what I thought she did not as yet have herself. Upon her entering, I remarked at hazard (and quite ludicrously) how small the bathroom of our new house is.

'Oh, baths—they should be large', said Eveline, divorcing the receptacle from the room, as it were, though not perhaps deliberately, and then she inclined her face to Maude and gave her an expectant look as might one actress to another who has lost her cue.

'Step-Papa told us that in Japan ladies and gentlemen bathe together', Maude said, and looked as pleased as a schoolgirl who has parsed a sentence correctly.

'Which we now sometimes do', added Eveline while I gazed at the pair askance and asked how that was possible. I meant in terms of the physical—of space—and perhaps should have added 'moral', but to do so with Eveline would have been absurd.—'A remarkable invention of my husband's; come and see', I was invited, whereupon the three of us went up.

On the first landing was a bathroom at the end of a long corridor. As we approached it, the door opened and there were clouds of steam through which a maid appeared in the manner of a vision at a pantomime. Her cap was floppy and her face was flushed.

'We shall bathe now, Mary', said Eveline.

'Yes, m'am—and shall I help you to undress'.

'Tomorrow, Mary—not today. *She has her fingers everywhere, the naughty girl, especially with Maude*', added Eveline *sotto voce* as the maid swept on, whereat we entered and the door was closed.

Ah, such a bathroom—such a bath! Maurice, it seemed, had had the sides removed from two quite large ones and then had the pair fastened together in some wise so that they formed a huge receptacle.

'It is a communal bath, my dear', said Eveline through the warm, pervasive steam, deliciously scented as it was. She and Maude then began to undress, I being invited to follow and to cast my clothes into one of four large baskets as they did. I apprehended from the number of baskets that the same number often shared the luxurious bathroom with its marble tiles, its lamps and chairs—a large chaise-longue pressed to one wall.

'There has been fun on that', Eveline said of the last-named when I cast my eyes along its length and breadth.

I did not hesitate to disrobe, wishing as I did to see both Eveline and Maude. Both had dark muffs and long and shapely legs. Maude's bottom was a rapture of firm flesh, as was her mother's. Maude's breasts were smallish—pumpkin firm—her mother's large, as are my own. We explored with seeking eyes each other's forms, our gazes lingering in between each other's legs. Or rather, Maude's and Eveline's to mine, and I to theirs.

'It is quite fun to do it in the bath', said Eveline at which Maude uttered, 'Oh, Mama!', and received a firm smack on her bottom cheeks.—'Get into the bath, my girl, and hold your back to us', she was told, whereat pouting she obeyed and sat there like an odalisque, tits half submerged beneath the water and her back against the side.

Eveline then approached me slowly and brought her nipples against mine.

'Two grown women—let me have your tongue the while I feel your lovely quim', she whispered, gliding her fingers underneath between my legs.

I was startled that Maude should be there, even though she could not see, and said without thought, 'Don't!', but said it softly to her mouth which brushed from side to side across my own, her hand fondling round my bottom cheeks.

'Mama, what are you doing? I don't want to have a bath', murmured Maude in something of a whining tone.

'Whatever I am doing, my dear, is not for you to be conscious of. Stay as you are and where you are. Now, Deirdre, open your legs a little more', came her imploring whisper. I shook my head, yet feebly, for my cheek was then against her own. Her fingertip had furrowed up between my lovelips and had found my spot. My knees began to bend; I could not help myself, but even so I murmured weakly, 'Don't!' again. I was caught between two hands that knew their skills.

'How quite adorable that you can still sound like an untried girl', said Eveline—and this for Maude to hear, which made me blush and tremble. I could hear myself breathing—always for me an amourously fateful sign. I wished to fondle her furred slit in turn, but was conscious of Maude's presence, though she was at least eight feet from us and showing us her back still, fingers paddling in the water as she sat.

My nipples stiffened, as did Eveline's, and memories of my wild youth filtered back.

'I would adore to watch you being fucked. Say that I

may', said Eveline, her long tongue flicking in my mouth, and I on the point of my orgasmic bliss.

'N . . . not with Maude there', I whispered back, and received her husky laugh into my mouth.

'In the bathroom—even as in bed—even upon the sofa in the drawing room—one does as one is told, requested, sought to do'.

'No . . . n . . . no, Eveline, stop it, do! HAAR!' All too soon I sprinkled on her busy hand and felt a fingertip within my nether rose at the same time. Thereat, too, came a sound. The door opened and Maurice was there! I swayed, my legs apart and weak. Four steps and he was upon us, and I thereupon exchanged from Eveline's arms to his, sagging against him in my amourous spillings while his lips took mine and he continued taking toll of that which his wife had so skillfully aroused.

I heard myself moaning 'No!' The sound was only in my mind. I heard a splash, and Maude jumped out. Maurice seemed oblivious to her presence as I, caught in a tide of passion, slumped to him and felt his penis vibrant up against my thigh.

'I hate you all!', I heard Maude say. Her mother evidently smacked her, for I heard that sound and then a squeal. I kept my eyes closed, lips a-swim. In a moment she had taken up her clothes, or part of them at least, and rushed without. There came the maid's voice saying, 'Miss, oh Miss, you're wet! I'll fetch a towel, Miss. Go into your room'.

I was sinking, I was lost. A rug received me and I lay, entirely helpless to resist as Maurice came upon me, trousers down, his huge prick burrowing within my oily nest while Eveline lay down beside the pair of us.

'What a fine woman, is she not, my love? Come, Deirdre dear, lift up your legs. Let him get in you to his balls, my sweet. Ah, there—he's in—right in—O lovely sight! No—keep your legs up, silly—yes, that's right'.

'Oh my god, oh my god, oh my god', I sobbed. My bottom bumped and squirmed upon the rug. The ceiling danced. Their lips were everywhere, he sucking my nipples, she upon my mouth, and I dissolving in a warm, lewd bliss as his deep-seeking piston worked its will of me.

And then unconscionably I began to cry—long-racking sobs that no doubt he mistook for passion's song. Eveline did not, I am sure of that, but continued nurturing my tongue with hers while Maurice quivered and ploughed on. I felt his pulsings huge, then with a groan he expended his thick jets of sperm in me and lay a-tremble on my vibrant form while tears cascaded down my cheeks and I lay like a stricken doe beneath his weight.

'It has been a long time for you, has it not?', he asked gently. His mouth replaced his wife's upon my own, and then he withdrew his steaming rod and rose to draw his trousers up.—'What a splendid fuck she is', he said and out he strode. Eveline hugged me for a moment and then helped me up.

'My dear', she said with deep concern and led me naked as we were along the landing to a bedroom which from its ornate furnishings, its mirrors and its lovely drapes I knew must be the one they shared. There I permitted her to pull me down upon the bed. She kissed my tears away and smoothed my hair.—'Was it so nice for you, or has it really been so long since you were threaded, Deirdre?', she asked gently, rolling her fleshy breasts to mine.

'I have sinned', I said, and sounded mournful at the least. I do not recall ever having said those words before. They are inimical to my nature, anyway. Were someone of a sensitive nature to read those words, they might well guess my state of mind. In having Maurice so suddenly upon me, and though I had much enjoyed his lusty cock, I had thought of Richard and had experienced once more the sense of true excitement blended into guilt.

'You have sinned? Have we then misunderstood you, dear? I did not mind at all, you silly thing. We do not fret at pleasure here, and nor must you'.

Her tongue was sweet, her eyes conveyed to mine a genuine desire to have me more amourously responsive than I was. And indeed now that we were alone again, belly to belly, thighs to thighs, I felt renewed stirrings in me, sought a curious protection in her arms and palmed her weighty bottom, felt it roll luxuriously and received her throaty chuckle in my mouth.

'Ah, now you are better, dear', she said, 'What was your upset? Was it because of Maude? I permit her certain things, I know. Perhaps I was too hasty. Was it that?'

'No, no, it was not quite, but evidently she dislikes me from the things she said'.

'Oh pouf! That was a tantrum only. You will soon see her in a different mood. Something else ails you, Deirdre, and I know it does. Confess to Eveline and you will feel the better for it. In my youth I cried sometimes', she added pensively, for frequently when seeking to know another's thoughts one wishes to express one's own, as if to say 'That happened to me, too!'

'I cannot tell you, Eveline'.

'Of course you can. It is something very naughty, is it not? Shall I tell you all the wicked things that I have done? Why, I could fill a book, my dear—and even Maude and the other girls have several chapters they could write. Are we not all cast in the same old mould? We Libertarians confess ourselves and feel the better for it. Maurice is the cockerel, my pet, and we the hens', she said and tickled me beneath my arms to bring my spirits back, which she succeeded in, for then I laughed and kissed her hugely, rubbed my bush to hers and savoured all the sensuousness of her full form.

I had done it with Richard, I said, amid a kiss, and said it hurriedly, excusingly. It burst out like a bubble from my mouth.

'Your son? Oho!', she laughed and rolled upon me, legs between my own. 'Your eyes are deep and lovely—do you know?', she asked playfully and rubbed her nose to mine, soothing her lovelips up against my own to afford me a swimmy sensation I could not resist.

'More than once', I said, and knew it for a sort of boast.

'If once were ever enough, Deirdre, we all would be half virgins, would we not? Is that your awful, secret sin? I have a score to match it, anyway. Does he do it to you nicely? Is he slow or quick? You have to tutor them, you know'.

'Oh, Eveline, really—stop it! Do you not really, really think it the most awful thing?'

'You are seeking reassurance, and you know it well, you minx. Are you not?', she asked me softly. Her lips slowly brushed my own, back-forth-back-forth—a quite delicious way to kiss.

'I suppose—but on the other hand', I mumbled.

'You can have it in either hand, dear', Eveline laughed, 'Come on, I'll make you come again, and then you'll change your mind on it. He must be good if Maurice made you think of it'.

'No, no, it wasn't that. Oh, Eveline, don't!'

Too late, too late. The bedsprings sang. We breathed into each other's mouth.

'You are a good fuck, darling, do not be ashamed of it. Cock has no conscience, neither have our quims', she mouthed. Then the sweet spillings overtook us once again. The lips of our cunnies splurged and kissed. Our bushes were sticky in a trice. The milk of love. How irresistible it is!

After we had long lain, kissed anew, she fetched our clothes, and asked, 'Do you feel better now that you have told me that?' Before I could reply—and really I did not know my own mind still—she went on, 'Darling, you must bring him here. One afternoon perhaps'.

'No, that would not be possible', I said, and wished devoutly I had not confessed.

'All things are possible, my love. We Libertarians do not put up bars against ourselves. Against outsiders often, yes, but not against ourselves. I count you one of us. Speak only here of love, desire. We hedonists must stick together, must we not?'

'You are incorrigible, Eveline!', I could not help but laugh.

'I always was. So, I suspect, were you. You only wish to have your sins confirmed. I know that feeling well enough. She who gives way to love gives way to life. Do not be broody. Take things as they come. There—what a splendid smile! You must come on Friday and meet Claudia'.

'And who is she?'

'A young actress—or would-be one. Her husband—a very likeable young rogue—wishes to see her being threaded. She will not, and does not know whether to play Miss Prim or Miss Improper. We shall see'.

'Eveline—you will not force her, surely?'

'Were you never forced, my dear? A little were you not? Never have your legs kicked? Were you not held down until the surging pleasure took you?' She looked straight into my eyes. Her nipples were still hard beneath her gown, as were my own. I imagined her for a moment talking thus in front of Phillip and could not prevent a smile.

'When one is young . . .', I said. My words fell limp.

'Claudia is twenty-*three*, my love. She flirts with the idea, though never would confess it. Some men call such women "cock-teasers". We shall have rare sport—I can tell you that'.

I murmured something, but I know not what. I am being drawn into a whirlpool now. I know not whether to go on Friday or not. I may see myself in Claudia. Perhaps that's what I fear.

CHAPTER SEVEN

Sylvia's Day-Book

thought before of looking *there*. It is a very big one, though, and gets all leathery sometimes. 'It is Nature, do not be afraid of it', they said. The saddle rubs me inbetween my legs and makes me feel all hot sometimes. Aunty Muriel says that is good for me and that I should keep my bottom moving back and forth like when she puts her tongue there underneath. Rose was in bed with them last night. I listened and I heard her moans. I am glad that she is naughty, just like me. I do not feel so bad about it now.

Phillip's Day-Book

There is no escape for me in my own house. Perhaps there never was—perhaps I am a prisoner in myself. There is both mockery and affection here which tosses me this way and that. I am pursued, entrapped, and know not where to turn, and spend much time upon my study couch in dismal thought while laughter sounds beyond, bites at my mind and makes me feel more churlish than I know myself to be. My writing has ceased. Even to me my manuscript appears more wooden that I thought it once to be. I read it no longer through my own, discerning eyes, but horridly through those of Muriel and Jane who tempt me frequently to write that which I will not do.

'Women have limbs, my dear, have lips. Portray them as they are and not as dummies such as may be seen in a dressmaker's window', I am told.

I loathe myself that I argue with them on this score, but silence cannot always be maintained. They have their tricks of making me reply by questions that appear at the first speaking innocent, and yet in truth are quite insidious.

'Can you not describe a woman's lips?', asked Jane. At first I would not reply, but upon her asking me again I replied in irritation that of course I could. Such is the writer's art, I said.

'Indeed? Describe mine, then, or Muriel's—or Sylvia's even. All lustrous, velvety and warm—a touch of honeyed moisture here and there. You see—I have no art with words such as you claim to have, yet I can say such as you do not write. As to a woman's thighs...'

'Please stop! I will not write of immoralities', I said as bleakly as I could.

The hour was late. She wore a peignoir. Through its folds—its misty folds, if she would have it so—I discerned that she wore little else save for her stockings and a pink chemise. With each movement of her legs I saw that which a gentleman should never see—that blur of sinful dark between her thighs. Her bosom, too, was almost visible.

'You are in purdah, Phillip. Some females should be, but males should not'.

So speaking, she moved round behind my back, for upon her entrance I had got up from the couch and taken a plain chair. In the moment that she became all but invisible, something dropped down about my face and wound itself about my neck, half throttling me. It was the silk cord from her peignoir. Frantically I strove to free it from my neck, begging her to cease this foolish game. My fingers tried to hook behind it, but could not.

'For heaven's sake, I cannot breathe', I gasped. The chair being hollow at the back, she pressed her knee through into me. At the same moment, Muriel entered, closed the door and advanced upon me. She, too, wore a peignoir and, beneath, had nothing on save for her gartered stockings and a pair of buttoned boots that reached up to her knees. My eyes bulged at the wicked sight of her. Once more I tried to claw the cord away. The pressure of Jane's knee was fearful in my back, and Muriel held a long cord in her hand.

In a flash, I was their prisoner, for Muriel swiftly knelt and tied my legs against those of the chair. O perfidy, O wretchedness! She knew too well I could not kick a woman thus, nor even beat her with my hands, much as I wished to. Vainly I strove, not using violence such as they, but all in vain. Jane twisted the cord with one hand and with her other seized my hair—I strangulated, gasping, helpless in their hands.

No, no—I will not write of this—a deed so terrible, so lewd. May the heavens fall upon them for their wickedness. I was left weak and stunned by that foul act that brought me to a pitch of miserable submission to their wills. My hands tremble even now to think of it.

Jane's Day-Book

What a splendid penis Phillip has! The dear, poor idiot, he tried to hide his pleasure at the last, but could not, fell to sobbing like a boy while Muriel drew on his reservoirs and sucked his sperm with her naughty quim. Had she so not exhausted him, I would have taken my toll, too. The chair bumped, though. I feared that Sylvia would wake. Besides, the floorboards creak too much in Phillip's study. We must not do it there again.

How wildly did he shake his head (or try to!) when Muriel cast her peignoir off and opened up his trouser buttons, nurturing his tool until it stood up stiff and ready for the game, the knob all purplish and sleek and swollen such as a healthy, eager female loves to see. The faint blue veins stood proud around the stem.

'And now, my love...', said Muriel. His legs being together, she was able to straddle him while standing up still and let her titties swing across his face, reaching beneath to fondle and position his stiff tool beneath the rolled lips underneath her bush.

Ah, how he gurgled, whined and whimpered when she did! Not hurrying, she then caressed his balls which were slightly squashed and so appealingly looked even bigger than they are, the skin as equally polished in that posture as his knob.

'In a moment, in a moment, Phillip', Muriel said, as though he too were eager for the fray. So clever she can be sometimes in saying such—the gentle voice, the luring touch. 'Twas she in truth who first seduced dear Uncle Reggie and then took me upon the bed with them.

'No!', Phillip managed to moan when at the last the pinky-purplish lips of Muriel's love-slit swallowed up his knob. Her eyes half closed, knees trembled, at that naughty and exquisite contact. Still she took her time, though, and sank very slowly down until his prick was sheathed and her bottom settled on his knees.

'Oh, it is nice!', she murmured. I could feel her head and loins a-swim as mine would have then been, and knew exactly how her cunny squeezed upon his embedded penis.

I had loosened the cord by then around his neck and laid my hands upon his shoulders, bent and kissed my sister on the lips. Our tongues toyed. Both her arms enfolded him and thus could hold his pinned.

'My god, my god!', he moaned—the foolish man who thus was led into such a Paradise!

'Give me a good fuck, Phillip, for you know you want to', Muriel breathed. Her hips worked gently up and down. I saw—just saw—his cock emerge and then sink up again into the clinging enclosure of her folds, his foolish face strained far away from hers.

'Do not hold him any longer, Jane. I will pump him; I will make him come', she said. Her voice was strong. She meant to milk him deeply, and she did. So hapless was he, though, and so excited (though he would deny that to the last, I'm sure) that he came too soon for her—before she even came herself.—'Oh, you fool, you fool!', she sobbed at him. I knew from his expression and the squeezing of her eyes that his thick jets were flooding her too soon.—'We shall have to teach him better, Jane', she said, but stayed upon him, wriggling her plump bottom all the time upon his knees, and he a-moaning like a long-lost child until at last it slipped out limp and wan, and dribbling at the nose, as Uncle Reggie used to say.

'You will sleep better now for that', said I to Phillip who did not seem to know or care that I untied his legs. He looked just like a mannikin whose strings have all been cut.

'You beasts—O filthy beasts', he moaned as we two

left. Muriel says that he will have to pay for that remark. I cannot blame her. He must be somehow set upon the path of true voluptuousness!

Deirdre's Day-Book

I lock my bedroom door now when I leave. Richard must not get in and hide again. I am determined to rescue myself from my perversity, in his respect at least, no matter what dear Eveline might coo.

But what a rich occasion Friday was! I know not the truth of all that happened, which itself excites. I had expected Claudia to be a rather brittle, hard young thing. Instead I found her small and slim and quiet—indeed, I read anxiety in her eyes. Her dress was a pretty blue, speckled with white as was the broad-brimmed hat she wore upon arrival. Long, white lace gloves adorned her arms up to her elbows and, this being afternoon, she naturally kept them on, which made her look adorable.

As to her form, she is superbly sculpted round her nether parts which are accentuated by her long, slim legs that form twin columns for her bulbous orb. Her nose is aquiline, eyelashes long, the upper lip quite small, the lower full and pleading to be sucked upon.

We were but five—two married pairs and I. The husband of Claudia—Ewan by name—is glib, of medium height, and reasonably fair to look upon. He is such a man, however—as I felt—from whom one would not buy a horse without making sure that all its legs belonged to it.

'This is my love. She has a mood of sweet compliance on her—do you not?', he asked and kissed her cheek, which small caress in front of others brought a flush upon her velvet skin.

'Please, Ewan, do not speak like that. I have no knowledge of what you speak, nor have our friends. We cannot stay but half an hour', Claudia said, and looked a little like a hunted doe, taking a seat as though it might not bear her weight.

'We were speaking of love, my pet', said Eveline, 'before you came, that is. I vowed to Deirdre here that she would see love flourish this afternoon. Let us—for fun, of course—make a small pact that at least we shall all kiss before you leave'.

And at that a sudden silence fell. All eyes were on poor Claudia whose white-gloved fingers twisted every way and whose blush was like a lantern in the room. She affected not to have heard and cast embarrassed eyes around as if for the first time conscious where she was.

'Well, my pet, what do you say?', Ewan asked bluffly, 'Who shall kiss you first? Shall I kiss Eveline? Will you? Or shall you throw your arms about the neck of Maurice who has longed to hold you these long months?'

Frozen in attitude, Claudia simply stared at him as if he were not real, as if indeed the whole thing were a dream to her. It was Eveline then who suggested I kiss Claudia first.

'And so we shall proceed, each one to each', said she while Claudia sank back into her chair and clutched its arms. She was truly speechless for the moment, at which I curiously felt impatience with her and not solicitude as I first felt that I might have done. She was not, after all, a virgin, nor was she immature.

The room stilled for a moment. All eyes looked at me save Claudia's which were fastened somewhere on the floor.

'I would like to kiss her very much', I said. I meant to add, 'if she agrees', but out of some perversity did not.

'She likes to have another's tongue between her lips', said Ewan, at which Claudia seemed to wake from out of her daze and squealed that she did not. How foolish that cry was. A more learned young woman would have said she did, and perhaps added something to the effect that she would permit no more than that. We cannot gauge the responses of others, however, by our own.

'Ewan, I am leaving—on my own', said Claudia desperately and got up, which I suspected was the last thing that she should have done, and I was right, for on her rising Maurice got behind her, seized her waist and pinned her arms down at her sides and told me literally to have at her.

Amid such screams as then were uttered, Eveline said calmly, 'Wait! Let me undo her dress', which she proceeded to amid long howls from Claudia. Her dress unbuttoned to the waist. She really should have known better than to wear one such. Her lovely tits were scooped out then from her chemise and showed her nipples, brown and small.

'Oh god! Oh god! Someone must save me! Help!', screamed Claudia while Eveline—forgetting my election to be first—bent and applied her warm lips to those sensitive points that, under the ministrations of her lips and tongue—soon rose up to sharp points while Claudia mewed and tried in vain to twist in Maurice's commanding grip.

Ah, that I had a writer's art to delineate, describe in perfect detail all that followed then. I confess to having savaged the young woman's mouth. I could not help myself. Alas, so often have I said that to myself, and yet it's true. She slobbered sobs and blurted protests underneath my searching lips, I palming her firm breasts while Eveline knelt beside the three of us and got her drawers down.

'Turn her a little, Maurice!', she commanded, and Claudia's half-smothered wails then turned to moans as her pussy yielded to the tongue that lapped with such small succulent sounds as put me in a frenzy of desire. Her moans were weakening by then. At last she acceded to my flickering tongue.

'We shall all have you now, my sweet', I murmured to her lax, warm mouth.

'Play with her Deirdre. She will soon be ready for the cock', said Eveline and, rising, took her dress off, presenting herself corseted and stockinged only. It was I who attended then to Claudia's muff, finding the honeyed stickiness between her thighs. Her knees were trembling. Maurice held her still. Out of the corner of my eye, I saw

Ewan take his boots and trousers off and Eveline playing with his prick, he fondling her bold, naked bottom cheeks, the two locked in an amourous embrace, at which Claudia needed to be supported more, for—seeing them—she sobbed most fearfully, though mingled with her sobs were other strains that one could not help but recognise.

Claudia then began at last to reach orgasmic bliss despite herself. I lapped her steadily and felt her salty spurts while Maurice twisted her neck round and seized her mouth—she utterly unable to resist.

Ah, what an orgy followed! Moaning her despair, Claudia was then bustled, wrestled, carried—oh, I know not what—to a sofa where, with bottom up, she received the burning, throbbing stave of Maurice's prick between her bottom cheeks. A long minute did he labour even to get his swollen crest within her tight, rebellious hole. She cried, she pleaded, even clutched my arm, but finally the rod was worked right in until his balls brushed to her bottom's bulge.

'No, no, no, NO!', a score of times she sobbed while Ewan mounted Eveline on the floor in such a position that the wicked pair could perfectly well, with worm's-eye view, witness the buggering of Claudia who afterwards, as it transpired, had refused to receive her husband in that wise.

Was this, then, a revenge on his part? Was it real? Or is she an actress of first rank? I confess to never having seen real tears from her—would have expected such if it were 'real', by which I mean to say was unrehearsed and thoroughly unexpected by the girl. She acceded to him after several manly thrusts and ceased to struggle, though her hips moved not to aid his pistoning of her fine, rumptious little bottom.

After he had come, withdrawn, she slumped down on her tummy, hid her face—would not be spoken to and lay like one who has gone to sleep of a sudden in a stranger's house. The two on the floor had separated meanwhile, lay replete.

'Poor Deirdre—only you remain unsatisfied. The men,

though, will recover soon', said Eveline, legs open boldly to our gaze.

I wanted her, in fact, to vanish—Maurice and Ewan, too, and to talk to Claudia, so much did I wish to know if she had been genuinely ravished or whether I was meant to be spectator to a play. I believe that, had I stayed, I would have known. I had a sense indeed that in some way I had been used. I merely smiled and shook my head and retreated to the hall to don my hat and gloves. No one, I noticed, called out after me. I expected Claudia to, in some strange way. She could scarcely not have realised that the curtain had not descended on her bottom yet.

I am left thus in some curiousity, and feel—although I think it an illusion—the eyes of Eveline on me from afar, though to what end, what purpose, I cannot guess.

I need a male tonight. O let me not be tempted—no!

CHAPTER EIGHT

Daisy Partridge's Day-Book

We are settled now. How nice and cosy the new house is! I love the winding stairs, the staircases. I have my own room now as well—at last! Mama had promised me one when we moved. She presented her calling card today to our nearest neighbours. They have a daughter near my own age, I believe. Papa says he saw her in a donkey-cart. I think he meant a pony cart! He is very vague is Papa, always mixing such things up. Uncle Arnold gave me a big kiss today. It was lucky Mama did not see. I know he kisses her as well. She says I am too grown-up for my age. I really don't know what that means. I told our governess. She says I mustn't talk of things like that. Jack wrote a note to her last night and put it underneath her door. It was VERY rude and said, 'You have a nice big bum'. He tried to disguise his writing, but she knew all right and spanked him for it with his trousers down. I know because I saw. His thing got stiff and stuck up underneath his shirt. I saw her holding it as well! It serves my brother right. I bet it hurt. His bottom was all red. Papa has often said he'll birch my own when I am 'bad'. I pray he never will—please no!

I wonder what that girl he saw is like?

Lady Celia Partridge's Day-Book

A rather curious household at the Mansfields', but the general atmosphere is nice. Or rather, I should say is nice in parts. Having been invited to take tea, I met the sisters. No Mama is spoken of. I wonder, is there perhaps a touch of scandal there? Had she been deceased, they would have surely said.

Mr. Phillip Mansfield is a studious-looking man. He quite reminds me of my brother George who failed at all things and has become an unpublished poet for his sins. Mr. Mansfield is EXCEEDINGLY quiet. I suspect him to be dominated by his sisters who betray great mischief, as I understand the term, and appear to be in permanent residence.

The daughter, Sylvia, is sweet. I have suggested that she meet with Daisy. Mr. Mansfield quite brightened up at that and has invited her immediately. He has great need of a companion for his daughter, so he said—and this I well understand. It does the girl no good to be alone all day with just adults. However, in so saying he gave his sisters a quite PECULIAR look. Perhaps it is they who do not want to be disturbed, yet gave quite the opposite impression to me. I DO find myself confused, but even so they are PERFECTLY proper people to know and have an excellent cuisine, I hear. I have invited them all to return my visit. The Misses Jane and Muriel accepted gladly, as did Sylvia. As for the master of the house, he seemed not to know his own mind and offered his apologies lest business take him off that day. In truth, he appears to be as vague as my dear husband is. There are times, however, when I do suspect that such indeterminacy veils such other thoughts as men may have.

Sir Roger Partridge's Day-Book

Met Mansfield today. Seems a frightfully reserved chap. Had a feeling that he didn't want to come. His sisters, though, are a very jolly pair. I ventured to show Muriel the conservatory. She admired some rather ripping orchids I have nurtured there. A splendid figure of womanhood she is. She stumbled on a broken pot that the gardener's boy had left upon the floor, which produced a very charming thrusting of her bosoms to my chest. I must say they are jolly firm, as is her bottom which I accidently clutched when she fell against me. I could not feel that she wore drawers beneath. She blushed and hid her face into my neck, I murmuring my profound apologies, but the dear creature did not seem at all to mind my absolutely unforeseen caress.

I have arranged with her, quite privately, to do a little hunting at some time—pursuing hares, or such. 'The poor little creatures—can we not *pretend* there is one?', she shyly asked. I must say I agreed to that since it will leave us without the diversion of the chase.

There is a remarkable resemblance in height, form and hair between Daisy and Sylvia. From the back they look like twins. I did not remark that to them, though, for young girls are peculiar in their ways and like to be thought of as quite different from the rest. I observed my thought to Muriel and Jane, and they concurred.

How fortunate one is to find such prepossessing females near!

Muriel's Day-Book

I sense that there is much worth in Roger despite his seeming absent-mindedness. Having fondled my bottom in the conservatory, he asked me, 'By jove, what am I doing? Frightfully sorry, dear lady, for that'. Even so, he had a good squeeze there and began to erupt a little, for

I felt it against my thigh. It seems years since I have brought forth a little blush. I was quite pleased with that.

Lady Partridge is quite sweet. I have yet to sum her up, for women are naturally cautious at the first. I believe there may be *possibilities* as equally there are in Daisy whose resemblance to Sylvia is marked. They could be exchanged quite neatly in the dark, I said to Jane, who laughed and asked me what I had in mind. I do not know as yet, though certain naughty thoughts arise. I shall go riding with Roger and have little doubt that we shall end up in what the French so charmingly call a *bosquet* or, in common parlance, among the bushes!

'I thought he would have asked me first', said Jane, but she is never really jealous of such things. Besides, as the older sister the privilege is mine to handle possibilities first.—'Of course, dear, but don't *exhaust* them', said she, though kissed me all the same.

We handled Phillip once again last night. I believe he may be 'waking up' a little bit. Jane saddled him and took the pleasure of his cock while I sat on his face and kept his nose stuck up between my bottom cheeks. We tackled him together in his bed long after Sylvia was fast asleep. The poor, dear man, he is quite terrified lest she should hear.

'You will do your duty by us, Phillip, dear. You have the first rights, have you not?', asked Jane to his despair. At that moment she was riding up and down upon his prick, jogging her naked bottom lusciously. I lifted up my bottom for a moment and he snorted, groaned, 'Leave me, leave me!' As he began to come, however, so he clutched up at my straddled thighs and, by determination or by accident, brought his tongue to flirt around my cunnylips which were exceedingly moist at that stage, and indeed I sprinkled him profusely while Jane wet his balls.

'There—are you not enjoying it, in truth?', I asked him afterwards, our naked bodies pressed on either side to his. We tease him much about dear Uncle Reggie—how he pumped us both. Jane lay behind him and held his arms while I manipulated his limp, sticky prick. It began half turgid once again, and much against his stubborn will.

'How dare you thus make me submit to you?', he moaned, but even in the moonlit room one could see that his face and neck were flushed. As much as he pretends to loathe it, even so he likes it when I cup his balls and Jane rubs his tool at the same time. Jane made him turn his neck and kiss her—said that she would scream for Sylvia if he did not. I held their heads together while he did and rubbed my treasure up against his cock, and then took a ribbon and bound it tightly round the root of it to keep it up.

'You naughty boy', we teased him then, and left him thus, all in a daze, I think.

Phillip's Day-Book

My forlorn, lost mood will never leave me now. I am convinced of that. I have become a plaything for the sinful pair. Thank God that none will ever know of this!

I thank the Heavens, too, for Daisy who is fast becoming a companion for dear Sylvia. Their innocent laughter often reaches me amidst my torments. Even so, young Daisy has become another lever that my sisters use. This afternoon they both invaded my study again, Muriel holding something crumpled in her hand. To my horror, they were a pair of her own drawers, and most expensive ones with short frilled legs.

'Come, Phillip, put them on', she said to my disgust. I steadfastly refused, of course, though was not made to combat wickedness of this dire sort, and prayed for the presence of my once-beloved who was veritably an angel beside this pair.

'You will wear them underneath your trousers. Otherwise we shall pull your garments down in front of Sylvia and Daisy', Jane declared.

I did not doubt them for a moment—or at least that

they might try, and show me thus as a shorn lamb, disgustingly, beyond all one's experience. Thereat Jane threw the door of my study open and called for Sylvia, albeit softly. Panic then was upon me like a net. I drew her back and slammed the door.

'Go out and I will do it', I declared. But no—we want to see you put them on, was said. I turned my back on them to do that shameful deed. The drawers are softer and more clinging than my normal, proper underwear.

'How sweet you look!', said Muriel and halted me from putting back my trousers on until I was 'inspected' by the pair and made to draw the knickers tightly up until my manhood formed a lump that was visible through the fine batiste. I begged them for the thousandth time to let me be. Muriel looked serious at that and told me to draw my trousers up. I am to be inspected day and night to ensure that I am wearing the ridiculous attire.

'You know the penalty', said Muriel.

I cannot bring myself to feel that I am any longer the possessor of my soul. I feel the drawers all day around my person. They produce the most peculiar sensation I have ever known. My testicles are constantly caressed by the material which has the same effect upon my other private parts. Dear Heavens, dare I write to Deirdre and beg her to return? I fear that if I do—and much I wish to now—I might be scorned by her as well. How desperately I have wandered from the true path that I set myself in life!

Muriel's Day-Book

A delightful ride with Roger. Truly, he has merit and does not rush his hedges nor such skirts as come to his attention. Upon his suggestion, we met discreetly at a halfway point and then circled around his private wood where we would not be disturbed, said he, for he had sent his foresters away.

We settled ourselves, after a fine, refreshing gallop, in

a clearing where the sun had enabled a small sward to grow. Delightfully springy it was too, being compounded of both moss and grass, and I asking him if he wished to discuss the condition of the Nation, or philosophy.

'The philosophy of affections', he replied and—we lying down—he cradled my head romantically on his arm and sought with gentlemanly caution underneath my skirt to an inch or two above my knees, I not disturbing his hand in its search.

Roger is a fine bookman seemingly and discoursed to me, while pecking lightly on my lips, of much that he has read of love's fine doings, even quoting passages therefrom that stirred me deeply while his fingers made a tour around my garters, felt my thighs above—not hastening but in a teasing way such as one rarely comes across with urgent males who are too quick to put the poker in. Thus did he speak to me of one Brantôme who wrote the 'Secret Lives of Ladies', so he said, and had much to plainly speak upon the things the long-gone ones had done, such as ladies 'frotting' quims to quims that were as frothy as with soap.

'I would not know of such', I smiled, but tipped my tongue between his lips to show him that I merely teased. There were gallants—so he told me Brantôme wrote, who fucked their ladies two by two, sometimes a wife and mistress in the self-same bed, and gentlemen who 'trod' their daughters first, before they wed.—'Oho! That is a gentlemanly thing to do?', I asked.

'I would not know of such', was his response in taunting echo of my own.

By then his hand reached my slit which he toyed with gently, seeking out my spot and bringing it to tingle to his touch so enervatingly that I squirmed and begged him with my eyes to do the deed. I must have received there many a fine prick, said he. He clearly sought me to respond with more impassioned words, but I would not. A woman knows a man the best when he does all the speaking at the first. As to himself, I asked, how many cunnies had he breached?

'Of late? A score or two'. He smiled and pretended a soft yawn upon my open mouth forcing my legs apart just as I wished him to, for such a move excites me much, reminds me of days past, my naughtiness.

'Tut-tut, you have not been over-busy then', I riposted whereat we exchanged tongues more. I drew my knees up. He uncovered me and tucked my gown around my waist, leaving my bottom naked on the sward.

'I shall be busier with you. Perhaps also with Jane, and . . . '

'Sylvia?' At last his penis had sprung out. I fondled its firm girth, soothed up and down the vibrant rod. Her name excited him the more. Even as I uttered it he got between my open legs and rubbed his crest against my furry mount.

'Has she been trodden yet?', he asked.

'Not yet. Has Daisy? What sweet legs, she has, what lovely tits. Have you not even brought her nipples up? Oh, Roger—put it in me now!'

'Wait, woman, wait', he answered me. I adore such mastery. All women do who are not dead to adoration of one's form. His bulbous knob had found the entrance to my honeypot. It parted the rolled lips and slipped within, then stayed itself most maddeningly despite my wrigglings. Both my wrists were gripped and held above my head, he arched upon me; self-possessed, all his supposed vagueness had gone. I knew it for a trick of his. Women can sometimes be so, too, when in the lure of some desire that they are minded not yet to express.

'Fuck me and you may have us both', I said.

'Both you and Jane—and Sylvia, also?' His prick moved in another inch. I squeezed upon it rapturously. No one had fucked me thus before. I knew the stimulating thrill of it. His voice was husky and dark as was my own.

'I want your cock more, Roger. No—not Sylvia. But Daisy, yes. How sweet to hear her whimper under you, but you must *promise* that you do it to her . . . OOOH!'

My words had such effect that he was in me to his balls in one long stroke, holding my wrists still, crushing me, and thus he pinned me, cheek to cheek, both of us breathing heavily.

'Stir your legs more, woman. Lift them up!'

'Won't—won't', I said like a young girl, and turned my face more into the soft sward as if I would deny him then my lips. His tongue entered my ear. I closed my eyes. I murmured it was naughty, wicked, bad. His prick stirred in me slowly, throbbing well. I held it clenched within my spongy grasp. What lovely little liquid sounds came as he moved! I hissed my breath in, stirred my bottom just a trifle then, but—as if regretful—let it plump again upon the grass and wore a dull, rebellious air.

At that, he clasped me firmly around the waist and rolled right over upon his back, carrying me with him with his prick still deeply sheathed so that it was I who straddled him. And thereupon he smacked my bottom hard and gasped, 'Now buck your bottom, woman, and get on with it!'

'YOO-OW! You beast!', I laughed. I slewed my hips up, down, and rode him well, sitting up straight and jogging as I did. The deepest penetration is secured that way, I think. I felt completely pierced, absorbed, fulfilled. I spurted, spattered love-juice on his pubic hairs, eyes rolling and my hair all wild. My moans betrayed me, for then he rolled right over once again and pinned me again beneath his virile form.

'Keep your legs open—wider—wide!', he gasped and mashed his lips most passionately to mine.

'Come in me—come!', I choked. The grass tickled underneath my bottom and the world was all a-heave.

'Wait, woman, wait', he groaned and stirred his throbbing pestle more. I had never felt myself so conquered since I was Sylvia's age, and loved each second of his savage thrusts, his mouth all over mine, his hands holding apart my bottom cheeks.

'Yes, sir, but do it, sir, please do', I whimpered like a girl again, for I felt that such play-acting pleased him so long as he remained the master of my hot, orgasmic fate.

It did indeed. 'You are a naughty little girl', he mouthed,

but still he would not—as it were—obey commands, and threshed me more before he came and shot his huge, warm jets within my clenching maw until both of us lay quivering in the gruelly pools of our delight.

His body crushed my own. With any other man I would have murmured, 'Get off, do!', but with Roger I remained quiescent, breathing softly till he drew his steaming penis out and knelt to button up his trouser front.

'You may rise now', he said to my faint astonishment, for though it was said gallantly, there was a strain of strong command in it. He sat to one side, back against a tree, and lit a cigar the while that I repaired myself. Then, having done so, I was ordered to sit down with him, his arm around my shoulders placed.

It was then that he commenced a discourse that I listened to with awe, for so many things he said about me were correct. I was the leader of a pack, he said, and Jane could well be my accomplice.

'At the moment, I suspect, you have young Sylvia in thrall. What of Mansfield himself? How does this come to be?'

I snuggled more into his arms and felt myself—as I so often have with men—superior.

'He, too. I keep him segregated from the girls', I said.

He appeared to read my mind on that, and nodded gravely, said I had done well.

'Pout your lips when I kiss you next', he said. I did so dutifully. He felt my breasts meanwhile and asked me many things about myself: when I was first mounted, how I had behaved—all such. His curiousity seemed endless on that score. When had I first taken the cock between my bottom cheeks, he asked. At seventeen, said I. And as to Jane? Yes, I had held her for her first. He stroked my cheek at that and smiled.—'All as I thought. I saw it in your eyes', said he.

A moment of silence passed between us then. My cunny pulsed agreeably. I saw some renewed stirrings of his cock and fingered it lightly through his trouser cloth.

'It shall be thus, my dear', he said at last, 'I shall have

you as often as I wish. Jane, too. As to Sylvia, she will be brought upon my cock in turn'.

'And that is ALL you wish?', I asked, yet felt a curious edge of fear as if I had committed an impertinence—a feeling I had never had before when with a male save for those times when Papa birched me and I would not take my drawers right off.

His fingers thereupon seized my chin and held my face right under his.

'You will not answer me in that wise, woman, when I speak!'

'So you will have us both, then—Jane and I? If such is your command, sir, yes, we will. Together if you wish—that would be nice'.

I spoke constrictedly. My mouth was pursed up by his grip.

'You have not mentioned Sylvia', said he.

'You may not have her—that is why. Not yet, at least. As to Daisy, you may have her on my bed, and if . . .' SMACK! 'OH!', I bleated. Suddenly he had me over on my belly, dress thrust up again, and SPLAT! SPLAT! SPLAT! his hand fell on my derriere.

'You will not entertain ideas of that sort, Muriel. That is for me to say. You understand?' SMACK! SPLATT! SMACK! SPLATT! Oh, my poor bottom burned!

'Yes, yes! Oh, Roger, do not beat me, please!'

At that he desisted, hauled me up again. I winced as my burning bum squashed on the grass. Indeed, I attempted tears, but none would come. How curious and astounding was the change in me—I who would have spat fire at any other man. I had not so been treated since my more tender years when I was broken-in as many young girls are, particularly in the countryside.

Would I continue to deal with Phillip, he then asked curiously.—'Of course', I said and waited on his further word.—'We shall see what we shall see', said he, then fell to tender kissing and caressing, which surprised me just as much, fondling my pussy through my pulled-down dress, and I his prick, but neither of us urgent to commence again.

Jane will scarce believe all this. Perhaps I had best not tell her yet.

CHAPTER NINE

Eveline's Day-Book

Claudia played her part superbly, but she always does. I believe she is quite *fixated* to this role and can probably play no other, but then she will never appear upon the stage as such. Her theatre is a drawing room.

Deirdre behaved extremely well and I have no doubt was quite convinced by Claudia's performance, as a few other of our friends have been. I expected her to stay, but discreetly she withdrew and thus—although she knows it not—has passed her test. Our small circle of Libertarians is comprised only of those who can behave when the time calls for it, and who will not blather to the world at large.

As to her confession on her second day here, that did intrigue me much. Young men are difficult to handle when drawn in on chance from outside. Perhaps her Richard may fill a role. Well, we shall see. I do not wish to interfere. Deirdre is obviously doubtful about her sin, but has not acted weakly, as perhaps she thinks. She had little solace from her husband, after all, and so should feel the minimum of remorse—if any, I would add, if such she needs to feel.

Deirdre's Day-Book

Richard is forlorn, the silly boy. 'Mama, do you not love me still?', he asked, thereby betraying that he had tried my bedroom door. I told him that I did, of course, but that we must not embrace so much. Immediately I said that, he embraced me, kissed me passionately and made to push me on the sofa where I would not go.

'I shall find a nice young lady for you', I declared, at which he flushed and said that was not what he wished. I was a little angry with him, for I had not demurred in letting him caress my bottom and my breasts the while we kissed. It should have been enough, I said. He stomped upstairs and slammed his door just like the naughty boy he is—though he is scarce a boy now, more a man.

Amy listens to all that happens. I am sure she does. I fret at that. She evidently takes after her father more than me—in some ways. I trust she will not prove as glacial as he. It will bode her no good in the end. I fear to talk to her about such things or she may well throw back at me my 'sins', and that would do no good at all.

Phillip's Day-Book

I am told by Jane to write a novel of erotic tone. How can I when it is quite against my will? 'Think and make notes', she said. I was locked in my room again today, my drawers on underneath my trousers. More and more I find myself sinking in a torpor of despair.

'You like to suffer, Phillip—that is certain', Jane said while I ground my teeth and could not bring myself to answer her. Can it be true? I tell myself that it cannot. If I am to be forced to write of women's limbs—and all such else as they would have me write—I know not how to formulate the words, nor how to strain myself to write them down.

Long did the paper lie in front of me untouched—

then squeals and cries came to me from below. I ventured to the window at a pace and in recording what I saw can scarcely hold my pen without a trembling now in all my limbs. There, on the sunlit lawn, dear Sylvia lay on her back, legs bared—indeed, her dress was round her waist. Upon her Daisy had been thrown—I swear she had—and showed a naked bottom to the world.

Over them both my sisters stood. Muriel had one foot planted in the small of Daisy's back, thus holding her upon my dearest girl, while Jane knelt and smacked Daisy's nether cheeks which, to my gaze, assumed a rosy hue. Resultantly, the poor child squealed although, to my amazement, several times she laughed as well and smothered Sylvia's lips beneath her own.

Of course, I could not bear to look for long. My damned drawers teased me as I watched, producing an eruption once again. Then Sylvia was made to raise her legs. Dear heavens, they had robbed her of her nether garment, too! No knickers were in evidence upon the grass, and so must have been cast off in the house—no doubt by the same threats that I receive.

How difficult it is to tear one's eyes away from that which one does not wish to see! I reeled back from the window—felt a fearful throbbing that I did not wish to feel. The sickliest sensations seized me, and I sat, whcreat, to my utmost dismay, I spilled into my drawers that manly substance which both Muriel and Jane extol from me, and thus sat weak in horrid, sticky state.

I would brace myself, humble myself, to write to Deirdre. Yet, what could I say—what could I say? I am caught in such a trap as no man ever could have been before.

I have failed to say that I saw Rose there, too—some distance from the scene, yet looking, smiling, with her finger in her mouth, the wanton that she too has now become.

Sylvia's Day-Book

My aunties are very naughty, making us do that upon the lawn today! Oh dear, I hope that no one ever finds that I have written this, but Daisy's thing kept rubbing to my own each time that Aunt Jane smacked her, and I got such funny feelings, too, just like when I'm in bed with them. Aunt Muriel told Daisy to put her tongue into my mouth. She did. It was quite nice, though—a nice licky-lick. Then she began to moan and twist about. Our hairs rubbed and she made me come, and did the same herself. Aunt Jane said that spanking often makes one do that. The most AWFUL thing was that I thought I glimpsed Papa looking from his window down on us, but he could not, of course, or he would have been awfully stern.

Afterwards I whispered to Aunt Jane that I thought I had seen him at his window, and she laughed and said that he liked looking at nice views. I think that was really horrid of her, yet she makes me laugh as well, so I do not think she meant it wickedly. She just says things that come into her head.

Daisy has been spanked by her Papa. She told me so. I wonder what it feels like to do that? I shouldn't think such things and yet I do. She said he made her take her drawers off, too. I can't imagine Papa ever doing that. I would blush ever so much, I'm sure. I told Daisy so. She said she expected he would like to, but I shushed her up. I told her that it wasn't true and that I wouldn't speak to her again for ten whole minutes. She said she didn't care, but waited that whole time for me to speak again!

Jane's Day-Book

Muriel has confided in me (after many hesitations, I believe) as to what passed between herself and Roger. I am not sure that she has told me all, but clearly he is both vigourous and brash, and not to say adventurous. I prefer, as she does, more spontaneoous events than was suggested in his conversation with her—if it can be called such! So does she, I know. Moreover, we have always marked out our own destinies in amourous affairs. 'I believe I am a little in love with him', she said. What nonsense! She is almost of that 'certain age', but of course I did not tell her that. He is certainly not to be made a 'free gift' of dear Sylvia who needs more tutoring yet, in any case. His advice about Phillip, though, was sound, though I am quite sure he merely believes that we have simply bullied our dear brother.

I am positive that Phillip is not yet fully aware that he wishes to be obedient to us. I found his drawers very patchy last night and asked him what he had been doing. He would not say. There is a look of shyness in his eyes when he is called a 'naughty boy' and he secretly likes to be called such, I think. I said to him that he must pay a penance for toying with himself (the which he vehemently denied) and must kneel and kiss my feet, my knees, my thighs.

After much hesitation he obeyed. I only have to mention Sylvia to him! His face worked slowly up beneath my skirt, whereat—he having reached my thighs—I clamped him tightly inbetween and made his ears to burn, which also made him groan. What a delicious feeling to hold a humbled male thus—even my own brother, I confess!

After two minutes or so of clamping him, I told him he might lick, but bent and held his hair lest he might struggle. Thereat I opened my legs wider and squashed my pussy down upon his mouth. He spluttered much, but finally acceded to my wish. Fortunately, Muriel did not interrupt. I held my legs straight and bent myself back a little, loosed his hair, and enjoyed his doglike licking thoroughly until I creamed his lips and tongue, made him stand up and lick his lips, which he did, much shamefaced.

His cock was very stiff after that exercise. I avoided touching it—felt that was best. I told him to go to bed and made my exit then. He looked forlorn and—for the first time—almost pleaded with his eyes for 'fond attention'. But he must learn: it is the only way. I who have been under men who ruffled me so much and often told me what to do am pleased that I can conquer one in turn! It is an utterly new experience. Muriel says it was her idea, but it was I who put the leash around dear Phillip first.

We had Rose in bed with us last night—I at her bouncy bottom while Muriel attended to her quim. After a few minutes of attention, she was very eager to have more and tongued us dutifully afterwards.

Deirdre's Day-Book

There is nothing for me but to go to Eveline and tell her what has passed, and which I hesitate to put to paper—but to leave blank pages now would only irritate me much in years to come, veiling my weakness, as I would be bound to think. I have no one else to confide in now but Eveline.

Richard brought home a friend of his—a youth of his own age, good looking and of good appearance. I judged him thus to be a nice young gentleman. Ah, how appearances deceive!

Richard asked me if his friend might stay the night, and I agreed. Amy retired to bed at ten. I believe she was taken with Jeremy who has an undoubted outward charm, but since I cannot tell her what has passed, I cannot warn her. Such is the web we weave, as the Bard said. But in truth I must castigate myself for having acted foolishly. 'Entertained' as I felt myself to be by the engaging chatter of Richard and his friend, I permitted myself too much indulgence both in wine and relaxation, and was scarcely aware of passing time.

At my age, of course, it is all too easy to imagine oneself as being able to bridge the gap between maturity and youth and to fancy oneself as being less than one's years, particularly when one is being lightly flattered, as I found myself to be by Jeremy who took upon himself the filling of our glasses—I having loosely given permission thereto, and the which I now regret. I was prettier than his own Mama, said he, at which I told him he should not say that, though even so (as I am sure all women do) accepted it as a compliment.

Our voices were hushed, for the hour was late. Several times I made to stir myself and rise but was seized by that torpor of langourousness that has too often been my undoing.

In providing me with a fifth or sixth glass (for I had lost count), Jeremy made so bold as to *accommodate* himself beside me on the chaise longue while Richard intimated his own devotion by settling himself at my feet. The conversation being but light (and often foolishly skittish on my part), I know not what we were discoursing on when Richard suddenly said, 'He wishes to kiss you, Mama', and I replying 'What?' rather than to offer an offhand reply, as I feel certain I would better to have done.

Indeed, I found myself endeavouring to gather further words which certainly evolved in my head but never appeared on the very lips that the wanton youth then attempted with his own. I confess that in the surprise of the moment—for the action followed within seconds of Richard's pronouncement—I made no move to evade the unbidden kiss that was one of undoubted, would-be passion. I recall uttering a small choking sound of surprise, but by then Jeremy's mouth was all over my own, the while—to my extreme amazement—Richard (being, as I have said in an inferior position on the floor close to my knees) moved his hands up beneath my skirt and commenced caressing my legs.

So feared was I that Jeremy would notice this rude gesture, that I pressed both away hastily, though this did not prevent Richard's friend from raining further temptestuous kisses on my averted neck.

I am not one given to great displays of temper. Even when in great discord with Phillip, I rarely raised my voice, but spoke coldly and quietly. In this particular circumstance, however, I blustered out some protest (though not in a common manner) and endeavoured both to show dismay and yet to try to make light of it at the same time, saying—no doubt feebly what a foolish boy Jeremy was. At the same time, my head was swirling somewhat with all the wine we had absorbed, which circumstance I can only extend as a frail excuse for the roguish pair as well.

I must to bed, I said, not wishing to confess even to myself that Jeremy had passed his hand across my breasts while kissing me, for I could not bring myself to say that outwardly.

'Mama, please stay and talk with us', Richard pleaded, but I would have none of that, merely saying that such foolishness was not proper and that it was time we all retired.

Thereupon I rose, settled my gown, and departed—leaving the two, as I thought, in a state of embarrassed, if not shamed, confusion. Such is the the wilful simplicity of the human mind, that—having entered the hall and hearing them whispering—I assumed them to be exchanging regrets and even arguments over what had passed. Reaching my room, I lit a cigarette and threw myself on my back on the bed while uncaringly casting ash upon the floor. That small detail comforts me for in retrospect it at least indicates to me what a carelessly foolish state of mind I was in, which is to say that I had not let anger overcome me as it should have done. I am weak. I am prone to make excuses for others. How else could I have endured a marriage as fruitless in responsive desire as I did?

Were I to search my soul, I would say that I am also given to believing that others are as I myself am. Therein, however, lies a betraying irony in the light of what was to occur.

I know not how to frame these passages, and yet would be a coward if I did not. Extinguishing the cigarette, half-smoked, I rid myself of my dress, my drawers and my chemise and—being naked to my waist corset and stockings—brushed my hair, though more in absent-mindedness than otherwise and conscious that my steps were not entirely steady. The floor itself appeared to waver underneath my feet, and yet I felt in no mood then for sleep, was restless, knew my cunny to be tingling just a little with desire, though I believe that normal in a woman such as I—which is not to denigrate myself, I trust.

My mind was mazed. Do I excuse myself? Perhaps I do. The door opened and I made to turn about. Before I could do so it had closed again, and there to my considerable dismay, astonishment—or call it what one will—were Jeremy and Richard, naked, with their penises erect, their faces flushed with fearful eagerness.

'Ah! How DARE you!', I remember uttering, but in that fraught moment they had advanced upon me. Richard clasped me round my waist and pressed his throbbing pego to my belly, bidding me to shush or Amy would be disturbed. I gasped, I thrust against him wildly, but to no effect. Indeed, such efforts as I made to free myself were entirely frustrated by Jeremy who took up post behind me and pressed his prick upright between my bottom cheeks.

Dear heavens, how loosely could my pen now run if I should let it!

'Get out! My god, get out!', I moaned while Richard tried to kiss me passionately. Their cocks rubbed fore and aft—aroused me all against my will, though weakened as it was by wine and thought. My wrists were gripped by Jeremy who held them tight down at my hips and coursed his knob up-down between my nether cheeks while Richard's pronged itself beneath my fur.

'Come, Mama, let us—do it, please!', choked Richard.

Thereupon I screeched unwittingly—the last cry of despair perhaps.

'Mama! What is it?', then came Amy's voice from behind her door, along the hall.

'It . . . t . . . trod upon a pin! Now, go to sleep!', I called, and knew perhaps that in my answer was surrender to their wickedness. They knew I dare not then cry out again. Such almost soundless struggles as I made availed me not, and I was urged and drawn on to the bed, cast down on my back thereon, my shoulders pinned by Richard while I gritted out my pleas to him. I threshed my legs, but Jeremy seized them underneath his arms and scissored them apart, then—falling on me—probed his penis to my nest.

I bucked. I clawed at Richard all in vain. The knob slipped in.

'I'll fuck her first, then you, old chap', said Jeremy.

'RI-CHARD!', I choked, but in the moment Jeremy was sheathed. Dear god, the stinging sweetness of that stiffened rod that pulsed its message to my clinging walls! —'Ah, no!', I heard myself moan out. The cry, however, was but a cloud of out-pulsed breath in Richard's mouth. Jeremy's belly flattened down on mine. His rod grooved slowly back and forth—and not, as I expected, with excited thrusts. He has clearly had a mentor of some sort, a married one, perhaps. Despite myself, I came. Almost at once I spilled and further oiled his prick.

'She's coming on, old chap, leave go of her. I have her now', said Jeremy.

Dear heavens, had they only held me all the time! I could at least have snuffed my conscience out. Richard leaned up, and Jeremy sleeked full upon my form. I blubbered, blustered, yet he too captured my weakling mouth and stung his tongue to mine, panting his pleasure and yet not beyond control. 'Twas I who slipped across that boundary with my acquiescence to the wicked deed. The working of our lips was heard, and all such soft and liquid sounds as come when mouths and naked bodies move in an abandoned unison.

Of the long hour that followed in that darkling room, I have but a mosaic of lewd memories. I moaned, I whimpered, sobbed—and yet to all their crudities of muffled speech I uttered not a word, was as a limp and willing plaything to the pair who spermed my nest in turn.

I was not spoken to by Jeremy. I was spoken *of*, and that alone intensified in a most curious way the dark excitement that I did not wish to feel. After both had spurted out their liquid treasures, I allowed my fingers to be drawn around their pricks—played with them feebly, as in some far dream, and yet I did. That, and their youthful ardour, brought them to a stand once more.

'I say, get her up on to her knees now, Richard. What an arse she has!', was said.

Inert and well-juiced as I was, I made to stall their efforts by dumb slothfulness, by mournful sounds that veiled my sad hypocrisy. As heavy as a sack full of potatoes was I rolled, urged up until my bottom bulbed to Jeremy who knelt behind me and, despite my gritting squeal, entered his knob between the deep cleft of my nether cheeks and forced the tight ring of my bottomhole. I jerked, or tried to, but he gripped my hips. In girlhood had I been invaded such, but never since. I grinched, I bit the pillow as the knob urged in, the helmet slipping past the rim, insinuating inwards till my breath puffed out. I bit the pillow, tried to glide down on my belly then, but Richard ringed my waist and held me up.

'Good fellow, Richard, hold her so. *I* have her now'.

'Oh no!', I sobbed—but did the words escape my lips, or sang they only in my head?

One long, slow thrust—a grunt—and he was in. His balls brushed underneath my sticky pouch, his hands replacing those of Richard where they clasped beneath the soft curve of my belly and thus held me corked. I whimpered. Thus we stayed, then he began to work it in and out with long, slow movements, making my head swim, feeling the suction of his penis there.

O dark miasma of desire—O dark! I heard my breath out—gasping, screwed the pillow up and strove not to cry out the secret pleasure I sustained.

'She's taking it, old chap, I knew she would!', gasped Jeremy, whose prick moved faster then, finding an easement in my narrow aperture, causing my fleshy buttocks on and on to slap against his belly as he worked.

'*Come—work your hips more, Deirdre!*' Ah that voice that came to me from a long, distant past, a bed squeak-creaking underneath my knees after the birch had done its burning work. . . .

Do I excuse myself? Excitement dons a mantle often of confused delight and shame that mingle even while the deed is being done. If such is my excuse, then it must be. One's emotions ofttimes are as hounds that willy-nilly chase the fox. I yielded, I received, first to the one, and then. . . . But no, I'll write no more of that. The morning, come dimly to my eyes at last, found me alone in my much-tousled bed, the stains of sin like puddles on the sheet.

I cried a little—silent tears—then heard the maid approach, and she surprised to find me clothed still in my corset with no nightgown on. I spoke not to her, though, save just to ask if all were up.

'Master Richard's guest has gone, m'am', I heard to my joy. The young rogue had risen early and had fled. My tears dried at the thought of that. He would live all day in fear of my appearance at his home—angel of vengeance with unfolded wings demanding audience with his Mama. Then came the sound of Richard's voice, asking the maid if I were yet awake. At that I sat up in the bed and called him in, to his astonishment, no doubt.

He entered like a vagrant, thief, as well he might—stood dolefully regarding me. I beckoned, motioned him to close the door. His eyes lit up. The dark deeds were forgiven, in his mind. My naked breasts loomed to his willing view. I kicked the sheet down idly and exposed myself, my dried bush well fluffed up and dark upon the white skin of my belly and between my thighs.

'Mama?' His voice was scarce more than a squeak.

I put my finger to my lips, brought him to kneel up on the bed and undid his trouser buttons carefully while motioning silence all the time.

How eagerly and with what wolfish grin he nodded then! I drew out his limp cock and fondled it, pushed down his trousers and caressed his balls. He thought himself in Paradise, of course, and grunted, and his face was flushed.

'Come dearest, lie beside me', I invited. For a second

then his eyes veiled over with an instinct that, alas for him, came much too late. No sooner had he come down to my side than I rolled upon him, clamped my hand over his mouth and—impressing my full weight upon his body, squeezed his balls as strongly as I could while agony showed in his bulging eyes. His face paled, was as white as was the sheet. His eyes rolled—then he lay in a limp faint for which I felt no pity, none at all. Indeed, I rose, began to dress myself. Long moments passed and then he groaned, eyelashes fluttering he doubled up his legs and lay in patent, searching pain which I ignored.

His groans, his whimpers, all were meant as pleas that found no home within my vengeful heart. Passing without, I took the key and locked him there within. When Amy asked me where he was, I said he had gone out a-riding with his friend.

'Oh, he is very nice, Mama, is Jeremy', she said.

I gave her no reply. Such was the only hint I could extend of my displeasure. Not till four hours later, and she out of sight, did I release Richard who had not dared to make a sound to expose his presence in my room. He slank into his own, head down, will get no word from me until I wish. I have not finished with him yet, and nor with Master Jeremy.

CHAPTER TEN

Richard's Day-Book

Mama is so furious with me that I have had to stay in my room all day, and told Amy I have a fever. I was only allowed soup. It is all Jeremy's fault. He told me he had done it before and that ladies always treat it as a jape afterwards. I do not know now if Mama wanted to or not. She was very quiet, but that was only because of Amy, I am sure. I have written her a note and said that I deserve to be beaten and have asked her forgiveness. I put it under her door. I know she found it because I listened very carefully and heard her unfolding the paper, but then I heard her turn the key in her lock. I have been afraid that she would go and see Jeremy's parents, but she did not leave the house. If something would happen, I would feel better. I don't care what it is. Mama's silence is awful.

Amy's Day-Book

Richard does not look at all himself and would hardly speak to me, though I only ventured once into his room. Mama says he may have something catching and that I must not stay. Tomorrow Mama and I are going into town.

I hope I see Jeremy. I think he is very handsome, but I do not think Mama thinks much of him.

Lady Celia's Day-Book

A visit from the Mansfield girl and ladies. Mr. Mansfield did not come; it was said that he was busy and extended his apologies. Sylvia is very sweet, but I find the Misses Mansfield rather forward. It is the way of some County folk apparently. They venture to speak of more intimate things than one is accustomed to. Thus, when I was showing them my dresses, both said what a fine figure I had and judged my age to be several years less than it is, about which I did not disabuse them. Muriel remarked that I have a fine bosom and what she described as a most fetching *embonpoint*, by which Roger later told me she intended my bottom.

That was not a very ladylike thing to say, I told him, whereat he said that to the contrary it was a fine compliment and that my bottom—as he insists on calling it now—is as sleek and firm as a Dutch cheese. He has many times attempted to enter my person there, but I have always desisted. 'It is the country fashion', he said, which I cannot bring myself to believe, nor that Nature intended such. I fear to think how he has come upon such knowledge and tackled him upon that while we were abed and he constantly fingering my aperture there. He said he had overheard such talk being put about in the tap-rooms locally and that it is called corking a female.

I continued to resist his efforts whereupon he spilled against my belly after rubbing furiously and becoming much more excited than I have ever known him do before. I trust that country life is not changing him. I have never known him be this way before. It was proper for him, of course, to accompany the ladies back to their residence, though he was overlong in returning, which I told him would tire Daisy out. She appears to be enjoying the company of Sylvia, though, and that pleases me. It is good for her to have someone of her own age. Girls grow up more quickly nowadays than they were wont to.

Daisy's Day-Book

I am going to ask Mama if I can stay a whole week with Sylvia. We have such a jolly time. Papa is much brightened up now that we have new friends. Mama was a little grumpy that we stayed so long, but Papa wished to talk business with Sylvia's aunties. I believe it was about their stable for they went in there while Sylvia and I stayed away in the garden. Sylvia said we must not play fingers and kisses, as we call it, in sight of her Papa's window again so went into the shrubbery. I like sucking her tongue and she likes sucking mine.

Oh dear, we forgot the passing of time, it was so nice and warm on the grass. We hardly had time to push down our dress before we were found, and Papa looked very flushed for he saw our legs, but Sylvia's aunties said all young ladies like to kiss and that we were not fret to show our jollity. Aunty Muriel is very friendly with Papa for she had her arm around him. Papa did not know what to say, and I myself was confused. She said that if we all kissed one another it would make it the same. Then everybody kissed everybody, and it was very nice. Papa only kissed me on the corner of the mouth and, while he was doing so, Aunty Muriel said she would smooth my dress down, but instead she pulled it up! Sylvia giggled. Papa said it was wrong.

We all had some lemonade and champagne mixed after that. I did not see Mr. Mansfield. He must work very hard. When we came home in the carriage, Papa said I am not to take offence at their jollities for it is the way of people hereabouts.

I did not know what to say, for he spoke to me very directly and I hoped and hoped he had not really seen what Sylvia and I were doing in the garden, so I said I did not mind. Papa said he could not hear me, though, with the noise of the carriage wheels, so I sat on his lap and said it again. He said it meant that I was growing up and that he would kiss me for that, which he did, and while he was doing so he felt my titties! I felt all sticky and warm and the carriage jogged us ever so much so I clung to him and bounced up and down and I could feel my titties swelling. Papa asked did I like it and I said yes, I did not mind, and he said we would do something nicer soon. He sucked my tongue like I do with Sylvia and her aunties! I felt swoony. I am sure now that he did see, so I could not say no. Oh, I did so much kissing today that I feel quite dizzy when I think of it. Aunty Jane said to play with myself when I think of nice things, so I do now.

Phillip's Day-Book

The doom of womanhood is upon me, if womanhood it is still to be called. I am to call both my sisters 'Mistress', I am told, and am to kneel whenever they enter my room. To my profound shame I find myself now doing so, my head first to be buried up under the skirt of one or the other and my ears painfully clenched between their thighs. At all such times now they wear drawers, the crotches of which frequently become moist when I am thus imprisoned.

'Hold your face up and sniff, but do not lick', I am told in the most severe tones. It is useless for me to beg (dear heavens, that I should use that word!) that I do not wish to do either. I am beginning to find a fearful, an utterly incomprehensible, feeling of comfort in having my face so clenched between their fulsome thighs—even, I note, to the use of that very adjective that they have bidden me both to use and to write.

I have not progressed scarce two paragraphs in my new writing, and such as I have miserably penned is scorned.

My day-book is henceforth to be read by them. I have no rights of privacy. Thus am I told to write herein that which I hesitate to set down on paper otherwise. I have smelled in their drawers an admixture of urine and muskiness such as evidently comes upon a woman when she is 'on heat'—oh, dreadful phrase, and one that they have put into my mouth as well as have caused to ease forth from my pen.

In my boyhood I several times heard rough fellows use the dreadful word 'fucking'. My sisters have extracted this confession from me. Deirdre frequently used it when she found herself in the throes of passion, and often wished me to repeat it, to say it to her then, but I would not.

It is, I am told now, an unseemly word for me to employ—though I never have save when Muriel and Jane both brought me to utter it after long ear-burning moments inbetween their undoubtedly strong legs. I am to speak instead of 'servicing' a female—which is to say to insert my penis in their persons (I shall be punished for not using the word I was told to) and to so modulate my movements as to accord them pleasure.

I am to be 'taught' this, and indeed have already, to my renewed despair, begun. This evening Jane knelt upon the couch in my study and presented her naked person to me in the shape of her posterior, having pushed her drawers down to her knees. Muriel meanwhile manipulated me through my drawers and then commanded me to push down and to mount the couch behind Jane who rested on her palms. By various tickling movements of Muriel's fingers I was then entered into Jane's person, or quim—the crest of my tool to very slowly enter until the whole of my penis was engorged in her 'clinging channel'.

The emotions, the sensations, that come upon me when I am sheathed thus in one or other of them are utterly indescribable and so far beyond the bounds of propriety—of morals such as they are properly known and understood in decent Society—are such as make my head reel. Bending behind me, Muriel felt for and held my testicles lightly while I was made to remain embedded in that spongy nest. (Their words again, not mine, of course.)

I was, I was told, to accord Jane fifty long slow strokes of my unfortunately stiffened penis—no more and no less before expelling my juices in her. My testicles being warning held, as I have said, Muriel then slapped my bare buttocks with her free hand and bid me commence. Ah, what an agony of sinful effort! I was made to remain with my torso upright and gazing ahead—not on the 'divine form' of Jane, as Muriel expressed it.

To my supreme agony of shame, Muriel's finger then inserted itself in my nether hole, which caused me excruciating sensations.

'Come on! Perform properly!', she snapped, and then began my enforced motions in and out of Jane's 'clinging maw' while she herself remained still save for occasional imperious movements of her hips, as if to indicate that my efforts were poor, Muriel's finger meanwhile moved back and forth in my posterior, making my embedded penis to feel even stiffer. Moreover, she counted relentlessly. Despite myself, despite all my efforts to remain calm and detached from these wicked proceedings, the urge of Nature came upon me too soon—encouraged wickedly as it was by certain interior clenchings of Jane's person.

My failure thus to accord with their wicked desires and instructions was total. At the count of thirty-one, when I was already at the limit of my endeavours to hold back my spermatic flood, I injected her helplessly and quivered and shuddered much as she sucked upon my jetting tool.

Thereupon, hearing my groans and Jane's murmurs, Muriel removed her finger and began slapping my buttocks hard, telling me—even while I expelled my sperm—what an idle, wicked and totally selfish dog I was not to be able to satisfy the demanding female in the way that she required.

Such are the sensations that so haplessly come upon one during the emission of one's sperm that I begged to be excused, though this did not alleviate the very hard smacks I received—'Just like the bad, naughty boy you are', said Muriel while Jane drew out the last quivering drops of my expended penis and declared that I had come a lot, but much too soon.

For a moment of terrible and unforgivable desire, I wished to remain sheathed in her, but I was made to withdraw and—while she rose—was put upon my belly and thrashed with one of my own straps until I sobbed. I pleaded—yes—for forgiveness. There was none.

'You will LEARN!', Muriel commanded me when she had at last finished assailing my heated buttocks which were torturously striped and hot from leather.

'He MUST learn', I heard Jane say as she pulled her drawers up, as I could hear by the sounds, for my shamed face was all but hidden from them. 'He has a good prick and he comes a lot. He can be put to servicing the girls when he is fit for it and controls himself,' she added.

'Control will come. We will see to it that it does', Muriel said. I was then given a kick and told to pull my drawers up. I stood quivering and weak with my back to the wicked pair, wondering of whom they had spoken. I wished to die, I said. They were the only words I uttered.

'To the contrary, Phillip, you are being guided into a life of usefulness. Males such as you, my dear, are but appendages to your prick. It is your prick that must be educated to perform its correct and proper duties such as your dear wife doubtless never received. You will in the future be put to females twice or thrice a day and will be expected to perform to their satisfaction. You will be slavish in your attentions to them, as you are to be to us. Fail and you will be even more frequently whipped. It is what you have always wished for yourself, had you but known it'.

'I have never...', I began, but such as I might have dared to protest was ignored. With a sweeping of their skirts they retired and closed the door, leaving me to such cogitations as even the great Dante did not envisage in his visions of the Inferno, albeit that in the middle of the journey of my life I, too, find myself in a dark forest whence there seems no escape.

I shall write to my once-beloved. It is my only hope.

I shall smuggle the letter out somehow, but who will put it to the post for me? I may be driven to ask Rose. A sovereign slipped into her hand should suffice to seal her lips. I shall ask Deirdre to return. We shall restore order to the house. I am sure that she will see the light. Ah alas!—I have forgotten that my day-book is now to be examined by Muriel and Jane. I must pen my letter immediately and somehow must get hold of Rose. I shall stand bold—shall expunge not a word of what I have now written here. My ears will burn between their thighs again, I know.

Muriel's Day-Book

Rose was quite taken aback last evening to have a sovereign pressed into her hand by Phillip, she believing that he required rather more special favours of her, which I suspected she would not be that unwilling to accord him. She, too, must learn however. In the event he but wished her to post a letter to Deirdre. Within half an hour I had handed it back to him, advising him that he might post it himself. Naturally he was covered in confusion, which is quite a proper state for him to be in!

'Are you then a prisoner in your house?', I mocked him. I had not ventured to unseal the envelope, nor would dream of doing so. I know our Phillip by now much better than I ever did. He is falling faster and faster into that very despond—as some men believe it to be—that in truth he wishes to immerse himself in.

Even two weeks ago a pert reply would have come upon his lips. Now, however, he merely mumbled something and made his way without—quite longing, I am sure, for me to call him back. I then read the last entry in his day-book. He betrays himself, though he knows it not, in the final sentence he has penned therein. That which he pretends to despise, to hate, to feel shame of, is that which he really now desires. He was not long gone.

Upon his ascending the stairs once again, I pointed to my bedroom and he went meekly within. Following him, I closed the door and turned the key. I would have my amusements occasionally without Jane there.

I advised him that I was going to teach him little tricks—that one snap of my thumb and finger would indicate my requirement to be licked and attended upon and that I would extend that part of my body which required such attention. Two clicks would mean that he was to service me, bearing in mind the required number of cock-strokes were to be given. His eyes have begun to grow a little hungrier now. I observed that as I disrobed before his eyes, retaining only my bootees and my brown, gartered stockings.

A motion of my hand caused him to kneel. This he has already learned. Straddling my legs and standing over him, I brought him to apply the tip of his tongue to my slit, whereat he had to sniff first. The motions of his tongue have become more agile, I notice—sweeping and curling in the appropriate manner of a trained hound that I once knew a lady to employ for that very purpose. I moved my belly occasionally, deliberately bumping it against his nose.

'Faster! You are making your Mistress come', I ordained. Hands on hips, I teased myself by weaving my bottom about so that one moment—as the exquisite climax of desire approached—his tongue swooped beneath my slit, and at another I withdrew from all but the very tip of it. An agony of pleasure seized me after a few moments of this voluptuous exercise. Grasping his ears, I brought his mouth to splurge under my cunnylips and squirted my fine juice of love over his tongue whereafter I turned, bent forward, and had him lick my bottom just as slavishly until my bottomhole was well lubricated by his saliva.

A sense of great satisfaction seized me. Alone with me, Phillip proved more suppliant and seemingly anxious to please than had Jane been there. Upon my facing him once more, with my bottom feeling pleasurably warm and wet, he bowed his head and remained kneeling with hands clasped.

'Show your Mistress what you have for her now', I murmured.

His hands twittered at his buttons, pushed his trousers down, and then his fine cambric drawers of which he now has three pairs, though has lamentably failed to note that fact in his day-book.

His penis stood very stiff. 'Are you a good doggy?', I enquired softly, for I have discovered that it is meaningful if one constantly changes one's tone of voice.

Phillip nodded but did not look up, despite the allure of my well-puffed quim. I teased him more then by rubbing my garters against his nose while taking purchase on his hair and holding his head up. I confess to a great desire to lie upon my back and have him mount me, yet it is frequently better to leave his cock in a state of suspense. I intend to work him well and believe that the day is not far off when his penis may be introduced very usefully into the younger ones. For the time being at least he may be regarded as the house stallion. That is how I wish it to be.

'You may leave now', I told him. There was little hiding of his disappointment. I made him turn and crawl on all fours to the door and there cover himself again before I bid him rise and dismissed him. His night would have been one of such desiring as he will never confess.

CHAPTER ELEVEN

Lady Celia's Day-Book

I am pursued by dreams and visions such as cloud my mind both with apprehension and delight. I am in such confusion as I have never known before. Two days ago Muriel Mansfield visited on her own. She was passing, so she said, and ventured to have herself announced. Being alone, I received her whereupon she greeted me by kissing me upon the mouth, to my great astonishment. She responded to the look of disconcerted wonder that I then could not contain by smiling and doffing her cloak and bonnet.

Tea being brought, we then discoursed on quite usual matters such as dress and so on, though all the time I felt myself as if being examined, and as if in turn I were examining her.

'I have upset you. Do you not like kissing other women?', she asked as soon as the maid had departed with the tea things.

I told her that I did not know of such things, which was true. My expression again must have shown it, for she laughed and asked me whether it repelled. I said that I did not know the answer to that.

'I believe you do', said she, 'but it is hidden in your mind. If I kiss you again when I leave, will you forgive me for my impertinence?'

Such a conversation never having entered before into my realms of experience, I was dumb and perhaps pursed my lips rather primly, for another aggravating smile appeared on her lips.

'It is not forbidden, you know', were her next words. Thereat, she rose, and I thinking that she was about to leave soon enough. Instead, she seated herself on the arm of my chair, drew my chin up and again impressed her mouth over my own in such a fashion that I clutched my both hands at the arms of the chair. Her tongue slid into my mouth for a moment and then retreated.—'You see how sweetly it disturbs?', she asked, for in the quickness of the moment I had not endeavoured to evade the strange and foreign-seeming kiss, and thus she evidently thought me entirely acquiescent.

I made to rise, but in that moment she removed herself from my immediate presence. And there came then from my own mouth one of those ridiculous interjections that have their origin without any seeming thought.—'I do not understand!', I uttered while she, turning away, picked up her long kid gloves. In that same moment a noise was heard without and Roger entered—and when I least wished him to. The door having been left ajar by the careless maid, he had overheard what I had said.

'Pray what is it you do not understand, dearest?', he enquired.

Perhaps I was saved for the moment by Muriel's otherwise most impolite interruption, since I would not have known how to answer him.

'Oh, something nice. But I must really leave now. Will you both forgive me?', she replied and swept up her feathered hat and was gone, leaving me to burst into tears which I refused to explain to Roger on any account, and he being left utterly bewildered and not a little concerned.

That night I entered into a dream in which Muriel was kissing me again, though for much longer. Indeed, I woke out of the dream with my entire body feeling overwarm and strange and clutched at Roger who awoke on the instant to ask me what the trouble was. Again I could not explain, but fortunately he fell asleep again almost immediately. The dream pursued me all day—not only the dream, but the actuality that had preceded it, those full moist lips upon my own and the impertinent flickering of a tongue in my mouth. Each time I thought of it my cheeks grew hot and I experienced a feeling of mingling outrage and unwanted pleasure that I could not bring myself to believe in.

I have always lived a virtuous life, as I have understood the word. I have fended off naughtinesses even from Roger who has sometimes become too wicked and brash in his desires. Yet as the night came on again, I fell into a curious despairing—that in truth was not completely so—that I would enter into the same dream again.

Indeed I did, save that this time both I and Muriel were undressed and pressed our naked forms together. Awakening from this dream, and it being morn, I began to roll restlessly about. Once more I awakened Roger and this time he would not be put off, indeed veritably bullied me into telling him what had passed, which I at last did, though brokenly and often almost incomprehensibly.

To all he listened quietly, however, stroking my face and form and in particular between my thighs where I was very moist. Raising his nightgown, he brought his penis to thrum against my belly and thereupon began to speak as I have never heard him do before. Strange words and phrases passed his lips and floated like down about my head. I was not to be disturbed, said he, for such desires between women were well-known and indeed universal. Kissing after all was a jollity and to be encouraged. It was a great prettiness for women to kiss, he averred, while I was protesting weakly that it was wicked and wrong and that I really had no desire to.

His voice then took on a more serious strain.—'I believe you have a considerable desire to pleasure yourself which until now has remained hidden in the depths of your being, my love. Deny it as you will, but at this very moment—awakening fresh from the most delightful and sensuous of dreams—your cunnylips pout like a young girl's and are sticky with desire. Feel how smoothly and easily my cock enters you', he intoned, rolling upon me before I could prepare a defense.

In but one second he was fully sheathed, our bellies close together and his fine eyes glowing down into mine. The gentle stirring and pulsing of his rod excited me madly and, though I did not wish to show it, I began to utter sounds of passion. Suavely and deeply his cock moved in me while my bottom cheeks rippled with pleasure and my breasts heaved, my nipples quickly springing erect.

'You will have her, my pet', he murmured, to which I moaned 'NO!', though not for long. His words had the same effect upon me as had her kisses—that is to say of apprehension and delight at the same time so that I knew not which way to turn between the two conflicting feelings.

'Yes!', he insisted. His loins began to work. My hips rolled with pleasure. I clasped my arms around his neck and came upon the instant, oiling his pistoning tool and thus silently confessing my arisen excitement which was fast overcoming its erstwhile twin.

'I must not! No, it is wicked!', I moaned, twisting and turning in my mind between the delirious actuality of what was happening and the wholly disturbing feelings that had otherwise been aroused in me.

'I will bring her to you, dearest', I heard and then my head sank back deeper into my pillow and I spilled yet again, though then in longer trills such as racked my entire form with electric sensations.

'No, yes!', I answered in one and the same breath. Thereupon Roger began to plough my clinging furrow deeply. We panted, we clasped one another in a frenzy of pleasure while the most sensuous and wicked phrases poured from his lips.

'Ah, what a superb fuck you are! What enchantment you will know!', he uttered, and then came the flood of his desiring in orgasmic bliss. Our bodies quivered together in delight, I creamed his prick again, received his last and thinner spurts, and then we both sank down in heavenly quiet.

Roger, though, was not long at his ease. More stirs in him than used to, I believe. The manly rod withdrew and he sat up, stirring his tousled hair, eyes crinkling in a smile.

'You shall have her today, my pet', he said and stepped from off the bed as though he had said something normal, ordinary.

'Dearest, no, I did not mean . . . !'

'I will bring her after lunch, my dear. You two will swim in delicious harmony, I know. 'Twill do you the very world of good. I shall take Daisy to their house and will not return for several hours. You will not be disturbed at all'.

'No, Roger, no—I cannot!'

'I say *yes*, you shall, you will, my dear. I promise you there shall be no reprise if you do not enjoy yourself'.

My remonstrances, my pleas, were all in vain. I am left alone now with my hour. I shall refuse to kiss her, that is all. I shall refuse.

Jane's Day-Book

Lady Celia is, then, to be brought into our little game. Muriel, as usual, has confided all in me. The lady is fit for tickling-up, she says, and then will be put to Phillip in a manner that she has refused her husband to this date. He will fill her plentifully in a few days, has not been allowed to eject his sperm and must contain himself for the event. Roger does not know this part of it as yet, though his dear wife will be returned to him perfectly whole, though with a very creamy hole! Meanwhile, Daisy, too, is to receive. We have worked it out between us, or I say we have—but dear Muriel says it was all her idea. I shall not say her nay to that; she always likes to have the upper hand.

Muriel's Day-Book

I have sometimes thought of myself that I am 'too many people' and have too many mixed desires. I have not said this to Jane or she might think me strange. Roger is at one moment one into whose arms I wish to fall for ever—yet at another I would have him in part at least as Phillip is. Let the wind take me, though, I do not care. It was I who suggested to him the seduction—if such it may be called at her age—of his wife. A fair creature she is and fit for greater pleasures than she has so far permitted to herself. As to Sylvia, I perhaps feel both resentment and jealousy at Roger's desiring of her when I would have thought I might have found excitement in the act.

Daisy looks prettier and fresher to my eyes each time I see her, though Roger appears confounded by my mentioning of her in the acts of love. I know not why save that he perhaps wishes to appear more virtuous than he is—or is it I who have unfolded his true character? I believed him shy at first, but one can never tell. I am thought to be most proper among those who do not know me well—which is as it should be, and this I always impress upon the girls. They take me seriously—I know they do. Such a sweet flush comes upon their cheeks when their titties and their pussies arc caressed. If anything, Daisy's nest is the slightly more plump of the two and is ready for a joust.

I shall have Celia tomorrow and trust that she is as fair unclothed as she appears in those expensive dresses that she wears. She is more susceptible than she believes herself to be. I shall much enjoy putting her up to Phillip. If it is needful to birch her first, I shall, but I do not think it will be. He is sufficiently well-trained to get his prick into her bottom smoothly now. It will do her a world of good, and will teach him, too, that there are such rewards for true obedience.

Aunty Muriel went to see Mama today. I believe they are going to be good friends. I hope so. I thought we were simply to collect her, but Papa then took me back, to my delight. However, it was not quite as I thought, for Aunt Jane was VERY naughty and said that as the house was quiet we could show our garters if we wished, and this said before Papa, and I did not know where to look and nor did Sylvia!

Papa said to let us be and said he wished to see the stable again with Aunt Jane, although I think it is very dull in there and rather like an old chapel. It smells of straw and horse manure.

'No, my dear, sometimes young ladies must do as they are required to', Aunt Jane said, or something like that she said, for I did not know where to put my eyes and ears, as we say. Well then, she said we might take our dresses off and made us stand up side by side. Papa said he would go out if we did, but he did not seem to know what to do. I do not know where Mr. Mansfield was. It was very quiet, and Rose was not there. Aunt Jane said we must do it and unbuttoned us both. I really wanted to hold hands with Sylvia and my face was red. To take our dresses off we both had to bend forward and I could not see Papa then and was glad of that, for I only had my chemise and stockings on, like Sylvia. Mama does not know that I do not wear drawers now.

Both our dresses tumbled on the floor, but when I straightened up I saw that Papa had gone out. He was in the garden and often turned his back on us but sometimes he looked through the window. We were not quick enough, said Aunt Jane, and had to take our chemises off as well! Oh horror to stand naked in our stockings and shoes! Papa looked again through the window, but only for a minute. Aunt Jane was DIPPY for she called to him that we wished to speak to him. He did not come at first, so again she called and then he returned, but stared at the carpet. He did not look up and asked what we wished to say. Oh, we covered our faces and could not speak!

Aunt Jane tutted and said we were being silly, but even so that we might all kiss and so make-up, though none of us had had a breeze. I wished to hide my front and so did Sylvia and so we turned and kissed each other. Aunt Jane said then to Papa to feel our bottoms and how nice and warm they were. I believe he did not wish to, but she made him do. Sylvia and I pressed together and giggled when he did. I felt his hand go underneath, but then he moved it quick away and went out of the room again.

Aunt Jane said then to us to dress and went off after him. I believe they walked around the stable, for we did not see them for almost an hour, and there was straw on Aunt Jane's skirt so I supposed she must have fallen down.

Papa kissed me in the carriage going home and said I was a good girl, and I sat upon his lap again. I did not wish to take my dress and chemise off, I said, but Aunt Jane had made me, though I said also it was by way of jollity, for such is the correct phrase for such things. She told me so. Suddenly a boldness came over me and I prayed him not to tell Mama that I was not wearing any drawers. Papa laughed at that, amid much kissing of my lips, and said that he could not in any case, for then it would be thought he had lifted up my dress. I very really blushed at that! How silly it did not occur to me. I hid my face and the carriage jogged us on, I bouncing up and down upon his lap and something very hard beneath me, too.

Then Papa asked, if he had seen me once, might he again? Oh how I blushed and hid my face the more, but then he did a funny thing and licked his tongue into my ear which made me wriggle, and asked again until I said he might if Mama were not there. At that he felt my breasts again and said they were quite swollen up. Did it feel nice, he asked, and I said yes. I felt all funny everywhere. My bottom jogged upon the hard thing underneath and Papa made some funny sounds. I leaned back and he kissed my titties through my dress!

Mama was in bed when we got home. I think she has a fever, for she looked so flushed. Aunt Muriel was buttoning up her dress and must have changed her clothes perhaps. She gave me a sweet smile and oh a big, big kiss and then she looked at Papa and said that he must see to me properly that night. I do not know what she meant by that. I think she really meant Mama, because she has a fever. She did not come down to dinner, anyway.

Lady Celia's Day-Book

O love, O lips, O wanton hands! I cannot believe what I have done, nor how sweet and insistent Muriel was. What lewdness did I entertain! I can scarce face my reflection in the mirror now. Her tongue was long and supple in my mouth. I thought us but to kiss, but she disrobed and had me do the same, despite all protestations that I made.

'Dearest, we are to have each other now. Your husband will not interfere', she said. How could she know? I wished to ask her that, but like a tigress, a devouring angel was she on my love-betraying form, my nipples stiff against her own, her belly working sleekly over mine until our love potions mingled in a flood and we lay panting in the aftermath.

I thought it done and that the dream was o'er. She told me then to swing my legs from off the bed. I thought us to get up, though dizzy was my head and stark with wickedness the brown tips of my breasts—my 'coral swellings', as she said. Upon my moving, though, she knelt beside the bed and lifted up my legs and . . . Oh! how dare I write of that, how dare! Her long tongue flickered where no mouth has ever been. I sighed, I moaned, could not contain myself. I have always thought that when orgasmic bliss has seized one and the juice is spilled, then all is done. It is not so for women, as she taught me then. Thrice more I spurted love's rain in her mouth, and then her lips came up to savage mine, our breasts a-bounce together; all was love. I swam in ecstasy, as Muriel avowed she did as well. We lay like two does, panting in the aftermath, our bushes sticky, kissing quim to quim—and I who never thought to use such words play with them now like trinkets of desire.

Roger was sweet to me, besides. 'Did you enjoy?', he asked, and that was all he asked. I nodded but I could not speak. I held his prick. He toyed with both my slit and with my bottomhole. I did not jerk, but even so I would not let him put it in me there, between my bottom cheeks, could not. 'Before the month is out you shall', he said. I know not what he meant by that. I was a lost woman, I said, for I felt a guilt, though he did not obtain any jealousy of Muriel as was evident from his soft words. He wished to ask me much, I know, but could not bring himself to do, and for myself I was—and am—too shy to speak. How unselfishly he has acted in the course of this astonishing event.

'I shall not do it again', I said, but hid my face, knew it to be a lie and felt an awful conscience over me. But even that he understood—the kind, dear, understanding man he is.

'Never say never, Celia', he said as he stroked my bottom lovingly. I knew not what to answer, so pretended sleep. I never knew myself before to be married to such an angel of a man.

Sir Roger's Day-Book

Dearest Celia, I will not have her undone in any wise, but only pleasured, and have told Muriel so.

'You shall have her bottom soon enough, if that is what you want', she said, and gave me a quite jealous look! I assured her that her own—bold and bumptious as it is and smooth as cream—was enough to satisfy any man, which much appeased her. How she pants when it is put up there—she bucks and whinnies like a mare while my prick soothes inbetween her ardent hemispheres.

She and Jane converse together of the most intimate things, I fear. Were it not for that my fondness as to Muriel would grow, I think. 'Is not Daisy nice and curly inbetween her thighs?', she asked. I said I had not looked, nor would. 'Oh, pouf, you felt their bottoms did you not?', she asked. I thought that indiscreet, but merely shook my head. I suspect she sensed an indiscretion then. I wished to ask if she had put her finger into Celia's bottom, but that would have been a caddish thing to ask. I marvel at my own terms of morality, and yet one can only be oneself.

I must speak to Daisy, for I fear the sisters' tongues. My resolution to have Jane and that sweet Sylvia as well has diminished slightly in the light of this, yet I am drawn to them in the same wise as Celia is to Muriel.

'You can have both of us together soon', said Muriel. I took offence at that and told her *I* would say so if I wished it to be so. Again she looked downcast. Her tongue does run away with her sometimes. She means no malice, that's the thing of it. I told her that I knew that well, and so excused her in a way. She sighed and lay within my arms.

'We two will always be both combatants and allies, dear', she said.

I thought that very true and praised her for her words.

'Oho, you like *some* things I say!', she laughed. She can be quite irresistible at times.

Daisy's Day-Book

If anyone asks me if Papa has kissed me on the lips, I am to swear that he has not. Papa has lectured me most solemnly on that. We had a SECRET MEETING in my room! I would not tell ANYONE in the WHOLE WORLD, I said, and that is true. Suppose you were spanked and made to say, he said. I would not even tell an ANGEL, I replied. It made him laugh. 'Then do not tell yourself, for you are one, my pet', he said. He seemed more jolly then—had had an anxious look before. I only had my nightgown on. He made to put his arms around me, but then he stopped and suddenly went out. I was very vexed. I'm sure he does not believe me after all.

CHAPTER TWELVE

Eveline's Day-Book

Listening to Deirdre's tale, one would think that the end of the world had come, though she made far more fuss of it than I suspect she really feels. Her need to unburden was greater than her need to receive 'grace', which I certainly was not going to accord her, as I said.

Did I not think it was wicked beyond belief, she asked. Fairly obviously she did not wish me to say yes to that. I explained to her—if explaining was ever needed—that she must bring herself to regard it as a libertine adventure of entirely impulsive origins. I confess I was rather pleased with that phrase, for I am sure she expected something much more open and unladylike.

Would she like me to deal with Master Richard? Her eyes lit up. Or was there a mite of anxiety in them at the same time? I impressed upon her that she need not be present, and that what I have in mind for him will but serve to teach him a lesson in the most knowledgeable way. Well, she has agreed. I am not to tell Maurice, she said, but 'Come, come', I replied, for if we are not libertarians then what are we? She became a little weepy—from love rather than remorse, I do believe. I had half intended confessing the truth to her about Claudia, but in the light of Deirdre's evidently mixed emotions decided against it. After all, the extremely naughty thought crosses my mind (not to say Maurice's as well) that there is yet Amy to be breached. We have yet to meet her, but from her mother's description, she sounds charmingly suitable for such conversions to our cause that we DO like to bring about.

Perhaps I should tell Claudia more about Deirdre. It is all getting to be quite an intriguing mix-up. There are distinct possibilities here, as Maurice avers, for of course I have told him all.

Richard's Day-Book

I am still in disgrace and must, I suppose, expect to be. I feel sure that if the worst had happened and Mama had gone to Jeremy's house, that I would have heard about it. I am to take some package or other to a lady she has met. Those are the only words Mama has spoken to me. I just said that I would and looked at her very pleadingly, but her eyes are as cold as ever. Amy asked me what was the matter and I told her to shut up. She is getting very bumptious and, I think, restless. She said to me that she hoped I hadn't 'done anything wrong' to Mama, and I asked her what she meant. I am afeared she has heard something. Jeremy was stupid. Amy said to me in reply that she knows all about these things but I don't think she does. I don't think anyone has even felt up her skirt. Her bum seems to have got a bit bigger. I told her so and she went red and rushed into her room and slammed the door. I bet she pulled up her skirts and had a look.

I heard mother say to her, 'You will be birched if you say things like that about your brother, Amy'. Perhaps Mama does not really think so bad of me as she makes out. I wish I knew. She will not allow me take the pony and trap to deliver the package. I shall have to travel on a horse bus with common people.

Richard went to deliver a package to a lady friend of Mama's, and he hasn't come back! I asked Mama if she were not worried. Mama said he was in good hands and would be looked after. I did not know he had not returned until I woke up this morning. This afternoon a gentleman called Maurice visited. I thought he was quite nice. He said that Richard was behaving himself. Well, that will make a change. I know he has been kissing Mama, but I am not going to say my other thoughts for I shall be told I am wicked.

Maurice—I thought his name was Mr. Maurice at first and apologised for calling him that. He said he did not mind, and when Mama was out of the room he said I am a very attractive girl! I think Jeremy liked me in the same way, too, but Mama will not hear HIS name spoken, and I cannot understand why. She says he was impolite to her. This was said while Maurice was listening, and when Mama was upstairs he told me that kissing and cuddling is sometimes thought impolite and asked me if I thought so.

I said I did not think so. I was blushing! He said he was pleased I was a sensible girl and that I was much like Mama in that respect. Very suddenly then he KISSED me and said 'Oh, you have a nice bottom, but do not tell your Mama I said so', and he put his hand there! I felt shy to move and did not know what to do. He said he could feel I had nice drawers on and did I always wear them. I did not know how to answer. He said I need not always, for they encumber young ladies. I felt very much a silly-head for not being able to speak. I thought it was rude for him to keep touching me there, but at the same time I thought it was rude if I said so.

By the time Mama returned downstairs, he had sat down again, and my bottom felt tingly as if his hand were still there. Mama excused herself and said she had a bad headache, so Maurice offered to take me for a drive. Mama did not seem sure about that. I think she was a bit jealous. She said I could go for an hour. I did not know whether I wanted to or not, but I like going out.

Maurice drove the pony trap himself and we went all along the lanes at SUCH a pace that I was breathless and my bonnet nearly flew off. Then we stopped on the verge of a little woodland. It was very pleasant among the trees. He tethered the pony and we had a little walk. I was VERY much praised for my conversation and my deportment. We sat down under an oak and he said my mouth and my eyes are very lovely! Then he made a joke and said he wished to be 'impolite' and kiss me and feel my BOTTOM again! I wanted to say no that time, but he would not let me and SMOTHERED me with kisses, saying I was RAPTUROUS!

Mama would die if she knew he felt up UNDER my skirt. I did not wish him to and struggled a bit, but he became stern and said to me to be still. He said he wished to feel my bottom through my drawers, which he did, all round and EVERYWHERE. I felt very strange because his finger was inbetween the halves of my bottom and rubbed me gently there. He said that if I stopped struggling it would be nice and that all mamas wished their daughters to learn it so, but always left it to gentlemen to teach them.

I could hardly speak because he was kissing me and FEELING me so much, even inbetween my legs! 'Oh no!', I said.—'Oh yes, my dear, for this is what you have to learn', said he. I thought of Mama and what she would think and said he mustn't do, or I would tell.

'Ah no, for then you would be most utterly and completely indiscreet and everyone will learn of it, which is to say your indiscretion. You would be scorned for that', he said.

I half believed him, half did not. Oh, what a tizzy I was in! Seeing my doubts, and my hand feebly thrusting at his own, he suddenly sat up and leaned against the tree and said I was not nice to him at all, which much confused me further, all in all.

I, too, sat up and began to smooth my dress. In a trice,

however, he had placed his arm about the back of my shoulders and made me to lie face down across his knees. Oh goodness, then he pulled my dress right up and smacked and smacked my knickered bottom till I sobbed for him to cease, so redhot did it feel. Real tears rolled down my cheeks. My bottom felt in flames!

'Sit up and learn that you have to obey your elders', then he said, and I still blubbering the while and not fit to sit upon my poor scorched bottom, but he made me do, then brought me to lean into him, spoke to me softly, helped to dry my tears. I was a young lady now, he said, and must do as all young ladies do, and if I told Mama how I had struggled she would laugh and say I was a baby still.

He fondled my titties as he spoke and I had to let him kiss my lips again. I wriggled all the time, though, while he did, because my bottom stung. I promised in the end I would not tell Mama. He said that all would scorn me if I did, and that everyone would remember it.

When we returned Mama said my eyes were a little red, but I told her that was because I had laughed so much and rubbed them. She was very pleased I had enjoyed myself, she said. I would have told her all that happened, but perhaps she will say that I am a baby after all. My bottom has got plumper—I am sure it has. I asked Mama if it stuck out. She laughed and said that all young ladies' should.

Sir Roger's Day-Book

What an odd chap Mansfield is—though it was said to me once that all chaps other than ourselves are odd. In his case, however, I believe it to be true. He has a wan, far look about him, and is most decidedly under the heels of his sisters.

Upon visiting them today I had little enough conversation with him, and all of it banal. On plea of seeing to his estate accounts, he then disappeared indoors again while I, the lone male among the females, enjoyed the sun and desultory conversation that went on. Muriel asked me whether I could tell Daisy and Sylvia apart in the dark. I knew very well what she meant thereby, or intended me to understand, but I replied jovially enough and said that I could distinguish them even by their toes. Jane, breaking in, asked me as to other parts of their anatomies, whereat I yawned and pretended not to hear. I obtain to the view that there are certain things that may be discussed in bed, or otherwise in a loving embrace, but not when one is sitting apart. A quaint view, perhaps; I am not sure.

Celia is to visit Muriel tomorrow. She was not unnaturally shy of doing so in my presence. She will not even have me transport her there, but Sylvia will come here via our carriage on its return journey. Indeed, it *would* be a great pleasure to have her! She has a most kissable mouth. I recall coming upon her and Daisy kissing on the lawn, their skirts much ruffled: a very pretty sylvan scene. No doubt young girls frequently amuse themselves in this way. I have heard a dozen stories and more of housemaids being found bussing one another when they had no man to do so.

The deuce of it is that I shall know well enough what Celia is at tomorrow and will think of it constantly. It makes a chap feel devilishly randy. Daisy has been a little sulky since my talk with her. I believe I handled it badly and should have put on a better humour rather than indulged myself in such serious vein. It is I who am to blame. I have already passed beyond the bounds of propriety by kissing her often enough and fondling her titties which are delightfully grown and round. Her nipples are responsive, by jove. I suspect they have been subject already to errant caressing by Muriel and Jane. It is no help to me that I tend to think of such and hence tend to get carried away when alone with her.

Maurice's Day-Book

What a delight to kiss and fondle a young girl who knows not whether to be pleased with it or not! Amy will prove a perfect subject for such games as we love to indulge in. I believe I had her in the right mood not to say a word to her Mama who in any case is sufficiently indulgent herself not to be able to cast stones.

Before we returned to the house, I told Amy with jovial lovingness that she has had her first smack-bottom, and may have more. Such confusion in her eyes! She is too shy to reject one's advances completely. Eveline will know how to handle her, and thus we shall progress her. One may anticipate quite a delightful future with such a nubile young subject. Provided one is sufficiently strict with her in moments of potential rebellion on her part, she will learn to yield.

Eveline's Day-Book

I must say that young Richard is a fine-looking youth and—as to be expected—charmingly awkward in my presence. He believed himself to be merely running an errand, on which however he was quickly disabused. Telling him that I had something to show him—which put him into much mystification—I led him up to the bedroom which is set aside for certain diversions and which even Maurice does not venture to enter, for I have made it my own domain.

There Claudia awaited, and in such attire, or lack of it, as caused Richard to gawp and his cheeks to assume a deep shade of pink. The basque that Claudia wore was black and trimmed with fine lace, the top flirting with her nipples, which are deliciously poky, and the bottom leaving her bush bared—or rather, it would have done had she not been wearing black silk drawers which matched her stockings. Black boots buttoned up to just below her knees completed as bewitching and commanding a picture of voluptuous femininity as one could hope to see.

While Richard continued to gawp, and Claudia rose from the single bed upon which she had been lounging, I locked the door. The sound thereof caused him to turn his head sharply while I maintained my 'cool look', as Maurice is pleased to call it.

'This is the one, then? Is he well-equipped?', Claudia asked, I having coached her well in all that was to pass.

This indeed was the miscreant, I replied. At that, something resembling a choked gurgle came from Richard whose legs trembled visibly. As to his being sufficiently well-equipped to be able to present himself properly to the most demanding of ladies, said I, we were about to discover.

Claudia then advanced upon him, swaying her hips until her belly all but touched his own while I went forward to his rear and clasped my arms about his waist which is of almost girlishly slim proportions. Had he but had his wits about him he would have realised that he was thus placed in the same position as the unwitting Deirdre had been.

'You will not speak nor raise protest or your Mama shall hear of it', I said.

'Oh, Madam, what are you at?', he gasped, for thereupon Claudia proceeded with fingers well-practised in such a task to undo all his buttons. Resultantly his trousers subsided to his ankles, his shirt being raised up and his penis and testicles bared for our attention. During this rapid process, I maintained one arm about his person while taking a firm grip on the back of his hair, which naturally caused him to yelp in surprise—and to utter pleas for mercy, indeed!

'Be quiet, you young brute, you are in training', Claudia hissed at him, and this leaving him quite dumbstruck, for at the same time she so expertly handled his cock that it rose in a trice to quite fine proportions. Indeed, I did have the passing thought that dear Deirdre has little to complain about.

'I have him; use the bottle', I told Claudia. It was unnecessary for me to so say, since she already knew our little plot, but needful for Master Richard to have two determined feminine voices at his ears.

'No!', came a whine from him, for she then turned and picked up a glass flask from the small cabinet at the foot of the bed. The mouth of the flask has a flare to it, the rim curving outwards, and has previously been used for such a task to which it was then to be devoted. To a cry from Richard, upon whose hair I maintained a painful tugging, the neck of the flask was slipped over the bulbous head of his aroused penis and the fleshy shaft sunk therein, leaving just sufficient of the base of his prick to be deftly fingered by Claudia.

Master Richard's knees yielded and quivered as she then began to frig him. The flask, being 'waisted' towards its centre, creates a partial vacuum within which draws upon the crest of a stiff penis and urges out the sperm.

His posture was, for him, awkward in the extreme, for I had by then pressed one knee into the back of his own and so kept him at balance and quite unable to resist Claudia's determined attentions. I doubt that three-quarters of a minute passed before he yielded his manhood and sprang some fine jets of come into the bottle where they formed a greyish pool. At that moment, of course, Richard was at his weakest and I had little difficulty in manacling his wrists behind him.

It was Claudia who held his hair in this brief process while maintaining the bottle well over his cock, though by then it had expelled its last spurts.

Stricken cries came from him upon our then forcing him down on his back on the bed where his legs hung limp over the sides and the flask tilted at an angle to his slowly diminishing cock.

'Mama!', he bleated wildly, to our mutual amusement.

'Your dear Mama would never wish to see such a dismal sight', said I, 'And heaven forfend that she ever should'. Then, turning to Claudia, I added for his benefit, 'His penis clearly needs exercising regularly. He must do better than this. What a feeble performance! Pray, dear, will you see to him upon the hour, each hour?'

'It will be my distinct pleasure. The rapscallion must surely have more in his balls than this or he will be no use to any of us. Why, I have a deerhound that can produce more!', Claudia jeered while Richard paled and flushed by turns and looked exactly like a maiden whose drawers have been taken down for the first time and, under inspection, knows not where to look.

'An hour then. I will leave him in your hands. He may be fed bread and milk, but nothing else. See to it that you perform better next time!', I told Richard sharply. 'Have him attend to toilet duties as well', I added in an equally severe tone to Claudia whose gaze was as unblinking as my own.

'To that purpose I shall put a collar and lead on him and have him crawl to the water-closet behind me', she said, and gave him a little kick on his ankles as though to emphasize the point, and this bringing a croaking plea from Richard to be 'allowed to go home'.

'You will be allowed only that which we desire', was my response and thereupon—having pointedly consulted a small clock on the cabinet—we left him to such a maze of thoughts as he must have found himself lost within: a captive in the house of strange, voluptuous females!

Four times today has he been milked of his sperm. Seemingly he could do no better than that and will sleep—still manacled—in an utterly weakened state. This, however, is but a beginning for Master Richard. I have always adhered to the view that a young male may become as much of a plaything for older females that a maiden sometimes does for her male elders. Maurice treads quietly past the door behind which I have Richard incarcerated and does not wish to see him. It is a little private business of my own, says he, and quite rightly. I allowed him to fête Claudia in bed tonight. She is always so sensuously wriggly between the pair of us.

As to Amy, Maurice has told me all. He is minded that I should take her in hand and prepare her for the sacrifice. I think not. I have Richard to attend to, not to say Deirdre. My hands are full in the most pleasant of ways. It would do well for Amy to be in the solemn presence of gentlemen only—a treat she will otherwise never have. I must say that Maurice looked rather pleased that I 'permit' that! Besides, it means that we need not have Amy here, for the time being at least, and this will avoid complications with Deirdre.

I may drop a hint to Deirdre that Amy must not be entirely neglected and, indeed, would be well to be 'diverted' in respect of naughty Richard's behaviour. Putting this to her as I shall, I believe she will allow herself to be convinced and may well be secretly comforted to have the otherwise difficult matter taken out of her hands.

We shall see!

CHAPTER THIRTEEN

Phillip's Day-Book

I am surrounded by that darkness into which I have allowed myself to be led. Dear Sylvia is to spend some time with her friend Daisy, for which I am grateful. Her eyes question me frequently, and I have naught to say that could be of comfort to her. The dread I have that she may discover my undoing causes me to relinquish myself more and more into the hands of Muriel and Jane.

A moment of extreme discomfort in every sense came upon me last evening when Sylvia ventured into my study to bid me good night. Her aunts had told her, she said, that my novel was progressing. The dear child appeared to have nothing else to say, and I did not doubt that my sisters had put her up to that remark. My desk being covered with paper on which I have endeavoured—though with little success—to ameliorate the wicked desires of Muriel and Jane, Sylvia perched herself lovingly on my lap and made attempt to peer at them, as if to express an interest in my work which she would not otherwise have.

Being unprepared for such, I made haste to cover them, which much put her out, and I endeavouring to explain that nothing was sufficiently good to be read yet.

'Well, Papa, they say you are a good writer, anyway', Sylvia said proudly, not having—to my relief—the forwardness to turn the papers over again to her view, though she looked a mite disappointed at my apparent secrecy. I was therefore put to the ludicrous exercise of explaining that I wanted her to read only the best I had written. This appeared to please her, for it gave upon her the role of a severe critic. What a ludicrous and shaming state of affairs! Moreover, she wriggled in her girlish way upon my lap all the time we were speaking, and in a manner that caused me some physical alarm. Her attire beneath her dresses is nowadays minimal and hence the warmth and roundness of her bottom exudes through the material.

At the same time I could not bring myself to push her off my lap, which brought me into severe physical embarrassment which I was afraid she could not fail to notice under her derriere. Nor could I retract my person from under her in the undue state of arousal to which I was in all innocence on her part being put.

It was then that Muriel intruded, telling Sylvia that she must hasten to bed and get her 'beauty sleep', as the foolish saying is. One last moist kiss from Sylvia's lips fell upon my own and then she scrambled off my lap, causing me to 'prong' visibly against her rising bottom cheeks. I flushed heavily, but fortunately she did not turn. Scarce had the door closed upon her, than Muriel cast her eyes down pointedly at my hapless state and declared her 'pleasure' that I 'have such a stiff attitude towards females'.

I replied not. I gritted my teeth and would have crossed my legs had my projection not been too painful for the task. I was then ordered to 'display' to her which I did, though in fear of Sylvia returning and seeing my near-bursting weapon. (I writhe to think that I shall be 'congratulated' by one or the other of my sisters on writing this).

My stiff cock was then handled gently and in the most fearfully exciting way. There are times—too many now—when one is forced beyond the barriers of pride and shame. Muriel leaned over my chair, her hand clasping my penis and rubbing up and down.

'Shall you come at a venture?', she laughed, thinking that a fine literary pun.

I shook my head. My cheeks were suffused. I knew well enough that in such moments now I am utterly weak in her hands. My hips began to jerk despite myself.

Poor, dear Sylvia—being made to sit upon his naughty big thing, I was told.

'No!', I choked.

Thereat she laughed her cruel laugh and, taking a cambric handkerchief from the neck of her dress, wrapped and tied it tightly about my quivering erection.

'No?, Very well, I shall leave it in this state, and I shall return in half an hour to make sure you have not messed into it', came her reply. She then swept out, leaving me bereft and with my testicles swollen with desire. Even as she closed the door I heard her calling down, 'Jane, there is something I wish to tell you'.

I had no need to try to guess what that might be. My name and dear Sylvia's would be used in the most untrue fashion. It was then, alas, that—my balls compressed on the chair and my prick having reached such a point of imminent effusion that it would not control itself—I spouted thickly into the enfolding handkerchief. The seat of my chair juddered beneath me, so violent was the spermatic explosion. Come dribbled back down my penis. Waves of exquisite pleasure were followed by a surging weakness amid which I knew to my horror that punishment was about to fall on me when Muriel returned. She would—and did—exult in my 'weakness' and 'the proof of her words'. I am a libertine who must be kept under control—so she and Jane proclaim, even though they know the truth of the matter.

Deirdre has not replied to my letter as yet, though still I live in hope. She was an angel of modesty compared with these. I care not that my sisters will read these words. They will chide me for the hypocrite that I am not, then make me lick their bottoms like a dog.

Celia's Day-Book

Through what an ordeal of explosive passions I have passed! I have cried, I have protested, I have loved, endured—and all this in one long, long day the like of which I never knew before.

Muriel cozened me at first with all her loving skills. Her tongue, her breasts, her thighs, her bottom, all were mine, as mine were hers. Naked we lay abed and cared not for the world. Our tongues entwined, our fingers sought. Several times she rummaged my nether hole and I protesting weakly that I did not like it there.

I must learn, said she, and this amid such flurryings of kissings, such rollings about upon the bed, that I could not bring myself to say nay to her.

'Let me give you the *feuille de rose*', she breathed. Not knowing what she meant I allowed myself to be manouevred up on to my knees, whereat she slid down behind me and lovingly applied the curled tip of her tongue between my bottom cheeks. Oh, the sensation!

'Stop! It is too nice!', I uttered incautiously, to which she replied, 'Of course, my sweet, but you have even better to learn'.

At that, a footfall was heard beyond the door and I made to start up, but Muriel was in truth upon me like lightning, first straddling my back and then quickly reversing herself upon it so that she faced towards my hips and pulled them up anew by main force of her arms. To my horror I then perceived the entry of a gentleman, totally naked and with his penis erect. Worse, he was not alone, nor was the manner of his entry any other than the strangest I have ever seen.

About his neck was a thick leather collar from which extended a steel chain, the free end of it being held in the hand of Muriel's sister who was garbed in but a filmy peignoir which, floating open, revealed her breasts and her dark bush.

'Quickly!', she rapped at him. He appeared to be in a

daze, much as I was myself at this turn of events. As for myself I bucked and endeavoured to throw Muriel off, much like a fretsome filly might, but the weight of her bottom on my back prevented the venture.

'Do not let him!', I screeched to no avail, for already he was taking postillion on the bed immediately behind me and—being commanded to by Jane—he assisted in raising my hips the more so that my shameless bottom was fully presented to him.

'I have oiled her bottom with my saliva just as you have his cock, dear—now put him to her. Her hole will be tight, for it has not been ventured before this. Monitor him! He has got to pleasure the darling lady thoroughly', Muriel uttered.

'NO!', I screeched, but already all was too late. The cheeks of my derriere were rudely parted. The crest of his penis, which was indeed moist, dared to assail me there. I cried, I pleaded, to no avail. If anything, Muriel took the saddle even more firmly, resting her knees on the bed on either side of me while my hapless bottom—receiving the first inch of his thick, fleshy pole—was held firmly.

Oh dear god, the sensations that came upon me with the entry of a man's prick into my most secret orifice! I felt at first a burning sensation. It was like receiving a cork—a long and much swollen cork. I heard him grunting. Three inches of pulsing desire embedded themselves and so held for a moment, 'that she might accomodate to it', said Jane who clearly exerted a strange control over the gentleman—if I can call him such.

'Work your prick back and forth a little—just a mite—then slowly give her more', Jane uttered while I moaned, closed my eyes and clenched my teeth at this rude, lewd invasion.

His cock moved back and forth an inch or two and indeed thankfully eased my passage a little so that the stinging sensation blurred and vanished. I felt curiously filled, plugged, yet it was nothing in comparison with what I endured as that erect penis then burrowed deeper, and I moaning out for it not to.

'Almost there!', Muriel exulted, leaning forward, as I felt her do, and having a prime view from above.

The male uttered some solemn imprecation that I did not catch. He was breathing heavily, as I myself began to. I felt his balls come to nestle under my sticky slit and knew him to be fully home, whereat he was told by Jane to 'hold' again while I endured the throbbings of his sheathed weapon which seemed to me to have so magically expanded my bottomhole.

'Now—work her slowly, for she is a divine creature whom you are not fit otherwise to touch', came from Jane.

As for myself I could have said nothing then. The total entry of his prick seemed to have driven all the breath from my body, though that was to be only a momentary feeling. After a seemingly endless moment of 'burying', he commenced slowly slewing it back and forth while I bit upon my knuckles at the sweet-surging sensation which I found to be utterly different and more *lewd* in feeling than having my cunny sluiced.

Our moans mingled. 'Work your hips gently back and forth, dearest', Muriel instructed me and gave my left buttock a little pinch to urge me on. I do not recall uttering any coherent words—only sounds and small cries which she afterwards averred were among the prettiest she had ever heard. To my shame I knew that I was beginning to surrender to the wicked act and to the ever-changing sensations it wrought in me.

A long, long minute of such slow pistoning passed the while that my bottomhole drew on his cock, for I could no longer help myself. Then an 'order' (I can call it no less) emanated from Jane, whereat he began to pump me with rather more rapid strokes, causing my bottom to smack against his belly as the cork surged back and forth.

Muriel thereupon unsaddled herself and slewed half beneath me, bringing her luscious mouth under mine.

'Enjoy!', she husked into my mouth. For a moment I fought between pretending prolonged dismay and the pleasure that had begun to steal into me. My breath puffed into her mouth, my bottom wriggled. Once more the sleek twirlings of her tongue invited reciprocating movement from my own. The male himself panted louder, enjoining Jane to say to him, 'Not too soon!'

'GOOOO!', I choked. In my own mind I uttered the most foolish of sounds, however well received they were by Muriel who fondled my dangling breasts at the same time and poured a heat of passion into my mouth so that I did not doubt the sincerity on her part that I should be pleasured and not, as I had first thought, but rudely assaulted.

My cunny tingled. It had done for some moments passed but then I became more aware of it. Muriel's hand reached blindly down under my belly, found my curls, and then my spot. No sooner had her fingertip circled it than I spurted a fine rain of lovejuice.

'Let him come now!', she uttered from beneath me.

At that a deep gurgling sound came from the gentleman.

'She is to receive every drop!', I heard Jane say, and at that he quivered mightily, drew my bottom cheeks deep into his stomach and loosed such a thick, warm flood such as I have never even known Roger to produce in my cunny. Ah yes . . . I have to confess that the feeling was delicious. It is true, as Jane said, that one can feel the injection of the male juices better there than in their 'proper' place. I felt every jet, every spurt, every renewal of the long threading, thick sperm until at the very last his pearly drops oozed into my tight orifice while he breathed above me as one who had run a long race.

'Out very slowly!', Jane commanded him, and as he obeyed, withdrawing inch by inch, so I felt the loss, the emptiness in my well-flooded bottom. The knob slipped without and I slumped, feeling his warm juices bubbling within in the most delicious fashion. I hid my flushed face, and my breasts wobbled as Muriel slipped out from under me and brought me to face her.

'You see how nice it is!', she smiled.

I knew not what to utter first. 'Who?', I asked stupidly,

squeezing my ardent nether cheeks together as the sensations continued pulsing within.

'It does not matter, my love, so long as you have enjoyed. Believe me, that was my sole intent. Let Roger be the future benefactor thereof. Offer your bottom to him henceforth and double your pleasures—as you may also do with other gentlemen I may introduce to you'.

'But you are making me into a wanton!', I protested.

'A wanton, indeed? What nonsense is that? It is a word coined by the prudish. It does not obtain to reality. Life is brief—enjoy it as you will, and let us have no truck with petty thoughts of the small-minded. You will carry home with you the most wondrous memories of pleasure such as I shall also hold. Much as I adore you, there are times when I wish you to be compliant, Celia, as a woman must be on occasion. Do you understand?'

She rolled upon me as she spoke and pinned me under her. The tip of her tongue coursed around the shape of my lips. Her stiff nipples stung my own.

'Yes, but...', I began weakly, at which she threw back her unpinned hair with a twist of her neck and but laughed at me lovingly.

'There are no *buts*, my sweet, only pleasure. I shall lead you to more. Trust me!'

'I want to, but I dare not', I replied, yet my eyes were as easily read as was my mind. Whatever else may have been said diffused itself in more prolonged kisses. Once more I spurted to her gentle rubbings and fell into a peaceful passivity, a dreamlike state in which I knew myself to be both lost and found.

As to my return, I found Roger pensive and feared that some change of mind would bring him to upbraid me. My fears were soon dispelled, however. Yet, guilt-ridden as I was, I sought to unburden myself by confessing fully all that had occurred, much as I knew that could incur his wrath. No sooner had I used the word 'confess', however, than he put his finger against my lips.

'Here is not a Court of Justice but a home of love; you have nothing to confess', he said. Even so, and sweet as were his words, I felt I could not hide from him that which I had virtually allowed to happen and which I had refused him for years.

'But dearest, I must tell you . . .', I began.

'No, you may not, Celia, for once a cupboard is opened, too much may tumble out. Is that not so? Have we not all something to confess? And shall we profit from so doing?'

I fell silent in his fond embrace. After such words, he can do no wrong in my eyes. The temptation—exceedingly strong to my surprise—fell upon me to invite his prick between my nether cheeks, yet by so doing, at such a time, I would in other ways be confessing. That passion will eventually tempt him to take me in that wise, I know. Let the moment come as it may. I shall not refuse him. Indeed I shall welcome the brute entry of his penis there—so unexpectedly have I become converted. If I have a confession to make to myself then it is that my bottom cheeks now squeeze pleasurably at the thought.

CHAPTER FOURTEEN

Sylvia's Day-Book

Daisy's Papa is so nice! I think she is naughtier than I am, or—Aunty Muriel would say—'more lively', though she says it with a twinkle in her eye. We had very happy hours at Daisy's house, especially as her Mama was not there to tell us to be quiet! We giggled a lot and talked about naughty things. I told her that Papa has a very big key in his pocket. 'Oh, you sillikins, that is not a key', she began when her Papa entered her bedroom to ask if we wanted some lemonade.

We clapped our hands and said yes, and he was so kind that he brought us a glass each himself, then asked, 'What is not a key?'. Oh, I blushed and so did Daisy. He seemed very amused at us and asked again, for he thought it was a riddle.

'Well, Papa, not all things that go into small holes are keys, are they?', she replied, whereat we both fell to giggling into our lemonade. Her Papa appeared a little stern at that. I believe he thought her flippant and RUDE. As to that he did not know, he said, and thereupon left us. Daisy was much put out, or really I should say dismayed and was all of a-tremble when I left lest she was to receive a spanking. I was glad that her Papa did not escort me home, but had a servant do so, for I feared he might ask me things I would find it MOST difficult to answer.

I do KNOW what Daisy meant. I only said it was a key to provoke her, I think. I like to talk naughtily. Aunt Muriel says it does no harm provided we take care of ourselves and do not let strange men invade the privacies beneath our skirts. She says that Papa is shy to kiss me goodnight, which I do believe, and that it is right I should sit on his lap. It felt ever so BIG under my bottom. I did not want to wriggle, but I did a little bit. Aunt Muriel came into bed with me afterwards and said I would stiffen up a statue! She and Aunty Jane always make me come with their tongues, and I like it. I feel ever so LUXURIOUS! They say it is the right feeling to have. Sometimes I lick Aunty Jane's while Aunty Muriel is licking mine. It is such a mix-up of legs. I think it's lovely.

Aunty Muriel says I now need a cock up my bottom while she is tonguing me! I am sure it would be too big to go up there, but she says not. I cannot imagine who would do that to me or if I would like it. Aunty Jane said in her very certain way, 'Oh you will LIKE it', but I am not sure.

Phillip's Day-Book

I am told I shall have nothing but bread and water unless I write of my incredible experience. I know not even who the lady was. Her bottom was lustrous, plump and firm. To be brought to invade the sanctity of that small hole between the cheeks seemed to me a sacrilege. Led in as I was like a hound, I dared offer no protest that would not have shamed me further. I feared at first that my knob would not enter, yet once past the rim it invaded that sleek and awesomely warm channel with greater ease than I would have thought possible.

What spell the dear lady was under, I know not, for her initial protests were vehement and full of despair. I felt for her, which is not to put a dire pun upon it. Once but an inch of my penis was embedded in her fundament, there was no retreating for either of us. Her aperture clenched around my penis like a rubber ring, yet even so it yielded to my inexorable urgings. By the time I had enforced a further inch in her bottom, the passage became magically easier. An insensate desire that I wished not to experience came over me at that point. My further entry was invited; I could feel it so. The moments of adjustment having been effected, I inserted the plunger to the full and held.

Oh the quivering of those bulbous cheeks into my belly! I felt the gentle tickling of her pubic hairs at my balls and drew in deep breaths of wonder at the subtle squeezings she effected around my embedded penis. My buttocks were then pinched by Jane and—being commanded to 'effect service'—I began pistoning my pego in and out of that warm and comforting enclosure which gripped me exquisitely with every full entry and at every emergence of my knob to the rim of her hole.

The dear lady began then to breathe heavily, as did I. It was all I could do to marshall my forces so that I would not expel my juices too soon. The sensation that stole over me was that she had become of a sudden the demanding one—the conquering female—whom I must serve to the best of my humble ability.

I ground my teeth in an effort to restrain my forces which have become the more excitable the longer I am in the disciplinary hands of my wicked sisters. Yes, indeed, they may read that I have called them that—but laughter will be their only response.

Upon being permitted to come, I expelled into the very depths of the lady's wriggling fundament more spermatic jets than I have ever known myself to loose forth. The while that I did, her bottomhole sucked greedily upon my foaming tool until every drop was expended, only a mistiness thereof being visible around the gently closing rim as my knob at last drooped its head and brushed her ivory-smooth cheeks in veritable homage.

Thereupon she sank down with a gratified sigh and hid her face, though I had already caught such glimpses of her in profile as to know her to be a true beauty. Alas, I had but done my duty and was not allowed to savour it, being thereupon led out.

At the least, I was neither tormented nor chided for my 'exercise', as they call it.

'Write well and you may even be praised', I am told. Even so, my lip curls with horror at that which has been forced to drip from my pen and whereby I am brought like a serf to earn my dinner. Rose brought it to me. In order to hide my shame, I pretend with her to great busyness all the time, and thus the reason why I so often eat at my desk.

An interruption, Jane entered and insisted on reading what I have written here. She did so very slowly and, I believe, passed over several passages twice. I waited with a certain trepidation for her verdict. Finally she placed my day-book down and gave me a look of some appraisal.

'You are a good boy at times; you are much improving, Phillip. We shall have great use for you', were her words to me. Seeing some gravy left upon the plate of my second course, she made me lick it off with my tongue until the plate was clean. How abhorrent!

I am to learn, says Muriel, to service females, without any form of bondage, must remain utterly silent during my working of them and must retire immediately afterwards unless I am bidden to stay. I am to obey simple and unvarying instructions. Thus 'Tongue one' means that I am to bring my own between a lady's thighs. 'Tongue two' intends that I treat the crevice between the bottom cheeks in like wise. I am given a list which I must study and memorise. 'Mouth number one', is the most hateful I can image. I cannot bring myself to describe it.

I have written several more letters to Deirdre, but have torn them all up. What is the use? I sometimes fear that I would not know what face to put on should she appear. I am not the same one whom she left, and scarcely know myself.

I was deeply concerned at Daisy's remarks about 'keys', yet found myself having to allay the fears of Celia who has clearly been up to much naughtiness with Muriel and—for all I know—Jane as well. No doubt the other of the voluptuous sisters was to form part of her confession. It is as well I would not listen to it for I may have found myself, in a moment of marital weakness and great confidence, expounding on my own sins. Celia now believes herself to be the less virtuous of we two. I can only gently persuade her that she is not, yet may be casting too much of a burden on her thereby.

As to Daisy, I fretted much at her indiscretion and while Celia went to bed—no doubt to recall the day's amourous events—I took myself to Daisy's room and found her in her night attire, gaining many glimpses of her slim naked form beneath the cotton by virtue of a lamp that shone behind her. The vista was bewitching. Her hips have a womanly curve already. I was much distracted while she was evidently apprehensive.

Being stood up at my entrance, she bowed her head, clasped her hands in front of her and looked as innocent as a choirgirl while I lectured her on the dangers of having a loose tongue.

'I did not mean what you thought, Papa', she complained moodily, but could not look up at me.

I asked her what she did mean, and there was silence. Her bare toes shuffled uneasily. I said that what she had said to Sylvia she might well say to others.

'No, I will not. Oh, I wish you to believe me. It was but a remark made in jest, Papa'.

'What did you intend by it?', I asked. How loosely the words tumbled from my lips, for I was seemingly inviting her to say that which I forbade her to.

'I was not talking about your . . . you . . .', she stumbled and all at once—and no doubt to hide her confusion—

flung her arms up about my neck, straining her face up to mine with the most devoted pleading in her eyes.

Oh, that she had not done so. In a second, and without thought save that she would not feel harassed by me, I returned her embrace and felt the pointed tips of her breasts piercing through her nightgown against my shirtfront, I having abandoned my jacket in my dressing room. Simultaneously our lips extended themselves towards each other's, her titties wobbling gently as she rose on tiptoe. All at once then my left hand cupped itself beneath her warm, tight bottom and felt the inviting silkiness of that pert bulb. A little wriggle of her hips gave assent to the caress so that in the haphazard delight of the moment I began to gather up the soft folds of her single garment at the back until her naked globe was poised like a ripe plum, a peach of perfect form, upon my palm.

'You are a naughty girl', I murmured to her sweet lips whence a sigh exhaled twixt my own. The tip of my forefinger, errant and lewd as it had become, worked gently into the springy parting of her nether cheeks and found the puckered rim of her most secret orifice where it circled tenderly, causing her to breathe excitedly into my mouth.

'This must stop', I choked, though even so my finger did not relinquish its gentle exploration. The rim appeared to my touch to moisten very slightly and even to open a little.

'Yes, Papa', came her quivering response, while in the very middle of those three small syllables the tip of her tongue flickered momentarily against mine and then shyly retreated. At that, our mouths veritably melted together and became as one, writhing and moving gently. In all my hypocrisy then I told myself that it was needful for me to teach her a lesson, and with that worked the first knuckle of my finger into her tight, warm hole, causing her breath to rush out anew.

'You see!', I gasped. With what lack of moral fiber I intended thus to 'admonish' her! What monumental self-indulgence and self-deceit was there!

'Haaar! Yeh-esss!', came her moan. Her lips wobbled

against mine, her hips worked as if fretfully, and I seizing upon that and keeping my finger embedded in her squeezing bottom, I told myself that she would soon cry out for relief. Perhaps she meant to. Her burning face hid itself against my chest and her arms tightened fearfully about my neck, she taking a step backwards so that I was forced by the constraint of her clinging grip to follow suit, whereat her knees bent against the side of the bed and we both tumbled thereon, my finger being forced out of her nether hole in the process.

'Very naughty', I exclaimed as though in further admonishment of her, yet in reality in the most stupid of fashions.

If I expected Daisy then to turn away from me and show much confusion, it was not to be. Her face—an oval of sweet wonder with its glistening lips parted—remained uppermost beneath my own. In our fall, her nightgown had rucked up and betrayed the warm sleekness of her bared thighs. Another inch or two and her pubic treasure would be revealed.

'Not naughty, Papa. Is it naughty?', she whispered with more allure than I would have thought a girl of her age capable of.

An utter helplessness of desire came over me. I endeavoured for the briefest of moments to raise myself from the languid invitation of her slim form, to desist from such an embrace. Instead I found myself sinking upon her, her nipples formed to sharp points that penetrated even my shirt. Again my treacherous left hand fumbled and sought, this time insinuating her nightgown upwards more until a froth of curls between her thighs hazed itself against my fingers. Amidst the intertwining hairs were two pulpy lips that exuded a veritable honey to my vagrant touch. Her bottom lifted and fell, as if eager to receive, causing a mist of moisture to be felt on my fingers.

'We dare not!', I groaned, but even as I did so her mouth touched to mine with a fearful admixture of innocence and sensuousness the while that her hand shyly but with dreadful inquisitiveness groped between our enlaced forms to touch the stiffly awoken rod of my penis which rammed upwards through my trouser cloth. My mouth opened, receiving the small warm snake of her tongue. The lightest of butterfly touches up and down my concealed rod sent agues of desire through me.

A humming noise emitted itself from her lips to mine. Drawing her further knee up, she parted her legs in the most abandoned of postures.

'B . . . big key!', she stammered, her sweet saliva intermingling with my own.

'Yes', murmured in return. All was lost and all a-whirl. I found her button and began to titillate it. A gasp broke from her and her head sank further back into the feather pillow while I, having a strange desire in that moment of madness to look into her eyes, raised myself a little, this also allowing her hand greater access to the most rigid portion of my anatomy. Curiously she threw her free arm across her eyes as though to deny to herself that which was occuring. I tried to take her arm away but she resisted. At the same time her other hand continued clasping as much as it could of my throbbing member.

'Take your nightgown off', I croaked.

She shook her head, still hiding half of her face. My fingers returned to tease her pulpy slit whose slightly raised mound looked utterly delicious. Her firm young bottom bucked anew, then her thighs clipped together, trapping my hand. Her back arched, elevating her derriere several inches off the bed. A low moan came from her. My held fingers felt a tremulous palpitation of her nest, and then she deluged them with a fine, urgent spray that evidently caused her such exquisite pleasure that she bit into her forearm.

'Hoo-hooo! Pa-pa!', she whimpered. Her arm slid away from her flushed visage and wound itself around my neck, drawing my mouth passionately upon hers. As urgently as any aroused female's fingers might, she frigged my prick through my trouser cloth, causing me to squirm in utter frustration.

'Give it to me!', I groaned and widened the angle of

her thighs more. Her tongue lashed my own. Our kisses were more torrid than any I had ever experienced, and so sweet was her mouth, half open as it was, that I felt myself to be as one drowning in a liquid paradise. I thrust her hand away from my crotch and began tearing wildly at my buttons. Alas, I scarce knew the fever point I had reached. The twisted nature of my trousers prevented more than three or four inches of my cock from emerging. The swollen crest brushed against her thigh. Immediately it did, Daisy rolled on her hip away from me, so presenting the cleft peach of her bottom. Whether such was intended as an offering or an expression of dismay that I was actually presenting myself to her, I do not know.

My hands dragged her nightgown high up, baring her swollen titties which I cupped fervently in my palms.

'Ooooh!', she uttered; her head bowed so that my kisses rained on the back of her neck.

The engorged crest of my cock was by then pressed upwards between the springy half-moons of her delightful derriere. It moved a fraction, excited to the uttermost by her exuding warmth, and then suddenly as a bullet is ejected from the barrel of a gun—so the first strings and pellets of my sperm released themselves, firing a hot stream of lava that spattered her bulbing cheeks and caused her to wriggle tightly against me, thus impelling further jets that spread a fine bubbling cream everywhere.

'Pa-PA! Naught-eee!', she whimpered, head bowed still when I wanted most to assuage my further desires upon her lips. My loins jerked as of some volition other than my own. Two further streams of sperm followed, and then the main pulsing was done. For long moments while I held her thus, all but captive with her tits in my hands, the ticking globs and drops continued to emerge until her bottom was veritably lathered. Then I quivered, stiffened my legs, and lay still. Small rivulets of come dribbled down from her pert cheeks to fall between the backs of her thighs and the fronts of my own, so closely did we remain interlocked.

A silence followed—a silence such as would wish to

repel any words that I might utter. Any such as might have come from me would have been of the utmost folly. Half shamefacedly, I relinquished her swollen bubbies and—feeling much like an intrusive tramp in my disarray—rose from the bed and adjusted my trousers while Daisy remained as I had left her.

'Sleep well', I said. No words ever sounded so abysmally doltish. Bending, I drew the bedclothes from under her—not without difficulty for she lay heavily—and covered her. 'Goodnight, my pet', I said, echoing my former stupidity of utterance.

A much muffled 'Goo-night' came from her. I tiptoed to the door, feeling like one who has stolen the fruits of heaven, as indeed I had. To my vast relief, Celia was dozing when I joined her in bed. Now and again she moved her bottom, but otherwise lay still. I have never known her do that before. I rested for a while on my back, staring with glazed eyes at the dim white ceiling. I had all but ravaged my dear, sweet pet—or had she been accomplice to my sins? The silence of the house was like a pall over me. Ridiculous thoughts ran through my mind like panic-driven sheep.

Should I return and apologise to Daisy? Despite my previous fondlings of her, how would our eyes meet in the morning—and what dare one say? Would she arise confused, and I much fallen in her estimation? I tore at that thought as one who tries to escape from a cell with bare fingers. At one moment I thought of the silky, firm bliss of her jutting young bottom and that she had not squealed and protested when I inserted my digit therein; at another I thought of the sense of remorse that would surely flood her soul. I, who had lectured her on being naughty, had now seemingly shed my disguise and stood before her as a lusting beast who has turned a merely amourous game—one of tender loving, as I had blithely told myself until then—into something of far more lewd and coarse intent. There was no doubt that Daisy had herself ventured willingly to the very cliff-edge of desire, yet it was I who had indicated the path.

Thus did I castigate myself, and it was long before I slept. Then, with the coming of a new day—and as is so often the case with the ever-hopeful mind—I told myself that all would soon be forgotten, that the waves of Time would wash over the beach of Life, as it were. Daisy would act as if nothing had passed, and I would do the same. I would kiss her still occasionally—and pray why not? I might even fondle her titties again, if she were minded to let me. Thus, and so ludicrously, did my thoughts again begin to run in all directions. I was as a man who has long wanted to do a certain thing and believes he has dissected it thoroughly and to his complete satisfaction. Then, upon taking the final step towards the fruition of his aim, he falters, becomes confused, knows not his own mind, and is caught between returning and venturing on.

I have this day been thus, and have received from Daisy only wan smiles and a few, broken words. At one moment, upon the first floor landing I endeavoured to approach her and to comfort any fears she might have. Before I could reach her, however, she turned into her room and locked her door. I have become lowly in her eyes, I fear, yet Time will heal all, and of that I am sure. She is unbreached still. May the Lord be thanked for that. Perhaps after all (for my hopes rise ever on) I have taught her the ways of men and have thus provided her with a better lesson than in truth I meant to do.

Richard's Day-Book

I am home again after three fearsome days. Mama does not care, for she asked me nothing about it. Amy was most inquisitive. I said that the family had merely taken a liking to me and that I had had a most jolly time riding and shooting.

This afternoon I overheard an altercation between Amy and Mama. The very husband of the principal lady who so ill-treated me may occasionally act as Amy's chaperone,

Mama said.—'But I don't like him', Amy complained, to which Mama replied very coolly that she had previously understood otherwise and that the company of a real man and a thorough gentleman at that (I believe she intended that remark slightingly against Papa) would do Amy a world of good and help to introduce her into Society. From such as Amy replied, she sounded half mollified and half not. I bet that chap is up to no good with her if he is anything like his 'good lady'.

She was anything but good to me. My thing is sore from all the times they made me do it—but not with them. Always in that horrid bottle, or in a thing they put over my prick like a sheathe. At times I felt very strange as if I did not know who I was. They said I am not very good at doing it, but I think I am. I was not even fed well until I was about to leave. I suppose they did not want me to complain to Mama about that, but I can say nothing to her. It would mean I would have to use words she does not like now, or so I feel.

I am to obey every woman, they said, but I do not intend to. Upon my return, I was only allowed to tell Mama that they wished me to return again. Indeed, they instructed me and said it will be the worse for me if I do not. Mama merely cut me off and said that of course I must do as I am asked. It is a stinker. They played with my cock all the time, and sometimes they twisted my balls. They said things I didn't understand, like I have to 'get the scent' of them. I believe they mean their knickers. What a disgusting way to behave! I never thought a woman could frighten me like that.

'All this serves you right', they said, but they did not say for what. They cannot know I was naughty with Mama for she would never have told them. She is too quiet and self-possessed now to do that. The knob of my prick is all red. Amy said I look 'weak', and I should jolly well think that I do. I heard a man in the house sometimes. It must be the same one that she was talking about to Mama, though I have only guessed that. We do not know many other people.

If I do have to go back there, I think I will run away to sea.

CHAPTER FIFTEEN

Stephen Brindley-Marshall's Day-Book

Maurice is a fine chap. I do not think our little 'Club' would exist without his meritorious efforts in seeking out and finding the occasional young lady for 'correction and treatment'. I keep a Minutes Book of all such events, but since it is the property of the members generally, it is often returned to me after long intervals and somewhat dog-eared.

I am told, by way of flattery which I am sure is intended to encourage me to make my memoirs of each pleasant session as detailed as possible, that I write exceedingly well. This I rather doubt, though I am happy to accommodate all who wish to revive memories of each occasion. For safety's sake, lest the minute book be lost—or worse, filched and destroyed by some irate and insensitive wife—I am now keeping a copy hereof, and thus am able to make an extra record of the initiation of one Amy Mansfield.

How the deuce he got hold of her (in every sense) I do not know. She is obviously a girl of excellent background, though with all the discretion whereby he ennobles his character he would say nothing of that, insisting that she must otherwise remain anonymous.

We met, as usual, in what we are pleased to call our Committee Room on the second floor of *The Boar's Head*.

The Manager thereof, having had his palm well oiled, is thoroughly discreet and happily makes an exceptional point of giving personal attention to Maurice and his protegées upon their arrival.

Amy was therefore treated royally upon arrival, being given a glass of punch and a few small comestibles before Maurice led her up into our presence, we being four altogether on this occasion, including Maurice. As is our manner, we seated ourselves on one side of a table, for the room is set out as a parlour of sorts, having no bed, but an expansive chaîse-longue which has previously accommodated several wriggling charmers.

Amy thus found herself confronted by solemn faces. Being led forward to the table by Maurice, she stood as shyly as they do, and in much wonderment as to why she was there and what was to occur.

Being the appointed spokesman on such occasions, I apprised her in measured tones that we gentlemen were present to further her education by methods which young ladies of good breeding were wont to understand was necessary to progress them on the road to life. At that, she turned her head and cast somewhat apprehensive glances at Maurice who stood close to her side and gave all impression of being a quasi-parental authority, as well in part a comforter by maintaining one arm loosely around her waist.

'S . . . sir?', she asked after I had concluded my little discourse.

'Yes?', I enquired politely.

'M . . . Mama has told me nothing of this', came her stammer.

'Of course not, my dear. Such are the family conventions that she would not do so, and hence in the absence of your esteemed father cannot offer the requisite guidance. In due course—and perhaps with the help of your—er—guardian, Maurice, you will learn that other young ladies of your age have passed through the same tests of obedience. Perhaps, Maurice, you will in due course, introduce her to such that she may be mollified and assured that no exception is being made in her case? You will? Thank you, dear fellow. And now, my dear, it is time for you to disrobe', said I.

How her pretty jaw dropped! She would have stepped backwards were it not for the restraining arm of Maurice who apprised her that she might wear her stockings and petticoat, but no more than that, for a physical examination of her person was requisite.

A deep blush settled upon her features. Her fingers twisted nervously and she cast imploring eyes upon me.

'I want... I want Mama', she bleated.

'Your dear mother is full cognisant with the affair. 'Twill take but thirty minutes of your time, my dear, in the natural course of things. Should you prove recalcitrant, then I fear your stay will be prolonged. These gentlemen are busy. Have they not put themselves out, wended themselves from their business affairs to attend upon you? Come now, off with your dress and your drawers'.

'But, but but...', stuttered Amy whose cheeks shone crimson.

I thereupon rose and gazed down on her with what Maurice is pleased to call my 'Magistrate's look'.

'If you do not, my dear, we shall find it necessary to undertake your disrobing ourselves. Do you wish that?'

'Oh no!' came her hurried response. Maurice thereupon loosed his arm from about her waist and bid her turn her back on us and go to the chaise longue where she was to present herself. Ah, what hesitant, mincing steps she took! Her blush was evident right down to her neck. Presenting her rear to us, she began with much trembling of fingers to unbutton herself. Thereat a hush fell upon the room. Such a spectacle is delicious to see for the first time. Inch by cautious inch her white-stockinged legs were revealed—first her slim, shapely calves, then the sweet indipping of the backs of her knees and then, oh heaven, the girlish swelling of her ivory thighs which sprang up in columns of unmarked purity above her stocking tops and garters.

Slowly, oh so slowly, her dress was worked from off

her shoulders and fell in a crumpled heap upon the floor. There was no petticoat such as Maurice had presaged. In place of such she wore a pretty bodice (laced at the front, as I could glimpse), and underskirt, and white drawers with flared frills to the legs which left a luring gap between them and her garters.

As we have previously experienced with such nubile female striplings, a low and tremulous murmur then came from her that she 'could not'. Maurice, calling upon a stern note in his voice, apprised her immediately that she must.

'Remove your drawers and underskirt. Show the gentlemen your bottom, girl!', he instructed.

Another bleat from Amy, but then without more ado, Maurice strode across and gave her bottom a firm smack which brought a foolish wail from her.

'Display yourself, Amy!', he barked.

Ah, how our eager eyes followed every movement of her hands then—the slow descending of her most intimate nether garment, the first appearance of the pleasingly deep cleft of her bottom which is indeed a 'cheeky' one, its hemispheres fulsomely rounded and with the most appealing dimple on the left cheek. Both half-moons sweep sharply under to the tiny creases they form at the tops of her thighs. I remark upon such always as little 'ticks' of Nature who donates Her approval to them as though to say a masterpiece of feminine sculpture has there been created—as in Amy's case indeed it has.

Her feet lifted one by one, struggling to release her shoes from the confines of the legs of her drawers and thus permitting an enticing view of the nest beneath her bulb.

Such little whimpers of dismay in so having to unveil herself to our view were silently ignored. Maurice stood by to give her bottom an encouraging smack again, but with a doleful hunching of her shoulders she then loosed her underskirt and allowed it to descend and take its place upon her discarded drawers and skirt. Her bodice was all that remained. At a whisper from Maurice, she tremblingly untied its frontal laces and let the sides hang away.

'Bend forward now, Amy, and place your palms flat upon the seat of the couch', Maurice uttered, accompanying his command with a SMACK! on her naked derriere as brought a mournful wail from her, though immediate obedience.

We three behind the table then rose. I, having the first honours as had been agreed on this occasion, produced from beneath my jacket a tawse which has by now done fair service in converting young ladies to their proper path in life. Amy, not knowing what was to occur next, remained as still as her modesty allowed, her bottom bulbing out towards us.

I approached her and swung the leather implement in readiness. A quick peep from beneath her arm and she observed it and uttered a dismayed squeak—indeed would have straightened up had not the hand of Maurice—who stood on her left side—settled gently on the nape of her neck and 'resettled' her.

'Be still now, Amy. You are about to receive your first lesson in the obedience of young females to the male', quoth he while I measured my first stroke and brought the tawse with a sharp crack across her fully-fleshed cheeks, this bringing an apparently surprised 'AH!' from her which gave proof to the fact that she had not been attended upon before.

It is the convention that each Club member provides each young entrant to our little circle with at least three strokes. Sometimes a chap gets carried away, of course. If the girl proves difficult she will receive much more. One fellow may give her a sixer while another may accord her even more. In general, a total of a dozen suffices to warm their bottoms sufficiently for other 'strokes' as are to follow.

Amy, I regret to say, proved a trifle difficult. Her hips weaved exceedingly at my third and fourth sweeps of the tawse which created a charming pink haze upon her velvety, firm cheeks. Her pleas for mercy sounded, premature as they were. Her sobs were most appealing, yet if discipline is to obtain then the initiate must necessarily receive a burning lesson.

I do not doubt that Amy did so. In all, and between us, she was accorded some eighteen strokes of the sharp-slapping leather before her rosy bottom was due to receive its final accolades. Amid all her wailings, her pleas, her broken sobs and cries, not a word had been uttered among us. Such is our way, and I deem it to be the proper one. No coarsities are exchanged; it would be a damned ungentlemanly thing to do anyway. It was sufficient that each of us was by then well upstanding in such parts of our persons as were to complete Amy's second stage of education.

In brief, I probed my knob first between the delicious young maiden's hotly burning cheeks, a modicum of unguent having been deftly applied by Maurice from a small pot to her puckered orifice while his free hand continued pressing her neck firmly down.

Ah, such a cry came from her pretty lips as my penis made its authoritative entry.

'No, no, no!', came her beseeching cry. She endeavoured to retract her hips, as all do at first, but I had taken a firm clasp around the front of her thighs and entered my piston slowly but firmly. Tight enough she was, by jove, and loud enough her cries until in due course I had so purposely plugged her that her nether cheeks came fully to rest against my belly.—'Tay-tay-take it out!', she moaned, though the sturdy intrusion of my prick had been finally eased by the applied lubricant around her bottomhole which had much assisted that initial breaching of her fine young bum.

'Oh-ho-ho!', she sobbed, but one is not to be put off by such girlish mewings as in due course are bound to transform themselves into more pleasurable sounds. My piston then began to do its work, though with due regard for her virginity I effected my task slowly, performing such long, deep strokes as caused her bubbling moans to sound endless. Her hips wriggled mutinously enough, but to no avail. Her soft cries were the only ones to break the solemn silence, save for my own occasional hurried breathing and the slight movements of the feet of my companions who waited to treat her royally as I was doing.

What electrical discharges and divine sensations I felt as at long last I provided her tight passage with my lubricating sperm! My vision dimmed as I finally brought the hot butterball of her bum tightly into me and expelled my juices.

'WHOOO!', came her expected cry as she felt herself being injected. Receiving my jets, she rubbed her arse cheeks against me in what I felt to be a rather promising manner, though whether in protest or desire it is rarely possible to tell on such initiatory occasions. Certainly I doused her sufficiently well for Hawkins to immediately take my place and equally certainly he entered her with more ease, though not without squeals of dismay from her, for she had thought the 'outrage' to be over.

Hawkins pumped her efficiently, and took as long about it as had I, whereupon—having loosed his spermatic treasures—came the turn of Madison-Brown who is rumoured to still accord his two married daughters such valedictory salutes when they visit him. 'A well-spermed bottom turneth not away the cock' has ever been his motto.

With the withdrawal of his spent penis, the young lady's first experience of the combats of Venus came temporarily to an end, as had already most of her whimpering utterances. Maurice permitted her to slump down upon the chaise-longue where, modesty abandoned, she lay upon her tum-tum and stirred not save for many a fervent squeezing of the cheeky halves of her well-creamed bottom.

We three then quietly retired, having done our duty by her. Maurice had not put his poker in to stir her fire, for whatever reason he saw best. He is a skilful fellow in such things and wished not, at that moment, to be seen as a villain of the piece but rather as an adjunct, an observer—though in all as a form of teacher and one who will benefit much thereafter, I am certain. He was not to be seen in her eyes as an accomplice, a bully-boy, but an arbiter. May we all learn a lesson therefrom!

'What have they done to me!', was Amy's first cry upon the departure of my learned companions.

I sighed a heartfelt sigh and stroked the silky surfaces of her bulb gently the while that she quivered. Her process of education as a young lady had begun, I said. She would tell her Mama, she whined.

That, said I, would be a monumental indiscretion on her part, as I had already conveyed to her before. Her Mama would be highly embarrassed to have her speak of the voluptuous details whereby she had been inducted into the first rites of Venus. It was expected of a young lady that she should remain quiet on such matters and not indulge in attempts to draw undue attention to herself. Her Mama, I continued, had been apprised of what was to pass and had accepted it as Amy's due—and so on and so on.

Much snivelling interrupted the flow of my soothing speech (or such I intended it to be), but no further protests being forthcoming I then proceeded to praise her in a manner which she least expected, saying that she had comported herself well and would be much admired for it by the gentlemen concerned in 'educating' her. I then raised her up and, sitting beside her, continued in like vein, caressing her titties whose nipples were well swollen and silently betokened a modicum of pleasure which she would have otherwise denied. I weighed the twin, gelatinous fruits on my palms and said they were the loveliest I had ever seen.

'I have been made to be wicked', she exclaimed, and I replying that nothing of the sort had occurred and that soon enough she would encounter others who had 'passed their examinations' in a like manner and were now ready to repeat the occasion more eagerly.

'Don't know any', she mumbled, but her tone sounded more placatory, and then added mournfully, 'My bottom hurts'.

I told her thereupon—ignoring any other intended implication of her words—that it might not be necessary to bring the tawse to her derriere if she showed herself to be more obedient. My tone being sharp enough, she knew not how to respond and said merely that she wished to go home.

'Shall you walk the long miles back and perhaps become prey to vagabonds, or shall I take you?', I asked—somewhat to her dismay that I should put such a question.

'Oh, you will take me!', she exclaimed, jumping up and half turning her back on me.

'Then you will ask properly, as a well-brought-up young lady should. Turn and face me', I commanded.

Her next movement was as expected. Obeying and blinking such tears from her eyes as she could manage to extol, she cupped her hands coyly in front of her Venus mound. Reaching forward, I smacked her wrists, causing her an expression of much dismay and her arms to flop to her sides.

Her tuft sprouts well for her age and is neatly triangular, being so straight across the top that one might think it to have been trimmed, were she not so naive. Her titties thrust forward well, and more so than one would suspect from the imprisoning gowns she wears.

'That is better, Amy. You will now make your request'.

Her eyes followed my own up and down her well-shaped form.—'Per-please will you take me home?', she asked. I parted my knees widely and drew her between them. Fanning my fingertips I ran them through her pubic curls, at which she sucked in her lower lip and stared above my head.

'*What* did you ask?', I enquired. Her thighs had parted a little in her forward motion. I effected a greater separation of them, stroking their warm, silky innerness in a silent gesture to her to keep them apart. Very slowly I turned my hand uppermost under her nest and, curling my forefinger, brushed it up between the moist, petulant lips to find her perky bud. Her tummy immediately tightened and then relaxed as I performed the most teasing of circular motions. Her eyes half closed and she began to sway a little.

'I w . . . want you to per-please t . . . t . . . take me home', she uttered in a very trembly tone. A sharp hissing sounded through her nostrils as I continued titillating her spot.

'In a moment, yes—in a moment, Amy'.

'Whaa . . . wha . . . whaaah . . .', came her otherwise incoherent moan. Her knees flexed a little. She knew not what to do with her hands. Despite herself, her hips began to work back and forth.

'Come on, now—come on, Amy', I urged softly. I passed my free hand around her, stroked her bulbing cheeks and caressed her sticky nether hole. Her mouth opened wide. Her eyelashes fluttered. Her eyes rolled up to show their pearly whites.

'Mer-mer-mer-mer . . . !', she whimpered, and thereupon spilled in a fine, abundant spray over my luring hand. The tiny drops pelleted in a quick shower on to my palm. Her knees buckled completely, and at that I pulled her further into me and sat her on my left thigh, causing the upper part of her yielding form to sink right back. My left arm behind her shoulders supported her. Her lips came open to my own. A further roving of my fingertip about her bud and she came again.

'Give me your tongue, Amy', I breathed into her mouth, knowing well how lost she was in the hot wilderness of desire. In the succeeding moments womanhood came fully upon her. Our kisses, our tonguings, were of the wildest. Then she collapsed as if in a swoon, I continuing to rain kisses on her distended nipples, soothing the lips of her pussy with my open palm while her belly shimmered.

It was needful, I felt, not to show too much abundance of tenderness thereafter. She is still in training. Once we had regained my carriage and were off, I reminded her quietly of such and asked whether she understood. Before she could find reply, I apprised her that she would for a few more weeks at least remain under discipline, but thereafter could choose her own lovers. That last word appeared to please her. A small, smug smile appeared briefly on her lips, though she sat modestly enough. Thereafter I did not pursue the subject. I feel as certain of her discretion as I do of her future obedience.

CHAPTER SIXTEEN

Eveline's Day-Book

So young Amy has been broken-in! I was delighted with Maurice's news and think it very sensitive of him not to have breached her himself. Deirdre must be informed of it some way. This task, it appears, is mine, for my dear husband opines that I shall be able to approach the matter better than he. He is right, I think, for were *he* to tell her then it would seem an act of bravado on his account. Deirdre is to bring Richard here tomorrow. I have so told her to do, and upon my assurance that he will *not* be permitted to exhibit himself before her. What is needful, as I expressed in my note to her, is that Richard is conscious of her *awareness* of his punishment merely by virtue of her presence in the house.

Maude is going to deal with him. She is much looking forward to it! So far, Maurice has but toyed, in a flirtatious way, with his stepdaughter, and this I have permitted. He has not got beneath her skirt, nor do I feel I wish him to. I sense that I am jealous in that particular respect. Maude is well-thighed and well-bosomed, and has a derriere that is frequently remarked upon by gentlemen.

Heaven knows she has been teased enough by the various things she has glimpsed. Maurice avers that she should go before his 'Committee'. I am undecided about that. Even if I agree, I do not wish him to be present other than to conduct her there and fetch her back. It would not be entirely proper, nor judicious, for him to view that which he did with Amy, however delectable the scene of utter abandon that must have occurred.

He asked me whether I minded his tickling her up. Of course I did not, I replied. Heaven knows that similar incidents in our lives together have been many! Besides, it will be nice to have her between us eventually with my tongue at her pussy and his cock in her mouth—such a sophisticated exercise, I always think. He must sperm her slit first though. I think that is best done upon her own bed. She will then carry sweet memories to sleep with her. By the same token as that of Richard, Amy must be brought to know that all is understood, otherwise we shall all get into the most fearful tangle. Perhaps we are already doing so. Maurice says I must not be faint of heart; in fact we have always proved ourselves quite efficient in tidying up such little matters.

Richard's Day-Book

So, Mama has been behind this all the time—or I am pretty sure she has. I never thought she could be so vengeful, though she put on a great air of pretending to know nothing about what was happening to me again.

Mama insisted on accompanying me there, much as I tried to get out of it. Amy wondered what was going on—and tried to come with us! It was the same lady there, Eveline she is called, and this time a girl not much older than my sister, called Maude.

No sooner had we arrived and got into the drawing room than the lady said to Mama, 'We will just take Richard upstairs and settle him'. Mama said nothing and appeared to be very interested in a lot of stupid flowers. I wanted to say I didn't want to go upstairs, but that would have made me look silly, and I bet they counted on my being polite.

We got up into that same room. I had my hair wrenched again. The lady asked me if I were going to be a baby and call for my mother. She knew I couldn't do that. They bound my arms to my sides with cord; it was a horrible experience. Then they laid me on that low, uncomfortable bed on my back and got out that dreadful bottle again. The lady said I was going to have plenty of time to fill it—as if I could, or anyone could!

Maude then knelt up over my face and pulled her skirt up. She didn't have any drawers on. In a minute she smothered my nose and mouth with her naked bum and squashed down hard on me while she put the bottle over my cock. Then the lady said she would leave me to her and went out to go down and rejoin Mama. It was the most terrible experience because I was half afraid that Mama would come up and laugh at me, but she didn't. The girl made me come into the bottle, like before. I didn't want to. It always feels tender after I've done it.

She took the bottle off and lifted her bum a bit so that I could breathe at last, but then she said that I was to lick right at her bumhole! I told her that was a dirty thing to do. She laughed and said, 'Well, I'll soon see to you', and began to rub my prick again. I begged her to stop and she said she would when I began licking her, so I had to do it and it was hateful.

At last she got off me. I can't imagine why a pretty girl does horrible things like that. She said she would see if she could make me come again—they call it 'milking'—in half an hour, and then she GAGGED me with a cloth!

I was left all alone again. It was awful. Right on the half hour she came back. I knew that because there was a clock on the cabinet facing me. I'm sure it was put like that on purpose for me to watch it. She called me a 'brute' and left my gag on while she frigged me again until I got stiff, but in the end I didn't come so much. She said, 'You'll have to do better than this', and sounded just like the lady does. Then to my horror she asked, 'Do you want to see your Mama now?'. I was in such a state that I shook my head wildly. I couldn't speak because of the gag.

Again she went out, saying she would visit me again. Before she did, she held the flask up and said critically that there wasn't much in it and that this time they were going to keep it until it was full! My trousers were pulled down to my ankles all the time and I felt stupid and wretched. At the door she hesitated and turned back and said she would take the gag off me because she was SURE (she said that very sarcastically) that I wouldn't call for my Mummy. Then she asked, 'Shall I ask her to come and see you?'

I begged her not to. She laughed and said that I was begging and that when she returned I was to beg her to make me come again, or she would call Mama. I didn't answer her. I just lay there and glared at her. I hated everybody, including Mama, but I don't now. It was nearly four hours before we left and I had to tidy myself before I went down, and all as if nothing had happened. Mama merely said to me in a very distant way, 'Are you ready?', and I couldn't say anything. I even half believed she didn't know what had gone on, and I was weak and sore again. I think she knew that. You can sense these things.

Amy wanted to know why she couldn't have come with us. Mama said to her that she would have her chance soon enough. I'd like to know what THAT means. I want to talk to Mama about this, but I don't know what to say. She just talks to me in the same, cold tone of voice all the time. If I ever see Jeremy again I shall really hit the bounder. He has kept out of my way and doesn't take the same morning ride as he used to. I know because I've watched out for him. I think he must sneak out of his house. He is an absolute rotter.

Eveline told me precisely what is being done to Richard. It will do him no harm, and will do him a world of good in learning to respect ladies, she said. Oh dear, I am beginning to feel sorry for him. She saw that and said I am not to.

I have such difficulties now about Amy—with her sensing things as she is, and besides which she is quieter even than she was. I asked her where she had been with Maurice, and she said in a very strange voice, 'Oh, it is nothing you don't know about, Mama.'

Eveline told me, in a very roundabout way at first, that it was time Amy is seen-to, or she may discover things I do not wish her to. Heaven forfend! I asked her what was I to do, to which Eveline replied that I should let Maurice take her in hand, and in such a way that I appear to know about it without referring to it! She said that I must not be too protective of dear Amy or the girl will end up frigid.

'Are you being entirely fair with her?', she asked me, which of course increased my sense of guilt. I said I would have to think about it. To that she replied gently, 'No, my dear, let action take its course'. It would be easy enough for me to bring her there, she said, but that was not the way it should be done, and Maurice will visit tomorrow. Oh, to what have I led myself! And, besides all this, I received an utterly ridiculous letter from Phillip, couched (as one would expect) in utterly wooden terms, to which I have no intention of responding. It is he who had led us all into this. Had he been more of a man, he might have given Amy a little lesson or two himself, and Richard would have been quite other than he has been.

I know not what to say to Richard. He is as mournful as a scolded dog. Eveline says that this is how it should be and that I must now learn to deal with the situation myself. She has told me how to, but I am not sure whether I can venture that. I am told to discard all my doubts and make myself as free in my ways as she. I rather thought that I had, which I said to her, whereat she laughed and told me not to sulk. Finally we went upstairs and tiptoed past the room where Richard was. I must say that he was VERY quiet. What a truly voluptuous experience it was to lie abed with her while we tongued each other's cunnies, and he in a nearby room lying with his trousers down! Eveline said it was 'deliciously complex' and told me of many other libertine adventures of a like kind she has brought about.

Such pleading little notes asking for forgiveness are slipped beneath my door by Richard. I know not what to do. I shall have to forgive him in the end, I know, but Eveline says that I am not to be 'soft' and that she will deal with him again, by which time, she says, he will remain infinitely more obedient and will obey my every command.

'And that, too, has possibilities, Deirdre', she said, which I told her was a very wicked thing to say. How dull it would be otherwise, she replied.

Maurice's Day-Book

'Let boldness be my friend', was the motto for today. Deirdre, having visited yesterday with her son (about whom I wish to know naught!), I returned today to her house to pay my respects to her.

Amy was all a-flush and a-blush, as may be imagined, though looking extremely attractive with her hair let down and wearing a wide-skirted blue and white dress which I half thought had been put on specially for the occasion. Perhaps Deirdre had given her a hint or two, or perhaps Amy expected another visit to 'the Committee'. At least I persuaded Eveline last night that it is time for her Maude to attend there, I agreeing upon her condition that I should remain outside while she is being 'seen to'. I am not without understanding in that. Maude is a little flightier than

Eveline imagines and, after her feathers have been smoothed, will take her injections with less fretfulness than did Amy. I have already tumbled the lovely girl several times and have, unknown to Eveline, had a good feel through her drawers both front and back. She has proven wriggly but langourous, and I do believe secretly thinks of it as a challenge that I should attend upon her occasionally as I so frequently do her adorable mother.

'It is too close to home', says Eveline when I have broached 'possibilities' to her. Latterly, of course, I have been able to remind her of her homilies in this respect to Deirdre, which DID cause her a little confusion, in particular as I am related to Maude only by marriage.—'Oh, that is different', replied Eveline with all the impenetrable logic of the female. I threaded her well and thoroughly last night and got her, as so often, to confess all her passions while we were in the throes of love. At the very height of it, and I about to spill my sperm into her clinging nest, I called her by Maude's name. Eyes rolling, she threshed her ardent bottom even more wildly and moaned 'Don't!' Afterwards she murmured, 'I suppose I cannot stop you now, dearest, but I do not want to know about it. When you do it to her, will you still love me just as much?'

Oh, what a sad, sweet question! I assured her that I would. —'I do believe you', she said, and then we fell to talking of naughtinesses again till both of us were stirred to fuck once more.

As to Amy, there would be no hesitations. Deirdre tactfully took up some crochet work and hence permitted me the lightest of conversations with Amy whose eyes found great difficulty in meeting mine—as well might be understood! We three having each enjoyed a glass of wine, I rose and said quietly that I would 'take Amy up'.

'Oh, you are going to have a little chat?', replied Deirdre. Amy blushed to her neck, I finding it necessary to draw her up from her chair. She bleated out a very small 'Mama!'—in a sort of squeak I would say—and to that Deirdre answered very mildly, 'Yes, dear'. Obviously Eveline's little 'chat' with HER did a world of good.

Amy was silent while I led her up, guiding her along by her elbow to her room where I closed the door. Immediately that I did, she backed away and exclaimed nervously, 'I did not tell Mama!'

I removed my jacket and cravat. Her room is a pretty one and has all the airs of young femininity, there being blue and silver paper upon the walls, a well-decorated little dressing table with spindly legs, and pillows upon her bed that are edged with lace. Brussels lace I believe it is called. A pair of white drawers with pink ribbons hung over the back of a wooden chair. They were spotless, and I wondered if she had previously taken them off.

Faced by my silence, Amy murmured plaintively, 'I don't want to do it again'. She clasped her fingers together and looked at me hopefully, I barring the door.

I reminded her what I had said about discipline, and told her moreover that were I her Papa, I would have attended on her sooner than this.

'*Would* you?', she asked and blushed. The fact that she glanced sideways down at her bed gave her thoughts away. As I approached so, so she stepped backwards to it, vaguely seeking to take hold of a support when there was none.

'How pretty you look', said I. One a little nervous flurrying of her hands, at first protective and then limp, and she was in my arms, palpitating like a bird.

'You mustn't. Mama is here', she said foolishly, but I had already begun to gather up the back of her loose dress, uttering the most comforting of sounds as I did so.—'B . . . b . . . but Mama . . .', she kept twittering as I descended her drawers and caressed the ivory cheeks of her bare bottom.

'I am permitted to birch or tawse you first—do you understand that, Amy?', I demanded sternly. Her head shook as if in assent. Holding her bottom cupped, I raised her chin and made her look at me. She had to learn, said I, to take the cock, as all young ladies must. Her lips tightened and she blinked. My hand was firm beneath her chin. With her drawers then spilled around her neat ankles and her white stockings shimmering in the morning light,

I could have cast her then and there upon the bed and threaded her without more ado. Was she going to be obedient, I asked. Her lips quivered. I then afforded her a resounding SMACK! on her bottom which caused her to squeal.

'OOOH-AH! Mama will have heard that!', she whimpered, trying to rub her bum, but I pushed her hand away.

'You are quite right. Let us therefore have no more nonsense, Amy. What sweet lips, you have—what lovely eyes! I am going to sperm your cunny, my pet, and not your adorable bottom, fit though it now is to take the manly tool. We are very proud of you, you know, to have offered yourself up so sweetly'—and that said to her great confusion and surprise. I fingered her rosette, causing her to jerk. She wished to drop her eyes from mine, but I would not let her. Thus Eveline has always advised me to do, and she is right.

The tip of my finger inserted itself gently. She grinched. The tip of her tongue, pink and moist, appeared between her teeth.

'You . . . you . . . said . . .', she stammered.

'Amy! Raise your dress to your waist and stand with your legs apart as far as your drawers will allow', I snapped. At that I loosed my broad belt from my waist and laid it meaningfully upon the end of her bed.

'OH-WER!', came her little cry, I having stepped back a pace or two. She clutched at the skirt of her dress and stared at me as though I were a visitor from another part of the Universe.

'It is that or the strap, Amy', I said, whereat she began hesitantly enough to unveil her legs which lack nothing in shapeliness. Her calves are slim, her thighs a little plumpish, which becomes her well. The thrust of her bottom is proud indeed. Making the most audible noises of swallowing, she at last displayed her pure white belly and well-fluffed bush to me, her feet inching apart the while until they could go no further.

'Now STAY so!', said I, and cast off my boots and trousers, bringing to her view as fine an erection as she will ever see. Seeing the swollen crest, the veins outstanding, she all but let drop her skirt, but then with some effort of will tucked it under again.

I had her walk forward to me then, as awkwardly as she had to in the imprisoning drawers. Upon my instruction, her fingers came timidly to my cock while she continued holding her dress gathered up to her navel with her other hand. I demanded to receive her lips and her tongue. A little quiver of desire seized her then. Her fingers moved up and down my rod more certainly with the coming together of our mouths. With one hand I stroked her silky bottom cheeks and with the other toyed with her muff. Her legs trembled. A faint stickiness exuded from her love-lips.

'Good girl, Amy', I breathed to her. Step by step I began edging her back to the bed. Upon finding herself on her back, her drawers swiftly removed and cast aside, her legs parted, she instinctively covered her eyes with her hands, her pretty cheeks much flushed. I would not have it so, though, and drew her palms away, placing her arms above her head. Thereupon I unfastened her corsage and brought her wondrous titties into the light. The rose nipples erected themselves quickly to my delicate, fleeting touches and in a moment were rubbery and stiff. Her breath began to come more quickly then and she gazed up at me imploringly. Her stockinged legs shifted and I thrust them wider apart again with a stern gesture until they lay limp, the pearly skin of her thighs swelling up above her gartered tops.

'Tongue now, Amy, play with my prick. There . . . good . . . feel my balls now . . .'

All such instructions did I give her until her belly shimmered the more eagerly. Stroking her slit as I was, I caused her bottom to writhe slowly, which I encouraged by whispers. Finally I rose upon her and half settled between her legs.

'Guide my knob into your slit, Amy', I insisted.

An incoherent sound came from her and her eyes half closed. Her belly was rippling with unspoken desire. Fumbling much, and in the shyest manner, she brought my crest to nestle against her seeping, pouting lips. The bulb entered and she gave a gasp and bit her wrist, but once more I placed her hands above her head and bid her draw her knees up a little. Ah, what a fuck she proved to be once the stem was finally embedded in her spongy dell! I cupped her warm bottom firmly then and slewed my prick very slowly back and forth at first until the slight arching of her back told me of her oncoming pleasure.

'You are being fucked at last, my sweet', I gritted into her mouth whence came delirious moans. Her cunny nipped upon me as I worked the exquisite smoothness of her warm, wet channel. She spilled and clung to me, returning tongue for tongue.—'Ask me to fuck you, Amy', I insisted—not mindlessly as one does in youth, but to a purpose, for Eveline wished it to be so and wished the girl to learn to form the words.

'F...f...f...!', was all she could manage, though. The delirium was upon her again. I felt her spatter my balls. The speed of our bout quickened, causing her bottom to bounce like a rubber ball on my palms while the bed squeaked endlessly. Deirdre could not have failed to hear it, but that too has been acounted a good thing by Eveline, 'for it left her in no doubts', as she said.

I marshalled my forces and kept the girl in a raging heat of pleasure until I apprised her that she was about to receive all the treasures of my balls.

'Say it again!', I commanded and this time a low, whimpering—indeed, urgent—'F...f...fuck MEE-EEEEH!' flooded my mouth while I in turn flooded her clinging nest with such bountiful spoutings as she could not fail to feel and indeed wriggled all the more upon receiving.

The impassioned workings of our tongues died away. She received my last strong jet and then what I often call its 'camp-followers'. Rolling over onto my hip, I remained nested in her until the final drops were expelled, we lying face to face while her breath broke in pleasurable sobs of release. Finally easing out of her, I cozened her, stroked her hot bottom all about and told her that she was proving the prettiest and most able of pupils.

'Oh, what will Mama say!', came her little cry.

'Nothing but good of you, Amy. Though it is not to be spoken of openly, it is understood. It is not infrequent for young ladies to be fêted while their Mamas wait placidly downstairs. I shall descend now. Nothing will be said. Indeed, she shall continue conversing as we did before. You will come down as sedately as you ascended and will comport yourself quietly. Is that understood?'

All the while I had been speaking, I had been cupping her pulpy, warm nest which had settled eagerly enough into my palm, the curls titillating my skin most charmingly.

'Yes', she murmured dutifully.

'There will be less fuss next time, Amy, will there not?'

'Yes'.

She hid her face away immediately, but I permitted that and—rising—I attired myself again, feeling a delicious glow in my loins, so worthy a young mount had she proven in the end. Indeed, I used those very words to her, which caused her to cover her eyes, though the gentle curving of her mouth showed no displeasure at my words of praise. Her knees were drawn up and her thighs tightly together as I quit the room. I felt that she was thus conserving in her throbbing quim that which she had so plentifully received.

'What a delightful girl she is!', I greeted Deirdre. Her crochet work was upon the floor. Her eyes looked a little glazed.

'Oh! I heard you!', she gasped.

'Shush!', I responded, and bent and kissed her. 'She has proven most responsive, if that comforts you', I added.

'I don't know what to think!', came her reply.

'I'll wager that your drawers are a little moist, Deirdre'.

'Oh!', she burst in dismay—or, I rather think, in mock dismay—and ran out through the morning room into the garden where I joined her and began immediately to talk about what a splendid showing of shrubs she has. I believe she was strangely grateful for that diversionary remark, for she immediately clasped my hand and squeezed it, but did not reply except to ask if Amy were all right.

'You will see for yourself that she, too, is now in full bloom', I said.

Indeed, I was right. Such is the adaptability of females and so vagrant are their moods that Amy appeared scarce fifteen minutes later looking far more self-possessed than I would have given her credit for.

'I have been tidying my room, Mama', she said, and therewith set a seal of sorts upon her growing tactfulness.

CHAPTER SEVENTEEN

Daisy's Day-Book

I am not going to write anything in my day-book because I wouldn't tell anyone IN THE WHOLE WORLD what happened. I felt ever so funny afterwards, but quite nice. I thought he was going to put... Oh, but I said I wouldn't say anything, so I won't. Mama seems to like going to see Aunty Muriel, but won't take me with her, so we go on different days, which I think is silly. I suppose they want to talk 'grown-up' talk—as if I am not grown-up myself now, but the trouble is that I can't tell Mama that. It IS a nuisance.

Papa seems in a very funny way, not knowing whether to look at me or not. He tried to talk to me upstairs, but I went into my room. I felt shy at first, but now I don't so much. Sometimes I think he just wanted to make me feel silly, and sometimes I don't. Aunty Jane says that if you are going to do a thing, then you should do it properly. She wasn't talking about me, of course, because I know she doesn't know. I hope they don't tickle me and try to make me talk. They do that sometimes, always asking me things, and it's not fair. I still think he could have put it ... Well... he COULD. Perhaps he didn't want to; I don't know. It's silly being stern with me, then doing that. I feel quite huffed about it, after all. I think he knows that, for

I gave him quite a LOOK, which was very daring of me, but I meant to do.

Maude's Day-Book

I had a lovely time playing with Richard, but I could not have done it if Mama had not tied him up. Or could I? I wonder. He is like all young men and does not know how to behave himself. I like older men because they are more interesting to talk to.

I have to go and see some gentlemen friends of Step-Papa's tomorrow, but I don't know why. Mama says that she does not know, except it is some business that a young lady has to know. Step-Papa told me to wear a waist corset and to lace it tight. What a funny thing to say! He has seen me in it once, though Mama does not know. I had my drawers on at the time, but nothing else. I let him feel my titties and we kissed. I do think he is nice; I do not mind. He felt my bottom, too, and put his finger in the 'groove', though only through my knickers. Was it nice, he asked. I wanted to say yes (it tickles funnily and makes me squirm), but I just said that I did not mind. —'What a lovely bulb you have', he said and caressed it all about and underneath. I felt quite swoony and wish that he would do it more, but Mama is jealous of him, I am sure. She wishes to pretend I don't know what she does! I have heard her kissing Deirdre Mansfield several times—and after that episode in the *bathroom* weeks ago, I don't know what to think. Or rather, yes I do, and that's the wicked part.

I hope these friends of Step-Papa's are nice to me. He says they will be 'in a special way', but does not tell me what it is.

Daisy has a fey look about her, and I am sure something has happened. I have teased her, and so has Jane, but can get no word from her. Should we put her up to Phillip? No, I think not—there are dangers there. It is exciting, though, to see him work a female. There is a little measure of cruelty in me, so Jane says, but I do not think it to be so. Celia, after all, enjoyed herself, and women frequently wish their struggle to be overcome. I know I did when less than half her age.

A letter arrived, addressed to me, from Deirdre. She is enjoying her newfound freedom and asks after Sylvia, of course, but not Phillip. Last night I made him do 'Mouth Number One'. Having filled myself with wine, and while Jane kept Sylvia occupied, I led him to the bathroom nearest to his room and made him strip and lie down in the bath upon his back.

He begins by being silent always, but then whines. He asked me what I meant to do.

'Mouth Number One', I said. He has the list and should have learned it all by now.

'Oh no!', he gasped and tried to rise, but I put one leg over the side of the bath and pinned him down.

'Down, cur! Have you not learned obedience yet?', I asked. And yet withal I felt a certain tenderness for him and bent and frigged his prick up to a fine good stand that mollified him, for he groaned a groan or two—no more. I spoke to him of Celia's bottom while I did. He grimaced, yet I sensed the pleasure he had had from it. He was a 'good boy' then and must be now, I said. My belly swilled with wine. I had to grit my teeth to hold myself, stripped as I was to just a petticoat. He likes to look up inbetween my legs more now. My straddled legs allowed him a perfect view. He gazed up at me blindly and licked his lips. The bath was cold beneath his back, he said, but I ignored that silly plea.

I worked my fingers up and down his prick and couched

his balls in my free hand. I swear they are now heavier from being exercised more than in the past, and told him so. I said—just to help bring him on—that he would have to give it soon to Sylvia.

'Do not speak so!', he begged.

'She will make you come a lot, you know', I teased. His eyes held dreams, his buttocks squirmed.

'You would not, Muriel—could not!'

"Then be a good boy and give me all, and I will give you something in return. Her cunny will be warm and tight, will suck you deeply in and . . .'

'AAAARGH!', he gurgled. Few men can resist erotic words when they are being frigged. Phillip is no exception now, though he once thought himself to be. His cock throbbed mightily—out shot the creamy jets. Descending on my hand, they splashed my wrist.—'Moo-moo-moo-Muriel!', he moaned and frothed the more, and then was limply done. I let it bubble on a bit, then wiped my fingers on a towel.

He who gives must receive, I said, and got into the bath, raised up my petticoat and lowered my waiting quim over his mouth. He kept his lips together at the first, but then I took his weakening cock and again twisted it.

'Phillip, don't be naughty', so I scolded him. I have the measure of him now. He adores to be spoken to like that, though might deny it in the light of day. I twisted more and caused his mouth to open wide, his lips on either side of my lovelips.—'This is called water games', I said, though never had I done such a thing before.

I held back for a moment, then I gushed. O golden rain descending forcefully into his mouth! He spluttered, gargled, choked. I held him still by force of my bottom's weight. His heels drummed on the bottom of the bath. I had not finished yet.

'Is it not good wine?', I laughed, and afforded him another flow—though lifting slightly, let it gush around his face, the golden spray and droplets sparkling on his skin, and more choked, anguished sounds from him.

I rose and clambered out and left him spluttering and

very wet. My wicked deed was done. A strange and perverse thrill it gave me, too. I threw a towel upon his limp, soaked form, told him to bathe and go to bed. It is better always to end curtly on such things. This I have learned with Phillip, at the least, and do not doubt that other men are so who come beneath a woman's heel.

'I must anoint him, too', says Jane who so often follows what I do.

'I think he will expect it now', I said. I believe that to be true. I believe that Phillip could not express himself successfully before with women, and that without his knowing it he wished to be conquered by them rather than conquer. He is happier in his dismay than he would be had he continued to live in what he thought of as his normal way. Last night I told Sylvia that we were going to play a silly game, and that upon entering her father's study to say goodnight to him, she was to tell him to rise upon her entrance.

As I expected, she was most doubtful of doing this, but was prodded in the right direction by Jane also—indeed we had to physically prod her up the stairs to do it! At his door she hesitated and I waved my hand at her insistently. She knocked and entered and I heard her voice say tightly, 'Papa, please stand up'. A minute later she was out, and with a huge smile on her face like a pauper who has found a ten-pound note.

'He did it!', she whispered in her wonderment.

'Of course. You must continue so to act', I said. I thereupon entered the study in turn and gave some mild praise to Phillip for performing correctly in the presence of a female.

'I was already standing up', he protested, which I knew was not true.

'Just continue to be obedient, Phillip, that is all'.

His knob protruded through his trousercloth. The excitement of submission brings him up as quickly as does anything. I have told Sylvia to rub herself against it next time—briefly, and no more than that. How shocked she looked, and all the questions in her eyes! Dear Jane, though, backed me up in that. How fortunate I am to have her with me all the time!

Sylvia's Day-Book

I do not know what to think sometimes. Things that I always thought were rude are not so, and neither are things that are naughty. These are just 'disguise words', both my aunties said to me. I really listen to them, though, I really do. They have to tell me things the men cannot, they said, and besides I am growing up and must get used to it. They make me say things like 'cock' and 'prick' when they are talking with me now. I think Daisy knows those words as well. I am going to ask her when she comes! I'm sure she'll say she does already know. She tries to be a clever puss sometimes, but I don't mind because I like her all the same.

I know how men put their stiff things in girls now. It can go up in my bottom, too, said Aunty Jane, told me that was why they put their fingers there when we're in bed together. Ooooh! I can't imagine anything so big in such a naughty place, but they said I'm going to have to do it soon. I don't know what to think of that.

I think I will tell Daisy—if I dare. Aunt Muriel thinks that she already knows. I asked her how she knew that, but she wouldn't say.

Deirdre's Day-Book

Three days have passed now since Richard's last visit. He is to go tomorrow again—for the last time, I hope. As to Amy, I knew not what to say to her after Maurice had departed. Finally I could not help myself and asked her if she felt happy. What a foolish thing to ask! She blushed and said she did and turned away. I know all the emotions in her heart as well as I know the springlike stirrings in her slender form.

I approached her and she kept her back to me. Maurice was a nice man I ventured. She but nodded and kept her shoulders tight. Suddenly she spun around and cuddled into me.

'Oh, Mama!', she said in wonderment.

'It is nice', I said. Another foolish thing to say, yet she understood as much from it as I wished her to. I wanted her reply in any case, to feel more settled in myself. It *was*, she said in a small voice, and to my great relief as well. It was always so, I said, and stroked her hair. I wanted her to feel appeased. Then Richard entered and he stared at us in our embrace and asked what was to do. Amy then burst at him to go away and told him he was stupid—but I understood the flaring of her feelings then. Richard looked sulky and went back upstairs where nowadays he spends much time a-brooding in his room. It is not good for him.

'I am sorry I said that to him', said Amy after he had gone. I told her that I understood. And then, in one of those bursts of false confidence that one sometimes has, I told her that if she enjoyed herself I did not mind. Her 'Yes, Mama' was one of as much relief to her as to me. I told her I would talk to Richard, and she then was pleased—so much so that she knew not how to put her face and whether to look serious or gay. My words have helped her, and that comforts me. She is more fit to deal with men; I realize that now, and Eveline was right.

I resolved to settle things with Richard, too. He sat all doleful on his bed. I told him Amy had apologised. He wanted then to say something, but could not find the words. His eyes settled on my middle part as if he no longer dared to look up or down. It is much better for him so to be. An awkward silence then obtained that I resented in myself and knew my weakness all again that Eveline does not always recognise.

'You had best come to my room when Amy is asleep tonight', I said. I walked out straight away and left my words to float about him as I knew they would. What a long day it was! I knew not how to be, but finally decided on the actions I must take. Retiring to my room at last, I remained clothed when Richard quietly slipped in and stood before me wonderingly, though with some hint of hope within his eyes.

I asked him if he would be good. He said he would. —'Then you will kneel and tell me so', I said, and felt a pleasure that I forced the words. He knelt at once! Oh joy that Eveline has trained him so. I walked around him slowly, let my skirt brush at his back (I am a better listener often than dear Eveline imagines that I am) and told him to get up, but not turn around.

He did so willingly to my surprise. His hands were clenched, the knuckles almost white. What was his state of mind, I wonder, then? Eveline says one never asks. It shows a weakness in such circumstance, she says.

The hardest part of my task was then to begin. To Richard's total amazement, I am sure, I told him to unbutton himself below, but otherwise not to move and not to turn. He did so, and his pego came out stiff. I saw it as I glanced around his side, for I was standing still behind him like some ever-watchful crone. The crest glowed wondrously but looked a little red—from too much rubbing, I believe.

'Now you will leave and go to bed', I said—but oh, with what a tremor in my voice! I tried much to disguise it, though.

I heard his teeth grind. 'Oh, Mama!', he pleaded. That I think of as the breaking point. Had I weakened then... but I did not, and felt a greater sense of freedom than I ever knew before. How strange!

I did not answer him. Cock showing still, he slouched out of my room and—in some burst of fitfulness—then went along the corridor and slammed his door.

'Oh, the noise!', called Amy from her room.

'He is a bad boy, Amy—I will see to him', I shouted back. It helped me to say that as well. She knew that I would then be in his room, as indeed I was in but a moment. Richard trembled at my entrance—had one hand upon his prick. He snatched it away and said in tones of anguish, 'Oh, Mama—I did not mean . . .'

I did not recognise myself as I thrust him down upon his bed, his buttocks uppermost, and pulled his trousers down. SMACK! went my hand and SMACK! again, and Amy joyfully calling out, 'Go on, Mama!'

'Shush! Go to sleep!', I told her back and smacked and smacked again while Richard yelped and rubbed his cock against the quilt. This taking my imagination, I took hold of it with my free hand and let it urge back-forth within my palm the while I spanked his reddened bottom more.

'WOH-WOH!', he yelped quite shamelessly. I heard Amy's door open at the same time. I told her to go back, but curiousity overcame her and she peeped within. Richard did not see her for his nose was buried in the quilt, his buttocks flaring from my heavy smacks. His cries were part of pain and part of pleasure all the time. Amy saw what I did and stared. I shook my head at her to go away and venged myself on Richard's bottom all the more.

'I can't, I can't!', he choked out. Oh, too late I made to take my hand away. He jetted, frothed, and spilled upon the bed, and Amy with her hand up to her mouth and standing in the doorway at the time. Still Richard did not see her, though. More wildly did I motion her to leave. The floorboards did not creak, at least. She stepped back then, and I with a very sticky hand was quick to follow, closing Richard's door and leaving him to sob. Downstairs into the dark I ran, and Amy following on her bare feet. I lit the gas lamps, could not speak, and poured myself some wine, wiping my wicked hand upon my gown. I did not think of it as wicked, though, but that it had done a useful task.

Amy went to the sideboard and poured herself some wine, then came and sat beside me on the couch. How different silences can be! This had no awkwardness in it and slowly I relaxed. The palm that I had spanked him with was stinging still, and Amy sucked her lower lip in, looked at it, and said, 'It's red!'—and then we started giggling, both of us and could not stop and had to wipe our eyes. I told her to be quiet, but that was all. Nothing was otherwise said. We were conspirators. I had not sinned in her eyes, but done right.

We ceased our giggles, finished off our wine, then went upstairs again, though on tiptoe. An awesome silence came from Richard's room. I kissed her at her door and said goodnight.—'Goodnight, Mama', she said in turn, and looked at me with reverence!

I feel delighted at the outcome of it all and cannot wait to tell Eveline what transpired. There will be no more nonsense now from Richard, that I know. This morning he was courtesy itself, and Amy did not laugh at him. She pretended that she did not know of it. I am very proud of her for that, and was quite cheery with Richard, to his great relief. The bubble has broken, and the very air seems freer now.

CHAPTER EIGHTEEN

Maurice's Day-Book

Maude's bottom has been breached, and very thoroughly, I hear. The chaps enjoyed themselves with her. She put up some resistance, not too much—just as I expected of the dear girl.

'She has a lovely bum, old fellow, you must try her out', was said to me in confidence afterwards. Eveline, being all a-flutter, followed behind us at a distance into town, saw me go in with Maude and then emerge. How bright her eyes were at the sight of me! I insisted that we take a drink downstairs in the hotel while Maude was receiving her first accolades. How squirmy Eveline was herself!

'What are they *doing* with her now?', she asked again, again, and looked up at the ceiling as she spoke.

'You may ask her, dear, when she comes down', said I. She—always confident at other times—was all a-twitter then, said she must leave. But no, I said. She had to stay, or she would think I might go up myself.

'Oh *you*—you'll do it with her now in any case', she pouted, sought assurance, but got none. I felt that I had shown my worth enough.

'Are we not libertarians still?', I asked. All in my mind, of course, the while we spoke were visions of Maude's bottom being plugged. Percy had her first, I learned. His prick is slightly smaller than the rest and made its entry with aplomb, burrowed between her cheeks and then was in. She jerked and moaned a lot at first, but took it well—did not strain forward as they sometimes do.

'Yes, but I want to go', said Eveline.

'She will come downstairs in a minute', I said, for forty minutes had already passed. They were not to linger afterwards with Maude, for I had told them so. In but five minutes they trooped down. Much flushed she was, and Stephen's arm around her waist. Turning the stairwell, she made to let him kiss her cheek, saw her Mama and blushed the deepest red, of course. Eveline stood stricken in the lobby. I did not. I offered up my bluffest smile and strode towards her, took her arm, complimented my companions, and led her swiftly out while Eveline slowly followed as if she did not belong! I, much amused, saw to their comfort in the carriage and back home we came—a fretsome journey at the first, for Eveline would not speak and nor would Maude which, as I saw it, gave the game away in a less tactful fashion than we like to do. Maude went upstairs and Eveline sat dumb once we were in.

'You are being silly, Eveline', I said.

'Perhaps I am. I don't know what to think. If you go in her room tonight...'

'I may', I interrupted puckishly.

'Oh, what? Oh, Maurice, no!'

'Get up! Come here!', I said. I never knew her to be so before. She obeyed me, though, and tucked into my arms, began to sob. I was not taken in by that.—'I said I *may*. I did not say I would', I said. I wiped her tiny tears and kissed her mouth. So fragrant was it with desire!

'I want it', she said moodily, tried not laugh. 'Go up and talk to Maude', I said. She would not go at first. I made her do, and left the house to ride about the grounds, saw to the fences, kept my mind alert, and then returned within the hour by when they had descended once again.

'Maude, you will kiss me first, and properly. Then I will take your mother up to bed', I said as bold as brass. I knew not any other way to handle it.

She got up slowly, walked with mincing steps. I wondered much what they had talked about. No sooner had she reached me than I took her in my arms and beckoned Eveline to us. Oh, what a LOOK she had upon her face like a schoolgirl who does not know whether to laugh or cry! I kissed their mouths—Maude first, then Eveline, and felt their bottoms gently as I did, then said to Eveline, 'Now, woman, come upstairs!'

Meekly she followed me.—'I love you so', she said and took her drawers off, lay upon the bed. I mounted her without preliminaries then and fucked her sturdily in silence, swallowing her moans. No word was said. I wanted it to be thus, and she as well, maybe. I do not know.

'There—you are done, and now be quiet', I said.

'Yes, Maurice', came her meek reply.

I shall have Maude soon enough. She knows it well. That is to say, that Eveline knows it well, but nothing need be said on it, and as to Maude, I know that fleeting look of hers, as if to say, 'You can, then, if you want'. I shall take my time about the matter, though. What the eye does not see, the heart cannot grieve over, so they say. Besides, a little secrecy will add a further mite of salt to it.

Deirdre's Day-Book

Eveline has told me what transpired with Maude—the whole of it, I'm sure of that, even to the moment when he kissed them both and felt their bottoms as he did. I must confess that I wondered for a while whether I was being made a confidante in this, or whether she wanted to confess! I think it was a little bit of both, and that amused me, I must say.

What did I think of it, she asked. I thought the same of her as of myself, I said, and told her how I handled Richard, which diverted her. I felt I had the uppermost for once. If one plays with people's lives, I said, one had to learn to have one's played with, too.

'Oh, Deirdre, you are wiser than I took you for', was her reply. She is clearly anxious about Maurice and her Maude, and fears she may be dispossessed of his affection if he gets too often with the girl.

I had to tell her that was nonsense to my ears, but even so she stayed uncertain. From what I have seen of Maurice, he is more obedient to her than she thinks, and this I told her first of all, then followed it with an outrageous plan which I am sure will work though, for it must. She listened open-mouthed, said several times, 'Oh, no!', but I insisted and went on and on—have almost turned the tables round on her.

'Now think about it, Eveline', I said. She looked dismayed, put out, and gazed askance at me that I should try to take the upper hand. If I let Amy do it, as I had, then she must do the same, I said, or all her 'principles' would go for naught. That hit 'below the mark', and yet I think it may have worked. It has given quite a new direction to her thoughts. I cannot wait to hear what now transpires!

Maude's Day-Book

Mama knew what had happened to me with those naughty men! I am to say that first, she says—for everything I write she wants to see. Today she spoke of it again and told me why I had to put my bottom up. Young ladies thus keep their virginity (officially) she said. It teaches them to be submissive also, at the first. She wanted to know whether all three of them had done it well and come in me. We have never talked like this before! I said they had, and pulled a face.

'You pushed your bottom out well, so I understand', Mama said next. I wanted to say no, that I did not. Those awful men have talked about me now! My bottom still feels funny. I can feel them put it in. I didn't mind the second, though. The third I was more ready for. His prick went up me easily. I had to tell her all of that! I whispered all the time and had to keep repeating what I said.—'There's a good girl', said Mama several times.

Having learned all that I could tell, she rose and smoothed her gown and said 'Good' in a funny voice. As she was going out, she turned and said, 'Maude, I may call you in tonight. You will come immediately, you hear?'

I thought she had 'traitored' on me—that I was to be birched. That made no sense, though, to my mind. I went up early last night and tried to go to sleep so that I would not hear her call me, but that did not work. She knocked upon my door and said, 'Now, come!' I only had my nightgown on and wondered much what was to do. Maurice was lying in the bed, his back to me. Mama said I would sleep that night with them! I wanted to say no, but then she pushed and made me fall on top of him! I rolled as quickly as I could and got between the sheets with Mama on my other side.

'Now go to sleep', she said. Our legs all touched and I could hardly move. I lay upon my back and stared the ceiling out. His toes touched mine, they tickled me, withdrew. His head drooped on my shoulder. Mama turned her back and made all sounds of going off to sleep while I lay rigid, didn't dare to move. Then Maurice put his hand upon my thigh and began to grope my nightie up! I could not move my arms to fend him off in case Mama should feel me do so. Inch by inch his hand crept underneath my flimsy covering and felt my thighs, all warm and moist with wonderment.

He *has* done that before, but not in bed. I have to write that down as well, Mama said. I think she scorns me for my wickedness. I hope she writes, 'I don't!' when she reads this!

Anyway, he did it to me. Mama was not asleep at all. That's all I need to write, Mama says, so I will. It is to remind me every day, of what I MUSTN'T do she says, but does NOT mind me being naughty otherwise! I can play with Richard, if I want. The way I did before? I am not sure. Mama says I must ask his Mama first. She said she'll do it for me if I don't. I'm sure I couldn't, so she'll have to, anyway. Are you reading this, Mama? I hope you are.

Maurice's Day-Book

Quelle nuit! A sudden turn-about by Eveline, so I thought, but the deuce of it, she was clever with it all the same. I knew naught of what was in her mind until she made my cock to stand in bed but would not have me touch her in return.

'No, dear, you are to nest in Maude tonight', she said to my astonishment, and then unveiled her plan with all the frankness that she has, concealing nothing of her thoughts and fears, much as I reassured her all the time.—'Even so, you will do it my way—do you understand, Maurice? We have not had secrecies as yet and will not have them in the future. I know females better than you do, my love, and will not have a daughter as a rival in my house, nor have you flit from my bed to her own. You will sperm her once within my sight, then I will deal with her myself. I will brook no intrigues after that with her unless I know of them beforehand and assent to them'.

'I adore you, Eveline. You are the very air I breathe', I said.

'That is as may be, dear. We have no jealousies as such, nor ever had—are fortunate in that. There will be girls the more, and ladies, too, but Maude just *once*. You understand?'

I said I did. Dammit, my prick was hard—she all the while a-squeezing, rubbing it. She would not even kiss me—kept her face away. I never really knew the like of it—we who have cozened several girls in bed between us and enjoyed our bouts of Venus with them all. With Maude, who is a most delicious fuck, she has this strange fear of propinquity, and perhaps also a needless fear that her daughter is a younger, fresher image of herself.

'I did not marry you for body only, but for mind and body both', I said, and overcame her strangeness for a moment in succeeding then to clasp her in my arms, my penis throbbing up against her thigh.

'You want to watch', I said. I knew her mind—the corners that the torch of words can quick illuminate.

'Perhaps'. Her honesty will always out. Her voice was thick and sludged against my mouth. She tried to turn her mind, could not. I felt her cheek hot-flushed to mine, then with resolve she slipped out of the bed and told me she would bring her in.

I will not venture into the preliminaries of Maude's wondering entrance and her careful shuffling into bed. Eveline pretended early sleep while very, very slowly I caressed the girl. Ah, what a fuck she proved! I have to say it now. Her cunny is well-furred, the lips quite tight. Several times before I ventured her did she choke down a moan or two, but lay still—petrified, I think, lest we should wake her Mama up.

I stroked her cunny gently—could not really reach the lips, save for the small, sweet junction at the top. She kept her thighs together all the time. But softly, softly did the trick. My knuckles stroked her face, around her mouth. Her legs then opened just a little bit—allowed my finger to invade the stickiness, the warmth I found. Twice did she shake her head, but then I brought her mouth to mine—tip of her tongue. How glorious that felt, and all in silence, all in seeming secrecy!

I levered out her thighs the more. Reluctantly she conceded. First I stroked her belly and her curls, then brought her hand down to my standing cock. She rubbed it gently while I teased her quim. My tongue intruded deep into her mouth. I rolled her slowly on her hip, was face to face with her and felt her bum.

'Mustn't!', she whispered softly in my ear.

A spoken signal was to have been mine. She did not know that, though, but Eveline could sense all that had occurred. The tiny movements of the bed, of hands, told all. A tigress then she turned, took Maude's shoulders and turned her down again upon her back.

'Ma-MA!', shrieked the young heroine of the piece.

'Now have her, darling—do her well', was said, whereat Maude tried to draw her legs up, keep them closed, but Eveline thrust the bedclothes down and pulled her daughter's nightdress up about her waist. O glory of bared belly, hips, dark bush and lustrous, silky thighs!—'Open them, Maude!', snapped Eveline and kept her pressure on Maude's shoulders all the time.

'Mama, I won't! Stop him! Oh, please!'

'Get on her Maurice, do, for goodness sake. Open her legs, my love, and put it in'.

'OOOH-WAH!' from Maude then as I parted her fine limbs, and though she twisted, jerked, I nubbed my charger to her fulsome nest, felt tickled by her curls and found the lips. My goodness, how she struggled, though! The sheet was rucked beneath us and the bed awry, the blankets falling on the floor.

'Maude! Will you stop it, you bad girl!', my wife hissed at her.

'Mama, I don't, I . . . OOOH! It's going in!'

Her body reared. I had to flatten her, put all my weight down on her, cupped her warm, sleek bum and grooved my penis slowly in her nest the while she hissed and spluttered, moaned, twisted her head this way and that. A jolting of my hips—one long, strong lunge—and I was sheathed, her belly under mine, my pubic hairs a-rasping to her own.

'I have her, Eveline!', I gasped.

'Mama! Oh, please! GOO-HOOO!'—I holding her flat under me, keeping my cock full-sheathed in that warm sponginess and raining kisses on her face and neck. My love sat up, legs twisted under her and gazed down on her daughter's face. Their mouths were open and their faces flushed. I worked Maude's nightgown up beneath her arms and tended to her nipples with my lips. She moaned and bucked still under my full weight, the big plum of her bottom on my palms.—'Oh, please don't do it to me—OOOH!'

I snorted with delight, I do confess—buried my face beside her head just for a moment, blind to Eveline whose breathing I could hear above. I felt Maude go a little limp and stirred my cock an inch or so.

'No!', came her bleat, but she was quieter then. I worked my piston out, then in again—felt the delirious thrill of it. Her cunny clenched, relaxed, and clenched again and held me in the tightest grip.—'Doh-doh-don't want to!', came a moan from Maude, but she was more quiescent then, could feel the inner throbbings of my prick.

I raised myself on one arm then—felt quite berserk with love for them, and to a cry from Eveline brought her down to lie alongside Maude.

'PMFFF!', choked my wife, her mouth beneath my own while I began to stir my prick the more in Maude's warm tunnel of delight. Ah, such an impassioned battle then began as I would have thought could be! My tongue found Eveline's. Maude's bum began to work. Despite herself, she could not stay her hips from responding to my slowly slewing prick. Her arms wound round my shoulders and her fingernails dug in my skin. Our bellies smacked together as we worked. I, slipping my left hand from beneath her wriggling bottom, found my wife's own sticky quim and fingered her ecstatically.

A moo-ing came from Eveline. Her own hips twisted, bumped to Maude's. I brought... dear heavens, yes, I brought their mouths together in the end. At first they would not, but I made them do. Or rather, I should say, their tongues touched but their lips would not. How curious—yet what a feverish flare of passion reigned! All three of us were lost. I felt Maude spurt, and Eveline too. They came again, again, all sobs and cries that floated like warm blossoms on the air. What juicy sounds, what anguished moans! My lips roamed both their mouths, our three tongues touched. Electric shocks! Maude's right leg hooked itself in wildness on her mother's, and I came, I came, I came, I came, until her cunny sucked in the last drops, and all was still, was very still, Maude's belly trembling under mine.

'Go to bed, Maude', came from Eveline at last. I had already rolled off from the girl and lay upon my back, replete.—'You will not do it with your Step-Papa again, you hear?', she murmured in a limp and broken tone, as if she had meant to say it all the time.

Maude vanished like a pale, half-naked wraith. Eveline flustered as I drew her to me, hid her face, then wound her arms about my neck.

'You did not whip her afterwards. You said you would—to teach her, dear', said I.

'I know'. A little mumble from her lips. 'You do not love me now, I know you don't', and mournful as a long-lost child her voice.

'Probably not. We shall divorce and I shall marry Maude', I smiled.

'S'pose it was nice with her', she said, and would not lift her face at all until I made her do and kissed her lips.

'Oh, FAR, far better than with you', I said.

'I hate you now, you know I do. You will not do it with her any more, you hear?'

'Bien entendu, pet—of course'. And so the badinage went on. She held me tightly till she slept. In the morning, to her great surprise, I spoke to Maude in front of her. I said that we would kiss occasionally as fondly as we always had, but that was all, and that was all.

'We are all at fault', said Eveline. The pair embraced, and all seems well.

Maude does possess a lovely bottom, though. Perhaps one day when Eveline is out. . . .

CHAPTER NINETEEN

Phillip's Day-Book

I am chided constantly for 'writing mournful things'—so Muriel puts it, and Jane, too. Their machinations now have cast a cloud upon the innocence of Sylvia. I know well what their game is even though I stand up now when she comes in my room. It is a courtesy to do, I tell myself. I have thought of her too long as still a child. Muriel has reminded me of that. She may be right. I give her that one point, though Sylvia is not eighteen yet, dammit, no.

Thus my resistance rises, yet it falls as soon as Muriel comes into me. Her eyes have that commanding look that I succumb to more and more. Ugh! horror of the bath and what she did! A monstrous happening. I all but drowned in that out-gushing from between her legs. Women pee far more strongly than do men. It is not fair to treat me so. I said as much to Jane. She simply smiled.

'You wish it so', she said, but I do not, and will say so to my dying breath.—'Do not be tiresome, Phillip', was her cool reply. She made me write down 'Women's pee' a hundred times just like a schoolboy—even made me count in front of her the stupid, silly lines I wrote. She was not satisfied, of course.—'*I must service Jane tonight*—write that', she said and on and on I had to pen the words while she took my free hand between her legs and had me soothe her thighs between. She knows the tempting of that well, so warm and silky is her skin above her stocking tops. My finger touched her crotch; I could not help. She had no drawers on, and I felt her curls.

Was I requested to do that, she asked. My pen ceased and I shook my head. The awful thought came like a big black bird upon my head that I wanted her to punish me. I swear I have not thought that before and was as one whose head is spinning, runs down a long corridor, in darkness fighting at the narrow walls.

She knew, she knew. She saw my face.

'It is time for you to speak your heart. Now, speak', she said. She spun my swivel chair around, brought me to face her, then with a lewd smile she raised her dress, exposed her quim, and brushed her fingers under it. She would not tell Muriel if I spoke, she said. O fool that I believed her then!—'Come on, or I shall whip you, Phillip, shall pull your trousers down in front of Sylvia and Rose. I mean it, and you know I will'.

Oh god, how cold her voice was then! Her thighs were straddled, and her finger moved. All crooked it moved beneath her cunnylips, teased at their pouting, worked among the curls that sprout upon her milk-white skin.

'I want to kiss your legs', I said. I swear I said it to divert. I swear I did not mean to say.

'And after that—what would you do? Come, speak up! I will make you write it down and leave it for the world to see. You want to fuck me, do you not? To get your naughty prick into my slit?'

'I want to kiss your legs', I said again. I mumbled it—would not say what she said.

'You are a *bad* boy, Phillip, are you not? All right—unbutton. Let me see your drawers. Do not get up, my lad—just push them down. Oho, your prick is getting stiff, I see! More, please—right down, I said. That's better. Now untie your drawers and push them under you in turn. I love to see your balls squashed on the seat. Now, push your bottom forward to the edge. Quickly, my boy, or I'll call Sylvia. I swear she wants to see it big'.

'Don't, please!', I groaned. Her will was done. I squatted awkwardly, displayed, both drawers and trousers wreathed below my knees, my penis like a flagpole sticking up.

'I will give it what it wants. Shall I?', she cooed. She tucked her dress up more and bared her hips, her garters silvery and pink, her stockings a dark blue against her skin. Ah, parting of her cuntlips that I saw! I am to write that down, and have. 'Mere words—what are mere words?', she asks, 'They are as fluff upon the wind. The doing of it is the thing'.

Oh treacherous her seeming-tender smile! She moved upon me, standing, her legs wide, the insides of her thighs outside my own, her hands clasped on my shoulders. Her bare bum hovered an inch above my standing prick. She reached behind her, reached far down, steadied my cock beneath her waiting quim. Her face grew florid, cheeks were puffed. Fool that I was, I should have known.

'I want to piss. Sit still!', she gritted then, the full weight of her arms upon my shoulders pressed. Her nose touched mine, lips sultry, half apart.—'Now—touch your tongue to mine', she breathed.

'Mistress!', I groaned. The word came out.

'Yes, Phillip, you're a good boy now'.

I groaned, I gritted, tip of tongue to tip, my face not daring to lean forward more. Peach of her slit that barely touched my quivering knob. She would not press it down, would not, but stayed thus, ever taunting me, faint tingling of saliva to my own.

'Ask me to wet your prick—come on!', she breathed.

I panted—felt my veins a-throb, then shamefully the words fell from my lips, causing my tongue to quiver more to hers, hearing her husky laughter. Then the stream! O golden gushing out upon my prick! The harshness of her pissing stung my tool, especially about the crest. My loins were drenched. I dared not even jerk. On, on it came, her belly puffed. I heard it trickle to the floor. It ran down in my trouser legs.

'Phillip, your tongue more! Ah! It's going in!'

It was. I felt the trembling of her knees, the clawing

of her fingers through my shirt. Her cunny opened like a rose, absorbed my stinging knob, then sheathed it in until her bum was full upon my thighs. Dear god, I jerked, I jetted straightaway, full up in her the wondrous lava spat. She moaned, to my delight, and pressed down more. Her face moved and she bit upon my ear. I squealed like a stuck pig and came the more, all quivering, all throbbing all the time. She moaned. At least she moaned. Was it desire? The last fell shoots of sperm, and I was done. She sighed a huge sigh, kept her saddle long, jerked up and down as though demanding more, and then unsheathed herself and stood, brushed back her hair, I dripping wet.

'Wash! Change your clothes!', she spat at me, and thrust her dress down as she spoke, then turned towards the door.

'Oh, Jane!', I groaned. Despair was on me deep.

'Yes? WHAT?', her voice snapped out.

'Nothing', I mumbled.

'Good', she said, and then was gone, and I left in my wan *douleur*—sickness of satisfaction and frustration, too. Yes—I confess that which I would not speak, and she may read here all she seeks to read.

'He would fuck us if we let him', Muriel said last night when they both stood over me.

'I know. He's dirty. Come to bed', said Jane.

Thus do they make my life despair. I had to lick their shoes the while they spoke. My once-beloved will never write, I know. I am left alone in sin and misery.

Sylvia's Day-Book

I spoke to Daisy, and she knows! I mean, she knows about men's *things*. I told her that I did as well. 'They put it in you if they can', she said. I went all red and said 'I know'. We both said 'cock' and 'prick'—tried not to laugh, then Aunty Muriel came in and BOTH of us went red. I KNEW she was going to ask us what we spoke about, and did. We would not tell her, though. At first she didn't seem to mind and said that girls should talk about all things—and things that HAPPENED to them just as much, she said.

'Have you been good?', she asked Daisy next, and Daisy said she had, but still blushed. I had a sudden feeling why she blushed. I'm sure she has not told me everything, but *I* did, and that isn't fair. I think Aunt Muriel thought so, too. She stared at her for a long time and said she wished to talk to her, and that I was to go into the garden with Aunty Jane.

Daisy looked very awed at that and twisted all her fingers round. Outside I then asked Aunty Jane what they would talk about. She would not say.—'Oh, Daisy is more advanced than you', she said.—'She ISN'T!', I replied. That made her laugh. It made me sulky, though.—'I told you that you will have it soon enough', she said, and then we heard a shriek from Daisy from upstairs! I wanted to run in. Aunt Jane said no.

'Why? Is she spanking her?', I asked. I could not understand at all.

'No, she is not. Look! Aren't the roses nice?'

I didn't care about the silly flowers. I wanted to know what was going on, but did not say so. Daisy didn't shriek again. The curtains of Papa's study were pulled to. Aunt Jane said I want not to look.

'Your Papa is working, dear', she said, sat down beside me and gave a funny smile. That's all that she would say except for ordinary things. A whole half hour we sat there—then Aunt Muriel called. Daisy had gone home, she said. Oh, I was really put out then. She hadn't even said good-bye, I said.

'She was too full to speak, I think', said Aunty Muriel—and laughed! When I see Daisy I will tell her off.

Phillip's Day-Book

Daisy! To what depths have they fallen now! I knew her by her footsteps, by her squeaks, and even by her body-scent which is different from Sylvia's. They did not think of that—that I would guess. I was blindfolded, strapped into my chair, was gagged and had my tool exposed.

I heard the scutterings of feet—heard my door open, heard her brought to me. A hand touched at my upright prong.—'Go on, go on, do as I told you to', said Muriel to her. O moist, warm rose of mouth upon my knob! O bliss the slow, sweet sucking up and down, the hissing of her breath from out her nose, the slippery sounds her young mouth made at its lewd task!

'He will come a lot—just let him come—suck on him when he does and drain his balls', I heard from Muriel.

The hissing sounds grew louder. Hot breath flowed with the saliva that my prick immersed itself within in that soft cave. Life flowed in me, pulsed out. I never knew such richness yet. My buttocks squirmed and tightened. Her lips slooped, made sucking noises, drew on me. Oh, frail am I that I should feel desire.

'Good girl! Now frig him with your fingers—quick!'

Dear heavens, how I came! Each surging jet of come leaped down her throat. I heard her gargle, choke, believe her head was pressed. More of my cock was drawn within. I felt the swimminess within her mouth, the glutinaceous flood from me that cloyed her tongue and onward flowed. She pumped my penis still with her slim hand, licking round my spilling knob as she was told, and left me empty as an unfilled sack, a weakness flowing through all my limbs.

Not until after she had gone was I released. I heard the carriage drive away. Then Muriel released me, did not speak except to scold me for what I have not written in my so-called book—a mess of papers that lie all about, all scribbled on and passages expunged. I am to begin again, she said, and has repeated it tonight. I am to 'lay the chapters out and make a framework of the plot'.

My head swirls and I cannot think of anything save that warm-sucking mouth. My penance is to brood on it, to think how lustfully I soiled her lips.

'Be careful that you get to work and write. The next young mouth may not be Daisy's', Jane said to me on reading this.

I try, I try. They will not stop at anything. I have no fear to write this; they will merely laugh and say that they agree with that.

Celia's Day-Book

I visited Mama today, and felt exactly like an actress who has somehow wandered into the wrong play and finds her lines are wrong, the scenery all changed. I am not what I was nor ever shall be again. I am drawn not only towards Muriel, but that which she holds out to me: the promises, the lure, of sins I otherwise would spurn. I know I would.

Daisy came back from there two days ago, all perky and a little flushed. I did not ask her what had passed. I almost feared to. Is that wrong of me? She is coming quickly into bloom more now.—'Let her grow up and let her be', says Jane. I suppose I must.

Was she hungry—had she eaten, I asked Daisy, though their hospitality is always good. I have had some perfectly delicious roast duck there—*à l'orange*—and cream puffs, too. Their cook is excellent.—'Did you have cream puffs, dear, today?', I asked. To my astonishment she went bright red, then said 'Oh yes, I did—cream puffs!', and ran upstairs. Some girls seem always at a silly age.

I remarked on this to Muriel who laughed.—'Cream puffs? Oh yes, she swallowed everything', she said, and mystified me more at that. Perhaps it is a private joke.

We kissed, spoke of obedience and love, or rather it

was she who linked them up.—'Would you enjoy to be obedient to me?', she asked. I knew of what she meant: that last time there. I asked her who the man had been. A distant relative of sorts, she said, then added, 'He is more obedient than you. But you already know that, Celia—have guessed. What say you then to your obedience?'

'I was', I blustered. How she makes me blush! Jane entered then into the morning room. I made to move from Muriel's arms on the couch, but could not. Jane asked if I were being 'good', then said, 'I want to kiss her, too'.

'Jane, don't be silly', I began, though not in protest but embarrassment. It was then as if we were schoolgirls at a romp. One held my arms, the other raised my skirt. I skittered, but did not cry out in case someone came in and saw. I struggled silently—half playfully, I felt—between the pair. Jane, to my horror, felt right up my legs and loosed my drawers and got them off one leg.

'Stop it!', I pleaded. Jane knelt up between my legs and thus kept them apart. My right leg slipped upon the floor. Muriel, who had held me, knelt beside the couch and pinned my shoulders with her hands.

'You are going to be fucked today. I want to watch you being fucked', she said.

'Don't speak to me like this!', I begged. She held my chin, my mouth beneath her own. My fallen leg was raised and Jane slipped down, bringing her face between my thighs. Her tongue lapped up and down my slit. I squirmed.

'First we will bring you on, my sweet, then you will take the cock, you understand?', asked Muriel.

'I thought—I thought you loved me, Muriel!'.

Jane held my bottom tightly underneath and mashed her mouth the more into my quim.

'I do, my pet, and love is sweet. It is a passion dark, contained—a mystery, if you wish it so. There, there—you see, your mouth is growing loose. One cannot help oneself, you know. No, Celia, don't struggle, just lie still. What a pretty noise her tongue makes at your slit!'

Such sounds as left my throat and entered hers were

both of passion and despair. Jane licked remorselessly. I quivered, came, and entered into clouds of soft delight, my garters rubbing to her cheeks, against her ears.

'With love you must surrender all', said Muriel. My eyes were closed. Was it myself who lay there or a wanton, weak, who let herself be made a plaything of? I thought of Roger, Daisy—the dear innocents—and I the one upon the loose.

'No! Stop! Get off!', I moaned, kicked with one foot and caught Jane on the hip. The transformation, sudden as it was, surprised the pair, and Jane said, 'Oh! That hurt!', and got up all bemused and stepped away. I pushed at Muriel and struggled up. She saw my expression and was much surprised.

'We only meant to entertain you, pet', she said.

'Yes, that was all', said Jane and tried to smile, rubbing her hip quite ruefully.

Abruptly I stood up and made to put my drawers back on, but Muriel said 'Oh, please!' and touched my arm. Her tone and touch placated, but still I clothed my bottom part and moved away from them to smooth my skirt. Jane said, with awkwardness, she would have coffee made, and went. A silence reigned, and I was very conscious of the tingling in my quim. I held my legs apart a little, strained my knees—a movement I could not disguise from her despite the covering of my skirt.

'It is nice when lovers are obedient—sometimes it is', Muriel said in a soft tone, came up behind me, put her arms about my waist.—'Because I love you, dear, I want to make you cry', she said. I understood that in a way. That was the curiousity of it.

'But not too much', I said. I knew not what to say. She made me turn about, reluctantly. Our lips met for a moment, then I dropped my head.

'If it is not too much then it is not obedience', she said, 'Why, if you held me down and let Roger have me, would I not obey?'

'Would you? And is that what you now want?', I asked. There was a slight snap in my voice at that. I felt a jealousy of both, could not command myself at all. Her titties bulbed to mine, made me feel weak. Our thighs pressed close, our bellies, too.—'Well, *do* you?', I repeated in a sulky tone.

'I want what you want, darling, that is all. You were superb the last time you were here. I want to see him work your pussy, too. I want to feel the sting of jealousy. Can you not understand that—strange as it may be? In pain is sometimes sweetness. Just to see a rearing penis nub between your lovelips, to see your mouth twist and explore the passioned heat within your eyes, to see your bubbies swell, your legs apart . . . Oh wanton, yes, and I would kiss your mouth, and wish I had a penis, too'.

'Would you?', I clothed my mind with questions to evade such other thoughts as I may have. Her palm explored my bottom gently as we spoke and pressed me deeper into her.

'Of course. Then you will make me do the same. May whip me if you wish'.

'With Roger?'

'Yes. I will not even look at him, I swear—will only look into your lovely eyes, and you will suck my nipples while he does, make me to lie there, wriggling as I shall . . .'

'No, stop!', I burst away from her, was moody once again. I did not have it in me to explore such things, I said. I put my back to her again and flushed. I felt myself to be upon the edge of a crevasse and swayed. I wanted to run out, and yet to stay. Once more she came to me and held my waist, my bottom pressed against her belly then.

'Don't go', she pleaded softly, 'Come upstairs'.

I shook my head. Her hands cupped both my breasts. I fought the wicked thoughts I should not have. My nipples came to points beneath her palms and prodded through the fine cloth of my gown. I leaned my head back, sighed, and closed my eyes.

'The man is up there, though', I said.

'Yes, Celia, he is. Come—please obey'.

Jane entered then, put down a tray, and looked at us and asked, 'Is she all right?'

'I'm not', I wished to say, but Muriel said, 'Yes, of course she is. We are taking her upstairs just as I said'.

'No, please!', O treacherous my weak and pleading voice, my feet that stumbled in between the pair! The hall, the stairs—how broad they had become! I pressed back feebly, but they led me on. The landing came to us and I began to cry, beseeched them softly as the bedroom neared.

'Oh, lovely tears, my love!', said Muriel and pulled me in. My sobs brought on my weakness more, I swear. The bed received me, down my drawers came once again, my skirt piled up about my waist, all done so smoothly, quickly.

'Please!', I begged, was shushed and then Jane left and returned in a minute with the naked male, blindfolded as he was, and chained and collared as a dog might be. Of course, I dared not speak lest he should one day know my voice again! My legs were skewed apart, he came between and settled on me heavily, but had his head held up and could not kiss.

It was Muriel who groped his pego, guided it within. I strained, I hissed out. In it slid, sleeked up within my nest and held, his balls beneath my bottom couched.

'Perform now slowly in the lady!', Jane said, holding taut his lead. My mouth was then absorbed by Muriel's. I knew not whether it was night or day. All was deep darkness, whirling tongues, the shunting of his cock within my quim. All was delirium, shame of excitement—even my own heart cannot dissemble all that I then felt. Upon his sperming me, he uttered a deep groan and loosed the heavy pellets of his come in such abundance that they flowed in one deep, creamy stream within my nest.

'What a good girl you are!', said Muriel afterwards, and held me like the lost one that I felt I was.

CHAPTER TWENTY

Muriel's Day-Book

Dear, youthful Daisy! I have stirred her well. She has the devil in her more than Sylvia. The latter is the quieter one, but she will make her way all right. And as to Celia, she walks upon a brink, yet so do I in more ways than I count, as things progress.

'Because you *love* her, so you wished to make her cry indeed!', said Jane of her, and gave a little sneer. She sees a change in me—I know not what. It was true, I said, and added that we did the same with Phillip, after all, to which she conceded I was right.

Daisy did well. I told Jane so.—'Well, it is Sylvia's turn', Jane said. I shrugged and did not answer her. A week ago I would have said to take her in to him. Do I grow older, old? Oh, surely not! I thought of Celia's warm tongue, her pulpy mouth. What curious fancies take one at such times.

'I shall take her in if you do not', said Jane. She held my hand. We stood as people in a likeness do, stared out into the garden and saw nothing there.—'You're in a curious mood', she said.—'Oh no, I'm not!', I said. We laughed and kissed. Today there is an absence of desire in me to do other than to bed with Celia and Roger both. I told Jane so and asked her why. She searched my eyes and looked away.

'You wish to escape', she said to my surprise.—'From what?', I asked. She shook her head, looked worried.—'I don't know', she said. We put our cheeks together and stood quiet. My old spirit returned when Sylvia went up tonight. I said to have her father stand again.

'I know. All right', she said in an old-fashioned way. I could not help but listen. They were very quiet. I heard the chair squeak, that was all. Ten minutes later she came out and went into her room, said naught. Jane went into him and returned after a long, long interval and said he was 'in fine array'. He had not come, was dying to.

'Be sure he doesn't, Jane', I said.—'Oh, you ARE strange today', she said, and went back into him and closed the door. Poor Phillip, how he groaned for all to hear! Rose asked if she might go in Sylvia's room. I said she might. I heard them whispering together. That will do no harm. All seems *distant* from me at the moment. Very curious! My mind dwells in another house. I must rid my mind of fancies about Celia and Roger. It is quite absurd. Do I love them both or do I seek protectiveness? I hardly know myself at all.

Roger's Day-Book

It was dark in her room. Dammit, I could not help myself. The curtains were drawn, the lamp was out. I blundered to her bed, felt a bare leg. She lay there naked and her bush was moist.

'There are riders at night', she said. Was there delirium? Mouth upon mouth all of a sudden then. I pushed my trousers down—was deep at fault. My prick sprang out as hard and firm as I have ever known it be. O fearsome rushings of our breaths, O sweet *douleur* of entering her nest, the bumpings, heavings, and her bottom sleek and wriggling on my brazen palms again. This time the turmoil and the storm carried the bridges all before it in the dark. Warm, wet and seeking caves of mouths, legs locked, arms locked, her honey trickling down my threshing cock—and bursting, O it burst, I burst and flooded her in a gigantic whirlwind of desire, she sobbing, drawing on my prick until my last, small pearls were spent, the jets gone on before, absorbed. And say goodnight with languid tongues, then—hesitating ('Yes!', she moaned), plunge in again and fill her spermy cave anew until all breath was gone from us, and we like stranded ones upon a shore, her slim legs wide apart beneath my own. And Celia returned, and it was light. How could it then have been so dark, or did I sleep and dream it all? My trouser-gap was rimed with white, dried sperm where I had buttoned-up again.

I tell myself I dream it. It was dark. Those heavy curtains that let in no light, save for a searching, sun-pierced slit. Say that I dreamt it, that my mind's awry. Hot points of nipples at my lips. Another guides my pen today. I am possessed and know myself to be.

Celia's Day-Book

Sometimes when all is quiet, too quiet, there brushes at the mouth, nose, eyes, a silence like to cobwebs. So it was when I returned, my heart a-bursting as it was. Roger, like a shipwrecked captain, stood within our doorway with his trousers off.

'Changing', he said, and I said yes. His prick was pendant, glistened in the light.—'Roger, I want to tell you, to confess', I said. He backed away and let his trousers fall. They crumpled on the floor. His boots were off.

'No, do not tell me for I must confess to you, I must. I want . . .' His voice trailed off, he looked bemused. Daisy was in her room, he said. He sounded anxious, and I knew my guilt the more. He had not known what to do in all the waiting hours, I told myself, and threw my arms about his neck.

'Confess—let me confess', I said.

'No, Celia, do not—for if we both—if we should both confess . . .'

'What have you done but wait?', I asked, and cried against his shoulder as I spoke. We had both sinned, he said. I knew him to mean that he had acquiesced in my dire sins, but to allay his fears said that I understood.

'Do you? And yet you cannot know', he groaned.—'What I have done to you? I do! I shall never go to her again, I promise, Roger. And besides . . .'—'Yes, what?' His voice was edged with fear. Oh, that I have brought him to such a precipice—he who is faithful to me to the end and succours my most sinful whims. I am the one who must have strength, I told myself.

'What is the hour? Is it not night?', he asked.

'It is but dusk. I meant not to be late'. I moved from him. His penis had not stirred for me, was coated as with frost or rime. I thought he had. . . . But he could *not*, would not. There is no other woman here. I would go to bed, I said—was tired. The day had such a dying fall! Dear Daisy did not come in to say goodnight. Perhaps she frets for me as well.

Deirdre's Day-Book

Vaguely I think of returning—yet what will be there but an emptiness? I languish without Sylvia—or is that my excuse? I would lose my freedom—would lose all. Muriel, in a letter, says that I stay best where I am, and that Sylvia will visit shortly here, but not alone, for Jane will come with her. I think that Muriel is right.

Dear Eveline, she has confessed to me all that was done.—'You brave one', so I said to her. Maurice appeared and asked us bluffly what we spoke about.—'Go on and tell him', Eveline said. I could not, though.—'We spoke of Maude', she said and then he laughed and said that he was glad the truth was out. He told me then what he had told them both, and Eveline looked quite proud at that.

'You *see*, we are libertarians to a fault', she said, though looked not as comfortable as she might. It was a strange day—empty in its way. I half expected what they said. I doubt the word of Maurice, though. A woman's instinct? Yes, perhaps. It is as much to say as, 'I will not eat another chocolate from that box'—and then within the very thought one's hand extends to it. I know. I have dipped into that box myself. The lure of sin is like the thought of Christmas to a child. If Richard only had a different face, ah then I know I would—tonight.

Eveline said that they will have a 'party' soon—'Just chosen guests', she said, and winked.

'Would Maude be there? Could she *not* be?', I asked. She flushed at that and looked away, Maurice said nothing but just hummed.—'Well—you could chaperone her in a special way', said Eveline and looked at Maurice straight. I think their house is built upon dry sand. He shrugged and said, 'Of course—what else?', but which question that he answered neither of us knew. I saw myself in mirrors all about and knew myself to be no better then they are.

Richard was in Amy's room when I returned. They both sat straight up on the bed.

'It is good for you to talk', I said. I cannot stop the world from going round. Richard jumped up and kissed me on the lips and said 'Mama', just like a parrot might while Amy simpered and looked down, fingered her dress which was much creased. Two dents showed in her pillows. That I saw. Maurice will have to see to her again. I know about 'the Committee' now, for Eveline has told me, has confessed that, too.

I took the key from Richard's door and locked him quietly in when he had gone to bed. He waited, thought I slept, then tried the door. I heard him grumbling to himself. Perhaps I should lock Amy in as well. They cannot have it as they will. Despite my sins I do not think myself so much a libertarian yet! And Eveline, I do believe, is having other thoughts as well concerning that, with Maude upon her mind. The biter who is bit knows well the pain.

We are 'between lives' in a strange, new way. Despite the badinage, assurances, all is not well. This irks. It should not. Is all spoiled? Maude is her daughter, after all, not mine. I may be kin but am not blood-kin to the girl.

Maude is provocative, besides, and gives me sidelong looks which do not help when Eveline is present, for I think she notices. I resolved to speak to Maude again, finding myself much between two stools, and thought thereby to quell my own desires by speaking to her sternly. Alas, she has her mother's ways. It did not work out as I thought. Perhaps in truth it worked out as I hoped. The human mind is, after all, a maze of 'Will' and 'Will not'—that cannot be helped. We all are as we are and must accept the fact.

Maude said that she would go to town today to buy some stockings and some shoes. For my part I said that I would be about the farm and would not be an hour or so. Taking horse, I followed Maude and caught her on the road, coming alongside her carriage and signalling our driver to stop at the next village, which he did. Maude thereupon got out and asked me with a knowing smile what I was at. I did not answer her at first but took her in a nearby inn, asked for a room and led her up.

'What is to do?', she asked and took her bonnet off. A comedy then followed, if such it can be called. We were to behave ourselves I said. I carried no conviction in my words, as well she knew.—'I know. I understand', she said, then looked towards the bed and added, 'You may kiss me, though. You said you would'.

A silence followed. For a moment we two stood apart.—'I wouldn't tell Mama, you know', she said, and stepped towards me, put her arms about my neck. Lord help me, in a moment we were down upon the bed, my hand beneath her skirt, her legs apart. Her tongue was wet and long within my mouth. She drew her further knee up, let me feel her quim.

'You have no drawers on, Maude'.

'I knew that you would follow me. Mama was naughty, watching. Why should I not be? Oh, let me touch your prick. I want to, please!'

'You bitch! How quickly have you learned!'

'I have good tutors, do I not?',—and all this said while down my trousers went, my cock couched in her smooth, warm palm and all a-sudden fever of desire. Ah, what a feline animal she proves to be! And I . . . I could not help myself. Her stockings rubbed my bared thighs as I entered her. Obscene words poured from both of us. The gentlemen had had her bottom, yes. She liked it, and I could as well. Her cunny was a mouth of hungriness much as her lips were under mine. Brazen her wriggling, wild her eyes. She wound her legs up round my hips and moaned her pleasure as we came in torrid torrents of ecstatic bliss, then lay a-panting, quiet and still the while I kissed her powdered cheeks.

'The coachman may suspect if we two dally long', I said at last.

'I know'. Her voice was sulky about that. She had a moody look as we both dressed and tidied up ourselves again.—'You do not love me after all', she said. Shades of her mother!

'Why do you think I did it to you?', I flared up. Oh, what a stupid thing to say!

'Oh, I thought you did it *with* me', she declared and swept out of the room, I following like some ridiculous suitor, much put out, and in a dungeon and confused. I rode straight off, came home and knew not how to be.

'What IS the matter with you?', Eveline asked. Maude, fortunately, did not return for a whole hour, so nothing was suspected, though there was no cause to be. I do not want another 'party' yet and have told Eveline so. She looked relieved. I am sure she knows it is because of Maude.

CHAPTER TWENTY-ONE

Deirdre's Day-Book

A week having passed since I visited Eveline, I decided to call upon her again. Intuition must have led me there. Oh, what a tizzy she was in! My suspicions as to Maurice and Maude were not unfounded after all. She had discovered them together in the summerhouse—foolish as they were to do it there, and these of course are my words and not hers.

Eveline sensed something as women do, pretended to go out and then went back. Not finding them in the house, she searched the grounds and saw all there was to see through a window of the garden-room. Maude, brazen as she is, was kneeling on the floor upon a mat, skirt up and no drawers on. Maurice was naked to his shirt and knelt behind her with his penis well embedded up between her bottom cheeks.

'My god, they *were* enjoying it', said Eveline, and wept. I had a mind to comfort her and smack her face at the same time—for what hypocrisy is here!

'Why, first of all you let him . . .', I began. She interrupted me and said, 'I know, I know. I was at fault. I thought that it would cure them in some wise—and so did you, my dear', she threw at me.

'Indeed, indeed', I said and sighed. I confess I had forgotten it was my idea, so much stirs in me nowadays.

As it appears, she marched straight in (and oh, the shock to both of them that must have been!), and just at the moment when Maurice was close upon his climax, too. Indeed, despite alarms he did not even stop, she says! Maude squealed and tried to pull away. He would not have it so and held her in, and even gritted out to Eveline, 'My love—come here!'

'Did you?', I asked. I tried to make a joke of it. Alas, she was not in the mood.

'You are on their side!', she declared, and fell into hysterics then, but calmed after I kissed and comforted her. She had stood there but for a moment, then walked out again and locked the house on them for several hours—forbade the servants even to open up to them.

This happened just the day before. Since then there has been silence in the house, Maude's bedroom door locked every night by Eveline (I did not tell her I have done the same with Richard, too) and Maurice despatched to a guest room to sleep.

Strange as the turns of life may be, I decided on the spot what I would do. That is to say, I shall go home—and take Maude with me, I told Eveline. Her eyes lit up. Her whole expression changed.

'Oh, Deirdre, will you do this for me? Yes!', she burst. Maude was upstairs 'in hiding' all the time. Bold as she may be with Maurice, she shows no effrontery with her Mama, and came down cautious as a cat who thinks that danger lurks somewhere.

'Maude, I understand that you would like to have a holiday', I said. She blinked. I noticed that she did not sit, and realised the discipline that Eveline has her under. Hands twisting, she stood quiet, and so I told her of my intentions, couching each phrase somewhere inbetween commands and quite polite requests. She could stay for several months, I said—would like the countryside, would have good friends in Amy, Sylvia and Richard, too. Her eyes glinted a little at his name. It shall not be, though, as she thinks.

We leave on Friday. Meanwhile I have written and

told Phillip so—also have sent a note to Muriel and Sylvia. How wonderful to be among my own things once again! I am more determined than I was before to have things my way. Phillip must respond to me or he will have his own bed just as Maurice has—though I do not think in Eveline's case that that will last for long. She will forgive him once Maude is away.

'Deal with her kindly, will you not?', asked Eveline anxiously. Her mood turned when she knew what was to be.

'You can have parties now again', I said.

'Perhaps. I think our lives have changed now, Deirdre'.

I think not—not in the long run. Leopards do not change their spots. Shall I?

Muriel's Day-Book

Deirdre to return! I am surprised at that. I had a note by messenger today—and such a ride he had of it. Two days upon the road. We paid the fellow well and lodged him in an inn. Jane says that I am growing soft. The second criticism she has made of me. I hope we are not getting quarrelsome.—'So much has changed', says Deirdre, and I wonder what she means?

Phillip is beside himself upon the news, and Sylvia has such a guilty look that I had to spend an hour or two placating her. Her Mama would need to know nothing of her naughtiness, I said, at which she looked relieved. Jane was precipitate, as I thought she well might be. I did not interfere two nights ago when she took her into Phillip—not, thank heavens, in his study, but upon pretence that another gentleman had just arrived and was waiting in the stable.

Blindfolded she took her in, and Phillip bound—and blinded also by a cloth whereby he also could not see at all —was 'succoured', which for once is Jane's word and not mine. Only her lips, of course, assailed his manly tool. More timid at the first than Daisy was, Sylvia had to have her mouth pressed down upon it several times. Jane held her wrists behind her back and brought her to drink every drop of the warm sperm he jetted out.

'She recognised his groans, I think', said Jane.

'He ought now NOT to groan', I said, but must confess I felt a mischief in me that he had, and so revealed himself, for Sylvia will now think that he did it voluntarily.

'What did you tell her afterwards?', I asked of Jane. She shrugged and said, 'Oh, that it's nice to do it sometimes'. I had to tell the dear, sweet girl the same. We still must stand as one, must Jane and I.

'Suppose Mama finds out', said Sylvia, after a long and blushing silence from her.

'She will not, dear, unless you tell her so. There is a silent understanding in such things. She knows you have to do such lovesome things', I said with a feyness that amused myself. Mischief arose in me. I asked, 'Did it feel bigger than you think? You've felt it underneath your bottom sometimes, have you not? My goodness, Sylvia, when I was your age and was birched, I had it right between my bottom cheeks. I felt so hot, but it was nice. Young ladies must be exercised, you know, to keep them fit for all that lies beyond'.

'So, darling, keep your bottom up just as you do with us', said Jane and bussed and tickled her until she laughed.

I shall to Celia's today, and have told Jane who pouted and was quite put out. I have assured her that I will not stay, and that we two will go as soon as Deirdre comes.

'There are more adventures in the world beyond', she said a little wistfully.

Roger and Celia could visit us, I said. She relented and agreed to that. The chain may not be broken after all, but many of its links are weak. If Roger were not married I would settle down with him. If Celia were not married . . . Oh, my poor head goes around, around. Jane cannot wait to pack. I understand that very well. I understand too much, perhaps. That is the trouble with me now. My headlong, hot desires have gone a different way to what I thought.

Phillip's Day-Book

Release! Yet do I want it? That's the nub of it. I am to keep my drawers on, I am told. To Deirdre that will be an outward sign of my conversion to a 'nobler cause'.

My sisters stood before me just this afternoon. I feared assault—desired it—but it did not come. I was lectured as a child might be, then made to kiss their feet again. They took their shoes off, made me suck their toes, or rather simply bid me to. I did. I savoured woman-taste again. Deirdre will expect the same, they said. I have no doubt that they have told her all. I both fear and need her presence as much as I did theirs.

'You must learn to live with what you have. We may return, may not', said Muriel. Her tone was formal as—strangely enough—I wished. Jane, too, was moderate and did not raise her skirt nor tease my penis which is to remain a willing tool of love, they said.

'Now rise and say you will obey your wife and female kin', said Jane.

Obeying, I forced out the words, yet found them not as fearsome as they would have been. It is my role, my duty—that I understand. The world has changed for me and I for it.

'You will express your gratitude to Sylvia when she comes in tonight. No more than that. Just use those words and say them humbly to her when you stand', was Muriel's command to me.

I did not answer at the first and she asked sharply, 'Well?' Dear god, I wanted to be tied up again, to have them treat me as they did, but neither moved and merely stared me out. I felt the curtains closing on a play that once had tortured me, yet brings me now a sense of strange release—a bursting out from deep within myself. I who was a mountain, as I thought, the tower of strength within the family realm, have now become a molehill and see womankind anew.

'I want to lick you everywhere—the both of you', I said. The words burst out.

'Answer the question, Phillip! What you want is quite beside the point. Have we not surely taught you that?'

'You have, yes. I am sorry. Please forgive. I meant to say I would adore to lick you—only that—and then would wait upon commands. I will, yes, I will simply say to Sylvia that I...'

'Am grateful! Say it out! Add no more words than that. You understand?

'That I am grateful. May I now, for the last time...'

'You may not, no. You have others to attend on now. Be patient, quiet, obey their words whatever they may be. Wait without hope, for hope there may not be. Wait upon love. Be doglike in their eyes. And that applies to Amy, too. You understand?'

'I understand.' The words were bitter aloes in my mouth, yet I knew myself to be as is a child whose pain is less than he pretends it is. I knew that they saw through me from their smiles. Then Muriel at last relented, made me kneel, raised up her skirts and clamped my ears between her thighs but would not let me lick beneath her quim, and nor would Jane who followed suit. I was inspected then, still kneeling as I was and quite bereft, the musky scents of them that stung my nostrils with desire. My penis, freed, reared up its glowing head. They would not touch it, though, would not. It quivered and the veins stood out.

'Make sure it does its work', said Jane. I had a feeling of too-tattered hope that she might stay within the room and 'deal with me'. Alas, they both went out and left me in my stance of penitence. How strangely, humbly, hopefully, I feel that my private parts no longer are my own! They belong to those who will command me now—and I their suitor, servitor and slave.

'Throw away your writings now. You have no need of them', said Muriel tonight. I thankfully destroyed them, yet may keep a secret diary of my own. A foxlike slyness has come over me. I shall read the day-books of the others when I can, and yet will keep a mask upon my face. A small, small victory will then be mine. I shall live two lives—yes, that's the trick of it. I shall be punished if they ever know, and that is what I know I need. O Deirdre's thighs . . . Will *she* know what to do?

Celia's Day-Book

A strange and sudden visit from Muriel who tried, as I did too, to keep herself composed and yet could not. She is departing! Oh the pain and yet the feeling of relief! We kissed, clung to each other, knew not how to be. Roger is teaching Daisy how to ride. The two had gone out earlier, she looking sweet in a new tricorne hat and a green velvet dress I bought for her.

'You may stay if you want', I said to Muriel. The words escaped my lips before I meant them, too.

'No—yes . . . I know not what to do!'. She wept. The stairs upwards to the bedroom drew us. O that they had not, for scarce had we undressed, lay down and fell to passionate caressing than Roger and Daisy came back home. Such startlements, such guilt! We sprang up naked, knew not what to do, our clothes pellmell upon the floor. Roger came up, but Daisy thankfully went to her room. My god, his eyes as he then saw us both!

'My loves!', he said, partly to my dismay that he should use the plural. Hard-nippled were our breasts. Brazen we looked.—'Oh god!', said Muriel, sat down upon the bed and wept. He had her nakedness before his eyes as well he did my own.

'Daisy!', I said and quickly locked the door.—'I must go!', said Muriel, snatched up her dress and was like a lost lamb. Roger was flushed and knew not how to be, nor I, though I flung my arms around his neck. Perhaps I tried to hide the sight of her. I thought he would get hard, but he did not. He had a look of some exhaustion on his face, from too much riding, I suppose.

'You love each other—that I understand', he said.

'You will never see me any more!', sobbed Muriel.

'She is leaving—going home', I said a little desperately.

'Yes', Roger said. He broke away from me, unlocked the door, was gone, and left us to our guilty thoughts. So hurriedly we dressed and then went down, and Muriel seized her cloak up straightaway and all was as a dream save that dear Roger smiled on us and said that all was well while Muriel declared that neither of us would see her anymore.

'Oh, what a nonsense! Celia will visit you, my dear, and I may, too, if I am so allowed'.

'Of course, of course', I said. Her smile broke through at that. We saw her off, waved to her carriage as she went. Daisy came running down and asked, 'Oh was that Aunty Muriel?'

It was, I said, but she could not stay long. Roger then went to see the horses groomed, so tactful is he. I much wanted then to be alone, and tidied up my bed lest Daisy see. Last night I gave him his well-won reward between my bottom cheeks at last. How lewdly did we talk when it was in!

'My love, my love', he panted on and on, and pumped me so majestically that all my guilt flew in that torrid bout, and I feel free at last and quite myself.

'You may do it next to Muriel', I said long moments after he had come. He did not answer, but he seemed content. He deserves all that I give to him—has been so faithful and so patient all the time. Besides, I may well do to her that which she did to me. I find new depths within myself the more I think of it.—'I want to make you cry', she said. How I would love to kiss her tears away!

Dare I tell Roger so? I wonder how he would react? I feel sure that when we visit her, I shall be more naughty than she was with me.

How curious it is that when we anticipate something, one tends to think, 'Yes, this is how I thought it would be', and at the same time also thinks the opposite!

Muriel and Jane were all prepared to leave. I sensed an undue haste in that, yet at the same time understood that they knew I wished to be alone with Phillip for a while.

How different he is! My goodness, he is quite another man, is timid, quiet, has lost his pompousness, and almost bowed to me when I came in! He kissed my hand and Amy's, too, which he has never done before.

'What have you done to him?', I asked Muriel, though more in joke than seriousness.—'We have taught him manners, dearest—taught him to comport himself with ladies as he should. Keep him in check', she told me, much to my surprise—and Phillip heard what we both said! I was bowled over, as men say, and asked him afterwards, when they had gone, if it were true.

'I have sinned', he said and kept his lips tight-pressed.

'Have you indeed!', I laughed. The old, old look came on his face, and yet it was not quite the same. There was a fearsomeness within his eyes I did not recognise from old. Muriel, of course, was very quiet. Richard behaved himself as quietly as he should and as I have now taught him he must be. Sylvia was shy, and Amy too. They ran upstairs together as girls will, and no doubt had *too* much to talk about! I wonder about that, but it cannot be helped. Amy will be discreet, I trust, and Richard dare not 'sleep-walk' with his father in the house.

Last night . . . I know not how to write about last night. Phillip stayed in his study and was quiet, and dinner was a mournful, almost silent thing. I knew I had to have it out with him. His mood is one of doglike watchfulness. Sylvia went in to bid him goodnight which I understood, for she must have made a habit of it now, and it is proper that she should. Amy must do the same in the future. We must be complete. I have an odd feeling I now must rule the house. Having handled Richard quite severely, it will please me to.

'Well?', I asked Phillip once he came to bed. He had gone into his dressing room to put his nightgown on, which he does but rarely, and today I found a pair of drawers in there, though hidden underneath a chair. I will tackle him on that, but for the nonce have found that Muriel was right. I wonder how she had a hand in this?

I asked him straightaway to tell me of his sins, for I dare not confess my own!

'I have mistreated you', he said and straightaway knelt down and kissed my feet.

'Phillip!', I gasped. In truth, I was not displeased. Would I forgive him, so he begged. I might, I said. I felt the strength of me as I had done with Richard when I spanked him hard. It may amuse me to do the same with Phillip now.

I would give thought to it, I said, and marvelled at the glorious feeling that I had. His prick was hard. I saw it when he rose, but out of mischief and revenge I pretended not to notice the projection underneath his night attire and said that I would sleep and think about our future on the morrow. In bed he did not try to touch me, but lay rigid—not in the old way but with a sort of humbleness that emanated like a cloud from him. Something has happened. What it is I do not know, and in the circumstances of my follies think it better that I do not ask. I know that in some way I have the upper hand—may take a lead from Eveline's book in the way she handled Richard first. As for *him*, the bad and wicked boy, I will have him up and lock the door and put him up to Maude. 'Twill do them good—will keep his hands away from Amy and from Sylvia. I mean to do it strictly, though—will have no looseness from him otherwise. He will see to her needs and his own and then they will behave themselves until the next time that I call them up.

Sylvia's Day-Book

How glad I am that dear Mama is back! What strangeness we have known, and I feel restless all the time. Aunt Muriel said that I would, and not to curb my instincts if I wanted to be naughty on the quiet.

Papa is very quiet still. I am glad of that. When I went to say goodnight to him, he straightaway stood up again. He asked me where Mama and Amy were. They both were in their rooms, I said, had shut their doors. I *wanted* to say that. I thought of what had happened in the stable and I almost blushed, but Aunt Jane said that I shouldn't now. I *did* guess when I heard him groan that time. Oh what a lot I swallowed, too!

Papa said next that he was very grateful to me, so I thought he read my thoughts! I didn't mind, I said, though then I thought that if he had *not* read my thoughts, then perhaps it was the wrong thing that I said. I said to him to sit. Aunt Muriel said I MUST say that. His face went awfully funny, but he did. I wanted to be kind, so sat upon his lap again and talked of dear Mama and Amy, too. I mentioned Richard just a little bit. I have a feeling Mama is put out with him. I 'spect that he was rude to her. He can be very *brash* at times.

Papa just listened to me, did not speak. Aunt Muriel said that when men are silent, that is good! Papa, though, was not always so. I think she lectured him and made him shy. A *part* of him, though, wasn't shy. I felt it underneath my bottom all the time and wriggled just to make it 'fit', as Aunt Jane said I should. It got so big!

Papa got flushed. I thought that he might birch me, but he never has. He asked Rose if she'd got her drawers on once! I think he's very naughty, too.

Daisy's Day-Book

I think Mama is being naughty! Perhaps it always happens with grown-ups. I heard a *little* what they said when Aunty Muriel was here. When Papa went downstairs I crept along and listened at the door and heard Mama say to her, 'Quickly, we must dress!' Oh goodness, he had seen them both undressed! Perhaps, though, Aunty Muriel was trying on a gown. I wish I knew, but cannot ask Papa.

Sylvia has invited me to stay with her—and her Mama is back! Papa says he will take me over there. I wonder if we'll stop awhile halfway? Mama wishes very much to know what Sylvia's Mama is like, so I will have to tell her everything of that. Papa is anxious that I do not say too much. He goes very late to bed now, sometimes when Mama's asleep, and then we have a lovely 'chat' which leaves me feeling very sticky in the end! I daren't, oh daren't, tell Sylvia. I hope she doesn't try to tease it out of me like her two aunties did, oh dear!

Deirdre's Day-Book

What a charming man is Roger, and how sweet young Daisy is! She has that look of innocence that Sylvia has. Long may they keep it so, and yet...

Phillip amuses me. I frigged him last night while he lay quite still. Occasionally he groaned. I shushed him when he did and he obeyed, save for some whimperings. Finally I rolled upon him, sheathed his cock and rode him as I wanted to—and O the sense of mastery it gave! The lamb, he did not even jerk the while I slewed my cunny up and down.

An inspiration struck me. I could not resist. He had not come as yet. I rested, gripping him within, my nipples sharp upon his chest, my thighs full weighted down upon his own.

'Have you been taught so? Tell me, Phillip', I commanded.

'Yes', he moaned.

'By Muriel? And Jane, perhaps? Come, Phillip, tell me, for I too have sinned'.

'Forgive me! Humble as I am, I have. They made me, Deirdre. First they . . .'

'Shush! I do not wish to know. Obedience is *all* for you henceforth. Obey myself and both the girls, and all will follow'.

Why I said the latter I will never understand, save that it seemed to set the seal upon his strange and craven attitude. Perhaps I thought he might adopt a sterner attitude towards them, seeking compensation in that wise, though I could not imagine it of him.

'I will, I will, I will obey you all!' Such was his cry and then he came and jetted his abundance deep within my slit, I sucking strongly with my cunnylips till all was done and the last pearls were spent.

Today though—ah!—Daisy's Papa asked me to show him round the grounds. Much taken with him, as I felt myself to be, we viewed the shrubbery, the lawns, the flowers, then strolled as if with one mind to the summer-house. The door closed, and I felt a girlishness upon me, but too late. Strong were his arms about me, warm his lips.

'Upon such brief acquaintance, sir?', I laughed.

'Given that it may be a lengthy one', he smiled and led me slowly to the waiting couch, swept up my dress without ado and tickled me delightfully between my legs.

'The girls! Beware in case they come—or even Phillip might', I breathed. His stiff prick touched my knuckles as we lay. I turned my hand and felt its length and girth. My fingers sought his buttons even as I spoke.

'I sent them to his study to discourse with him and told them to amuse themselves, my dear. I have a feeling that may take a little time'.

'Roger! What *do* you mean?', I gasped, and yet withal I laughed despite myself and arched my back to let him loose my drawers, had in a vision Phillip lying all quiescent with his prick in my nest, saying 'I will, I will, I will!'

The devil take me—I am lost again, should write no more, should write no more. This is a house of secrets now.